"Full of warmth, pathos, history, and humor, not to mention a cast of delightfully quirky characters, and a math lesson or two; all together, a winning equation! When Rojstaczer writes about mathematics, you'd think he was writing about poetry."

—Jonathan Evison, author of *West of Here* and *The Revised Fundamentals of Caregiving*

"Here is the rare book that invites us into the romance of pure mathematics and the very human company of those who spend their decades unknotting the abstractions that describe our reality." —Lore Segal, author of *Shakespeare's Kitchen*

"This funny, moving, perceptive look at one man's relationship to his eccentric mother and the legacy of her genius succeeds to the *nth* degree. Rojstaczer is a wise, warm-hearted, and wonderful new writer." —Eric Puchner, author of *Model Home*

"Stuart Rojstaczer has written a mathematician's history of the family, full of challenging equations, emotional calculus, and unexpected conclusions. *The Mathematician's Shiva* is intricate, intelligent, and funny, a pleasure to read."

—Roxana Robinson, author of *Sparta*

"At last! The long hoped for proof that a group of people even crazier than Yiddish-speakers can, in fact, exist."

—Michael Wex, author of *Born to Kvetch*

"High math, Eastern European history, and American culture converge in this hugely entertaining debut. . . . [A] multilayered story of family, genius, and loss." —*Publishers Weekly*

PENGUIN BOOKS

The Mathematician's Shiva

Stuart Rojstaczer was born in Milwaukee, Wisconsin. For many years, he was a professor of geophysics at Duke University. He has written for the *New York Times* and *Washington Post*, and his scientific research has been published in many journals, including *Science* and *Nature*. He lives with his wife in Northern California. This is his first published novel.

The
Mathematician's
Shiva

STUART ROJSTACZER

PENGUIN BOOKS

PENGUIN BOOKS
Published by the Penguin Group
Penguin Group (USA) LLC
375 Hudson Street
New York, New York 10014

USA | Canada | UK | Ireland | Australia | New Zealand | India | South Africa | China
penguin.com
A Penguin Random House Company

First published in Penguin Books 2014

ISBN 978-0-14-312631-7

Printed in the United States of America
1 3 5 7 9 10 8 6 4 2

Set in Warnock Pro
Designed by Alissa Rose Theodor

In memory of my father, who was a wonderful storyteller, my mother, who believed fervently in the beauty of life, and my brother, who was my guide to all things American

First you must know your mental capacities and your natural talents: you will find this out when you study all mathematical sciences. . . .

—Maimonides

It's always the same story full of confusions, nuisances, pressures, willy-nilly journeys, annoyances, disputes, kinks in well-made plans, jolts, itches, and bewilderment.

—Mendele

The

Mathematician's

Shiva

PART 1

THE FAMILY

CHAPTER 1

Tonight It's Just Us

"**H**ow's your mother?" Yakov Epshtein asked. Yakov's goatee was flecked with gray. Over the years his cheeks had ballooned and taken on a happy glow. His clothing choices for work had migrated from a cheap sagging suit, pressed white shirt, and thrift-store tie circa 1984 to a polo shirt and jeans with tasseled loafers sans socks. He was waiting, perhaps, for the day that global warming would bring the ocean to the Great Plains. This miracle, if it took place, would be welcome to Yakov but not necessary. Life in America had been good.

I was in Yakov's office, its well-worn vinyl floor covered with the grime of twenty years of use slightly mitigated by perfunctory cleaning. It was early afternoon eleven years ago, in the winter of 2001. The wind outside barely blew. The sky was crystal blue. Looking through the double-paned glass, those inexperienced with the Midwest might be fooled into thinking it was warm outside, at least warm for January. Both Yakov and I knew better. "My mother is hanging in there," I said. "You know her. She's not going down until she's ready."

"A remarkable woman." Yakov was from Russia. When a Russian mathematician mentioned my mother, this phrase "remarkable woman" would often follow. It was a phrase my father would use as well, but often in a sarcastic way.

Yakov had come to the United States in 1986 and taught at the University of Nebraska in Lincoln. He was lucky to have eventually found this job. Many of my parents' acquaintances who had emigrated from Russia in the 1970s and 1980s were doing things far afield from mathematics in order to put food on the table. I, unlike Yakov, had come to the United States as a young child. My memories of the former Soviet Union were fuzzy at best. Given what I had heard about Russia from my parents and their friends, I knew that this fuzziness was not a bad thing.

I was giving a talk at Nebraska's atmospheric sciences department, but when people in the math department heard I was coming, they filled up half of my appointment schedule. I was used to this. It was never about me. It was about my mother. She was the stuff of legend.

She was five foot eight, a tall glass of water by European (and maybe even American) standards, who tended to tower over men, including my father, in her heels. She favored gray or burgundy suits tailored by a local dressmaker and owned well over two hundred pairs of shoes, an obsession that she said derived from her poverty during World War II. She would probably have been even taller had she not starved during the war. My mother never needed a microphone. When she spoke it was with the cadence of an oracle. She had been banned from teaching calculus at her university simply because she scared the hell out of freshmen.

When my mother was ten years old, she was living in an Arctic Circle work camp where her father, a Jewish Pole/Russian (every decade or so, control of his hometown would change from one country to the other), was sentenced to hard labor for being a capitalist Enemy of the People. At school on the frozen tundra along the

Barents Sea, my mother showed a remarkable facility for mathematics. In Russia, math is not just a means to an end. It's a glorious art. Suddenly, my mother's family got a little bit of meat and flour in addition to their wrinkled potatoes and onions. Another Enemy of the People, a professor of mathematics, was told to tutor my mother three times a week. Like many, he never made it back home.

My mother, formerly a Pole, then a full-fledged citizen of the glorious USSR due to the Soviet annexation of her hometown after the war, was sent to Moscow for further study in 1945. These were heady times in Russian mathematics, and the most admired mathematician of all was her advisor, the great Kolmogorov. My mother began to publish papers when she was sixteen. She defected to the West in 1951, after giving a talk in East Berlin. My mother became a tenured professor at the University of Wisconsin at the age of twenty-two. At twenty-eight, she was offered a tenured professorship at Princeton, which somehow promised to ignore its rules on nepotism and hire my father as well. She turned them down. Like Kolmogorov and many of his acolytes, she believed that cold weather was required for the creative mind. New Jersey simply was too warm. Plus, according to her, Princeton was a haven for anti-Semites, and she'd already had her fill of that in Russia and Poland. She stayed in Wisconsin.

In 1999, after sixty-nine years without a single major health issue, my mother was diagnosed with advanced lung cancer. Her doctor told her to expect to live three to six months. "Nonsense," she said. "I have a good year of things to do."

A year and a half later, she was down to eighty-five pounds. As I walked out of Yakov's office, I got the call on my cell phone. "I'm going to die today," she said.

"I'm in Nebraska. I have a talk at three."

"Forget the talk."

I asked Yakov to give me a ride to the Lincoln airport. There was a rumor that my mother was working on a solution to a heretofore unsolved, century-old, vexing mathematical problem that she was cheating death to finish. I didn't know how this rumor started. It couldn't possibly have been true. But every mathematician I had talked to for the last two years, including Yakov, had mentioned it. I could sense the excitement in their voices. A once-in-a-century problem finally solved. The worldwide mathematical community would be in a rare upbeat mood, maybe even completely euphoric, for a year at least. "She must have finished today," Yakov said about the rumored proof. "A remarkable woman."

My mother lived alone. Fifteen years earlier, she had come home for lunch, found my father screwing an undergraduate on the leather couch, and threw him out. She called me on the phone at the time. If she possessed any sense of loss or grief, it wasn't present in her voice. "He was fucking someone on my furniture. And she wasn't even that good-looking," she said. My father's side of the story was a bit different. They never formally divorced. Such legalities were either beneath them or beyond them. On the day of my own wedding, my father looked more bewildered than anything else. My mother cried.

The closest I could get to Madison on quick notice was Chicago, a town that is physiographically as dreadfully boring as Lincoln but makes up for it by housing several million more people. When you grow up in the Midwest, every mound and depression become a cause for celebration. The long winters and tedium of the landscape can lead you to drink a ridiculous amount of alcohol. On that front, my family fit right in. I rented a boxy American sedan and headed out on the interstate, where I got another call.

"Where are you?"

"On the border."

"Drive faster."

"I'm going ninety-five, Mother."

"I didn't ask how fast you were driving. Drive faster."

"Who's with you?"

"No one."

"I thought Cynthia was with you."

"She left. She couldn't stand the stress. I went to the bathroom. I was shitting blood. She walked out."

"She walked out?"

"Yes, she walked out. What was I supposed to do? Bring her back in the house? I didn't want that painted doll around anyway."

"I'll drive faster."

"That's what I told you." Once during a chemotherapy session, my mother had said that if I didn't speak to my father after she died, she would rise out of the grave to slap me. "He's your father. He's a bastard sometimes. But he is your father." With most people threats like this would be considered idle. But with my mother perhaps anything was possible.

I whizzed by car after car at a speed that should have caused a cop or two to pull me over, and became half convinced that this was a day I was immune to such quotidian barriers. I thought about my family. It was small by any standard, shrunken to a handful by Hitler, Stalin, and divorce. There was my father, with whom I had issues. What son doesn't? There was my mother, whose most notable feature was a towering intellect. Then there was Cynthia, who had heedlessly walked out on a dying relative because she couldn't take the stress. That was my aunt. There was also a cousin, Bruce, but he had left the madhouse of Madison long ago for a different kind of insanity. He produced television shows in Los Angeles. His credits could often be found at the end of Grammy Awards and Barbra Streisand/Beyoncé/The-New-Singing-Sensation specials. There was also my uncle, my mother's kid brother and Cynthia's husband, who, under circumstances far more dire than my mother's, had miraculously survived the war. He owned a liquor distributorship in town. Finally, there was an ex-wife and child for me, but our relationship was nil and had been so for more than twenty-five years.

My mother lived in the same house she had bought with my father back in 1954, a bungalow near the zoo and walking distance to the synagogue. Yes, my mother was very religious. She rarely missed Sabbath morning prayers. Many mathematicians found this unbelievable.

Some people fondly or not so fondly remember roosters waking them up in the morning. For me it was the barking sea lions of the zoo whose sounds readily crashed through my second-story windows in both summer and winter. After I left, my bedroom gradually filled with journals and books, overflow from my mother's office at the university. Then there was my mother's opus on bookshelves as well, her family history. We are not a tidy family. The acrid air produced by the yellowing paper of those volumes kept all but my mother and the occasional dedicated visiting scholar out of my old room. When I visited, I slept on the living room couch.

We moved my mother's bed downstairs into the sunroom off the kitchen when she got sick. It just made things more convenient. Everything she needed was within thirty steps. She even had an electric kettle for tea next to her bed and a spigot that a kind and handy neighbor had jury-rigged into the room.

When I walked into the house, I saw her propped up in her bed, almost completely hidden by a thick, ivory-white down comforter. It was something she had never needed or had when she was healthy. She was now so thin that I barely recognized her. Her long blond hair, which had never grayed, was not in her signature schoolgirl/Valkyrie—take your pick—braids, but fell raggedly over her shoulders.

For a year after she was diagnosed, I would come every other week for her chemotherapy sessions. As the months wore on, though, my work at the University of Alabama piled up. I tried to achieve balance, but I'm not good at multitasking. Neither are my mother and father. My research program lost a huge chunk of funding. I had to let a postdoc go. OK, I am not my mother in terms of intellect or achievement, but who is? Everyone, even self-acknowledged minor scientists like me, needs a little sunlight to shine on their ego. My visits to Madison went down to once a month.

When my mother noticed me, she turned her head slightly, her eyelids opening as if from a long deep sleep. "My Sashaleh," she said.

I walked up to her and touched her cheek. Her skin felt smooth and paper thin. "A woman shouldn't die alone. It isn't natural," she said. "I don't want to be in pain. I want morphine. That's it. Morphine if I need it." I called up the hospital. The ambulance came and two men in stiff orange shirts with typical barrel-like Wisconsin bodies hauled her out. How much beer, schnapps, and pizza must one drink and eat on a daily basis to maintain such a size?

They carried her carefully along the ice-covered sidewalk and then, out of habit I guess, drove the sixty seconds to the hospital as if they were NASCAR drivers. When my mother was wheeled around the cold hospital halls—barely lit, with the kind of fluorescent lighting that makes even the healthy look sick—she seemed both lost and terrified, an emotional state that I had never before witnessed in her.

"I haven't been here since the oven blew up." We were at St. Mary's, walking distance to our house.

"That was, what, forty years ago?"

"Forty-two. The idiots called me into the room and told me you had a broken leg. Burns on your face, and they told me you needed a cast."

"They mixed up the files."

"This is a good place to be, actually. At the university hospital they might try to keep me going for a few days. Here, they don't know what they are doing. If they tried to save my life, they might just kill me outright instead."

"You sure you don't want to keep going?"

"No. I'm done. I suppose this is better than at home," she said and looked at the morphine drip. "I could have used this yesterday, too. I hurt like hell. Did you give them the papers?"

"They're on file."

"Show the nurse the papers. These idiots cannot be trusted to do anything right. I don't want some tube down me. Who are you calling?" she asked as I dialed on my cell.

"Father."

"He won't come. He hates hospitals." In the war, my father, who was, and I mean this as a compliment, the best liar I have ever met, faked his way into being an orderly in a hospital. The job, far from the front, likely saved his life. But he had no idea how to minister to the sick, and he probably killed more than one or two men because of his incompetence.

"I don't need to say good-bye to her," my father said on the phone. "I already did."

"I'm not asking you to come for her. I'm asking you to come for me."

"That's different, I suppose." He came, but it took an hour. As always, he was impeccably dressed. A well-pressed dark suit. A starched white shirt. A blue-and-black bow tie. A blue pocket square. His face freshly shaved. His dyed hair combed over his still visible shiny bald spot. My father was a charming anachronism. My mother and I and a few dozen undergraduate women were probably the only people in this country who ever saw my father in anything less than formal attire.

My uncle Shlomo, who had been at a liquor convention in Detroit, apparently drove at something approaching the speed of sound on I-94—he didn't need encouragement like me in that regard—as soon as he heard and arrived almost at the same minute as my father. Cynthia, though, was still suffering from stress. Bruce was taking a red-eye from LA. So was Anna, more or less our family's adopted daughter, and reminder, as if my parents needed any, of the hell of Russia and the heaven of the United States. But neither Bruce nor Anna would see my mother alive, I knew. My uncle gave his sister a hug that rattled the bed and kissed her softly on her cheeks and lips. "You really want to die today?" he asked.

"I don't have a choice. I've already lost a lot of blood."

"They could give you more. Blood. They have lots of that. Blood is cheap." My uncle put a bottle of vodka on the nightstand. A nurse walked in to protest as he opened it. My uncle looked completely different than my mother, with dark Mediterranean skin and a perpetual five o'clock shadow. His curly thick black hair, graying in streaks, was combed straight back. When he looked at the nurse, he did so with the exact same expression that my mother had used, intentionally or not, to scare thousands of undergraduates over the years. The nurse scurried down the hall.

"Rachela, we should take off your jewelry," my uncle said. He pronounced her name like it would have been pronounced in her hometown, *Rookh-eh-leh*. "Otherwise the *ganovim* at the funeral home will steal it."

"He's right," my father said.

"Of course, he's right. Shlomo knows these things." She smiled faintly. "It's getting hard to talk."

"Don't talk then," Shlomo said. "Just listen."

"I'll have plenty of time to listen when the worms crawl into my grave. A little vodka would help."

My uncle took the bottle to her lips and she had a sip. Then he lifted the bottle high and poured a shot down his throat.

"That's better," he said. "This is hard, you know. I can't believe it." He passed me the bottle. I drank with my uncle, which was nothing new. Even my father, Viktor, drank, although he refused to drink from the bottle straight and got a cup from a drawer in the room.

"Viktor, that's a urine sample cup," my uncle said.

"So?'

"This is good vodka. It isn't piss. I'm not pouring good vodka into a piss cup."

"All of a sudden you have principles?"

"All of a sudden you don't have any class?"

"It's a cup. I need a cup. The bottle already has your spit on it."

"Enough, you two," I said and looked at my mother.

"It's like old times." She smiled and coughed.

I took the bottle from my uncle and poured vodka to the top of my father's urine cup. "I'm going to spill good vodka," he said.

"It won't be the first time," I said.

He drank it down in one gulp. A smile flashed from his thin lips.

"It is good."

"I told you it was. My sister is dying. I'm not going to bring cheap stuff."

Three minutes later my father asked for more. "I want to make a toast," he said. My mother's monitor beeped as he raised his cup. "To my Rachela. Who gave me love, gave me a son, and had the strength to cheat death."

"The vodka is making you sentimental," my mother said.

"Yes, it is. I didn't want to be here, you know. A dying woman. A hospital. A depressing thing. But I'm glad I came. Tomorrow it will be chaos. All of those mathematicians. Tonight it's just us."

"I'll have another sip," my mother said. My uncle dutifully obliged. "This bottle won't last," she said.

"I have a case in the car."

"You should get more."

"You won't die while I'm gone? I want to see your last breath. I don't know why I just said that. But I think it won't hurt so much if I do."

"I promise. I'll wait until you get back."

Shlomo walked out of the room. A nurse entered. "Is there anything I can do to help?"

My mother laughed. "Help? I'm here already. That's enough. Go help someone who needs it."

"Okeydokey," the nurse said and walked out.

"There's a cross over my bed, isn't there?" my mother asked. I nodded.

"Take it down. I don't want Yozl Pandrik looking down at me when I die." I walked over to the bed, reached high, and yanked. Jesus wouldn't come down.

"He's nailed to the wall. I could have told you that," my father said.

"Take a towel and cover him up. I won't see him in the next life. I don't want to see him in this one either."

"Don't start, Rachela," my father said. He was slurring his words. He poured the last of the bottle into his cup.

"You're right," my mother said. My father pulled out his notebook from his suit pocket. He could work anywhere, and sometimes worked better drunk than sober.

"Riemann?" I asked.

"No, something else."

"It's always been Riemann," I said. My father had been trying to solve the Riemann Hypothesis, a major problem in mathematics, for thirty years. He certainly wasn't alone. But to try to achieve something massively significant in a field where you're by and large useless after your fortieth birthday—and my father was seventy-seven—is the height of both delusion and optimism. That said, old mathematicians tended to shrivel up entirely intellectually. At least he was trying.

"Today it's Navier-Stokes," he said. This too was one of the great unsolved problems in mathematics.

"You have a big appetite, but you don't know anything about partial differential equations."

"And you do?"

"I know how to use them. Mother is the one who knows how to analyze them. And you're at Wisconsin, not Minnesota."

"Minnesota is for the dull witted," my mother said. "Enough talk about nonsense. Now that you two are here, I want to say something."

"Go ahead, Rachela," my father said.

"I want to say the obvious. OK, this family isn't the best. But neither is it the worst. We have our strengths. We are still close. I will die happy knowing this."

"I'm glad you think we're still close," I said. Why did I say such a pissy thing? After all, my mother was dying. I should have let her be and enjoyed my last hours with the one person that I loved more than myself. I am not always proud of my behavior.

"You know what I'm saying. Don't be an idiot. Not with me. Not with your father."

"Mother told me she would rise from the grave if I didn't spend time with you after," I said to my father.

"I'm an atheist. I don't believe in such things," my father said.

"He'll spend time with you," she said. "He's gotten old. He needs you. And you have the American sickness of niceness. You don't hold a grudge."

"And you'll rise from the grave if I do hold a grudge?"

"Sure. If Yozl Pandrik can do it, then why not me? Go get the towel." I walked into the bathroom and grabbed two brown paper towels.

"*Pani Karnokovitch?*" a man asked from the hall entrance. My mother spoke four languages fluently: English, Russian, Yiddish, and Polish. Her Hebrew and German weren't half bad, either. But Polish was her mother tongue, and she spoke it like the dukes and duchesses of old. It was a formal style of speaking, long forgotten. My knowledge of Polish is spotty, and as a result, I never understood much of what she said when she talked to Poles. My father, a Russian native, was a little better. My uncle, who lived in Poland until 1957, of course was fluent. When I heard the words "Mrs. Karnokovitch" in Polish, I turned around.

"*Tak. Proszę niech ksiądz wejdzie* [Yes, it's me. Please come inside, Father]," my mother said.

His name was Father Rudnicki. I didn't know him.

I walked over to the priest, and shook his hand after I stuffed the paper towels into my sport coat's interior left pocket. My father looked up from his notebook and mentally recorded the priest's presence. "This is my son. He lives in Tuscaloosa," he said. "I've never been."

"You're a long way from home," Father Rudnicki said to me. "I understand it's very pretty there."

"He studies hurricanes, flies inside them to make measurements. It causes us a great deal of worry." My father went back to his notebook.

"It's good to have parents who care about you," the priest said.

"Even at fifty-one, yes, I think it's probably true," I said.

A nurse with a golden smile walked in. "Is everything OK here?"

"I think everything is fine," the priest said. "Nurse, did you know that Professor Karnokovitch is a hero in her Polish homeland. Please be good to her."

"I didn't know."

"It's fine what she's doing," my mother said. "A few more hours and the blood will drain out of me. I can say good-bye."

"You still have your sense of humor, *Pani* Karnokovitch."

"It's not really humor," she said. "It's a statement of fact."

"I'm sorry."

"You shouldn't be. I've had a full life. I can go now without any regrets."

"How do you know my mother?" I asked.

"Through the diocese." My mother, while working on her family history, had managed to wrangle the Wisconsin Catholic Diocese to help find records of her family in Poland. "I happened to see her name on the list of patients. Of course I had to come visit."

"It's good you're here, *proszę księdza*," my mother said. "Sit down. We have no more chairs, but you can sit on the bed if that is OK with you."

"Of course."

"My brother. You've never met him, but you'll like him. He will be back soon. I do have a request, *proszę księdza*."

"Anything."

"The cross above my bed. As you know, I'm not a Christian."

"Yes, I'm aware."

"My son and husband say it's nailed to the wall."

"That is correct." My father once again joined the conversation. "She'd like it removed, *proszę księdza*."

"Thank you, Viktor," my mother said.

I looked at my parents and then watched the priest, taken aback by the sheer nerve of my mother and father. This was a time for me to stay in the background. My parents were conjuring forth something from a place I could only witness with a mixture of worry and admiration, but never fully understand.

My mother had what in Yiddish are called *bzikes*—it comes from the Polish word *bziki* and "issues" I guess is the closest translation—and she had so many of them that some might have viewed her as an impossible walking tic. My father, when they were together, off and on accommodated, no, more like celebrated, every one of these *bzikes*. I think I know exactly why. Her craziness was happily wed to her intellect. There are no reasonable geniuses in this world, I am convinced.

"My wife, may the Lord bless her, is of the same faith as our Lord Christ. She has brightened the world in her own special way," my father said. "Her views are peculiar, I know, *Księże Rudnicki*. But whatever fate befalls her in the world to come, she deserves to die with the dignity that comes of her own faith, yes?"

"Mister Karnokovitch," said Father Rudnicki. "You know I cannot do this."

"Yes, I understand. You cannot personally do such a thing. To be truthful, being of the same faith as you, neither can I. But for my son such a thing is possible. Perhaps you can arrange to have someone in the hospital provide him with the necessary tools."

"I couldn't even watch your son do this, to be honest."

"I understand this, too. You do not have to be here when it happens. But it is a dying woman's request."

"I'll see what I can do," Father Rudnicki said and walked out of the room.

"He will be back, I'm sure," my father said.

"No doubt," said my mother. "And if not, Shlomo, I'm sure, has tools in his car."

CHAPTER 2

Early Training

I remember it this way. My father and I are sitting at the kitchen table. I am six years old, small for my age. One of my hands is playing with my long blond curly hair. The other holds a red pencil with white lettering. My hand-eye coordination is not the best, but my father, who sits next to me, doesn't seem to mind my poor handwriting. In my spiral notebook, he has drawn a picture like this:

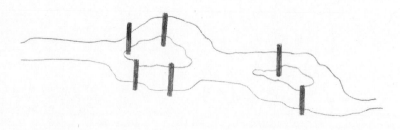

He tells me a story about a boy who lives in a city with six bridges. There are two islands in this city. On one of these islands there is a chocolate store. The only store on the other island has bananas. The boy wants to make chocolate-covered bananas. My father knows I like these things, of course. That's why he's added this detail.

"What's the boy's name?" I ask.

"He's a boy. Just a boy like you. Does it really matter what his name is?"

"Yes, I want to know."

"OK, then I'll tell you. The boy who likes chocolate-covered bananas is named Leo. He is a German boy. Eventually he will grow up and move to Russia. He will become a very famous man."

"Like a prince?"

"No, not like a prince. He will become famous for being very clever. Like your mother. A prince in Russia will adore him and give him everything he needs."

"He can have whatever he wants?"

"Within reason, yes."

"I want to be like him."

"Of course you do. He had a good life. As a child in Germany, he liked to walk around his city. Back then children could walk wherever they wanted. Not like now."

"What's the name of the city?"

"Königsberg."

"And he wants to make chocolate-covered bananas all by himself?" The thought of doing such a thing, of course, excites me.

"Yes, he knows how to do this. He is a very clever boy."

"Can you show me how to make them?"

"Of course. If you can show me that you're as clever as this Leo."

"What made him so clever?"

"Well, once a week his mother gave him enough money to buy one banana and the chocolate to cover it. Some weeks he would go to the chocolate store first. Other weeks he would go to the banana store first. He'd do this on the way back home from school, and he would always walk across all six bridges in his city along the way. He liked to look at the water.

"But here's what made him clever. He never crossed the same bridge twice."

"That sounds easy. Anybody could do that," I say. I start to imagine making my chocolate-covered banana, my father showing me how.

"Is it? Show me."

I look at the drawing, chewing on the back of my pencil, tasting and sensing with anxiety the mix of metal and spongy plastic against my small teeth. How did Leo do such a thing? I think of myself in a city from long ago crossing from bridge to bridge. It isn't hard to imagine. I have a glorious image of wooden arch bridges, the water under them crystal clear, abundant with jumping, silvery fish.

At first I make a mistake. I assume that the school and the house are on the same side of the river. I can't find a way this boy Leo did this trick.

"Leo is very smart." I'm so disappointed. In your youth, failure is never tempered. It always feels monumentally horrible, irrevocable, and complete (at least for an hour or two it does). I'll never learn how to make chocolate-covered bananas! But then, and this is how it always works if it does work at all, the solution comes to me visually. "His school and house are on different sides of the river?"

"Yes." My father shows a glint of a smile. I can always recognize that look, the way his face stretches taut. This is my father when he is lost in the moment. He knows I'm on the right track now.

I take the pencil out of my mouth and draw a path. "That's easy. I could do that, too. There are lots of ways."

"You're a clever boy," my father says.

I'm pleased with myself. In hindsight, I usually view my childhood ego as some monstrous thing. I thought that not only would I achieve greatness, but that I fully deserved it. My grandfather Aaron—who lived in our home through my childhood and beyond—called me his *ayzene kepl*, his little iron head. When I first heard this phrase translated, I thought he was teasing and calling me stupid. But I was quickly reassured that this was a good thing. I had something substantial in there, the mind of someone older.

"Can we make bananas now?"

"One. Just one. Just like Leo." That's what we do. We walk to a store on Regent Street and buy one Cadbury chocolate bar, its gold foil signifying its luxury. Then we walk to Park Street to the closest grocery, and buy one banana. We stand in the kitchen, and my father tells me that chocolate must be steamed to be melted. I stand over the stove on a chair and watch the chocolate liquefy and spread in the stainless steel pan, glistening and sending forth wisps of vaporized oil as it melts. My father has no taste for chocolate. It's my mother's weakness, not his. He eats apples, sometimes whole onions, after he peels the outer skin into a thin spiral with a pocketknife. But this land of plenty we live in never ceases to give him pleasure. I can tell he's enjoying this activity because he now has the ability, within reason, to buy anything he wants and can do something as whimsical as cover a banana in chocolate.

Years later, I'll remember this day and realize that the Leo in this story is Leonhardt Euler. In truth he's not a boy walking across bridges but a man, one of the finest mathematicians ever known. He will found a field of study in the eighteenth century, topology, which will consume the mental energy of many friends of my parents. And yes, it will also take up the mind of the great Kolmogorov for some years, a restless mind that will touch almost all of mathematics.

If you think it's torture to put a kid through such an exercise, I vehemently disagree. My father is teaching me to be a mathematician, and like most any other skill or art—and mathematics is definitely an art—those who learn early have an innate advantage. The tennis players you watch at Wimbledon and the quarterbacks you see in the Super Bowl are never taught their craft for the first time in high school or college. Why should it be any different for mathematics?

Just so you know, my father was being easy on me. The problem Euler faced was actually ridiculously and hideously more difficult. Euler wanted to cross seven bridges, not six, in his hometown of Königsberg. The real answer to the actual problem—crossing seven bridges—is that it doesn't have an answer. It is impossible to walk across seven bridges without using one of them twice. Euler proved this to be so. If my father had given me, at the age of six, this impossible problem, tried to get me to realize the problem was impossible, and prove it was so, now that would have been torture.

A proof. An ironclad irrefutable statement of what is or isn't possible. For three centuries at least, mathematics has been all about that one thing, and every new proof is celebrated by the community. Even minor proofs get a few minutes of sunshine.

I'm not a mathematician. Despite my early training, I don't have my parents' talent. I am good. I am clever. I am certainly not brilliant. But like my parents, I have a love for the elegance of proofs, their absoluteness.

Over the course of my childhood I will be introduced not only to little Leo but to little Isaac (Newton), Blaise (Pascal), Pierre (de Fermat), René (Descartes), Gottfried (Leibniz), and many more, all of these mathematicians playing the role of resourceful and independent boys, and all giving me the idea that solving problems always came with tangible rewards. Ah, if only life were so simple. Then there were the men and women, real men and women of today, not imagined boys, who came to visit us, and they knew the names of these mathematicians as well. In contrast to my father's fastidiousness, many seemed unable to even tie their shoes correctly.

When my father warned of the horde of mathematicians that would descend upon our house after my mother's death, I knew what to expect. They would be grieving, but not like my family. They would be mourning not my mother but the loss of ideas, the loss of intellect. They would no longer be able to sit in a room with her and feel the magical presence of someone with the talent to find the hidden gem in what is thought to be all dross.

The Hasidic Jews have a word, *dveykus*, for men who always possess the spirit of God inside them. My mother, unlike my grandfather, did not believe in such things literally, but when it came to understanding mathematics, she knew that she possessed the equivalent of *dveykus*. Like a *rebbe* with acolytes who feel blessed just to be around someone whose goodness and spirituality are always present, my mother had her followers. I had been with them all of my childhood. They sought me out for my secondhand *dveykus* even as an adult. Now they would come and I would have to be their gracious host for seven days, the days of shiva that are a traditional part of Jewish mourning. My uncle called them the *szaleńcy*, the crazy people. Yet he would supply the vodka, and soothe them in his own way.

But I am getting ahead of myself. In this story, my mother isn't even dead yet, and already I'm talking about her shiva. We need to go back to the hospital.

CHAPTER 3

Without Yozl Pandrik

The cross over my mother's bed, it turned out, was not hard to remove. Father Rudnicki came back with a screwdriver surprisingly quickly, handed it to me, and stepped out for a few minutes as I pried Jesus easily from the drywall. He left barely a mark on the glossy pale paint.

"Give him to me," my uncle, who had returned with two fresh bottles of vodka, said. Unlike my mother, my uncle had not lived above the Arctic Circle during the war. Instead, he ended up housed in a convent in the Polish city of Tomaszów-Lubelski. My uncle delicately fingered the crucifix in his hands. "They are giving Jesus six-pack abs nowadays," he said. "In Poland, he was a skinny little thing. Here he looks like he has been pumping iron with what's his name."

"Schwarzenegger?" I asked.

"Yes, that's the one."

My uncle walked up to Father Rudnicki when he came back, his instinctive childhood deference to all men and women who served the faith fully intact. "I do apologize for my sister, Father. She is not always respectful of others. But she does have a good heart."

"I know she does, Mr. Czerneski." They continued their conversation in Polish and, of course, along the way my uncle managed to pull another urine cup from a drawer and offer Father Rudnicki a well-earned drink. My uncle has no mathematical skills whatsoever, but he does know many languages. Polish, Russian, German, Hungarian, Hebrew, Yiddish, and even a language that seems to be one long whisper to me, Lithuanian. Though he came to the United States at the age of twenty, his English is without even a trace of an accent, except when he is drunk or tired.

My uncle had come to the United States in 1957, traveling from Warsaw to Chicago with a vague notion that he had relatives somewhere in this too large country. He knew, although he never practiced the religion, that he was Jewish, which is why the Polish government had let him travel in the first place. Back then they were always eager to remove whatever physical reminders—people, buildings, and even tombstones—remained of their once bountiful Jewish past.

His plan was simple. Go to the cities with the biggest Polish populations and search for his family. What better place to start than Chicago? But there were no Czerneskis in the Chicago phone book, and no synagogue had any recollection of anyone by that name. He found a job mopping the floor and washing glasses at a rickety bar owned by a childless couple born near his hometown. On a winter day, a Polish mathematician visiting Chicago walked inside. He and my uncle struck up a conversation. When my uncle mentioned his name, the mathematician remembered the papers of Rachela Karnokovitch from her unmarried days.

"It's a name well-known in mathematics, Czerneski. There's a paper by Kolmogorov and Czerneski. A classic in its field. Perhaps you are related."

"Could be. Is he living?"

"It's a she, not a he. She's in Wisconsin now."

I have actually met this mathematician and that was the story he told me about the first time he encountered my uncle. My uncle's version is a bit different, less matter-of-fact. In my uncle's version, he goes to the Chicago city library researching anything about anyone with the name of Czerneski. In a Russian book he finds a reference to a mathematician, R. P. Czerneski, student of Kolmogorov. He finds this "classic paper" written in German for the periodical *Mathematische Zeitschrift*. He cannot, of course, understand its contents, but somehow my uncle feels that this paper is significant to him. He cuts it out with a razor blade and carries it in his coat pocket for days. Then the Polish mathematician shows up in the bar. He shows the man the article and is told that the author, a woman, lives in the United States.

Whose story is correct? It doesn't really matter, does it? Now the stories converge, more or less. My uncle hears the woman's first name, Rachela, and though he cannot remember anything at all from his days as a young boy in Vladimir-Volynski, this name conjures forth an image of a girl with pale skin and the lightest of hair, holding him. He's seen this image before in his mind and in his dreams. Until now, he thought it was an angel holding him as a young boy, comforting him, protecting him. He always imagined that this angel had wings. But in the bar, when he hears the name Rachela, the image appears again and the wings are not there. It's not an angel that is holding him. This is how memory works, I know, full of clichés precisely because the pictures we hold in our minds are usually the most trite.

"You've met this Rachela?" my uncle asked the professor.

"Yes. She is without peer. Born in Poland. Educated in Moscow."

"Born in Vladimir-Volynski, yes? Jewish, but with the face of a Pole, broad, not like mine."

"How do you know this?"

"That woman is my sister." As my uncle said this he reached out and hugged the mathematician. I know this bone-crushing hug, its ability to force every molecule of oxygen out of your lungs and make you understand that true vitality requires some awareness that life is both fragile and temporary. My uncle is binary. He is either at rest or fully alive.

Now I am not trying to pull your heartstrings with this tale of long-lost siblings finding each other. It is not my style to dwell on the sentimental, but neither can I avoid it. I am stone-cold sober as I write this part of my story, although I do admittedly drink too much sometimes. My uncle is an emotional man through and through. With my parents, I can, if I wish, be distracted from their tumult and raw nerves by their work, so elegant, pure, and beautiful. But there is no other side to my uncle. Just thinking of him immediately makes me think of his rough beard scratching against my cheeks as he holds me and kisses one side, then the other. Through all of his years, he has attracted women who would, if asked, do anything in their power to come to his aid. I know exactly why. Who can resist such a life force?

After the mathematician left the bar, my uncle called the home of Rachela Karnokovitch in Madison, Wisconsin. His English was still rudimentary, so he began in Polish. He introduced himself and told my mother where he was born. You'd think my mother would have been surprised by this call. What were the odds of such a thing happening? But no. This most logical of women was always sure, somehow, that her brother survived. Every Yom

Kippur she would light a *yahrtzeit* [memorial day] candle for her mother. But she was convinced her brother, little Shlomo, still lived. When she prayed it wasn't for his life. It was for the hope that one day she would see him again.

The conversation fell into the familiar almost immediately as my uncle heard that perfect accent of eastern Poland. His money was running out—this was back in the days of AT&T's monopoly, when phone calls even over distances of 120 miles could quickly eat at daily wages—and he told his sister to call him back. He waited for what seemed like a ridiculous amount of time in the frigid Chicago telephone booth, the vapor from his lungs forming clouds, and when the phone rang, he brought the receiver to his ears, longing to hear that voice again. My mother told him the story of his childhood, of the planes flying overhead in 1939 and how their mother, literally hedging her bets and not believing her little boy had the strength to travel to the unknown in Russia, left him behind with her sister in Vladimir-Volynski.

My uncle was two years old at the time. And the only real memory he had of his days in Vladimir-Volynski started to make sense as he heard this story. Images will come to him over the next year. His earliest memory is from 1941. A dark-haired woman is holding him against her breast on a clear day in an open, grass-covered field. There is the sound of gunfire and the woman falls. He clings to her body even as she falls into a pit, and pretends to sleep, hoping that perhaps if he simply closes his eyes he can will this moment away. He remembers the musty smell of the dirt covering him, and the stillness all around him as he gasps for air and starts to claw at the dirt above, trying to find light.

This is my uncle's will at work even at the age of four. He will somehow manage to dig himself out of the ground by his small fingers, pruney, no doubt, from the moisture in the soil, and find the air to breathe. He will run from this killing field—today covered in chest-high grass in the summers and marked with a single concrete memorial pillar, Soviet in its pragmatism and with a few misspellings—into the surrounding forest and survive by himself for he doesn't know how many days. A Polish family will find him as they flee, not from the Germans, but rather from Ukrainian fascists practicing their own brand of ethnic cleansing.

In the hospital, my uncle told the priest a short version of this story. He ended it with a sentiment that I'd heard many times from him. "I've already been dead and buried. There is nothing anyone can do that can possibly shock me." But in my mother's hospital room, my uncle was undeniably fearful, and he was talking at a fast clip.

"Have you been to Poland, Father Rudnicki?" my uncle asked.

"No. I've never found the opportunity."

"I should take you. I haven't been in so long. Sasha as well. Maybe even Viktor. My son Bruce. It would be a good idea. Rachela would like it. All of us together."

"I would, to tell you the truth," my mother said.

"I barely speak a word of Polish, Shlomo," my father said. "I'm over seventy years old. You want to drag me back to a place where you can still smell horseshit in the streets?"

"It wouldn't be so bad," my mother said. "You'd be a tourist, not a citizen. If Cynthia came with you. Now that would be funny. That I would like to see. I wish I could watch from above. The *lalka* in her high heels trying so artfully to avoid the piles on the cobbles."

"Cynthia in Poland," my uncle said. "That is funny."

"You should take her," my mother said.

"No. It's a man's thing, this trip. But you could go with us, for sure. If I tell you we'll all go tomorrow, will you let them fill you back up with blood?"

"It's not that simple, Shlomo. No. I'm done. This is a good way to go, actually. I have people I love around me. The morphine makes me feel dreamy. Sashaleh, what do the pressure numbers say?"

"They keep dropping."

"I know. You keep looking at them. You think they are going to go higher by some miracle?"

"I can always hope, Mother."

"You've been a good son, the numbers can drop. It's OK." She looked at the rings on her fingers. "Shlomo, you can take off the jewelry now."

My uncle rose out of his chair and kissed his sister on the forehead. My mother loved jewelry. The thicker the gold and the bigger the gem, the better she liked it. It wasn't so much about display. "Even in this country, you never know," she said. "You might need to leave in a hurry. Gold is always valuable."

I watched my uncle take the heavy gold necklace with its opal pendant from my mother's neck. My mother lifted up her hands and he began to pull off the rings. She had a small lapis lazuli ring from her childhood, the only piece of jewelry they hadn't sold during the war. Although it had been stretched, all of her adulthood it had fit snug on her right pinkie. Now it was so loose that it came off without any effort. One finger at a time, the rings were removed, including the gold band and diamond she always wore. My uncle stood up, handed them to me, grabbed me by my shoulders, and sobbed against my shirt.

My father looked up from his chair. "Shlomo, you've been a good brother. You don't have to cry."

I looked at my mother. She had closed her eyes when she lifted up her hands for her brother. That physical act had required one last push, one last use of the mental will and emotional strength for which she was admired and held in awe. She would never open her eyes again.

CHAPTER 4

From *A Lifetime in Mathematics* by Rachela Karnokovitch: The Bear

I remember a good deal about our trip to Vorkuta. It was in 1940, in April, I believe, about the time of my tenth birthday. No one celebrated such things in my part of Poland, even in well-to-do homes like ours. It would have been considered decadent and indulgent to bestow such attention on a child. It was a time of war as well.

We had been living in Odessa. My father, ever resourceful, had in advance of the war obtained a letter offering him a place to live, should he need it, from a Karlin-Stolin sect rabbi in Belarus. He presented this letter to a Soviet officer in Vladimir-Volynski, and I don't know why—no one was being allowed to leave, even those who tried to bribe officials—he stamped our papers. Even the guards looked surprised as they inspected our documents at the Belarus border.

We spent roughly a week in the rabbi's house in Motal. In exchange, my father gave the rabbi gold. But there was no food. It was the first time in my life I had felt hunger. That's what I remember, the gnawing at my stomach, oh so fierce. I was a spoiled child back then, used to getting everything I wanted, and was so angry with my mother and father. Didn't they know I needed food? I thought of my brother, still in Vladimir-Volynski, and was terribly jealous. Our aunt was childless and she would give us little chocolates when we visited. He was undoubtedly in luxurious comfort with our aunt and here I was in a house full of children, all so quiet, subdued, and worried as they felt emptiness in their stomachs. We were disappearing little by little from our hunger. One day, we knew, we would be gone entirely.

My father was desperate to find someplace, anyplace, where he could find a way to make enough money for us to live. There was no black market of suitable size in Motal for my father to trade. We traveled on false papers to Odessa, where my mother had a distant cousin. They were not happy to have us in their tiny cinder-block apartment. Refugees were everywhere, hungry, looking for any bit of food or clothing. It was dangerous to walk outside even in daylight. Grown women, grandmothers, would force you down to the ground and steal the shoes from your feet. The police and soldiers would watch the lawlessness apathetically, spending most of their time trying to find cigarettes and women.

There was a place my father would go to trade, a square just a little walk from the main port. His Russian was poor at the time and the others didn't trust him. They viewed my father as an interloper who would take away their business. While he traded, I would sit in the stairwell of the apartment building by myself during the day, trying to avoid the angry stares, and worse, of my cousins. Here it was, out of pure unrelenting boredom, the absence of any stimulus whatsoever in my life for hours on end, that I began to amuse myself with what I learned is called topology.

The apartment building was constructed in a haphazard way, typical of what was found throughout the Soviet Union. As a result, the stairs were not predictable. Sometimes there would be twenty-two steps from one floor to another. Others would have twenty-three. The heights of these steps would be short or tall willy-nilly, and the lack of predictability would make people stumble even if they took care to watch their feet while they walked.

I thought there was some beauty in this randomness, something wondrously different from exactitude and predictability. Plus, I was surefooted and would delight in seeing my mean cousins end up with bruises. I started to think of staircases where there was no pattern to their ascent. I wrote down crude formulae to describe these stairs of my imagination. Unbeknownst to me, I was re-creating something devised by a Russian mathematician who died of starvation in World War I, Georg Cantor.

I'd sit on the cold cement stairs and imagine this unpredictable world. Hours would pass. There was my hunger, there were my thoughts, and if I thought hard enough, I could, moment by moment, forget my hunger. I was beginning to expand these pattern-less staircases into three dimensions, instead of one, spiraling upward—which is actually a trivial exercise—when my father was arrested as a capitalist for his trading. Two days later we were in a cattle car, bound for somewhere beyond Kotlas.

It was on that train that I began to change as a person. I started to be an adult. I had no choice. There was the light barely coming in from the slits between the boards, the cold at night. Everything was working to dull my senses, to make even the most mundane thought difficult to create. You tried to keep warm, huddling together with your family. There was one bucket in a corner where you had to do your business. At stops along the way, someone would throw the mess out and it would fill again on the next leg of our journey. The stench mixed with the vapors of people's faint breaths. The first time I had to go, my father walked with me to that bucket, trying to give me just the most meager amount of privacy, and I felt so grateful to him. He was a small man, graying and balding at an early age, but I could feel his strength. I knew he would take care of me no matter what.

Our life from now on would be hell. Of this I was certain. My mother was already showing signs that she would not be able to find the will to live through this ordeal. She would separate from us two, her head down, and it was as if something as involuntary as breathing was already becoming too difficult for her.

My father and I didn't talk much on this journey. Our conversations consisted of terse sentences, and were confined to the moments when we needed something. No one talked. What was there to say?

But at a stop in the Urals, I don't know where, we did talk. Someone randomly was given one loaf of bread and a jug of water for all thirty of us to share. The mood was tense. When would we, if ever, get more food? The car door was open, and I whispered to my father that we should just run, that it couldn't be worse than what was going to happen to us if we stayed on the train. He said, "No, Rachela. Look outside, what do you see?" I looked and saw nothing but stunted trees.

"No, look more carefully. There's a bear," he said and pointed into the distance.

"I see it, Father, yes."

"We see one. But there are many. They are hungry, hungrier than us. And they are waiting here for one reason, for someone to do just as you suggest."

"They would eat us, Father?"

"Yes, that bear. He is waiting to eat us. We are better off staying put. As bad as our life will be, we'll have a place to live. There will be bears there, too. But we can shut the door and keep them out."

I looked outside. The bear was still in the distance. He was emaciated. He would eat us for certain, I thought. Then the door shut and we were on our way to Vorkuta.

CHAPTER 5

Impossible Problems

Königsberg was not only the birthplace of my childhood "buddy" Leonhardt Euler but, as fortune would have it, also was home to one of the greatest mathematicians of the twentieth century, David Hilbert. Whether he, like little Leo, avoided crossing bridges twice is unknown. Probably not. Hilbert was a thoroughly purposeful man who perhaps, even as a child, would frown upon such a frivolous use of the mind. My father, certainly, never introduced Hilbert during his lessons to me. Even he wasn't inclined to dwell on killjoys. But he should have made an exception for Hilbert. My father knew, after all, that my mother had spent many years working on two of Hilbert's unsolved problems, one of them being the monstrously difficult Hilbert's sixth.

Hilbert would spend his entire career at the University of Göttingen. Hilbert's gift consisted not only of the ability to solve immensely difficult problems, but also the insight to identify what was *worth solving* in mathematics. He laid a road map for the work of future mathematicians that is still used today.

Even I, a mere user of mathematics, am under Hilbert's influence. Every student who wishes to understand the mathematics behind physical processes still passes through him or, more precisely, through Hilbert and his student Courant's textbook, *Methods of Mathematical Physics*. A textbook that is still useful ninety years after it is first published is unheard of. Yet I have Courant and Hilbert's textbook on my shelf. My students have this textbook on their shelves. My mother also had it, in the original German, on hers.

I open up this textbook now, dear reader. It's been decades since I've looked at even one page. The book is made of the good stuff: a sewn binding, thick acid-free paper, and a utilitarian gray canvas cloth cover with black-and-red lettering. It isn't an inviting text. Instead its appearance says "I know I'm important. Who the hell are you?"

I open a page at random, read the words, and look at the equations. Oh my, I had to struggle mightily to comprehend this material, but it was well worth the effort. It changed how I thought about math forever. I fully understood, in a way that I previously knew only vaguely, that math was about the ability to transform symbolism into palpable mental images. This is what my father had been trying to teach me when I was young. This is where genius lay. Hilbert had this ability. Whoever has the best visceral understanding of what seems to most to be abstract and obtuse wins in the battle to solve seemingly impossible mathematical problems.

For example, consider this equation, a formula that guides me in virtually everything I study:

$$\rho Dv/Dt = -\nabla p + \nabla \cdot T + f$$

Yes, OK, reader, I know you are probably sweating almost instantly at the sight of such a thing. You are thinking perhaps, "Why does this author show us such opaque symbolism? Forget this book by this middle-aged man raised by eccentric mathematicians (as if there are any other kind). One of his parents is already dead in this story and she was probably the most interesting character of the lot."

Why am I making your life difficult? Because while maybe math is shit to you, it isn't to me, and it wasn't to my mother or father. It is like breathing to us, and to ignore math in this story would be akin to listening to Frank Zappa without ever having taken hallucinogens, an incomplete experience.

Dear reader, don't panic. Newton was barely past twenty when he invented calculus. It's pure adolescent whimsy at work. Think of the language of mathematics as shorthand that has been around for centuries, the equivalent of teenage texting, but for geeks. Yes, I know you don't know half the text abbreviations that your teenage children use, but you can figure out their argot if pressed, can you not? You can figure out this one as well.

As my father noted to the priest at the hospital, I study the movement of air and water in our atmosphere. To study it, I fly into hurricanes and make measurements, which actually isn't as dangerous as it sounds. It's certainly less harrowing than experiencing the full blast of a hurricane on land.

The equation above has a name, it's so famous: Navier-Stokes. People like me routinely use this equation to describe the chaotic motion of air and water like that found in hurricanes. You've seen videos and pictures of such natural calamities, no doubt. Perhaps—and this would be unfortunate—you've experienced such danger firsthand.

Let's say we have a hurricane and we want to make some predictions as to where this horrible thing will move and how nasty its winds will be. If you live near a coastline, you, no doubt, would love to have such a prediction. Right now, unfortunately, I can say with complete certainty that I will never be able to provide one, although perhaps the students of the students of my students will be successful. Right now I am trying to understand what happens within a 10 inch by 10 inch by 10 inch piece of a hurricane. That may sound depressing, the idea of studying such a little speck of a big nasty storm, but the good news is that I'm making progress! To be of use to you, we will have to get much better at understanding my little 1,000-cubic-inch box, and then eventually move up to boxes 1,000 cubic miles in size. It will be awhile.

In the meantime, the National Hurricane Center makes predictions that essentially assume a hurricane is a solid cork floating in a swirling but well-behaved soup of water-loaded air. How well do these cork predictions work? Not well at all. Hurricanes aren't corks. They are not floating in a well-behaved soup. The soup is a mess, as is the hurricane, which is not surprising, since trying to make a distinction between the hurricane and what surrounds it is never precise.

I wish to describe and predict where a fluid particle inside my 1,000-cubic-inch box inside a hurricane will go. So everything in that bit of geek texting above called the Navier-Stokes equation relates to either the nature of the fluid or how fast it's moving. ρ is how dense the fluid is, p is its pressure, v is its velocity, and t is time. The equation states that if you want to know how the velocities of a fluid change with time, you need to keep track of how the fluid's pressure changes with space and the stresses, T, and external forces, f, on that fluid.

It is routine for upper-class undergraduates who are concerned with fluid dynamics to derive the Navier-Stokes equation, known for more than 150 years, on their own. It is simple to do this, actually. You don't even have to know anything about fluid dynamics. Just start out assuming Newton is right and apply Newton's fundamental laws to fluids. Voilà. But please don't misunderstand and think that just because it is easy to do, this work is trivial. It took more than 150 years to go from Newton to Navier-Stokes, and the work involved the best and the brightest mathematicians of Europe, including Leonhardt Euler.

I am happy to use the Navier-Stokes equation. But I am not a mathematician. I'm a user of Navier-Stokes, not an inspector of its correctness. David Hilbert was, however, an inspector. In 1900, he announced to the world that there were twenty-three major problems in mathematics that awaited solutions. One of those problems, number six, expresses the need to prove the fundamental correctness of using equations like Navier-Stokes to describe the physical behavior of materials. Then, in 2000, one hundred years after Hilbert, a group of mathematicians examined the future of mathematics again. Many of Hilbert's problems had in fact been solved at least partially over the interim years. But Hilbert's sixth remained a complete enigma. In a nutshell, the new committee dramatically reduced the scope of Hilbert's original problem to something more manageable than all equations used to describe physical processes. They chose just one equation—perhaps the most important and certainly one of the most baffling—Navier-Stokes.

The fact is that when your geeky college niece or nephew or my students derive this equation from Newton's laws (with the help of Euler's work), they are making assumptions about the behavior of fluids that are so naïve as to be ridiculous.

Think of a hurricane, the water and air violently going every which way with a mixture of order and chaos. We call this mixture of movement, this wildly erratic dance of fluids, turbulence. You know this word from air travel, and it never means anything good. But to me, it means something beautiful. Without it, understanding hurricanes would be boring. Mathematicians' worries about this equation would be the height of neurosis.

Add turbulence and mathematicians' concerns are quite sane. The committee of 2000 thought they were so appropriate that they offered $1 million, a Millennium Prize, to anyone who could show that the Navier-Stokes equation was indeed appropriate for all conditions, even turbulent ones. You can do a lot with $1 million, of course. But the money associated with a Millennium Prize isn't really an incentive. It's used as a symbol of importance, to show that a community views the solution of a problem to be so enormously difficult that it is willing to offer a ridiculous amount of money to anyone who can solve it.

Even before this million-dollar prize was offered it was recognized just how near impossible this problem was. Hilbert knew it. Kolmogorov, who had studied turbulence, knew it. My mother, who studied turbulence with Kolmogorov and unlike him continued her research in this field, of course knew it as well.

It is one thing to derive this equation and another to truly understand it. When I see the Navier-Stokes equation, it comes to life for me. It's not just an abstract combination of symbols that will eventually produce numbers. It is a living and breathing

description of fluids dancing in space to whatever may be whip-
ping them around. I can see the fluids. I can imagine clearly the
forces upon them as they move in a way that is semi-ordered but
ultimately unpredictable.

Actually, it's more than this. The big D in the Navier-Stokes
equation is called the material derivative, and it refers to watching
velocities of fluid change not from a fixed reference frame but
from one in which you are riding with the storm. When I think of
Navier-Stokes, sometimes I imagine myself as a Lilliputian in a
tiny canoe that has been lifted up and tossed high into the hurricane. The wind is so strong that it lifts my cheeks, distorting them
as if the storm were a real-life version of a fun-house mirror. I
watch as the fluids careen against and flow around me.

As well as I can visualize these fluids dancing, I know that my
mother could see them even better. She couldn't describe what
she saw to me in any concrete way, but I know from her work just
how much more ornate, nuanced, and ultimately more accurate
her vision was than mine. That's why she was a mathematician,
the best of her generation. That's, obviously, why I am not.

The problem of the universal appropriateness of the use of the
Navier-Stokes equation was the problem that my mother was rumored to have cheated death to solve. Where does such a crazy
idea come from? I submit to you the following evidence: my
mother, a seventy-year-old woman, ill, taking medications several
times a day that made her throw up, weak, unable to realistically
command anywhere near the concentration required to solve
such a problem, and far too old, even if healthy, to have the fresh-
ness of mind to make any headway on such a task. Who could

possibly think my mother could somehow capture the magic necessary to answer a question that had baffled mathematicians, the greatest and brightest minds, for more than a century? Here is one simple answer. Mathematicians can think like this. Impossible problems perhaps require impossible scenarios. Since no one young and healthy had solved this problem, perhaps someone old and sick, by sheer will, could.

Here is another answer. Only crazy people can think like this. And mathematicians are, as my uncle would say, *szaleńcy*, inherently crazy dreamers. They have no real sense of what can and can't be done. They work on impossible problems because they are impossible people. As I've noted, there are likely no reasonable geniuses in this world. While there are, I know from personal experience, some reasonable mathematicians, they are not at the forefront of their profession but mere worker bees. Even most worker bees in mathematics are hopeless as fully functioning human beings.

For better or worse, I'm stuck with them. They are all I've ever known. I grew up around them. They are my family. I love them wholeheartedly. After a brief and unsuccessful effort at trying to pull away from this intensely dysfunctional culture obsessed with abstraction, I even ended up marrying into it.

Yes, I have, with one exception, avoided any discussion of my own relationships, past and present. I certainly haven't forgotten about them, especially my life with my ex. You don't forget even two years of marriage. In my August years, my memories of that time are, strangely, far more vivid than they were thirty years ago. Oh Catherine. Perhaps you will pick up this book if only to see where you are mentioned. Here. This is the first real time. Catherine. Scan this text and find your name. You were my first, and for many years I thought you'd be my only, true romantic love.

Seven days in a house full of mathematicians who would pry up floorboards looking for hidden notes. Seven days with a father who had a difficult time forgiving me for abandoning what he worked so hard to train me to do. I wished out of both selfishness, so I could have avoided these days, and of course out of love, that my mother had proven to be immortal.

CHAPTER 6

When Someone Famous Dies

My mother's mentor, the great Kolmogorov, died in Moscow in 1987. Of course, the Russians, out of spite, denied my mother's request to attend the funeral. Whenever her name was mentioned in official Russian publications prior to 1989, they either pretended her career as a mathematician abruptly ended for no apparent reason in 1951 or simply made note of her first position after defecting, a lectureship at Ludwig Maximilian University in Munich. To someone in the West, this mention of her work in Germany would not be understood as anything out of the ordinary. But for a Russian it was an obvious and telltale slur. My mother was the lowest of the low, someone who abandoned communism and allied herself with Russia's truly worst and most vile enemy, the German Republic.

The rejection of my mother's request actually was, in hindsight, of no consequence. It was foggy in Moscow around the time of Kolmogorov's funeral, so foggy that planes could not land. My mother would probably have missed the event even if she had tried to attend. But she heard, of course, what had transpired. People came when they could by train, and the initial crowd, already large, eventually became an unmanageable sea of mathematicians, Soviet apparatchiks, and admirers not simply of the mathematical mind of Kolmogorov, but of his amazing political skill. How on earth did he, of all people, manage to avoid being exiled or worse during the bleak days of the 1950s, when anyone with any intellect was automatically targeted as an Enemy of the People?

Even Premier Gorbachev, fancying himself a bit of an intellectual, attended and spoke at this event. One could say without much distortion and hyperbole that Kolmogorov represented the best of what the USSR could offer both as an intellectual and as a citizen who profoundly shaped Russian education. A bastard son of humble beginnings who was nurtured with care by the Soviet system and gave so much back in return out of gratitude, it was perhaps to be expected that since his youth coincided with the rise of communism, his death would essentially be aligned with its collapse.

America obviously is not Russia. Mathematics does not hold any magnetic appeal. No, here it is strictly billionaires, football players, and movie stars who are of interest to the public. Certainly President Clinton, who had in 1993 awarded my mother a National Medal of Science for her achievements, was not going to attend her funeral in a Midwestern state where he knew his token presence would give Democrats no political advantage. He had other things on his mind, no doubt.

Besides, according to my mother, they had had an odd exchange at the medal ceremony. She was waiting in line in the Rose Room of the White House next to someone who had discovered, among other things, a new comet. Clinton chatted amiably with "Mr. Comet Man," giving him a big frat-brother pat on the back as he complimented him on his "eagle eye." He then moved to my mother, and struggled to find an entryway into conversation. "You know, Doctor K.," he said, giving an aw-shucks grin, "I hear you're just great with numbers." Clinton began to tell my mother of a recurring dream. He is in an elevator of an impossibly tall building. He keeps rising higher and higher alone in this elevator, the numbers signifying what floor he is on getting bigger and bigger. "What do you think it means, Doctor K.?"

"Well, I'm a mathematician, not a psychoanalyst," my mother said. "But it would seem that your subconscious is telling you that you are in over your head in your present job."

Clinton looked at my mother quizzically, and then grimaced, his jawbone clearly visible. The silence was palpable until Mrs. Clinton, standing behind him, broke into her signature, wineglass-breaking laughter. "Oh, it's a joke!" President Clinton smiled, hearing his wife's appreciation of my mother's dry humor. "You had me there, Doctor K.!" President Clinton placed his hand on my mother's shoulder briefly and then walked on. Mrs. Clinton gave a nod and a conspiratorial grin that my mother returned. My mother interpreted this brief wordless exchange as an indication that Hillary well understood that her husband, like most men lost in their egos and need for constant praise, was incapable of anything but obvious thought.

The *New York Times*, of course, had an obituary of my mother with a photograph taken by a White House photographer from that 1993 event. My mother never, ever smiled in a photograph. I have hundreds of pictures of her, and in almost every one there is that same look of scrutiny on her face. It's as if she is challenging the photographer to go ahead and try to take a decent picture of her. The *Times* called her, "The greatest female mathematician of her generation, and perhaps the greatest of any generation." My father, upon reading these words, looked hurt and turned indignant. "What is this qualification 'female'? What do these idiots know of mathematics? There will not be another like her for two hundred years, maybe longer."

But he had a right to be pissy. We were at my mother's home—a place from which he had been banished for many years, until my mother became sick—and the onslaught of phone calls, e-mails, and knocks on the door was already overwhelming. My cell phone mailbox had become completely filled in a matter of hours, mostly with condolences and requests for funeral information from Slavic-accented mathematicians.

"I want a private service," I said to my father. "Just us. The family."

"Good luck with that," my father said. "You know better than to ask for such a thing."

"You want to go with us to the funeral home and to find a plot?"

"No. I don't care for cemeteries. That is something Shlomo is best at doing, anyway."

"I'm going to buy two plots, you know. Together. You and Mother."

"Yes, I understand. Rachela already told me. You can put me in a Jewish cemetery, I suppose. I won't be able to object when the time comes, anyway."

"I'll need your signature attesting to your Jewish faith."

"You aren't telling me anything I didn't already figure out. It's a good thing I'm an atheist. You, however, have to play whack-a-mole with your sins." He gave me an ironic grin. Did I view the prospect of burying my father, who wasn't even circumcised, in a Jewish cemetery a sin? The answer is definitely not. He belonged next to my mother despite their many years apart. I would pay some extra money to the director of the funeral home so he would allow for this travesty. Yes, I knew I would be doing this not just for my mother. Mostly I was being selfish. I wanted to visit one place and one place only when, in the future, I would come back. Although I had no doubt that death was, aside from the recycling of carbon, a final act, I still needed to remember who these two people were.

Besides, it's not a Russian thing to follow rules, unless of course not following them will likely mean prison or worse. Many rules are in fact inherently stupid. Look at this rule about burial. You are required to be of the faith to be buried in a Jewish cemetery. The logic of such a rule, perhaps obvious to you, seems nonexistent to me. My father, like my mother, would end up a pile of bones soon enough. Did it really matter whether the penis once attached to my father's bones had a foreskin? After a few years underground, what evidence would there be of his Jewishness or lack thereof?

But my father was right. I do play whack-a-mole with my sins. I try to be a good person for, as the tacky Christmas song goes, goodness sake. Unfortunately, I don't possess the strength of will to avoid even the most common and obvious of pitfalls. So I do pray. I am, in fact, a praying atheist, and I'm sure there are many like me, although it's not a population that is measured in any census of which I am aware. What does prayer provide me, the most ordinary of sinners? A sense that my frailty is communal, a sense that I shouldn't be singled out for my human failures, or my attempts, however pathetic, to rid myself of them.

I prayed in Tuscaloosa regularly, most Friday nights at a tiny synagogue in a building that once housed a Jewish dry goods store. I certainly know how to pray according to the rules. In my teens, my mother sent me off to a Jewish high school in Chicago for a proper education. The idea was that rigor of any stripe would be lacking in the public high schools of Madison. The first time I went to the Tuscaloosa synagogue, the rabbi was out of town, and the synagogue president was on the *bima* [podium] valiantly trying to lead the services in a halting Hebrew with a crib sheet. I looked up from the second row and began to play the role of prompter, mouthing the syllables so she could see. After that incident I was more or less thrust into the role of assistant rabbi, which meant from then on I sometimes led services in the rabbi's absence.

Word of my semi-prowess in prayer and in Hebrew seemed to spread magically outside the barely existent Jewish community of Tuscaloosa into the general populace. Three blue-haired, Bible-toting ladies started to come by my house occasionally on Sundays.

With a mixture of the earnestness of faith and the bossiness of a healthy old age, they would show me passages that interested them in a dark brown, leather-bound King James Old Testament. They wanted to know, "What's it say in the original?" I would pull out my Five Books of Moses and translate the contents directly from the Hebrew for comparison. I never tried to tell them that the Hebrew from which I was reading was essentially a translation as well. I admired them for their faith and desire, however mis-guided, to get to know something akin to the true story.

I met my uncle at the synagogue, where we prayed, as is cus-tomary for those in mourning. I hadn't been there in a long time, and the old guys—some of the same old guys who were already stooped over and tiny when I was a kid—gave me a nod of aware-ness before we began. Then, after, they all shook my hand and told me what a wonderful woman my mother had been.

My uncle and I drove to the cemetery, the hot air in his

Lincoln Town Car blasting and keeping us remarkably warm despite the cold outside. "She wanted a plain pine box, you know," I said. "Just some rope around it. That's it."

"People will think we're being cheap. We need to do something a little better," my uncle said.

"OK, whatever."

"The governor call you?"

"The governor? Maybe. There were a lot of messages. I couldn't possibly listen to all of them."

"Dombrowski himself was on the phone. Not an aide. He was asking about the funeral." My uncle tapped his wedding ring against the steering wheel.

"You know him?"

"I give him money, but no, I don't really know him. I just shake his hand at dinners. He wants to give a speech."

"My mother know him?"

"Definitely not."

"He wants to turn my mother's funeral into a political event?" I turned to face my uncle, who continued to look straight ahead.

"Yes, something about Badger Ingenuity." There it was, that ungainly phrase, Badger Ingenuity. How the governor loved to use it when extolling the virtues of my home state. Manufacturing—upon which Wisconsin employment was more dependent than any other state in the Union—was plummeting due to the nation's push to have all of our jobs moved to China in the name of globalization, aka "let's accelerate corporate profits at the expense of the American worker." Governor Dombrowski, who claimed to be a distant relative of Copernicus, was forever trying to promote high-tech in Wisconsin.

While no national politician would be concerned with the death of a great mathematical mind, a Wisconsin politician was perhaps another matter. Home to a mere five million people, the state is best known for cheese, beer, and consuming an ungodly amount of alcohol per capita, in particular 25 percent of the nation's brandy. And what of Wisconsin's famous sons and daughters? Liberace. Hildegaard. Spencer Tracy. James Lovell. The Violent Femmes. The long-standing replacement guitarist for the rock band Genesis, I've forgotten his name. Gene Wilder. A book of famous Wisconsinites would be laughably thin, and most of those who might be included were, in truth, cultural obscurities.

Then there are the intellectual achievements of those from the Badger State. How many gleaming medals of anything have University of Wisconsin professors been awarded by the White House? One, to my mother. How many Nobel prizes? One, to Howard Terman, who died in the 1970s. Wisconsin did not apparently have much of a history of Badger Ingenuity.

"The man is an idiot," I said.

"Yes, but he is also the governor."

"What did you tell him?"

"I told him we would be honored to attend a separate memorial service at the capitol if he would like to arrange it."

"And I suppose you want me to fly in for such an event, yes?"

"Of course. It's the governor. They have to plan this and that. Maybe in a month they will hold it."

"And why do you want this to happen?"

"Now is not the time to discuss such things." I suppose I should have been angry with my uncle for trying to turn my mother's death into an opportunity for business. But this was who he was.

Despite, and maybe because of, growing up in a communist country, my uncle was inherently entrepreneurial. At least he was being honest with me. For now.

"It's the third funeral for our family in this country," my uncle said as we got out of the car. He reached down and picked up two stones. We walked to his first wife's grave, the red granite carved on the right-hand side, the empty shiny surface on the left. "I'll end up here, too, eh?" my uncle said. "I wanted to buy a plot for your mother when I bought these two. Right here." He pointed to a plot on the right, filled, next to his first wife. His father's tombstone was on the left. "But she said no. Now we'll have to be buried apart."

The air was cold against my cheeks. I could feel the hardness of the frozen ground through the soles of my shoes. After a century of use, the cemetery was almost completely full. In another few years, a new cemetery would open miles away from this one. My uncle placed jagged stones on his father's and wife's graves and recited a prayer. "Your mother was a good sister-in-law to her."

"She reminded Mom of her past, I think."

"Reminded me, also. Your *zaydeh* loved her so much, like she was his own daughter."

There was a steady drone of cars and trucks from the neighboring street. We walked to the sparsely filled part of the cemetery, the only portion with Russian-style tombstones. The portraits of the dead were etched on the granite. Some of the smiles were hideously spooky, perhaps even too scary for a Halloween midnight cemetery visit. I didn't know any of these faces. These were the graves of recent émigrés, most of whom had come to this country already middle-aged or old. They had tried to eke out at least a few final pleasant years in the paradise of the United

States. "What about here?" I asked my uncle, the designated de-
cider of all things practical in my family.

"No way!"

"Why not?"

"Look at who is already buried next door."

"Sam Wasserman. So?" I looked at the tombstone, the letters
in Hebrew telling me his birthplace. I thought of him years ago
standing on the *bima*, the synagogue president for what seemed
like forever. "He was born in Poland, like you, like your sister. He's
landsleit."

"That son of a bitch was the reason Cynthia and I couldn't get
married in *shul*. We had to rent a hall because of that bastard."

"You'll be buried thirty yards away."

"Yeah, but every time I visit my sister I need to be reminded of
him? And all those years not letting your mother read the Torah
because she was a woman. Like we were Orthodox or something.
Like we were still back in Poland. Your mother knew *Tanach* better than that bastard ever did!"

I was not going to get anywhere with my uncle in this mood.
"OK. It's important to you, I know. Pick a place."

My uncle walked between the sparely populated tombstones,
carefully inspecting all the names. If he was cold, it didn't show.
But me? After twenty-five years in Tuscaloosa, I was shivering despite the long cashmere coat borrowed from my uncle. He stopped
and started again and again. Finally, a look of satisfaction appeared
on his face. "Here. The Ornsteins. They will be good neighbors."

CHAPTER 7

From *A Lifetime in Mathematics* by Rachela Karnokovitch: Hunger

There are far too many people who know this feeling, far too many children. At any given time on this planet, maybe a billion people will be experiencing what we felt. Hunger. I hope you've never experienced it. I don't mean, "I'm hungry. I need to open the refrigerator and get something." That kind of signal is actually good, your body telling you it is tuned to your needs.

I mean pure hunger, not a transmission from your brain to get out of your chair and find some fuel for your body. Pure hunger is something different entirely. I'll try to explain to those who haven't felt it, but doubt I'll succeed.

I want you to follow my instructions. Take your eyes off this page when I tell you to do so. Look at the room around you. Wherever you are, simply open your eyes and look, listen, smell, and think whatever thoughts come your way. Maybe, since you likely are a mathematician if you are reading this, you are thinking about a problem you have been incrementally inching toward completing. I know you and how you think, don't I?

Take it all in. Then imagine all of your awareness disappearing. Your eyes work, yes, but they don't really see anything. Your brain won't let you process such information. The smells, they are gone, too. Your ears, they work simply to warn you of danger. Your thoughts, all of them are so uncomplicated and pure. Your mind cares nothing for mathematics. All is about the numbness inside you. This is what I mean by the purity of hunger.

You are truly in hibernation. Everything has slowed, because any processing, physical or mental, requires energy, and that, if you are truly nutrient-deprived, is precisely what you don't possess.

Stop here. Now take your eyes off this page. Forget about my story. Try to imagine this purity of absence. Do it. Try to do this for five minutes.

Now you're back. Maybe you can understand now, although I sincerely doubt it. But if you have managed to feel just a sliver of pure hunger, it's horrible, isn't it? Also, it's not like giving birth, where the mind can purposely forget all the pain so that you will do it again. It's not like that at all. Pure hunger is never forgotten. The memory of that feeling is placed in a part of your brain that allows for perfect permanent storage and almost instant recall. You never want to experience such a sense of deprivation again.

It can get worse than this, the retardation of everything, the numbing of your fingertips to go with the dull feeling in your belly. There is hunger beyond what I've described. I've never felt it, but I know people who survived the war under even worse conditions than my father and I did. They have told me what happens next. Even in the presence of food, the brain doesn't respond. Everything completely shuts down and your mind simply waits—without even the energy left for dread—for the time when everything expires.

As I've said, my body never shut down quite completely like this. We would have something to eat every day, just never enough. When I saw any food, a few crumbs of stale bread, some heated water containing the thinnest hint of something, even when that water was heated only with bones, my mind would spring up again. My purpose day-to-day was to eat and to have the sensory ability to find something that could potentially be edible.

When did this happen? We were near the Barents Sea during the war, north of the Arctic Circle. My father worked in the mines every day. There were clearings in the woods where the Soviets had built quarters for the miners and their families. There were no fences to keep us in. Where would we have gone?

In every clearing there were about six low-lying structures, long sheds. They possessed no windows. These sheds, covered in tar paper, had been broken up into four single-roomed living quarters, each with a wood-burning stove. The beds were made of louse-covered cloths filled with straw on wooden frames. The floor consisted of rough planks of wood. To keep the lice down— but certainly not to eliminate them—we'd put each leg of our beds into a cup and then fill that cup with kerosene. It was a trick that someone taught us early on. Before then, I can't begin to describe the agony of the itching and bites.

At first, we suffered tolerable deprivation mixed with an almost unbearable loss of dignity. It would get worse, although we couldn't imagine how. I had grown up so fast in just two months, had lost the demanding princess inside me. Unlike my mother, I completely stopped crying. It's not that I didn't want to do so. I just couldn't. The feeling of hurt would come to my eyes, I could definitely sense it, but nothing would happen. I had been transformed into a hardened adult, someone fully accepting of tragedy and disappointment. I understood the limitations present in the world. I could cope with anything, or so I thought.

One can, I suppose, invent silver linings just because they

provide some sort of meaning to tragedy and make the horrible palatable. But I don't think I'm doing this when I say that without those days above the Arctic Circle I wouldn't have accomplished much. I know exactly what direction my life would have taken without the war. I would have remained a spoiled child, growing up in my provincial Polish town with my little dog walking beside me on my visits to the town square.

The ties to my Christian friends would have been magically cut in my early teens, just like they had been cut with my mother and her friends at that age, and I would have accepted this change as inevitable and somehow natural. I would have lived my comfortable Jewish life with the overarching sense that it was my destiny.

The world of Jewish privilege in my hometown was available, of course, only to a few. There were twenty thousand Jews in my sthtetl, and what did I know of them? Our own house, lovely, one of the most beautiful in town, was made of stone. A wall of that same stone, perhaps three meters high, surrounded our rear yard. This was my world. I don't see how or why I would have left it even in marriage and beyond. I would have married into a similar family, taken care of a similar lovely house, brought up my own children, and continued to live a life of luxury, free from anything approaching intellectual thought.

Remember, my first mathematical stirrings did not take place until relatively late. I was already nine years old, almost ancient by standard measures. My dear mentor Kolmogorov was four when he began to examine the rudiments of number theory, or so he told me. Other mathematicians will tell you similar stories. But me? I needed the deprivation of war to let my mind be idle enough to discover the world of mathematics on my own.

How would this have happened in dear, provincial Vladimir-Volynski, with my days filled with things I thought were so important, like whether Katya and Brecca (Where are they now, I wonder?) would get permission to travel with my mother and me to Lvov to buy some Italian shoes for the school year. I would think of the colors I would try on, the wonderful softness of the leather. How could mathematics have entered a mind filled with such banal detail?

I needed a war to make me into a mathematician. I needed deprivation to make me appreciate every little gift, every tiny increment—like a crumb of food, yes—of understanding while solving a problem. I don't believe a spoiled child, even one encouraged to pursue the intellectual world, can ever be anything more than a second-rate mathematician. This is what war gave me, a life of the mind that would sustain me almost always.

There we were, in a place far, far from anything. As I said, at first the deprivation was tolerable. We had food, though barely enough to get by. We had wood for our stove. I would attend school, and this is where my talent was discovered. My teacher somehow knew I possessed this ability in mathematics. I don't know how. She was from Ukraine. I remember her well, still, how she tied her hair in a braided bun. I had never seen this before. It was a style from the eastern part of her own country. For many years, I have worn my hair in that style in her honor.

I did mathematics while the other children played. Almost all of the children in our part of the camp were Jewish like me, yes, but most didn't know Polish aside from a few words. They were barely competent with Russian, struggling in school just to comprehend what our teacher said. They spoke Yiddish, a language that I barely knew, and with an accent not from my region, not with closed vowels, but something broader. Initially, I couldn't understand them, and first impressions leave an indelible mark. They would taunt me: "Little Christian Rachela with the blond hair." "Your name is Jewish, but you can't be." "Your father is Jewish but not your mother." "Stuck with the Jews you are, now you know what it's like."

Even had I wanted to, the other children wouldn't let me play with them most days. But I was already occupied with something serious. I began to work on more topology problems. This was my entry into the world of mathematics, spatial relationships in the real world. I understand why my son studies what he does. It comes from me. Fortunately and unfortunately, he never had to endure hunger, never had to live without.

My teacher told the authorities about my gift. Somehow she knew I was not simply talented, but a prodigy. The food came, little scraps of horrible meat, but still I was so proud of what I managed to provide my family. Mrs. Sharekhova, you are long gone from this world, I know. But you were a splendid, observant teacher. What brought you to that forsaken edge of the earth?

My mother would die that spring after a long, hard winter. So did almost everyone, it seemed. The rations became smaller and smaller. The wood allotments shrank as well. We were cold. We were starving, all of us. That's when cholera came. My mathematics stopped, the only time in sixty years that this has happened. When hunger and death come there isn't room for anything else.

CHAPTER 8

The Ballerina

My mother hated Russia, more specifically the USSR. Despite the fact that the Soviet state identified her gift for mathematics and provided her with a world-class education under the tutelage of one of the best minds of the twentieth century, mere mention of the Soviet Union would cause bile to rise in my mother. It was all about her own mother, who died of cholera near the Barents Sea. Such deaths weren't unusual, certainly. Stalin was responsible for the death of perhaps as many as forty million.

That my grandmother, whom I, of course, never met, was one of many who died because of Stalin's cruelty did not diminish its impact on my mother. I understand this a bit. It has been eleven years since my mother's death, and while I had the gift of being with her well into my adulthood, I still feel the loss of her presence. Had I, like her, been ten years old, sent to a barren, frigid landscape, and watched my mother die because of the absence of even rudimentary sanitation—something that should be a given in any truly civilized country, war or not—I would no doubt be angry for life.

My mother harbored this hatred of the Soviet Union from her childhood onward and defected to the West as soon as she possibly could. Her husband and her toddler son, me of course, were in Moscow at the time. That's why the Soviets had no fear about her going to Berlin to give a talk in 1951. Yes, my mother left both my father and me behind when she defected. It seems to be a family tradition, this leaving the son behind. Perhaps this is why my uncle and I are so close.

Years later she tried to explain her defection to me. It wasn't just the oppressive nature of communism. She had no intellectual future in Russia. "Women in American universities complain about being treated like dirt today," she said. "They have no idea what it was like for me back then, even after I married. In the West, as bad as it was for women, it was heaven in comparison. Sure American men thought they could intimidate me. But I'd lived through war. I had starved. American male mathematicians back then, and even now, the obnoxious ones, you can still see their mothers' milk on their lips. What can they possibly do to scare me? Little crying babies they are. British mathematicians, too."

I was in good hands, she said, and she was convinced that she would never get my father to defect willingly. She had to force the issue by going ahead of him, and she was confident he would follow. "Your father is a resourceful man when he needs to be. I knew he would find a way. But those two years being away from you were harder than anything, absolutely anything else, I have lived through."

I could have challenged this assertion of my mother, I suppose. Really now. Leaving me was more difficult than starving along the Barents Sea? But I didn't have a child then. I didn't know, even vaguely, the difference between physical deprivation and the emotional loss of one's child, even when you know that child is healthy and well.

I don't remember much of the years without my mother. The

facts consist mostly of what others have told me. I don't remember missing my mother, although I do remember my father telling me that one day soon we'd all be together again. Here are the facts, a bit inadequate and random. My father lost his position at Moscow State University because of my mother's defection. Kolmogorov couldn't help my father, except perhaps to save him from being arrested and imprisoned. Daily, the NKVD watched us.

How we lived those two years without any real income is testimony to my father's strength of will and cunning. But it is more than this. How he implemented his plan to get us out of the Soviet Union required a singleness of purpose few possess. For those two years, our little apartment became an English-only zone. I am perhaps one of a handful of Russian citizens, well, former Soviet citizens to be precise, whose true first language was English. This was part of his plan, for me to speak as if I were an American, without even a trace of an accent. Where did he get the books and tapes for this major effort at subterfuge? I don't know to this day.

My father insists that at the age of three I spoke English with the casual, lazy tongue of an American sitcom child actor, but I find this hard to believe. At any rate, all those years in the little Moscow of the United States—my parents' Madison bungalow, with its frequent Russian visitors receiving my mother's kindness—partly reversed my father's hard work. Today most everyone knows I'm an immigrant from the second I open my mouth.

I will explain later exactly how my father and I defected. Again, it's nothing I remember. But I am told that I was ecstatic to come to a land where everyone spoke "my language." I was happy, of course, to see my mother. What child wouldn't be?

As I write this, I am a little past sixty years of age, and the fact is that my happiness over my arrival in this country has never left. I consider myself a very fortunate man. Where would I be in Russia today? Nowhere enviable, no doubt. But here I have much for which to be thankful. Like my mother, I possess an intense patriotic fervor. Sometimes I cry at baseball games when I sing "The Star-Spangled Banner" along with everyone else. My hyperpatriotism is one of the few things I share with most of my old Southern neighbors.

But my mother's patriotism, wed to her extreme antipathy toward the Soviet Union, possessed her to do things well beyond crying while singing about our great country. She wanted to share her patriotism for the wonderful USA with more Russians, as many as she could convince to abandon their Soviet home. This meant that just about every Russian citizen who managed to reach our modest city during the Cold War would encounter my mother and her larger-than-life presence. They would receive a speech from her that changed frequently in its particulars but always contained the same message: defect and stay in the paradise of America.

Whenever there was a Russian cultural event, we would be there. A ballet. A circus. A concert. A poetry reading. Russian ice skaters in tacky costumes dancing to Frank Sinatra. Some of these performances, even the highest of the high, on the part of Russian artists were painfully comical. For example, the Moscow State Symphony came to Madison when I was eight or so and played in the university stock pavilion, the only place large enough to house the thousands of music lovers excited about the prospect of hearing a world-class orchestra. The venue, of course, smelled like the barn it was and, worse yet, in the middle of Tchaikovsky's Fifth

Symphony, with the strings bowing vigorously and the cymbals crashing, a nearby train with perhaps one-hundred-plus cars' worth of coal and whatnot whistled its presence. The conductor, infuriated by the disturbance, stopped the orchestra in mid-measure, and waited a full five minutes for the train to pass. The orchestra never returned to our humble city.

We would drive to Chicago—my father gleefully speeding down US 20, then years later even more happily driving on the brand-new racetrack called I-90—to see Russian performers. These trips had only a little to do with cultural enrichment. My mother was on a political mission. We would always find a way to talk to the performers.

My mother's Russian was impeccable, the Russian of the elite, educated class. Russia, a country that for decades was supposedly about classlessness, is perhaps the most class-aware country I know. Accents, diction, and grammar provide a sharp dividing line and always have. Backstage at intermission or after the show, the sincerity and expert basis of my mother's pronouncements to these performers was accepted without question. She would talk to the artists as my father and I idly stood by. The appreciation in the performers' eyes, hearing my mother heap praise, was often palpable. But it was never long lasting. In the uneven light that seems to exist backstage in all concert halls, the inevitable would happen. My mother would pause from her stream of compliments, breathe in the stale indoor air, and then change her tone.

"You poor things. You are like circus animals, in a way. Forced to travel and parade your beauty and talent only to be put back in a cage after the show. I know. I was like you. But now, here, I am free. My name is Rachela Karnokovitch. I was a student of the great Kolmogorov in Moscow. But here I am free to do whatever I wish. I can accomplish so much more than I ever could in Russia. And you can, too. . . ."

Usually, well before she reached this part of her standard speech, the blue suits with their pale skin, bad breath, and yellowed teeth would come forth and gently try to move my mother along. Also usually, well before this portion of her speech, the appreciative glow on the artists' faces would change to panic at the thought of what punishments might await them as a result of this random, contaminating encounter with my mother. Sometimes the panic would escalate into hysterical shouts of disavowal in Russian. "I don't know this person! I've never met her! She came from I-don't-know-where!"

My mother, my father, and I would walk away. My mother would forcibly remove the hand of the KGB man against her elbow. "I don't need your help, you bastard," she would growl. Then the litany would fly from her lips. "You dogs! In Russia, I had to be polite to you, smile at you. But here it's different. Here, you have to be pleasant to me. How many have you murdered, you bastards? How many have you imprisoned? Here on Earth you are almighty. But in the world to come you will burn forever!"

These events would repeat themselves at almost every concert we attended. Even as a child, I couldn't understand why the KGB didn't have a picture of my mother, so that they could intercept her before she made their work so difficult. The look of satisfaction on my mother's face as we walked back to our seats would be absolute.

But every once in a while the script would change. The blue suits would be doing lord knows what. They wouldn't be paying attention as my mother beckoned an artist to defect. Even rarer still, the performer's eyes would lock into my mother's stare as if hypnotized, as if this were a dream come true. A woman was telling him in perfect Russian what he had been thinking for years, reading his mind. At such times my mother would pass a piece of paper into the hand of the artist quickly, with a nod. "You call," she would say. "You call me whenever and wherever. I will take care of you. I will make sure you are safe."

As a child, these "successful" exchanges filled me with pure panic. They were far worse than the embarrassment of being whisked away by the KGB. What if a call from one of these adult urchins did come? What trouble would my mother, so fervent in her anticommunism, get us into? The frequent intrusions of mathematicians visiting our house and sleeping on our living room couch or, worse yet, taking over my bed and making me sleep on the couch, were bad enough. I thought ahead and had visions of being exiled to our living room couch for years, usurped by a new needy member of our "family."

My mother was bound to succeed sooner or later. Two years after she handed a ballerina a slip of paper with the alphanumeric string HI4-6572, the HI standing for Hilltop, it happened. I, at the tender age of thirteen, picked up the phone and heard the panicky voice of Anna Laknova, who, like my mother and Kolmogorov, was brought up from the dust and, through the Soviet system, polished into a shining jewel of talent. Disappointed to hear someone who obviously was not an adult, Anna demanded to speak to my mother.

"She is at her office at the university," I said, thinking I was talking to yet another Russian mathematician.

"Ay, ay, ay, she said she would be here. She would take care of me." And I knew instantly what this was about.

"You are in what city? Chicago?"

"Yes."

"Where?" I could sense she was worried about giving this information. "I'm the boy who was with my mother and father backstage," I tried to explain. "I will go to my mother's office. We will drive to meet you. But you need to tell me where."

My uncle drove the first new car he ever owned, a Chevy Impala. My mother rode shotgun, and I sat in the back of the car reading Gogol or some other Russian writer. In our home, reading was more important than conversation. When there were no guests at night, sometimes the only noises you could hear were the creaking of chairs, the sipping of tea, and the almost silent sound of pages being turned.

I was having a hard time concentrating, though. I was giddy. I might have to live on the living room couch for the rest of my years at home, but this was something far better than watching a TV spy thriller like *The Man from U.N.C.L.E.* We were a part of a real piece of Iron Curtain intrigue. Plus I could tell that my mother was so proud of me for keeping my wits and writing down everything we needed for this freedom mission: the name of the woman, the exact address where she was hiding, and the precise meeting time.

But the truth was that—like most events that sound so exciting on paper—picking up this ballerina was a mundane thing. We parked our car along an elm-lined street of three-story brick apartment buildings, were buzzed into one of them, a door was opened, and there she was, a frightened woman perhaps twenty-one years old in the apartment of a Polish hotel maid.

OK, it was not entirely mundane. This ballerina was, to a thirteen-year-old boy, the quintessence of beauty, lean and graceful, delicately featured, exuding natural elegance, her long dark hair in a bun. We took her to an FBI office in Chicago, where she formally defected, and we filled out what seemed like a ream's worth of papers attesting to our willingness—without any promise of help or aid on the part of the U.S. government—to house and protect this defector from harm until she would be formally accepted as a legal resident of the United States.

They would become a formidable pair, my mother and Anna. Physically, they were so different. My mother towered over her dark-haired, olive-skinned, diminutive ward. In other ways, too, they contrasted. My mother had her overpowering intellect. Anna, so self-possessed that she scared all but the most confident and foolish of men, had her physicality. Perhaps you could count me as one of the foolish ones. Unlike any of the others, she would never toss me aside when she grew bored. I was as close to a brother as she would have. Tell me, what man doesn't want a self-assured, beautiful sister who men look upon with desire? You are the one man with whom she shares her secrets. You are the one who has a piece of her heart forever.

Anna's defection was a two-inch story in major newspapers across the country. It was something buried on page fourteen, next to ads for things like Pall Mall cigarettes. Who cares about ballerinas, even world-class ones, in this oh-so-practical country?

Anna would go on to perform in New York for many years,

and then move to Los Angeles to marry a movie director. This marriage—one of three total—would last for six years. She taught dance, and even worked with my cousin for a time, helping out with choreography for his TV specials. She would usually come to Madison once a year to spend time with the family that had generously given her a new home. After my mother was diagnosed, Anna started calling her once or twice a week and flying in on occasional weekends.

When I got a call on my cell, I heard the sadness in her voice, the same sadness I felt. "Is Bruce with you?" I asked.

"He'll be here later tonight," Anna said.

"It's good. I need you both here. It would be too hard without you," I said, lapsing into Russian, something I rarely do on my own.

CHAPTER 9

In My Room

When a family sits shiva, you have to do some rudimentary things to prepare the house. You cover mirrors, so as not to look at your dreadful personage. You cover photos, too. Why should anyone be reminded of any events of the past? You do that enough in your head without visual cues. I think this rule should apply more widely. Add bookcases to the list. Why would I want to be reminded of the books I read as a child in my mother's house?

I took over my old room, mercifully absent of anything from my childhood. There was a picture of my mother and my grandfather on a desk. That was it for memories. Those two were now gone. How many people were left who remembered them together? Me and maybe a dozen others. In another thirty years, the number would be zero.

I dragged an air mattress up the stairs that Uncle Shlomo managed to borrow from someone, blew it up, and put it dead center in the room. A week here would be fine, I thought, as I looked out through the lace curtains to the icy backyard and the park beyond. Bruce took over my mother's bedroom. Anna was supposed to be in there, but Bruce protested that he was not going to sleep in the sunroom because it housed a "dead person's bed."

"My mother died in the hospital, not here," I said.

"It's a sickbed. What's the difference?"

"You can't contract cancer from a bed, Bruce."

"You a physician all of a sudden?"

Bruce was by far the most American of us, the only one who had actually been born in this cherished land. In the world of Los Angeles, no one would guess that he was related to people like us. His cultural divorce—ultimately superficial—took place when he went to college. When he came back home from Williams his first year, he talked like a Boston Brahmin. After his junior year in Italy, he took on an Italian accent that he kept well into his mid-twenties. But in Madison, he tended to regress. This town was not good for him. I knew this. Even his father knew this. When Shlomo, with whom Bruce had long reconciled after some very tempestuous teen years, invited him to stay at his house—a faux-palatial estate with Ionic columns, marble floors, and a couple of gilt statues of Roman women in various classical poses—he knew what the answer would be. Anna, however, was far less patient. "You're being a big baby," she said, and reluctantly swapped rooms with Bruce.

My room had once been my haven. I would come home from Chicago—where I was living my ironic life of religious instruction mixed with a nascent atheism and a lust for the daughter of a delightful and naïve couple—and spend hours in my room alone. I'd read novels and philosophy and write thoughts that at the time seemed profound. When I read these heartfelt musings now they seem ridiculously morose and infantile.

No one seemed to be worried about—or maybe no one noticed—my descent into teenage narcissism except my grandfather, for whom we had made an expansive room out of the attic. Grandpa

Aaron was a pragmatic man. He was not a poker player, a bridge player, or a chess player. He liked to read the news. He read *Barron's* from cover to cover. In a home full of distracted people, he made up for us all. He was our chief financial officer and invested my parents' money well. My grandfather opened the door of my room one day without knocking—privacy was nothing my family believed in—and maybe if I had been reading Gorki or Flaubert or Turgenev, he would have just shrugged. But he saw the name on the cover of the book hiding my face and erupted.

"Kafka! What goddamn sixteen-year-old boy reads Kafka? Out!"

"What do you mean?"

"Out! Out of this house! Do something! Play some stupid game, baseball or something. Go *shtup* a girl. Don't read this dreck!" He reached over and grabbed the book from my hands. "Kafka was a *mamzer.*"

"What do you mean? How can you say that? It's not like you knew him, *zaydeh.*"

"Get the hell out, I tell you. Look at this stupid writing," he said, thumbing through the pages, then resting on one. " 'K. looked at the judge' . . . *yob tvoiu mat.* That idiot sat in his apartment all day making up dreck like this. Depressing stuff. You want to be an idiot like him?"

I looked at my grandfather. He wasn't talking abstractly or making assumptions. That wasn't his style. "You really knew him, didn't you?" I was getting excited.

"Kafka was Czech. I'm Polish. Why would I know him? I heard of him, certainly. I knew *of* him. I forced myself to read his dreck a long time ago."

"He was a genius, *zaydeh*."

"Genius? What the hell are you talking about? Your mother, that's genius. Kafka? A scribbler for the depressed, lost, and spoiled. Worthless dreck."

"So why did you read him?"

"Out! You get the hell out of here. You writing depressing shit like this, too?"

"I'm trying, yeah."

"No. Not in this family. I will not have a Kafka in my family. Out!" My grandfather ripped the cover from the binding of *The Trial* and threw it into the hallway. "That man caused enough trouble when he was alive. Screwed up a girl from my hometown."

"But you said you didn't know him."

"No. I didn't. But there was a girl from Komorow, a *dorf* not far from where I was born. She knew him. Screwed up her life forever."

"She knew Kafka?"

"Yeah, she knew Kafka and I knew her. Beautiful girl. So intelligent. She could talk about anything in such a beautiful Polish. Broke her mother and father's heart. She moved to goddamn Prague to take care of that sick *mamzer*."

"She was a nurse?"

"A nurse? What kind of nitwit grandson do I have? A nurse. Yeah, right. Like Rebecca Weidman in Chicago. She a nurse to you?"

"She's a friend."

"A friend. A special kind of friend." My grandfather was chuckling. "Pretty good deal you got down there. I got to hand it to you. You eat Mrs. Weidman's *shabbas* meal, say a few prayers, and then, you little devil, what do you do? You didn't get this from me or your mother, that's for sure."

"She's just a friend is all, *zaydeh*. I don't know where you get such ideas."

"You're worse than Kafka. Little liar to your *zaydeh*. Out!"

I never found out how my grandfather learned about Rebecca and me. But the network of Polish-Jewish émigrés in the Midwest was tight. Fortunately, Dr. Weidman and his wife were born in the United States, and both their parents were long deceased. If the grapevine hadn't passed them by, I can well imagine what I would have had to endure.

At first, I didn't believe my grandfather's story about a girl he knew falling for Kafka, but it more or less checked out. Dora Diamant, daughter of a well-to-do devout family, was the girl in question. She managed to make it to England before the war. Perhaps there were only two degrees of separation between myself and my hero. But with my family, you never know. The details that define the stories of our lives are malleable. If it isn't science or math, it's fair game to be trampled upon, stretched, wrung out of its water, and rehydrated with vodka. My grandfather, like everyone in my family, was a skilled liar. Maybe my *zaydeh* had simply heard about this girl and appropriated the story in an effort, no matter how ineffectual and ridiculous on the surface, to teach me a life lesson.

He was in the living room when I decided to find out what was what.

"You knew Dora Diamant?"

"You still reading that little *mamzer* Kafka?" He put down his newspaper and took off his glasses.

"Yeah. He's brilliant. Way ahead of his time."

"So you say. Man wakes up as a cockroach. This is brilliant? A stupid joke, really. Dora Diamant? She could have had anything she wanted. She was beautiful, she was smart, from a good family. And what happened? She fell in love with a sick man who for amusement told stories about insects that people take seriously. The joke is on us."

"Did you really know her?"

"Know? Idiot, I was supposed to be married to her, is the truth. My father and her father got together. I was eighteen. She was fourteen. It was planned in advance. Sixteen years old and she runs off to Prague to be with that little *mamzer*."

"So you and Kafka were in a love triangle."

"Love triangle. What kind of dreck are you telling me, Sashaleh? She was supposed to marry me. It had nothing to do with love. A triangle needs three vertices. There was no triangle."

"So you had to find someone else?"

"No, my father had to find someone else. He found your grandmother. My father's brother's daughter."

"You were cousins?"

"Yeah, cousins. Dora made a mess of the whole thing. My stock as a potential husband was down. My father did what he could to find a suitable match."

"We're like rednecks then, *zaydeh*."

"What are you talking about? I was educated well. I know six languages. I manage the family investment portfolio. Your mother and father are both professors. Your mother is brilliant. We are not rednecks, anything but."

"But you married a first cousin."

"That was done in Poland. Royalty did such things, too. Dukes,

duchesses, princes, princesses. It was a custom. We aren't rednecks. We're European. Big difference."

"You ever meet her again? After the war?"

"You've got to be kidding. What would we talk about? It's been
fifty years. What did you find out about her, anyway? She ever
marry and have children?"

"Never married. She had one child. Died in England, I think."

"See. That *mamzer* screwed her up for life with his stupid stories. You writing stories about turning into a cockroach?"

"No. Different stuff."

"A ladybug maybe? A tuna fish?"

"*Zaydeh*, don't tease me. It's hard to write. It's hard to find the
right words."

"Good. You don't have it in you, to tell you the truth. I wrote
some nonsense too when I was your age. You'll get over it. You'll
be a mathematician or something. But a scribbler? You have an
ayzene kepl, not something full of craziness."

Maybe this is the kind of stuff you'd expect to think about
when your mother has just died and you glance at a photo of your
mother and grandfather that you have neglected to cover up for
the shiva. I knew the photo on the desk in my old room was a
reunion portrait taken in Forest Hills, Queens, in 1952. My
grandfather's war story differed from my mother's once Stalin
"liberated" all Polish citizens from the work camps in 1941. He
was conscripted into the Russian army—leaving my mother with
a refugee family also from Vladimir-Volynski—and sent to over-
see missile production near Samarkand. When the war ended, he
went west, back to Vladimir-Volynski briefly, and upon hearing

the stories of the mass murder there, continued into Poland, certain that his son was dead and that the family that kept his daughter would travel to the West just like he was doing. After all, it was the most logical step. But he was mistaken in this assumption. It was one of the few times my grandfather ever made a truly bad guess. His daughter was in Moscow studying. The family that took care of her during the war, not nearly as resourceful as my grandfather, could not manage to cross the border into Poland and lived a precarious existence in Kiev.

My grandfather emigrated from Germany to the United States in 1949, two years before my mother defected. The presence of my grandfather in the West, something she discovered in 1948, made it somewhat less surprising that my mother defected and temporarily abandoned her husband and son. With my grandfather present, she would not be completely alone. The photo in my room was taken when my mother was twenty-two years old. She had not seen her father in more than ten years. They walked into a photo studio on Queens Boulevard, and my mother was not in braids as per usual, but instead was trying hard to look mature and stylish, with her hair held in a bun in back à la Grace Kelly. With money from the immigration charity HIAS and in anticipation of moving to Madison to take her American academic job, she had bought her first American outfit, an elegant summer dress with a little lace trim. My grandfather was in a wide-lapelled jacket and tie, his fedora at a tilt. Both of them looked damn good. America had agreed with them instantly. They were easily taking root, as would I, and as would my uncle and father. We were a naturally adaptable, if too small, family.

Years after the Kafka discussions with my grandfather I would have a dream. It was morning in my dream. I was waking up. But something was different. I had lost forty pounds. My gut was cramping. I looked at my skin and it didn't have its Alabama tan, but rather was a sickening white. I got up, hunched over because of my aching *kishkes*, went to the bathroom, and looked at myself in the mirror. Shit. I was in trouble. I looked at my elfin ears, pointy chin, and Talmudic-scholar eyes. This was not me in the least. Put my real self in Brighton Beach with my broad shoulders, thick thighs, high cheeks, and broad forehead, and I will not infrequently get mistaken for a member of the Russian mob. What a stupid thing, I thought. I had woken up as Franz Kafka. This wasn't profound. It was just a stupid sight gag.

My subconscious, like a good mathematician trying to work on a proof, borrowed heavily from my recurring teaching anxiety dream, in which I try to teach a full lecture hall about a topic I have never studied. In the Kafka dream I walked into a graduate-level class on mesoscale climate modeling—something I do know a great deal about—but without any ability to speak English. The students had no idea, of course, who I was.

My subconscious must have been in a cheery mood, though, and had no desire to scare me about my new body and loss of what was, more or less, my first language. What is modeling? Mathematics. An epsilon is an epsilon. A delta is a delta. In my dream I lectured as I furiously wrote the appropriate equations on the board. The graduate students didn't hesitate to follow my lead, and seemed to understand what I was trying to convey far better than on my English-speaking days. I walked out of the lecture hall with the air of an omnipotent Herr Professor and thought that this was pretty good. Kafka would have been proud of me.

I sat in my office after the lecture, and started to cramp anew. Now I really understood why Kafka wrote on and on about his *kishkes* for so many pages in his diaries. Maybe he wasn't simply being self-indulgent. He truly had serious physical troubles. But while I had Kafka's body, I had none of his kvetchiness and probably none of his artistry. My grandfather was absolutely right. Could Kafka have written the series of partial differential equations that I had laid down for fifty minutes straight in a lecture hall? No way, no how. I was a problem solver, not a dweller on the topic of the human condition, which is after all an impossible problem to solve. I felt the twisting, turning, churning, and lurching in my lower abdomen—an unrelenting, dreadful ride on a rickety roller coaster—and while I tried to overcome the necessity of bending over and succumbing to the pain, thought of one word: "Metamucil." They didn't have such stuff in Kafka's time, powdered fiber to mix with your orange juice to make your intestinal tract joyous.

That would do the trick, I was certain. Poor Kafka. No wonder he wrote such tortured material. Perhaps with enough Metamucil his writing would have been happier. Perhaps he wouldn't have written at all. I woke up thinking of a happier Kafka, one my grandfather would approve of, one who wouldn't steal my grandfather's betrothed, and one who couldn't possibly nourish the soul of a sixteen-year-old son of mathematicians stewing in his room.

CHAPTER 10

The Younger Generation

We sat in the restaurant of our youth, a little acrid-smelling coffee shop where the china clanged constantly in the background, and ate our greasy breakfast.

"I can't believe I ate this crap when I was young," Bruce said.

"You were a little wide back then, too," I said.

"You don't need to remind me. I swear, a week here and no one in LA will even so much as say hi to me."

"Well, the lighting is better in most of LA than here. It gives you a warmer glow. You're staying the whole week?"

"Of course he is. I told him he had to," Anna said. Bruce is the baby of the family. In this trio, I am the accommodating de facto middle brother and Anna is not only the family symbol of the folly and tragedy of the Soviet Union, but also the stronger and older sister. What she says goes almost always.

We were the younger generation of this small but never quiet family. This meant that in addition to being subservient to elders at all times, it was our job to decipher the mysterious and inexplicable ways of American culture in the day-to-day.

Here is an example. Suppose you are my uncle and are running a business, in this case a liquor business. In most countries this is a very corrupt enterprise. It's that way in America, too. If you are a liquor distributor working your way up in the world, you need to somehow, obviously, distribute your liquor to retail shops and bars, otherwise you won't make any money. Without distribution you are kaput, not a very inviting prospect.

Now suppose you are my uncle and have started this liquor distributorship from scratch. By clawing and pure luck—with the help of a tiny but enterprising brewery that wishes to expand its domain beyond its one tiny college town of Whitewater, Wisconsin—you hope to become something of a powerhouse. How do you do this?

My uncle struggled to get his beer into bars. His larger competitor kept him down. I suppose he could have, with some money, brought Slavic galoots from Chicago into town to force-feed the bars some Whitewater-produced beer, but for how long could such strong-arm tactics be successful? There had to be another way, a way supplied by an American-educated nephew. Through my uncle I am responsible, at the hormone-raging age of fifteen, for stealing an idea from Florida college spring breaks and bringing it to Wisconsin: the bikini contest.

"And college girls will do this? Wear next to nothing in a room full of drunk men?" my uncle asked in response to my suggestion on how to encourage bars to introduce his precious "imported" beer.

"Not at first, no. But you know, if you could find some girls, pay them at first, pretend college girls."

"*Kurvehs?*"

"Yeah, *kurvehs*, but not like that. Not to, you know, do anything except wear bikinis."

"Probably they'd do that for cheap. I could bring them up. From Chicago. A weekend. Winter when business is slow."

"Plenty of *kurvehs* in Madison, I think."

"I like the ones from Chicago better. They speak my language. Here they barely speak English even though they are native-born."

That's how my uncle's business began to flourish, and such "creativity" on my part defined my role in my family as an ersatz American ambassador and interpreter. It became Bruce's role later on. Anna's specialty was the interpretation of all things about American women. At breakfast that morning we were trying to figure out how to keep my mother's funeral from turning into a Russian theatrical tragedy.

"Your mother would have wanted a private ceremony, there is no doubt," Anna said.

"My father says that's impossible. He's probably right. I have had I don't know how many, maybe four hundred messages and e-mails, from every fucking mathematician on this planet. Even Zhelezniak called."

"Who's Zhelezniak?" Bruce asked.

"Vladimir Zhelezniak. Mother hated him."

"Russian?"

"Of course he's Russian, you idiot," Anna said. "Who else is named Vladimir?"

"He was my mother's mortal intellectual enemy," I said.

"It wasn't intellectual. It was personal," Anna said.

"Personal. Now I'm interested," Bruce said. "What did he do to Aunt Rachela?"

"It doesn't matter. He's the least of our troubles. Four hundred mathematicians, give or take, want to fly in. You'd think they'd come, cry, and just go back home. But no. They want to linger," I said.

"Linger?" Bruce asked.

"Yeah, they want to sit shiva."

"All four hundred?"

"No, they aren't all Jewish, of course. But they all seem to know about sitting shiva. Or many do, at any rate."

"They are worse than dancers. We know physical limitations, at least. The body doesn't always do what we want. But these people. What do they know about what isn't possible?" Anna asked.

"You were married to one. You should understand," I said.

"So were you," Anna said. "She call?"

"No."

"She's a strange one," Anna said. "She must know."

"Anyway, it's not just the shiva. There are these crazy rumors about my mother working on a proof."

"Navier-Stokes, I like how it flows off the tongue," Bruce said.

"How did you know this?" I asked.

"My dad. He was always so proud of his sister. Plus, people have called me about it."

"Who?"

"I don't remember fucking names. But they called. My assistant answered. Always these buy-me-a-vowel names."

"You should talk."

"At least I have some e's and an i. Some of those names, fuck, it's like five or six consonants in a row. Besides, I'm a Charles now, not a Czerneski."

"Did Otrnlov call?"

"Maybe. Who's he?"

"You'll see him. He's crazier than crazy. He's one of those who has asked if the casket will be open."

"Why?"

"Why? I've tried to think why. I don't think they want to see the body. They want to see what might be buried with the body."

"What do you mean?"

"This rumor has gone into another dimension overnight. My mother has solved Navier-Stokes, supposedly, definitely. And in an act of complete selfishness she has decided to bury it with her."

"Who can possibly think like this?" Anna asked.

"It's something my mother apparently said at a conference once. She said . . . I don't know exactly what actually. Something to the effect that if she would manage to solve Navier-Stokes, it would be for her own intellectual curiosity and development, not for any recognition. I don't want them poking in my mother's coffin trying to find a phantom manuscript. I don't want them anywhere near her coffin, as a matter of fact."

"It would be desirable to have some dignity," Anna said.

"I'll do whatever you want me to," Bruce said.

"OK, four hundred people, perhaps, at this memorial service. They are all her children or relatives in some intellectual way. Plus the stupid governor wants to do something, but he will have to wait his turn. The coffin will be sealed. Those bastards' imaginations can continue to run wild. I don't care."

"That's a plan. I can work that plan. This is easy. You should try handling Streisand's entourage."

"You're in charge of getting this thing together. The hall. The rabbi. It's all yours," I said to Bruce.

"It's what I do best," Bruce said, and for the first time since he arrived showed off his gleaming white teeth. He is not a man who likes to be idle, even in mourning.

"I know. Like your father," I said.

CHAPTER 11

The Ballerina, Part 2

"You're tired, Sasha," Anna said.

"Of course. It's not like I didn't expect this to happen. But when it does happen it's a different story."

"You know she was a great woman with a wonderful heart."

"I know. But she's gone. Absolutely gone. Fifty-one years of my life she was this undeniable presence. Now that space, everything about it, it's not empty, but it's not the same. It's not, I don't know, glowing like it did. Shit, I know I must be feeling bad. I'm speaking in metaphors. Who does that except the depressed or overbearing?"

"She was really a mother to me, too."

We were walking in Vilas Park, a short distance from my mother's bungalow. Bruce was on the phone arranging every detail imaginable, leaving nothing for anyone else to do. Even the head of the funeral home was left mostly idle. Bruce had looked at the casket his father and I had picked out and given it thumbs-down because of its excessive gleam. "Too Vegas," he said. "My aunt was not that kind of woman."

Bruce was having a casket shipped from Chicago that had been inspected by a friend. The flowers were being driven in from Chicago as well. At his father's behest, Bruce was also taking over organizing the governor's planned memorial service at the end of the month. Bruce adored my mother. He, in fact, had lived in our home for a year when I was already grown and living in Tuscaloosa.

Bruce would not be the only child to occupy that room after me. My mother was in the habit of picking up strays of all kinds, dogs, cats, birds, and, for brief periods, even the occasional wayward child.

Of course, there was Pascha the parrot, an African gray. She had been sitting on her perch in the kitchen ever since I went to high school in Chicago. All these decades and this bird was still living, fastidiously cleaning its feathers, and occasionally chattering in the high Polish of my mother's youth. My mother had a gift for nurturing those she deemed worthy.

Perhaps her greatest nurturing project of all was Anna, who, on the face of it, needed little care. She was a grown woman of twenty-one when she defected. Like my mother and many others, she had been picked by the Soviet system at an early age to use her talent for the glory of Russia. The Soviets were exemplary at finding and nurturing this 0.001 percent of the population with artistic and intellectual skills. Sadly they also sent a stream of the grown ones to prison and sometimes death for no reason, except, of course, extreme paranoia.

For decades they were on the phone frequently, my mother and Anna. My mother dispensed advice, only some of which was heeded. "You spend too much time worrying about men, Anna. They are all alike. Pretty boring, really. Just pick one and keep him," she said to her more than once.

Anna was born not in Russia but in Uzbekistan, and was orphaned at the age of three. Usually, people like this never thought of defecting. Stalin and the Soviet system were their parents, good parents who had brought them up with pride and discipline. They gave them a sweet life in Moscow far afield from the destitution of their youth. But Anna was different.

I could sense her will, her inability to go with the flow, early on when she lived with us that first summer. Russian men came to us from Chicago and the East Coast with sincere efforts to chart her course in the artistic world of the United States. Their eyes gleamed with the expectation of something intimate in exchange. She swatted them away without any pretense of being polite. If they persisted, she'd roll out the insults. *"Da poshel ty na kher so svoim utiugom* [Get the hell out of here and don't forget to take your dick with you]."

She was going to make her own way in this new world. Born in 1941, she had never known who her father was, but her blue eyes indicated clearly that he was not an Uzbek. Her silhouette, wiry, also told anyone who paid attention to such things that she was partly of foreign blood. "I could be Jewish like you," she once said to me. "You never know. There were all kinds of people in Uzbekistan during the war. The first time I met your mother and looked into her eyes, I felt something special. Like we belonged together." My mother believed much the same thing.

We walked hand in hand, like we were young again, along the path into the little local zoo. "It's hard for me," Anna said. "I could tell your mother anything."

"You can tell me anything, too," I said.

"No, you're a man. It's different. Yeah, I can tell you. But listening. You don't hear what your mother heard."

"Yeah, it's true." I looked at the scene in front of us, a strange mix of African savanna and crusty snow. "We're kind of like these monkeys. It's fucking cold. It's fucking sad."

"I would come to this zoo a lot when I first came here," Anna said. "Maybe because of what your mother told me when I first met her. In Russia, I was like a cat in a cage."

"She was never too subtle about Russia, was she? She'd come here, too, especially in winter. Watch the bears."

"It's funny, the bears," Anna said. "We spent so many years killing them all off and now we save a few just to lord over them. It's a sick affair when you think about it."

We made our way over to the bear display. I waved my hand to them in a mock show of kinship. "At least these aren't freezing like the African charismatic megafauna," I said. "Sure, they are behind a wall. They don't get enough exercise. But they get all the food they need. Pampered, with servants, really. This is kind of like a resort for them. Probably they get on the scale at night and worry about their weight."

"You don't know anything about it, Sasha. You never were caged in your life. Don't be silly. But your mother did like bears, it's true. It's a Russian thing, I guess. I like them, too. Another thing you couldn't possibly understand."

"My passport says I fully understand. Plus, I'm good at clichés."

"It's cliché because it's true. Maybe you do understand. Your accent is shit, though. Even in Uzbekistan they probably still speak Russian better than you."

"Yeah, probably. Look at that one over there."

"The light brown one? With the missing fur?"

"Yeah, that one. Mangy or something. That was Mother's favorite. We'd come here before her chemotherapy sessions. She'd stand and watch him carefully. I swear he'd watch her back."

"He's watching you now."

"Maybe he's watching both of us," I said. "I'm sorry to inform you, dear bear, but your number one fan will not be coming to see you again."

"Now you're talking to a bear instead of me?"

"He's a Kodiak. Probably in the old days, the Russians up there in Alaska, they talked to his ancestors. I'm continuing a proud tradition."

"If you had children, you wouldn't be talking to bears. You'd be with someone fresh and young, someone with a little of your mother inside. A new generation."

"I have a child."

She rolled her eyes. "Like you even know him or her."

"Anna, you know you're making me feel bad, right?"

"I'm not trying to do that. I'm trying to talk sense to you when your guard is down. You still have time. You're still young. People live forever nowadays. Find yourself someone already. It's well past ridiculous."

"What is ridiculous?"

"I've been married three times. I have both two children and two grandchildren."

"And a third grandchild will come sometime this month, although I shouldn't congratulate you before it happens."

"No, you shouldn't."

"Is this some sort of race?"

"No, it's not a race. But I lived. I didn't stop. I had my work, sure. But I tell you, even today at my age, I know that I am still capable of falling in love completely, openly. You are, too."

"Now you're talking nonsense."

"No, you're the one talking to bears. I'm talking to you. Look at me, Sasha." She pulled the arms of my topcoat, turning me toward her. She was still strong. My shoulders lurched forward. "Look at me, not the stupid bear."

I looked down at her. I hadn't looked at anyone like that in years. It's not like I hadn't been up close to a woman. If anything, I'd seen far too many faces.

I wasn't looking at Anna like I did at other women. I wasn't trying to determine the precise spot on her skin that needed a touch of my fingertips. No, I was looking at someone whose face I already knew well but through age and time looked both familiar and strangely new. I took it all in the way, perhaps, someone takes in new scenery as they cross over a hill on a day when the sun's light is just so, exposing every detail.

There was a little scar above Anna's right eye, just a light-colored line on her otherwise olive skin that even when she was young would form into a wrinkle when she raised her brow. She didn't know how she got it, she said. There were her rounded cheekbones, oddly similar to those of my mother, high on her face and broad as if they were specifically designed to allow her cheeks to be warmed by the sun. I knew these features well. I could have re-called them any time I wished. But there were also the shadows and lines that had developed over time, different than mine, finer and deeper etches along the lids of her eyes, furrows where there had once been the subtlest pair of curves accentuating her chin and lips.

"You're smiling at me," I said.

"It feels good to smile. I didn't know until recently."

"You're becoming an American, it seems."

"No, never. Not that. It's good to be here, though. You're the American, not me."

"Not really."

"Maybe not really. Not among women."

"How am I with women?"

"Big phony. A Russian accent comes out of nowhere. Your eyes droop sad like a puppy. I know you."

"You're amused by my behavior, are you?"

"Yes, very amused. Was at any rate. But don't you think it's getting old? Tell me true now."

"And what about you. Three husbands. Five years and then what, poof? You throw them out."

"That's over. I'm going to find myself a real man, successful, and hold onto him no matter what. I'm getting too old to be alone. Look at me. I'm telling the truth."

"You are. I can see it. I really can. I guess I'll be going to a wedding soon."

"One more, yes. I want a big one. One last big wedding."

"Could be you and me."

"That's disgusting. Incest almost. Your mother wouldn't approve. I'm going to find someone who knows he's getting something special."

"The bear is what's watching us, not my mother."

"Forget the bear. You and your fucking bear. Smile for me, Sasha."

"Like this?"

"No, not like that. That's stupid. A real smile. Not some fake thing. I've seen you do it. I know you can do it."

"I need to think of something good, Anna." I closed my eyes and tried to conjure up something that would make me smile the way that I knew Anna wanted me to. "Tell me what to think."

"I don't know. Maybe the pond over there next to the road. Where we used to go sometimes that first winter, when you were little. You'd put on your skates in the warming house and then show me how good you were on the ice. Little boy showing off. Remember?"

"Yeah, sure, I remember."

"I'd watch you skate. You were so happy. That's the kind of smile I want to see."

I concentrated as best I could. The cold air is, indeed, ideal for isolating thoughts and maybe even acting on them, if not physically, at least emotionally and mentally. In my mind I was a kid skating backward on the ice, knowing someone beautiful was giving me a visual embrace. What boy wouldn't smile in response to that?

"That was better," Anna said. "I saw the little boy in you. It was nice to see. No disappointments. A big future ahead of you."

"My future turned out quite well. I don't have many disappointments. It's true, don't you think?"

"Sure. You did what your mother wanted. What your father wanted. I'm not sure you've done what you wanted."

"My father wanted me to become a mathematician. I disobeyed him."

"And your mother? Did you ever disobey her?"

"Who could ever disobey her? She was in charge of it all. Me, you, my father, Shlomo, Bruce, everybody. She was the boss. You don't disobey the boss."

"Well, maybe now you can be your own boss."

"I could be independently employed, it's true. But you're the one sounding like the boss now. You wanted me to smile for you. I smiled. What do you want next?"

"OK, if I'm the boss, will you listen to me?"

"I've been listening to you since I was a boy. I'm certainly not going to stop now."

CHAPTER 12

A Confession

Did my accent really get heavier when I was flirting? Did I get all affected playing the immigrant card, and meld phony vulnerability with slightly questionable exoticism? Of course. I did it because it worked.

Up until the year 2001, I had loved three women in my life. One was my former wife. The other two, my mother and Anna, would frequently repeat the claim that I had given up on love. I didn't think that was right.

I had honestly tried to love sometimes. OK, there had also been times when I met a woman and had just wanted her physically. It was also true that I'd sometimes been a rat, feigning love, or at least emotional interest, in order to get inside a woman's dress. But that hadn't been typical. I hadn't been a player in the American way, serially acquiring and dumping women in an effort to collect an ever-increasing number of experiences. I admit, though, that it looked the same in terms of the balance sheet.

Before I begin to talk about my era of phony love, I should spend some time talking about when I wasn't a phony. Catherine Hampstead was originally from Ross, California. When I met her she was beginning her Ph.D. studies in mathematics at the University of Wisconsin. I was working on my Ph.D. in meteorology, a pursuit that caused my father to rage not infrequently about me squandering my talent in mathematics. I wooed Cathy, married her, and for nearly two years we lived in youthful harmony. Then one afternoon, in a roomful of mathematicians, her life fell apart, and our marriage soon went with it.

It all started when this bright, beautiful woman failed her Ph.D. prelims. Walking into that room, she was confident and radiant. I could tell that she was also nervous and probably so could her Ph.D. committee. Who wouldn't be? But she had never failed at anything before. We were certain it wasn't going to happen then. Like an imprudent couple that invests its nest egg in an IPO whose value, despite months of glowing press, falls precipitously at the opening bell of the stock market and continues to decline day after day, we were stunned and devastated. It didn't help matters that her Ph.D. advisor was also my mother.

All Ph.D. students must take prelims after they take courses for a year or two. They study for a few months, and then five or six professors grill them orally for a few hours. It's a painful experience even when they pass. It's supposed to be painful. I know. I've sat on scores of these exams and was once, of course, a Ph.D. student myself. It isn't a fair fight, really. Five or six very bright people who have studied your subject area for a combined 50 to 150 years are bound to ask you questions that make you seem like an idiot. Passing means that you are only a partial idiot. The good news is that after you suffer this humiliation, you are free to write your dissertation, and you can do that just about anywhere. On the other hand, failure means your attempt to earn a Ph.D. is done. Kaput. You can, of course, retake the exam, but not many people choose to do so.

On the day before her prelims, Catherine had a promising

future as a professor in mathematics. A loving family, supportive of all she did, had nurtured her dreams. At Wellesley, where Catherine had been an undergraduate, mathematics students were rare, but because there were no men, at least they weren't ostracized. Briefly I nurtured her dreams as well. It certainly helped that I was someone who knew a bit about the difficulties women had as mathematicians and knew more than a bit about the difficulties of mathematics in general. But after her prelims, she didn't have a promising future. Over a period of four hours, her dreams went poof.

This profound disappointment, so unexpected, was the first real test of our marriage. We failed that test as badly as she failed her prelims. New marriages need nurturing, of course. They are tender little plants that do not do well under stress. Our environmental conditions had been, in hindsight, hostile.

We were living in a drafty apartment in Madison, Wisconsin, close enough to Lake Mendota to catch the howling wind off the water. It was cold, the kind of gray fall cold filled with moisture. The apartment, with the furnace blowing, barely managed to inch up to sixty, according to the thermometer. I didn't trust what that thermometer said. The building, built in the 1920s, wasn't really an apartment complex, but rather was a large house that had been cut up into six units in a haphazard way. We were on the first floor, in Unit 3, which had two windows, one in the tiny kitchen and one in the bedroom.

Desperate to keep what little warmth there was inside the apartment, I had covered the windows in thick, clear plastic bought from a hardware store. Partly I had done this because Catherine had been uncharacteristically complaining about sweating all the time and was keeping those windows open when I wasn't around. I wasn't sure why she was always warm. She was pregnant when she started opening the windows. The logic at the time was that we would have our first child early, when Catherine was still a student. That way, when eventually she took an academic position, the child would be a few years old, ready for day care and then school.

The student health service, filled with trainees and burnouts from real hospitals, wasn't about to investigate why Catherine was hot all the time. I was obsessed with finishing my Ph.D. so I could take my job in Tuscaloosa—whose warm climate I was already beginning to think was a decidedly good thing—and wasn't paying much attention either. We had four goals that year. A very ambitious and organized couple we were. Goal one—Catherine passing her prelims—had not been achieved. But to my mind, that didn't obviate the need to succeed at goals two through four. I needed to pass my dissertation defense and graduate. Cletus the Fetus, our name for the bulge in Catherine's belly, needed to be born. Then, after all that, we, a lovely young couple with a beautiful baby in tow, needed to move to Tuscaloosa.

I was focused, oh so focused, on my dissertation. I ascribed Catherine's burning up day and night to having two heat masses, the fetus and her together. She was kind of a double furnace, I thought to myself, taking in fuel for two bodies and burning calories for two as well. Why shouldn't she be warm? This would not be the first time I would twist physics to rationalize why I was ignoring a serious problem.

My wife, formerly laconic, was also talking at the clip of a coffee-crazed TV host trying to squeeze in a bit of information before a commercial break. I ascribed this change to the unhappiness of failure. She was unhappy with her uncertain future, unhappy with my mother, and unhappy with my family, who she wanted nothing to do with after her exam. That was my internal pronouncement, although of course I couldn't say so out loud. But I wanted to. Simply. Plainly, in a way anyone who grew up in a family like mine would say it. "You're unhappy, I know. You've failed your Ph.D. prelim, I know. I believe in you. I love you. It will take time to get over this. But you will." Except at the time, I didn't know if indeed she would get over her failure. Plus, here is a horrible thing. Her failure was something I didn't even want to be around. She knew it. I knew it. I wanted positive stories to keep me going and help me finish. There Catherine was, overheated emotionally and physically, trying to comprehend the newness of bearing a child and the newness of having no academic future in mathematics. Where was I? Busy, busy, busy at work.

Catherine wasn't found to be an incompetent mathematician. My mother, a harsh judge in all things mathematical, would never have said such a thing, because it wasn't true. Rather, the committee told Catherine after the exam that she was bright, of course. Her grades were testimony to that. But there was a difference between being bright and possessing those sparks of ideas that lead to original thought. She was not an original thinker, my Catherine. She was instead a "mimic." That's the word my mother used after the exam. Using that word was cruel. My mother would say that she was only being honest, that there is no value in sugarcoating the truth. I think it's just easier to be mean. To have a light touch takes work.

Is it fair to expect every Ph.D. student in mathematics to possess originality? Again, according to my mother, there were plenty who didn't—most in fact did not—but not under her watch. "We have to be better. Women cannot be ordinary in this business. They must tower above everyone else to survive." That was what she said to me way back when. We were in her house in the kitchen. This was a sober discussion between a mother and a son. We weren't drinking vodka, but tea. I can remember her saying these words. I can remember also erupting, standing up and shouting. I screamed not in English, but in the dirty and gruff weathered language of where I was born. "I don't give a shit about what it takes for a woman to survive. Even if it's true, Catherine is not just a student of yours. This is your daughter-in-law. Exceptions have to be made for family."

"What do you know about family?" my mother replied. "You bring in this girl to join us. You don't ask me or your father about her. You just announce it, you're getting married. Two years you've been married to this girl who has nothing in common with you or me or your father or anyone else we know and love. She has led a life of ease, of no hardship, of no struggle. She can't do the work, this little doll of yours. I don't need dolls."

In the space of thirty seconds my mother had condemned not only my wife's intellectual abilities, but also my judgment in choosing a life partner. I knew it was only going to go downhill from there. Somehow I did manage to find the strength to try and challenge my mother not as a son tries the patience of a parent, but as an adult who questions the judgment and fairness of another. "Maybe she can do the work," I said. "But you don't want her to. Maybe you've decided she's a little no-brained *lalka* because it's convenient for you. It lets you knock your daughter-in-law down to a manageable size."

There was a look my mother showed when confronted with what she deemed to be arrogance mixed with idiocy. It was as if you could feel her presence leave, that it was not worth her while to even hear another word. "I don't mix the personal with the professional, Sasha. Not in that way. Now you are being ridiculous." There was no anger in her voice. As far as she was concerned, I was the equivalent of a love-struck teenager who thought he knew all about life.

I cannot remember a single time when I won an argument with my mother. Perhaps this was the last moment I seriously tried. I certainly can't say I was alone in my futility. If my father ever won an argument, it didn't happen while I was present. He could be a formidable adversary, but in comparison to my mother, he was always a distant second. Everyone was. I stopped screaming and stomped out of her house.

So there was the added tragedy of Catherine's failure. She was being held to a very high standard, an absurd standard, really. At the time I thought I had learned an obvious lesson. Do not fall in love with someone when that love is heavily dependent on the goodwill and kindness of your parents. Find someone else. It's a stupid thing to expect a family to help you tie up your love life into a nice bow, and smart people do stupid things far more often than most people realize.

Now, looking back, I don't think that's the lesson that I should have learned. I should have understood that when you love someone, and they are being subjected to cruelty, you need to do whatever you can to shield them, to defend them, even if the source of that cruelty, maybe especially if the source of that cruelty, is your own mother. This is your obligation. There are no exceptions.

My mother wasn't the only one with a talent for condemnation. Catherine had it as well. I heard her words after a return from a late-night trip to the basement of the computer science building. I had been trying to code solutions to moisture movement in clouds using the Navier-Stokes equation night after night for months with little success. I came home, as per usual, at 4:00 A.M., and Catherine wasn't at all happy. "I could do your fucking work," she said. "It's as stupid as making ketchup. You have a fucking recipe. You put it in a computer. Big fucking deal. You only have to use half your brain to do this. And you don't even have the fucking heart to use the other half for me."

I'd heard similar sentiments—not the love part, but the idea that I was slumming intellectually—from other mathematicians, including my father. "What is Rachela Karnokovitch's son doing with applied mathematics studying clouds and turbulence? What a waste of talent!" That was the gist of this argument. It wasn't true, and even if it was, it's nothing you want to hear from someone you love.

I do what I do not to avoid mathematics. If I loved mathematics, I'd be happy being a mediocre mathematician (just like many a mediocre actor is happy to be performing on stage in Tuscaloosa or Madison instead of Broadway or Hollywood). When my wife said her words, they hurt. I looked at the bulge in my wife's belly and thought, "Thank god this baby-to-be isn't hearing and seeing this, two people who are beginning to hate each other."

But the other half of her argument, my absent "fucking heart" was absolutely correct. I was focusing all my efforts on my dissertation not because I had to, but because it was easier than looking at the pain on my wife's face, easier than having to concentrate to hear her rapid-fire sentences about how she was hot, how she was uncomfortable, and how my mother hated her. I was refusing to help her in a time of manifest need. What was wrong with me?

That night, during and after the shouting back and forth, I looked beyond myself for the first time in weeks. The windows were open yet again, and the thin plastic window covering was holding the cold back a bit. I heard Catherine's words, coming at me so fast, and I didn't just listen to their content but to the intent behind them. Her face was flushed, of course, but I also saw that her hair was thinning. I reached out to hold her and felt her heart beating fast, like she had just run a marathon, and I knew instantly that my "theory" about her dual heat masses was stupid beyond belief. She was physically ill.

We didn't go to sleep that night. I took Catherine to the hospital and insisted I be with her in the examining room. They took her pulse, 140 beats per minute. The doctor—about fifty years old with an accent that I knew instantly was from Chicago's West Side—looked at Catherine's body, so skinny for someone pregnant. Despite eating prodigious amounts of cheese, something she always adored, she had barely gained weight. This doctor, unlike those at student health, knew what he was doing. "Your eyes, they're bulging. Are you receiving prenatal care?" he asked.

"Of course," Catherine said.

"Well, it hasn't been good care. We're going to take a blood sample. I'd bet my left nut that you're hyperthyroid." That's how doctors talked back then. They still smoked. As in mathematics, there were few women in the medical field, and the men all seemed to behave like gods. These displays of braggadocio look vain and ridiculous in retrospect. Be that as it may, the doctor could keep his left nut. The blood sample proved he was right.

Medication was carefully administered. Catherine's heart rate dropped. The constant patter stopped as well. There was half-hearted talk of having her retake her Ph.D. prelim, that her medical condition might have impaired her, but it was quickly dropped. So was our marriage. I continued to work on my dissertation with fervor. Catherine went back to beautiful California, to the lovely home of her parents in Marin County. Then she went somewhere else. New Zealand is where I guessed—that was where all her relatives were—but I didn't inquire about the details. My mother was right in one way. My Catherine was not one to fight back from blows either intellectual or emotional. "We don't think it would be a good idea for you to contact her anymore," her parents told me when I called after she moved out of their home and I tried to get her new phone number. They were always so polite. They simply couldn't just tell me to fuck off.

I would be at best obtuse if I didn't also recognize that my failure didn't end with Catherine's leaving. I can't understand to this day why for decades I was not willing to make the slightest effort to find her. It was as if I took her parents' desire for me to disappear as some sort of edict from on high. I, of course, did not forget that Catherine would give birth to a child, our child. But what was once so real quickly transformed into the fuzzy and theoretical. What kind of pathology led me to let go completely, to have no need or desire to come face-to-face and touch or even hear the voice or see a picture of my own child? I still don't understand it to this day. Yes, Catherine left and made no contact with me, but a real man with a real heart would not have let that deter him.

My wife left, papers were eventually signed, and somehow I managed casually and coldly to erase two years of my life. I found the perverse will to forget that I was a father to someone who undoubtedly wondered who I was and felt my absence with at least a touch of sadness.

After Catherine left Madison, it took only a little amount of time before I began a new era, the phony era, of my love life. It was winter, and it was even colder, of course, than in the fall. One Saturday night I was in bed feeling crappy. Being on the first floor of the building meant that the heat rose to the upstairs units almost as fast as it blew into the apartment from the anemic vents. The large house had not a stitch of insulation, and its exterior was covered in red tar paper made to look like brick. Outside it hadn't risen above freezing in forty or so days. It was maybe fifty degrees in my apartment, and I heaped blanket upon blanket on my body.

I knew I wouldn't get a smidgen of sleep that night. I decided to put on my clothes and go back to the basement of the computer science building to my faithful DECwriters and debug my code, which had a habit of blowing up sometimes. It wasn't blowing up in the traditional way of having numbers go to infinity. Instead, the numbers oscillated. These oscillations were, you could bet your left nut on it, driving me to complete distraction.

It was probably minus-twenty-five degrees outside, which my mother would have told you—like Zhelezniak and Kolmogorov and I don't know how many Russian mathematicians—is fantastic weather for clearing your mind. It's the best weather for coming up with original ideas and problem solving.

I walked around the Capitol building and looked up at Miss Forward, lit up on the dome and pointing west. It was where I knew my soon-to-be ex-wife had gone. But that's not really what I was thinking about. Just random thoughts went through my head. There was an album that I was listening to nonstop at the time, a jazz album mixed with modern African rhythms. They were so exotic to me, these patterns. The rhythms went in and out like waves at the seashore.

Then it came to me. Those rhythms were like my fucking computer program output. There was nothing wrong with what I had done. My computer code was good. The oscillations were real. They were meant to be there. Idiot. The solution was meant to oscillate. Idiot. There was nothing that needed to be fixed.

I'd already written two chapters of my dissertation. Those chapters examining data from low-altitude balloons during storms were adequate science. They represented the kind of journeyman work that used to get people decent but not particularly prestigious assistant professor jobs at places like the University of Alabama. Nowadays everybody and their mother gets Ph.D.'s, professorships are hard to come by, and work like I'd done in those two chapters would get me a decent but not particularly prestigious postdoc at a place like the University of Alabama.

This third and final chapter of my dissertation was special. I knew it would be. I was trying to simulate the movement of air and moisture in a way that mimicked—yes, that word so negative in my mother's lexicon but so positive for a person concerned with computer simulations of nature—the observations from those balloons. Using computers to solve equations that, as Hilbert had noted long before, still needed to be tied to the founda-

tions of mathematics was heady stuff when I was a student. I
didn't know what I would find. My advisor thought I was crazy for
doing this work, that my first two chapters were more than enough
to make a dissertation, that I already had a job, and that I was
simply trying to do the impossible. But I had the liberty to do such
work through the munificence of a National Science Foundation
scholarship and computer time that cost little if you ran your pro-
grams after midnight.

No one had found anything like this before in computer simulations of the atmosphere. All I had left to do was prove that these
solutions were indeed real. Not many atmospheric scientists could
prove such a thing. But an atmospheric scientist who had been
pushed to pursue pure mathematics and had "rebelled" to study
something rooted in the physical world could certainly do so. The
mathematical proof turned out to be fairly trivial.

It had been a bad few months, a horrible few months, in fact. I
kept working through it all because my computer program, however problematic, was something tangible. Solving equations is
not an abstract thing. To even a mediocre mathematician like me,
an equation is as solid as an oak tree in my mind. If it wasn't, I
couldn't solve it. People's emotions are, on the other hand, much
more abstract. You, or at least I, can go crazy chasing after such
vaporous things.

I knew then and there that my last chapter was essentially
done. I also knew that this would be the kind of work that would
draw attention to me in ways that it rarely did to any newly minted
Ph.D. in my field. My personal life was rotten, but my professional
life was about to take a hugely positive turn. As I walked down the
beginning of State Street, I decided to celebrate. The bars would

be open for another half hour or so, and I needed to take advantage of what they had to offer.

I walked into the first bar I saw, a narrow little Greek joint next to an old movie theater from the Depression era. I sat down next to a woman maybe thirty years old, with dark hair and ivory skin. To me she looked old, of course. "You look cold," she said.

"Yeah, cold and happy."

"You like the cold, I guess."

"Well, you know, I'm Russian. I'm used to it." I dropped into my ridiculous Russian accent. The woman was intrigued. My little act worked. We all have tricks to make up for our inadequacies. I drank vodka, of course. She drank gin. The woman had been married and divorced. I had been married and would soon be divorced. We had so much in common. The bar closed and we walked together in the cold air. We continued our conversation in my apartment.

Now how do I put this in a nice way? Well, I can't. I absolutely cannot put this in any way that makes me seem like anything but a jerk. Here it is, though. All of my life, I had been surrounded by smart people, smart women. Intellect is everything to me. Even drunk, it's everything to me. Here I was with a woman who couldn't possibly understand the first thing about what I did intellectually. But she was impressed in a way that no woman had ever been impressed with me. When I told her what I did, her eyes grew big, and she said, "Oh, you must be a big brain." I liked that. Yes, it's trivial and petty to like such stupid flattery, but I liked it.

I liked her, too. Laura, her name was. She had two children and a lousy, mean ex-husband who made me seem like an angel in comparison. It was easy to be with Laura. She expected so little of me that it was a relief. Here's another thing. American women can be so optimistic about what the next minute of life will bring. Where does this sense of a better world just around the corner come from, anyway? It's a wondrous bit of character, this optimism and hope. No one in my family possesses it. We pound and pound and work until something breaks and a little opening of light appears.

I suppose it could be called optimism that we assume we can see that light eventually. But no, it's really different. It's not American at all. It's our egos at work, not blind optimism about the world around us. It's the idea that despite all the obvious and unforeseen obstacles, we will manage to beat the devil. It's desperation that fuels us.

But not Laura. She felt that her life on this Earth would change for the better one day. It was a feeling she held as deeply as the devout believe in God. This was something new to me, this belief in the power of positive thinking. I couldn't believe it myself, but to be around that glow was life affirming. Who wouldn't want that?

I never saw Laura after I moved to Tuscaloosa. I never tried to meet her when I came to visit my parents. Years later I got an e-mail from her. She had seen me on a CNN show about a hurricane that had hit the Gulf Coast. "I always knew you'd be famous someday," she wrote.

There would be other Lauras in Tuscaloosa. Of course they had different names. I liked the women in Alabama a great deal. I liked the flattery they dished out, little pieces of candy to make a man feel strong and powerful.

This is what Anna and my mother meant about me giving up on love. But I didn't really think that was true. I had given up on the kind of romantic love they wanted for me, yes. Their ideal was that I should find an equal, someone strong and as intense and powerful as they were. Anything less was unacceptable. The truth was that I didn't believe I possessed the strength to be with someone like that, at least romantically. I'd tried that once. Catherine was like them in her own way, independent and judging others by lofty standards.

How many demanding women can one man have in his life? How many judgments can be made on him before he starts to feel their weight and feels inadequate, clumsy, and lacking? I had two women like this. Their constant evaluations of me were something that, while difficult, were also valued because they pushed me to do more. At the time I was convinced that there would be no more Catherines in my life. Instead, there would be only Lauras. These women weren't trying to achieve anything artistically or intellectually, weren't striving to live the kind of life that leads to write-ups in magazines and in the *New York Times*, and weren't even consciously trying to make the world a slightly better place. They wanted their houses to look nice. They wanted their children to be respectful. They starved themselves to keep their figures and spent copious amounts of money on clothes and makeup. My mother couldn't understand my attraction to these *lalkas* and neither could Anna. My father was indifferent. My uncle understood perfectly.

"Not every man needs to find a woman who understands him. Sasha already has that anyway," he would say to my mother in my defense. Thank you, Uncle Shlomo. You know what it's like to be ordinary.

PART 2

THE
MATHEMATICIANS

CHAPTER 13

The Gathering

The mathematicians arrived. They came to the land of Badger Ingenuity on flight after flight on a ridiculously cold day. A Canadian high-pressure mass descended on my home state, and it looked like it would stay put for at least the entire shiva. This was a good thing in a way. It wouldn't snow. The sky would remain blue day after day. If we were lucky and ventured north a bit outside of town, we might even be able to get a peek at the northern lights at night. But the absence of clouds meant a prolonged period of temperatures below zero, perhaps minus twenty in the wee hours of the morning. I was going to freeze to death. Bruce, too. We had become weather wimps, and in our family, being a wimp about anything was a definite black mark. We had both heard the withering criticism about any of our complaints as children. "You're kvetching over this? Over this? Have a soldier put the muzzle of a rifle to your nose and then you'll have something to complain about." We couldn't compete against our parents' past misery, and they never let us forget it.

Some flew directly to Madison. Others found their way through Milwaukee or Chicago. Calls came from the most narcissistic and cheap of the bunch to provide a free airport shuttle service and housing. I had no patience for such nonsense. I could feel a crustiness that I had worked so hard to smooth over in Tuscaloosa return quickly. Maybe I was even emboldened by the absence of the crustiest of the crusty, my dearly departed mother. Whatever the reason, I dealt curtly with these *shnorers* and would say, "This isn't a wedding, you cheap bastard. It's a funeral." I would speak sometimes in English, but usually in Russian. "Rent a car. Take a cab. Walk. I don't care. Mooch off your math friends in Madison. There's a HoJo's walking distance, more or less, to the synagogue if you need it." I didn't wait for any response before I hung up.

Our block of rooms reserved at the HoJo's by the math department's secretary—or I should say the H Jo's, since the "o" light in the "Howard" had burned out twenty years before and had never been replaced—filled up quickly. One of the sweetest mathematicians on this planet, Ollie Knutson, came forward to organize the logistics of housing these people and shuttling them around town. Ollie was a number theorist of considerable note who had "come home" from UCLA to take a professorship. His father, like my parents, had been a part of the faculty in the math department since the 1950s. Ollie was a saint that week. I can well imagine what he endured.

They came from Russia, France, Israel, Korea, Germany, and Japan to pay their respects to one of the two students of Kolmogorov who probably exceeded the genius of the master. The other one? Vladimir Zhelezniak, sly, humorous, self-deprecating, everything my mother was not. He was also my mother's mortal enemy. Zhelezniak would be there as well. "He'll come to dance on my grave, that one," my mother said to me when she was sick. She rarely mentioned his name, but every time I heard something negative about "that one" or "him" or "the bastard" as a child, I knew to whom she was referring. "Don't give him the satisfaction."

I'd never met Zhelezniak. I'd seen pictures of him, beagle-faced with sad, big eyes. His bald crown was fringed with curls. A man possessing a face like his, so obviously Semitic to the Russian eye, would have had a difficult time as a child and a young man, I knew. He would have had to prove himself quietly and never make himself and his genius too visible, except in the presence of someone like Kolmogorov. My mother's beloved great Kolmogorov didn't give a shit who your parents or grandparents were, and only cared about the size of your brain. At nineteen, Zhelezniak shocked the mathematical world by solving Hilbert's thirteenth problem. My mother, however, was not shocked. She was outraged.

It was 1957. I was eight years old. My mother was on the phone in the kitchen with Kolmogorov himself. Who knows how many Soviet agents were listening along? My mother complained bitterly about being usurped, about being unrecognized for a major contribution to solving this problem that she made in 1947 but had not published. Why hadn't she published it? It wasn't close to the full solution. In my mother's opinion, no proof was worth publishing unless it was substantially completed. Kolmogorov knew what my mother had done. He passed her partial solution on to Zhelezniak, who finished her work. In my mother's opinion, a nineteen-year-old boy was taking credit for everything because that's the way the Soviets wanted it. It was a good piece of propaganda for them. "This will never happen again," she swore. "My work will not be stolen. Never." I didn't hear the other half of the conversation from Kolmogorov, but I could tell that he was trying to console her. His efforts weren't working.

My mother had other enemies as well, although in the balance, she had many more friends. Her warmth and coldness were without pattern. Of course, she was warm to me nearly always. I was her flesh and blood. She remained warm to my father as well, even after they separated. I think this was partly in recognition of his having to deal with her difficult nature for so many years. Her brother and her father, too, she always held dear, as well as Bruce and Anna. But with strangers, you never knew how my mother would react. She would make snap judgments, and once those judgments were made, they did not change. A person was wonderful or they were an idiot or selfish or amusing or creative. Everyone she met was put in a pigeonhole almost instantly. Emotional nuance? I don't think she had time for it.

According to my mother, Vladimir Zhelezniak was an unrepentant thief. That he continued to excel in mathematics for decades following his solution of Hilbert's thirteenth problem, just as she had following her solution to Hilbert's fifteenth problem at a similar age, meant nothing.

My mother's mercurial nature, I'm sure, added to her allure in the mathematical world. She wasn't just a mathematical genius but one about whom stories could be told. There were lots of them. Here's one that involves Zhelezniak. It took place in 1968 in France, a crazy time of student riots. Nowadays, when you go to the University of Paris and notice its proto-IKEA tackiness and ugliness, you can blame it on that terrible year. After the riots, French muckamucks quietly made sure that any new parts of the university would have campus layouts designed to make it difficult for students to congregate in large numbers.

The unruly demonstrations in Paris and elsewhere in the 1960s and 1970s were predictably accompanied by a period of overheated sexual behavior throughout the West. My mother found the sexual revolution to be crass and tasteless. It was all too mechanical and depressing for her. She brought along a female Ph.D. student to give a talk at the Paris conference. Part of my mother's job, or at least she thought it was part of her job, was to make sure that her students didn't do something stupid at these conferences that they would later regret. "They should have 'premorse,' but not remorse," was how she put it.

Zhelezniak approached the Ph.D. student to compliment her on her presentation. Perhaps he was trying to do more. Who knows really, but when my mother saw Zhelezniak with her student at a table during a break in the proceedings, she seethed. I've seen that look in her eyes. I can well imagine her grimace as she looked around the room. Her eyes spotted the carafes of coffee in the center table—bad coffee can be found in France as easily as it can be found elsewhere—and her plan immediately came into focus.

She grabbed a carafe, walked over to them, and asked Zhelezniak if he would like more coffee. Perhaps this was the first time my mother had said a word directly to Zhelezniak in eleven years. Zhelezniak held out his cup. My mother promptly dumped the entire pot into his lap.

Acts like this—one great mind dumping hot coffee into the lap of an adversary—can be, and usually are, remembered for decades in academic circles. The truth was that she hated the notoriety caused by her flare-ups.

"Everyone thinks their children are special," my grandfather once said to me. "They delude themselves about their sons and daughters, their beauty, their minds." He said that in Russia people thought he was deluding himself about Rachela, who to most simply looked lost, absent from the world. But he knew. "I could see her mind working like a machine," he said. "When Grozslev came to our little hovel and began to give your mother lessons, his face that first day had such a surprised look. 'What have we here?' That look said it all."

"We do not come from stupid people," my grandfather would sometimes say to me when he sensed that I was showing signs of "being an American," which to him was any sign that I was relaxing my mind and resolve. That is certainly true. Stupidity also was not present in any of my mother's friends or admirers, at least when it came to mathematics. Some had talents in other realms as well. Music, of course. Painting and sculpture, too. Some were engaging conversationalists, and others managed to operate in the real world with ease and without a trace of overt strangeness, without giving away the fact that they were different.

"They're here." My father called me from his office. "All of them. They are crawling around the building like giant ants."

"Why don't you leave? Go home. You can come here if you want."

"I have work to do. Serious work. I need an office. A chalkboard. A desk. Something austere and uncomfortable. I've shut the door. Locked it. Those bastards keep knocking. They know I'm here. Some want to get into your mother's office. They want the key."

"Tell Marie not to give them access. No way. Ollie, too."

"I know, I know. I called to tell you about Otrnlov. I heard he's coming to the house. He's walking over right now."

Konstantin Otrnlov. It was a name I knew well. From a theoretical standpoint, it's perhaps expected that a great mathematician would attract a crazy acolyte or two. As a practical matter, these acolytes can be at best a pain in the ass and at worst dangerous. Konstantin Otrnlov wasn't sane, was devoted to my mother, and you never knew just what he might do.

Otrnlov had come to the United States from Latvia in 1978, and while he had been unable to obtain a position at an American university, he eventually earned a tidy sum of money with a carpet business in New Jersey. It was enough to allow him to return part-time to his love, mathematics. His admiration for my mother turned into an obsession in about 1990. He proposed marriage to my mother. He mailed her jewelry, which she would promptly return. He even bought her a car, which he tried to give her at a conference. One summer he rented a house across the street from my mother, living there when he wasn't in New Jersey. My mother ignored him. He was never let into our house.

My mother viewed Otrnlov's obsession as harmless until 1998, when he apparently anointed himself protector of all things Karnokovitch and physically attacked a mathematician at a conference for the sin of asking my mother a question that Otrnlov deemed hostile. Otrnlov was not a small man. I'm sure those blows hurt.

"You be careful with him," my father said. "He has some ridiculous idea that the proof is in the house. Anyone else home?"

"Bruce is, yes. Anna is visiting an old friend."

"Tell Bruce to get out of there fast."

"He's in the tub trying to warm up."

"Otrnlov's ideas. I've heard some of them. After Otrnlov leaves, throw Bruce out of the fucking tub, give him the keys to the car, and tell him to go somewhere, anywhere. I am not kidding."

"Anna has the car."

"*Yob tvoiu mat.* If Otrnlov asks about Bruce or Shlomo, tell him you don't know anything. You don't know where they are. Tell him that Bruce took off and went somewhere. Do not tell Otrnlov that Bruce is in the house. Understand?"

"Why?"

"I don't have time to explain it. I need to get back to work. But Ollie knows."

As my father hung up, I looked out the window and waited. It was a twenty-minute walk from Van Vleck Hall to our house. He'd arrive soon enough.

Otrnlov did love my mother. It was a deranged love, certainly, but he had come to Madison to honor her. With the others I was beginning to think that the hoopla was less about my mother than it was about the field of mathematics itself.

Imagine mathematics as a canvas where every mathematician of worth fills the missing white spaces. Hilbert came along in the twentieth century to do something no one had done well before. He assessed the canvas of mathematics and identified what white space was left. Since Hilbert, much of that white space had already been filled by both those painting details with the smallest of brushes, people like my father, and those who filled in the bigger blank spaces, people like Kolmogorov, Zhelezniak, and my mother.

Eventually, the canvas would be full, essentially complete in all its beauty. What would be left would be trivial. Mathematics had already gotten to the point where the canvas looked beautiful. My mother knew it. "It's a good thing I came when I did," she said. "Since the 1970s, what have been the discoveries? Not much."

Partly people were coming to honor my mother, sure, but they were also coming out of nostalgia for a time when mathematics was still great, when one highly skilled and gifted mind could do so many remarkable and exquisite things.

At the time of my mother's death, Otrnlov reportedly was working on a biography about her. I knew that he had gone through each and every article and word my mother had ever published. I'd heard that he'd wanted to write about my mother's personal life as well, but if so, he hadn't contacted me yet. I knew that when he did I wouldn't cooperate.

Otrnlov walked up to my mother's house in a New York Giants parka. A fedora covered his still-full head of hair. His thick mustache had turned completely gray since the last time I had seen him. I swear I could smell him on the other side of the door, which I wasn't going to open. I waited for a knock.

"Otrnlov. Get the fuck out of here," I shouted.

"Sashaleh, is that you?"

"Yes, of course. Who else? Now get the fuck out of here and don't come back."

"I just came to say hello to you, Sashaleh. Your father said I should come by."

"Get out. I'm going to call the police."

"Your cousin is here, too?"

"No."

"I'd like to talk to him. Where is he?"

"Crazy man. I'm not going to tell you where Bruce is."

"Sashaleh, this is no way to treat a friend of the family, someone who loved your mother as much as anyone. I've come all this way, ignoring important business, to pay my respects."

"Tomorrow at the funeral, I'm going to have a cop put you against the wall and have you spread your legs like a whore as he pats you down. If he finds anything, a gun, a knife, so much as a nail clippers, I'm going to have him haul you away. Understand?"

"Yes, I understand, Sashaleh. I don't have anything. I just came to say good-bye to the greatest mathematician of the twentieth century. That's all. Just to say good-bye."

"I'm not opening up the casket, either. Not for anyone. Now you get the fuck away from here and don't come back."

"I understand, Sashaleh, but I do have a small request."

"You don't get requests."

"Please, Sashaleh. I knew your mother for so long. She is like family to me. Dear family."

"No, crazy man. She was not like family to you."

"She was. You can't deny it."

"I don't care what I can and can't deny."

"I would like to give a short speech at the funeral, Sashaleh. Your father said it would be OK."

"No. It's not OK. No speech. No nothing. You come to the ceremony. You listen. You pray. You leave. The burial is private. Understand, crazy man?"

"This is not right. I did so much for your dear mother. I loved her."

"Get away from the door and go back to the university or I'll call the cops."

"Your mother would be crying if she heard you right now, Sashaleh. I can see her tears, I swear."

"I'm calling the cops on my cell."

"Don't call anyone. It's OK. I'll leave. I'll see you tomorrow, Sashaleh."

"OK. Tomorrow. Now get the fuck away from here and don't come back." I could sense Otrnlov turning around and moving away from the door with his plodding steps. I called Ollie on my cell as I, through the living room curtains, watched Otrnlov walk along the sidewalk and thought, good riddance. Ollie gave me the lowdown on Otrnlov's crazy ideas.

I went upstairs to see Bruce, who was in an old satin bathrobe of my father's, reading a manuscript in my mother's bed.

"What was that about?"

"What was it about? Maybe I just saved your life."

"Thanks, I guess."

"I'm not joking. I need to find a picture of the guy who was at the door just now."

"The one you were shouting at?"

"Yeah, that one. He thinks you have a copy of the proof my mother supposedly solved, and you're hiding it until you make a movie about it."

"Oh, he is crazy. This is amusing." Bruce was grinning.

"It's not amusing, Bruce. This is serious. The guy, his name is Otrnlov. I don't know what he is capable of doing. But his head is full of loose screws."

"A movie about your mother wouldn't sell, you know." The following year, when the movie *A Beautiful Mind* came out, Bruce would change his opinion about the prospects of a successful biopic about my mother. On this topic, maybe Otrnlov wasn't so crazy after all.

"I'm going to print out a picture for you. Don't get near Otrn-lov. Keep your distance."

"You look bad, Sashaleh."

"My mother died. How am I supposed to look?"

"No, not grieving bad. You look angry and upset, bad. I haven't seen you like this in a long time."

"I am angry. I am upset. My mother dies and I have to deal with these idiots."

"It's entertainment, Sasha. You know that. We're going to put on a show for them. Make a good strudel. Then we can be ourselves."

"Well, there have to be rules about this strudel. I'm going to campus. I'm laying down the law. You think I stand a chance of getting through to them?"

Bruce paused before he said a word, something uncharacteristic of him. He tilted his head and looked upward. Then and there, he reminded me a bit of Pascha the parrot when someone she liked was approaching her cage.

"Not a chance in hell," he said. "I don't get why you'd even try."

CHAPTER 14

Laying Down the Law

"I t's been a long time since we've had to deal with such a thing," my father said. I was in his office, having walked in a rage from my mother's home to Van Vleck Hall. A utilitarian tower built during the boom years in state funding of the university, the building was named after an alum and former faculty member who went on to MIT and won a Nobel Prize in physics. Nowadays, new buildings on state campuses like Wisconsin and Alabama tend to be architectural wonders funded by and named for near-billionaire alums who believe that, through their donations to their alma maters, they will leave monuments to their amazing monetary success that will last as long as the pyramids of Giza. The truth is that, more than likely, one hundred years or so into the future, their campus buildings will be torn down and replaced by something newer and fancier funded by near-trillionaires (since being a billionaire by then will be equivalent to being a mere mortal millionaire today). Thank god no one tells them this.

"Twenty years," I said. "A little longer. That's when Zaydeh Aaron died."

"Yes, that's right. He would never admit it, but he had the mind of a mathematician."

"Probably so. But that wasn't true for Aunt Zloteh," I said.

"Oh no, not her." My father smiled. Even my father, with the natural eye of a critic, always viewed my late aunt with a positive glow.

One of the advantages or disadvantages, depending on your view I suppose, of coming from a small family is that hardly anyone dies and you rarely mourn. I say it depends on your point of view, because births and weddings, happy occurrences, are infrequent as well. But grief always hits hard and somehow lingers longer than exultation in your mind and heart, or at least it does with me.

My aunt and grandfather died over a two-month period when I was in my late twenties. That year of funerals was a hard time for my mother. It was during a year of cicadas, and they were everywhere at my aunt's funeral, crunching under the soles of shoes. With the death of my aunt, my uncle Shlomo, for a time, became a broken man. It was the only period in my life when I saw him defeated by anything. After the funeral he went into a drunk that lasted a year and a half. A trio of Greek brothers, former owners of a couple of unsuccessful dive bars in the area who Shlomo had hired years before, held his business together.

Two months later, when my grandfather, walking like he always did in the morning to pick up his copy of the *Wall Street Journal* at Mac's, had an aneurysm and instantly died, I think my uncle barely noticed. In fact, the day of that funeral, I had to go to his house, sober him up a bit, throw him in the shower, and help him get dressed. He said not a word during the entire ceremony. When he took a shovel of dirt to the casket, I looked at his ashen face, literally gray. It was if his capillaries had retreated deep within his skin, and I thought that he would soon follow both of them, my grandfather in that deep hole, my aunt no more than ten feet away.

For my mother, it was the one-two punch of those deaths that knocked her back. My aunt had been born in a Polish partisan encampment during the war, but her family was from a *dorf* not far from my mother's hometown. They were like sisters, those two, and over the years had developed their own private language. I remember well listening to their mixture of Yiddish and Polish as they sat at the kitchen table drinking tea.

My aunt was a social creature in ways my mother could never be. She lived in the here and now, and was almost always impossibly optimistic about the future of mankind. When I was in my teens, I started to read Chekhov and noticed his fondness for including a female character in plays and stories like *The Three Sisters'* Irina, someone who believed with every bit of her being, despite all evidence to the contrary, that the future would bring a better world. I thought, "Oh, Chekhov maybe had an aunt like mine." He could have, for all I know, but more than likely Irina was a stand-in for Chekhov himself. My aunt was joyful, her presence made others instantly feel better about themselves, and she died too young.

When my aunt died, we lost our little good luck charm, although Bruce, once you scratch away his hip exterior and stupid French cigarettes, is like his mother in a lot of ways. Aunt Zloteh always had such consistent *goyishe mazel* that when she came back from the doctor with her diagnosis of cancer, we, a family that always defers to rational science, were half convinced that the doctors were completely wrong. Maybe if my aunt had lived a good many years, my mother wouldn't have been so devastated by the death of her father at a naturally ripe age. But nature rarely gives us convenient respites, and tragic events, just like celebrations, seem to get bunched together.

"I wish Rachela would have believed in the afterlife," my father said. "She would have been comforted a bit by thinking she was going to join those two."

"They were a good trio. They understood each other."

"It's true. But I'll tell you this. I'm not going anytime soon. I swear I'm going to hang around and torture you for another ten years at least."

"You're moving to Tuscaloosa?" I didn't know if his brand of torture could be conducted over a long distance.

"You've got to be kidding. It's too warm down there."

"You've never been. How would you know?"

"I'm not an idiot. I don't have to visit. All I have to do is look at Weather dot com. I don't know how you can do any decent work in such a climate."

"It's true, you can't ski there."

"How long has it been since you've put on a pair of skis, anyway?" My father looked genuinely curious as to what my answer would be.

"Downhill? Two years ago, maybe."

"No, not downhill. Any idiot can be hauled like a garbage can up a mountain just so he can let gravity slide him down. I mean up and down both. On a cold clear day."

"Cross-country? Forever."

"I'm going to take you out on a pair of skis again. I still went out with your mother, you know, when she was sick. I didn't think it was a good idea, actually. But she insisted. She needed to think clearly."

"Math still?"

"A little. She thought mostly about other things. Family history. You."

"I'm a grown man. I live eight hundred miles away. I'm not a well-posed problem."

"A mother still worries. Always."

"And a father?"

"No, not me. I don't worry about you. I raised you. You grew up. My biological purpose on this planet ended a long time ago. And you, your biological purpose. You didn't follow through on that."

"I did. At least one time."

"Not that I can see. Not that anyone in your family can see." My father gave me the look of a scold.

"It's true. I let my *nakhes* slip away. But your biological purpose seems to be quite intact given the way you still chase after skirts."

"That's different. That has nothing to do with my biological purpose. It's for pleasure."

"Mistakes happen. Those little guys can still swim. Even at your age." The thought of him fathering a child made me panic a bit.

"No, they can't. Not for twenty years."

"What? You never told me."

"Why would I tell you? Is it a requirement in this country that a father and son engage in locker room conversation?"

"It hurt?"

"What? The surgery?"

"Yes, the snipping. They say you get elephant balls for a few days after." I shouldn't have been taunting my father, but I couldn't help it.

"A lovely image you've just conjured up. This isn't my kind of conversation. You know it isn't."

"True. I didn't come here to discuss your fertility, anyway."

"So why did you come?"

"I need to lay down the law with these idiots. I don't want tomorrow to turn into a circus."

"You can't control these cockroaches. You know that. Your mother's death has been like turning on a light in an apartment bathroom at night. It's making these crazy people scurry around furiously."

"I'm still going to lay down the law. Ollie's rounding them all up. We're going to meet in Room B102."

"I don't know if you can fit them all in there." My father seemed surprised by my resolve.

"Ollie says it seats 350."

"All those great minds. Not a one of them with a milligram worth of common sense. You really think you can make them behave?"

"I'm going to try in a half hour."

"I was going to say it's your funeral, but that would be in bad taste, I know."

"I need the keys to Mom's office. I need to figure out what I'm going to say to these *szaleńcy*."

"They keep trying to get in there. They think there is some great secret to be discovered." He didn't hide his disgust.

"You been in there lately?"

"No."

"Maybe there is. You never know."

"I know," my father said as he tossed me the key. "There's nothing there."

My mother and father had offices on different floors. It had always been so, even before Van Vleck Hall had been erected. The place was showing its wear, I noticed. It was as if deferred maintenance were a requirement for running a modern public university. I walked into my mother's office and sensed that no one had been inside for weeks at least.

I could see the dust in the air, visible in the rays of light that came through the slits in the blinds. I walked to the windows, turned the plastic rod, not surprisingly the same make of plastic rod as in my own office, and looked outside for a bit.

My mother's desk was filled with piles of research papers and books checked out of the library. She had a thing about file cabinets, absolutely hated them. There was something about having a metal or wood case filled with papers that she found offensive. Why? I don't know. It was the same with raisins. It's just how she was, and the fact of the matter is that when you achieve a certain level of fame and notoriety—even in the obscure world of mathematics—you're given license to act on your whims and neuroses with abandon.

In her office, my mother had filled her open-wall shelves with orange faux–leather bound banker's boxes. The boxes were in turn filled with copies of papers, works in progress, and letters. One of these boxes was on her desk. It turned out that my father had been wrong about the absence of secrets in my mother's office. At least I was surprised. The box was labeled, *Papers of A.K.* A for Alexander, my legal first name. K for Karnokovitch.

I knew the research papers contained in that box, of course. I never sent her copies of my writing. She never asked for them, either. But here they were, Xeroxed copies of my papers, the ones where I was first author, at any rate. One of the papers had been pulled out, and I could see my mother's handwriting on the margins. She wasn't just collecting my papers. She was analyzing them.

We never talked about my work, although she would show up sometimes when I gave visiting lectures in the atmospheric sciences department at Wisconsin. One time by happenstance we were both giving lectures at the University of Arizona, and she suggested that we come to each other's talks. I remember my mother walking into the cinder-block lecture hall of the atmospheric sciences department with a troupe of skinny young male mathematicians, pathetic bodyguards of a sort. I looked at her in the middle of the lecture hall as I began and smiled. I knew why mother had brought her Arizona colleagues. She was *kvelling*, plain and simple.

Many years later, when my mother was already sick, I gave a talk in Wisconsin, and she again appeared. There was again a troupe of mathematicians with her, but this time their purpose was practical. They were making sure she was OK. In the middle of my lecture, she bolted from the room and went out a side door, only to show up again, her makeup redone, ten minutes later. I asked her about it after the lecture. "I had to throw up," she said matter-of-factly.

Did I *kvell* at my mother's lectures? Of course, or as they say in my home state, you betcha. She was more than just a mother to me, just like she was more than just a wife to my father and more than just a sister to my uncle. She was our source of pride, the standard-bearer of our family's *yikhes*, our family's bloodline. If anyone doubted that our gene pool was worth continuing for another millennium, we could always point to her. The world was lucky to have my mother. I was lucky to be her son. You betcha, indeed.

But getting into the *kishkes* of one of my papers—this one had been written in 1982—was about something more than just *kvelling*. She was using my work for something. I thought of Einstein and his progeny. His son Hans, like me, didn't even try to follow in the footsteps of his father (and mother) but ran away at an oblique angle to become a fluid dynamicist. He studied the motion of water in rivers. The great Einstein went to the trouble of doing a bit of research in his son's field, and even wrote a paper on the topic of why rivers meander. Perhaps my mother was trying to do something similar. Whatever the reason she was looking at my work, the recognition that she was in such close intellectual proximity to me lifted my heart, and I forgot, for a moment, my grief.

Mourning. Who can possibly be good at such an awful endeavor? Your heart really does feel heavy. That's not some poetic metaphor. Your skin feels absent of moisture. Your breath is shallow and you literally ache as you try to take more air into your lungs. Everything slows down and your senses dull. It's a coping mechanism, I guess, and a good one. Who wants to be aware during such a time? Your mind, if it were fully alert, would send you the images and feelings of a real-life horror show.

I just needed to get through tomorrow in one piece, I thought.

I needed to recite one speech at the funeral, and I didn't really care if it was anything close to perfect. I needed to make sure these mathematicians would be kind enough to sit in one place for one hour and keep their mouths shut.

I walked into Room B102, and there they were. The mathematicians. I knew many of them by sight. Ollie walked up to me, and somehow, the sight of his familiar shiny bald head made me feel better. I had known this man for forever. We'd even played in Little League together.

"I'm sorry for your loss, Sasha."

"Thank you, Ollie. They're all here, I see. I know getting them together must not have been easy," I said, shaking Ollie's hand.

"It wasn't that hard, really. Anything you need? A microphone, maybe?"

"I'm like my mother, you know. I can get along very well without one."

I looked out at the crowd. My father stood by the back door eyeing me. In the front sat Yakov Epshtein from Nebraska, his plump face absent its usual glow. Vladimir Zhelezniak, whom I had never met, sat along one aisle. Peter Orlansky from Princeton, someone who had written well over two dozen papers with my mother, looked down as I recognized him. Many of these people had known me when I was a child and teen. But that was way back when, decades ago.

Three hundred people sat enveloped by the stale air and deathly lighting that are a staple of college lecture halls everywhere. There was no sign of Otrnlov. I didn't know if this was a good thing. They were all so quiet, these mathematicians. They were obviously in mourning, too. My father walked from the back of the room to the podium. I watched him carefully. He was seventy-seven years old, and he still strode with the confidence of a man who believed his body would never betray him.

"My son would like to say a few words to you. I ask that you listen carefully." He nodded to me and walked off to the side. I took a breath. I could feel the ache inside my lungs. A quad muscle in my thigh began to tremble. I thought of my grandfather and what he would have said to me had he been there: "*Shtark zich.*" Make yourself strong.

"I know many of you, quite a few for many years. I know you have come here to honor the life of my mother. And to mourn, as well. I can sense the sadness in this room, and to tell you the truth, it's a comfort to feel that sadness from you, to know that my loss, the loss of my father, and of my family, is shared by many others.

"Here is another truth, though. I would have wished that my mother's ceremony be a private one. I wanted to have just my family say good-bye. But call after call convinced me otherwise. You all wanted to come. And the fact is that a lot of you would not have listened to me had I told you no. You would have come anyway. So to tell you the truth, I am stuck with you. I'm trying to make the best of a less than desirable situation.

"Tomorrow we will mourn and honor my mother. I want to emphasize this word 'honor.' It implies dignity. If my mother believed in anything, it was that, dignity. She expected me to rise up above ordinary behavior and behave in a civilized, dignified manner. To respect others. To live and think carefully. To use my mind in a productive way. Always.

"Just two hours ago, at my mother's house, all my fears that the presence of all of you would turn what should be a dignified event into a circus of craziness, all of my worries that the egotism of this group would simply not allow my mother's funeral to be a source of comfort to those who loved her, rose up. I will not tolerate it. I deserve better. My father deserves better. My family deserves better. Do you understand?"

Peter Orlansky stood up. He was an odd duck who never looked into anyone's eyes, and true to form he looked down at his shoes as he spoke. I looked at him, so tall with broad shoulders. His black hair was still thick. The years had aged him less than most. "Sasha, we are all here to pay our respects. To honor your mother. To honor your family. Whatever you want, we will do."

"Good. What do I want, then? Tomorrow. I want you to sit down and stay down. I don't want a word out of you. I don't want any speeches from you. You will listen. You will sit as if there is glue on your feet. When it's over, you will walk out quietly."

Zhelezniak then stood up. The entire room seemed to stiffen as it sensed his presence. He looked at me with his beagle eyes. "Professor Karnokovitch, I know we've never met. Excuse me for this indulgence. Your mother was no ordinary woman. In fact, there has never been a woman like her before in mathematics. Never. There may not be a woman like her again for hundreds of years. You probably know your mother and I were not friends. But the fact is that your mother was adored by all of us for her intellect, which was superior to all of ours. We will never see another mind like hers in our lifetime. Allow us the privilege to honor her as well."

"I heard something of this sort two hours ago."

"Otrnlov is crazy, Sasha," Yakov said without standing, his voice booming in the hall. "Don't confuse us with him. OK, I know none of us is really normal. But we are caring human beings just like you. It's true we don't deserve a part in this funeral. We know that. We'll be happy to just sit in our seats, glue on our feet if you want. But we are asking you to give us more. We would be grateful if you did. She is your mother, yes, we know. But we loved her, too. We would like to say good-bye to her in a respectful and dignified manner."

"There will be not a word from any mathematician save for my father, if he wishes, at the funeral."

"As you wish, Sasha. We understand," Yakov said. "We've discussed this amongst ourselves. We don't really need to say anything then. But we do need to mourn. And one day. Just one day. By Jewish law it isn't enough. Some of us want to sit after."

"I've heard that you want to sit shiva with us. It's an absurd idea."

"But as you said yourself, you can feel the sadness in this room," Zhelezniak said. "We can all feel it. We have lost something truly magical and wonderful. It will take a long time to recover."

I looked at my father. I wanted to see something in his eyes, a recognition that he knew just how outrageous this request was. Instead he opened his mouth before I could say anything. "Not all of you are crazy, it's true. A few of you were loved by my wife as if you were family. That's true, too."

"Thank you, Viktor, for your understanding," Peter Orlansky said. "It will just be six of us. We've decided amongst ourselves whom it will be."

"Six." I sighed.

"Technically, eight," Yakov said. "We drew lots. The Karanskys. One of them drew for all three."

A trio stood up, all of them from New York City with full black beards. I knew them, had seen them last when I gave a talk at Columbia a few years back. The Karansky triplets. Three Israeli brothers, born in Minsk, with joint appointments at the Technion in Haifa and at the Courant Institute at NYU. All three specialized in partial differential equations, and they almost always published together. My mother had written recommendation letters for all of them, and positive tenure appointment letters as well. She had, for some reason, decided that not only were these three young men excellent mathematicians, but they were also worthy of entry into her small circle of professional confidants.

"Six, eight. Why not twelve, or fourteen, or twenty?"

"Don't be mad, Sasha," my father said.

"OK, the Karanskys. Who else?"

"Me," Yakov said. "Orlansky. Zhelezniak. Ben-Zvi. Ito."

I knew all the names. All but Zhelezniak had published papers with my mother. Except for the Karanskys and Zhelezniak, these were people I'd known in some way for decades. Was Zhelezniak there to, as my mother thought, dance on her grave? I knew that wasn't the case. My view was that he was a fellow great student of the great Kolmogorov. He was a near intellectual peer who had come at considerable expense to pay his respects. "It's a Jewish event, you know. My mother was a deeply religious person," I said, as a last line of defense.

"Sasha, we have a similar ceremony in Buddhism following the death of a loved one," Ren Ito said. "I would be honored." Ito. He had lived in our sunroom for six months during a sabbatical in 1957. In World War II, he had been removed from graduate school at Berkeley and sent to a Japanese confinement camp in the

Central Valley of California for two years. How could I refuse such a good, gentle man pushing eighty years old?

"I don't want a public word out of any of you tomorrow. I swear if anything happens tomorrow, no shiva, no nothing. Understand?"

"Nothing will happen tomorrow," Yakov said. "You just have to trust us."

"What about Otrnlov?" I asked.

CHAPTER 15

The Women

My *zaydeh* Aaron used to say, *"A mensch tracht un Gott lacht."* You can make all the plans in the world, but God will fuck them up and be happy about it. I had planned to bury my mother quickly and with little in the way of embellishment. I thought, *ich hob getracht*, that for a week I would grieve in the comfort of my family the way everyone should have a right to grieve. Then I'd fly home for a month, immerse myself in work, the best medicine for mourning anyone could possibly devise, and come back one more time to face the Hollywood (truly) production of a memorial ceremony for my mother at the capitol. But that plan was gone. Now I was on to plan B, not a very good plan at all in my opinion. Plus I had to worry about Otrnlov. One of the Karanskys said he thought Otrnlov had gone to my uncle's house.

I called my uncle on his cell. He didn't answer, nor did he quickly call back as per usual. That was a bad sign. My uncle loved his cell phone. He always possessed the latest model and was one of those men who, in the company of other men, got pleasure from showing off just what his little gadget could do. My uncle was clearly avoiding me.

Then there was the fact that Anna was angry about the news of the expanded shiva. You never wanted to provoke her. It wasn't just the emotional toll. She was a thrower. My mother had a lovely, very breakable set of dishware that I had hoped to bring back to Tuscaloosa. Once, while living in Manhattan, Anna threw a frying pan at her second husband's head. He ducked. The pan continued to sail, crashed through a window, and descended to Amsterdam Avenue, where it burst through the roof of a parked cab. Luckily no one was injured.

I shouldn't single Anna out. None of us had anything in the way of equanimity even on good days. But I had to try for her sake. Back at my mother's house I was beginning to think that it might be best to simply be selfless. As Bruce noted, we were making what he called a strudel, a Hollywood show. If I needed time to reflect, I could hole up in my house in Tuscaloosa for a week after this circus was over.

Anna was smoking one of Bruce's French cigarettes in the living room and was pacing the wooden floor in her flats. She was dyeing her hair again, blond this time, and the contrast between the lightness of her hair and the darkness of her skin made her seem otherworldly. She looked like someone capable of making bold and accurate predictions.

"I'm not going to spend seven days with a bunch of misfits who think they are princes of the planet because they can play with numbers," she said.

"They won't live here. They'll come in the day. They'll leave at night. It'll be OK, I promise."

"What can you possibly promise? Be realistic." Anna gave me a dismissive look while she drew in some smoke.

"I can't promise they'll be human beings during the day, no. But I can promise that we'll have peace when they are gone."

"Avi will be one of them, yes?" The Avi in question was Abraham

Ben-Zvi, Anna's first husband. She had that knowing, big sister tone in her voice. I was starting to feel like I was fifteen again.

"Yes."

"You want me to believe that this was something done at random, cooked up by drawing straws? Those fucking mathematicians. They think they are entitled to lie because what they are working on is so important. Zealots all of them."

"I do admit it doesn't make any sense. Look at those names. They got together and decided. They didn't draw anything. I'm sure you're right."

"Of course I'm right. And you agreed to this craziness. You told me this would be a 'dignified event.' That's what you said. And I was stupid enough to believe you."

"Well, my father opened his big trap." I gave Anna a pleading look.

"They probably talked to him before. Probably more than eight wanted to be here. Maybe one hundred. Who knows with those crazy people." Anna was inclined to believe in conspiracy theories.

"Ask him. He might tell you the truth."

"Your father? Does he tell anyone the truth about such things?"

"Not usually, no."

"And what about you? Do you tell the truth?"

"In this case, yes."

Anna, standing in the center of the living room, looked up at me. "You're telling the truth. You're pretty good at lying, but fortunately you have a certain tell. It's not there."

"What is it?"

"I'm not going to tell you. I shouldn't have even mentioned it.

That was stupid of me. Your mother told me about it. I didn't notice it myself. I doubt anyone else would. After all, a mother knows best about a child, yes?"

"Usually, yes."

"But not always in your case, actually. She was a wonderful woman. But she didn't always do right by you." I saw a little tenderness in Anna's eyes just then, but I didn't like the idea that I was like a mistreated pet.

"I know she wasn't perfect."

"She made you into a confirmed bachelor with a child you don't know."

"No one could have predicted that Catherine would go to the other side of the earth." I could have pointed out that no Slav or Eastern European Jew could have predicted this. We expect and demand people to maintain bonds with family. It doesn't matter whether you love or hate your relatives, even ones you've legally divorced. As long as there are children involved, you stick together. Of course, my mother didn't follow this rule when it came to me, but there were extenuating (read: Soviet) circumstances.

"That's the family excuse. I loved your mother as much as anybody. Still do. I used to make that excuse, too. Maybe I love your mother more now that I see her more clearly, mistakes and all."

"Maybe you do. I know the mistakes, too. But my mother didn't make me into anything. I've made the choices I've wanted to make. Did she have a tell?"

"Your mother?" She raised an eyebrow. She never liked to divulge any secrets she knew about my mother, even to me.

"Yeah, when she lied."

"I don't know." I knew this was a lie. "Who the hell is coming to the door, anyway?" She pointed to the walkway, but I didn't have quite the view she did.

"Not Otrnlov, I hope."

"No, a group of women," Anna said, looking through the living room window. "All of them need to learn how to dress."

"Mathematicians, no doubt."

"No doubt. And if any one of them starts complaining about my cigarette, I'm going to kick all those bitches out. I'm not in a mood."

Of course they were mathematicians. I knew two of them, Patricia O'Connell and Eva Steinberg, both former students of my mother. Jane Sempralini I knew only from hearing her name now and then. Virginia Potter, who seemed to pay attention to her appearance more than most, was completely new. The rest? There were so few women in mathematics when I was a kid that it's not surprising that the rest were young, at most thirty years old. They all had been in the lecture hall with me just an hour ago. They, too, had not been pleased by what had transpired.

"Eight men, and not a single woman," Steinberg said succinctly, airing her complaint in the living room. She was clearly the leader of this troop. Eva Steinberg was my age. When I was a child in Russia, she was living in a refugee camp in Germany. She took a job at Michigan after she graduated and became the first female professor to obtain tenure in their mathematics department. "Your mother meant so much to us. You have no idea just how much."

I knew this was true. My mother broke barriers, although she didn't break them for all time or for everyone. The second female mathematician elected to the National Academy of Sciences—my mother was the first—was American-born Julia Bowman Robinson. Despite having been a central figure in solving Hilbert's tenth problem, Robinson did not have a real academic job when she was voted into the academy. At the time of her election, reporters tried to find her at the University of California–Berkeley, which was the institutional affiliation she gave on all her papers. They were told that no one by that name existed on the faculty or staff. Julia Bowman Robinson had a desk in a shared departmental office and taught classes on occasion. Most people knew her not as a mathematician of first rank, but as Professor Raphael Robinson's devoted, loving wife.

Anna was standing and smoking, watching these women sitting on the couch and on the wing chairs pleading their case to me not politely but indignantly. "It would be a good idea, actually," Anna said.

"What?" I said, turning around and looking at her.

"Having them here. It would be good."

"Why would having six more people in an already crowded house that is supposedly in dignified mourning be a good idea?" My sense that there were six mathematicians in the room disappeared. Anna was sucking all the oxygen out of the room physically and metaphorically.

"It would be a good idea for me," Anna said. "Think, Sasha. I have to be here for seven days surrounded by the kind of men you have to force to take a shower more than once a month. It's oppressive. I have my own grief to deal with, a private grief, and I have to have my ex-husband and his cronies around, too?"

"How is turning this house into an even tighter sardine can of mathematicians going to help?"

"Idiot. They'll be forced to behave better, those boys who think they are men. With just me around, they'll behave like I'm an intruder." Anna looked at the other women in the room, and for the first time since I had been back from campus, actually smiled. "How many of you are there?" she asked no one in particular.

"Well, there are us six, plus we think it would be only fair for two others to attend," O'Connell said.

"It seems fair to me as well," Anna said and nodded approvingly.

"Twenty-two people in this house for seven days. What's fair about that?"

"Plus, the men are all kind of long in the tooth. When is the last time they did anything original?" Eva asked.

"The Karanskys. They're thirty-five at most," I said.

"They're on the downward spiral," Eva said. "I've been there. I know. Nothing new will be forthcoming from them, just ideas they thought of that they haven't finished yet. All ages should be represented."

"All I see are two people younger than the Karanskys," I said.

"We'll bring in two more. Your mother was like a god to these young ones." I knew the type. They had begun to invade Tuscaloosa, these young professors. Male and female, they were all so skinny, fit, and earnest, and so remarkably free of anxiety. When you asked them what they liked to do, they had two answers, their work and running. They ran an ungodly number of miles every week not to avert a health crisis, but simply because they loved to run. Who understood them? Endorphins saturated their blood, mixed with the caffeine from their no-fat lattes. A new generation had arrived, and it quite frankly was superior, if much more boring, than my own.

I looked at one of the young women suspiciously. Maybe she was twenty-eight. The makeup on her face was so unnecessary. There was not a single mark of age on her dewy skin. I looked closely at her face again for the slightest of signs that she was a Member of the Tribe.

"Do you even know what a shiva is?" I asked her.

"It's a seven-day-long ceremony in honor of the loss of a loved one."

"And did you even know my mother, much less love her?"

"I didn't know her. But she was an example of what we can all do. Except she did it when it was almost impossible. She was amazing."

"She was a remarkable woman, it's true. But I hate to tell you, she's not a good role model. What my mother did intellectually, you couldn't do, never will. You need to find more ordinary role models, and I'm not interested in turning my mother's shiva into a display of political correctness."

"Sasha, forget political correctness," Anna said. "Think of me and all those men. My ex-husband. It will be unbearable. And as you said, they won't be here all the time. Just during the day. At night, they'll stay wherever."

"Just these six, then," I said. "Only because of Anna. No more than that. The boat is now full. And at dinnertime you are all gone."

"Most of us are at the Howard Johnson's," Steinberg said.

"Oh, that's a disgusting hotel." Anna shook her head.

"It's not that bad," Steinberg said.

"Professor Steinberg, even when Soviet artists would travel here on tour, we stayed in better places. Seven days in such a pigsty!" Anna nodded sympathetically. "We will find you better. We'll ask Sasha's uncle. He is a very resourceful person."

"That he is. But he's not answering phone calls right now."

"Oh, not really. He called me before you came. His Russian is not as good as he makes out it seems. He needed me to do some translating. You should probably head over there."

CHAPTER 16

The Prisoner

I can tell you the exact moment I became interested in meteorology. I was eight years old. It was in June during a year with an early summer when even Wisconsin was hot and muggy. Moisture clung to your skin, and at night thunderstorms lit up the sky.

We are, as a family, not fond of hot weather, although of course I changed my opinion on this subject as an adult. My mother was convinced that the heat fouled your brain. She used her summers to do things that didn't require much thought and were strictly for pleasure. For a while, in the good Russian tradition, we had an American version of a dacha, a little cabin on a lake about one hour north of Madison. Every summer we would haul up there for a month or two. My father would abandon his suits and ties, and would even forgo his comb-over as he took dips in the lake or went fishing in our little rowboat. My grandfather would sit at the kitchen table and do his annual dusting and cleaning of our investment portfolio. My mother would fry up the bluegill and perch my father and I caught, although my father was almost always far more successful than I was.

There is a Russian phrase that my father was fond of that is difficult to give life to in English, *bez truda ne vytaschish i rybku iz pruda*. It takes work to pull a fish out of the water. I suppose it's the equivalent of no pain, no gain. But according to my father, this phrase isn't really talking about pain and it's not talking about fishing the way Americans think of it. No, it's about diving deep to find a carp in one of those murky steppe lakes left by glaciers ten thousand years ago. You have to feel with your hands on the lake bottom without sight of what you are looking for, and hold your breath all the while. Then, somehow, upon feeling that familiar slick skin in the slimy muck, you need to reach for the gill of the fish and literally haul him up with you to the surface. That is indeed work, and I think it has everything to do with scientific discovery. You have to know what you are seeking, are often blind, and have to rely on the feel that comes with experience. Even then, when you finally have something tangible in your grasp, you still have a lot of work and struggle. Immigrants to this country and their children tend to understand this. Americans? Not really. It's why they don't often excel in science.

We were fishing, my father and I, on one of those unbearably hot days when in the afternoon the clouds formed into thunderheads. My father insisted that we continue to do exactly what we had started to do in the morning, weather be damned. As I was casting, I saw a tornado start to form in the distance. At first it was a little gray wisp high in the air, but then it lengthened. Finally its tip hit the water. It was as menacingly elegant as a cobra.

"*Papa, smotri,*" I said.

"Oh my, this I've never seen."

"What is it?"

"Tornado, but on the water."

The sky was changing color by the instant, turning from ash gray to olive green. I should have been scared, but instead I was entranced. Something almost as powerful as human love filled me. The wind whipped my T-shirt as I watched the funnel in the distance. I barely helped to gather up our fishing gear.

Right then and there I wanted to know everything about how tornadoes formed. I wanted to know how air and moisture organized in this way. Even today, I think it's remarkable that it does so. What starts out as a small disturbance cascades under the right and oh so rare conditions. The odds of this cascade of events happening are minuscule, and we know this because little wisps of moisture and air are present with us all the time.

Tornadoes are a good metaphor for how bad things happen in our lives. They build from small disturbances that usually don't mean a thing and almost always dissipate. But somehow one particular random bad event attracts others, and all of them together grow and attract more nasty stuff. Once it gets up to a critical size, the odds of it growing even larger are no longer remote.

I drove to my uncle's house and thought of Otrnlov and the out-of-control shiva. I walked inside. Otrnlov was sprawled on my uncle's dining room carpet, unconscious.

"What do you suggest we do with this *szaleniec*, Sashaleh?" My uncle looked at me as if I might actually have some useful contribution to solving the problem at hand.

"You're the one with the practical ideas in this family."

"Usually, yes."

"And this isn't like usual?"

"No, it isn't. I have enough to deal with with Cynthia. You have to deal with him."

"Where's Cynthia?"

"I don't know. Somewhere in here, I think. I didn't hear her car. You know, I should have never married that woman. But she has a reason to be upset now." Cynthia was American-born. My uncle had built this house for her. It was an effort at building a life completely different than anything he had experienced before. Like most efforts at reinvention, it was a failure. You could say that my entire family had reinvented itself by coming to America, but it wouldn't be true. We simply came here and did exactly as before, more or less. America accepted us, unbridled and untamed. "His name is Otrnlov, you say?"

"Yeah, Konstantin Otrnlov."

"A man walks up to my house, my wife answers, and he starts threatening her. I hear the shouting, see his hands on Cynthia. He's lucky to still be alive."

"What did you hit him with?"

"Baseball bat. I always keep a few around. I'm in the liquor business. You never know who's going to come to the door."

"You knock him out then and there?"

"No. I got him off Cynthia first. I tried to get him to explain himself. He talked. Then he reached for something in his jacket. I thought it might be a gun. That's when I hit him."

"Did he actually have a gun?"

"Sort of. A staple gun," my uncle said, and pointed to the loaded "weapon" on the dining room table.

"He was going to shoot you with a staple gun?"

"Don't laugh. You could blind someone with that."

"He's out cold. Thank god he's still breathing."

"The bat is metal. What do you expect? Not all crazy people have crazy strength, you know. That's just in the movies. He was drunk, screaming mostly in Russian but nothing I could understand. I thought it was some crazy dialect I'd never heard."

"Anna said that."

"He was using all kinds of Latvian words, it turns out. Anna couldn't understand him either, but she could tell he was from Latvia from his accent."

"He's not saying anything anymore. He was looking for Bruce, probably. I should have called you."

"Yes, you should have. Definitely should have. And now this *szaleniec* is your responsibility."

"I could call the police." Even I knew this was a lousy idea.

"This Otrnlov have a criminal record? He's done this before?"

"I don't think so, no. He hit another mathematician once, but that guy didn't press charges."

"So what are they going to do with him? And we have a funeral tomorrow. We have more important things to do than deal with this Otrnlov and cops."

"I'll call his daughter. Have her retrieve him."

"She nearby?"

"New Jersey."

"That's not nearby. That's a day away even by plane." My uncle sighed. "This family is hopeless. OK, we switch. You deal with Cynthia. She always liked you pretty well. Probably she likes you more than she likes me right now. I'll deal with Otrnlov."

"You sure?"

"You find Cynthia. She's in here somewhere. I know it. It's too cold for her to go out. I'll get this Otrnlov taken care of today and have his daughter pick him up tomorrow. You know her number?" My uncle took hold of his cell phone, and eagerly waited for me to give him the ten digits that he could enter into his little phone bank.

My uncle had met Cynthia in Florida when he was on vacation. She was from Dallas, Texas, and on a business trip. An interior decorator twenty years younger than my uncle, Cynthia was about to be married to a longtime friend of her mother's family. According to my uncle, she was not particularly looking forward to this marriage, or at least she was getting cold feet. My uncle, a confident, tall dark man, came into her life and offered her an exotic alternative.

Finding anyone in my uncle's house was not easy. The walls were thick, the hallways long, and any name shouted out would not likely be heard by its intended target. When my uncle built this house, a Roman library–inspired home of five thousand square feet, it was one of the most ostentatious in Madison. But over the space of a few short years, it became accepted as somewhat tasteful in comparison to the newer, monstrous, Disney-inspired castles that were being built on the fringes of town.

I opened the door into the greenhouse. Now, dear reader, don't try to read symbolism into this. Cynthia Czerneski was in the greenhouse, yes, but she is not a hothouse flower from the South trying desperately to survive the cold of Wisconsin. This story is not a Tennessee Williams play. Cynthia Czerneski does not depend on the kindness of strangers.

But here is some information about me. People do believe in my kindness, or at least women of a certain age do. I don't understand it myself. Physically, I don't possess any characteristics that could be associated with softness. I have a Dracula-like widow's peak. My face is more or less blocklike. I am broad-shouldered and have the short, marchlike stride of a boxer. It's as if I'm ready to do battle at any moment. If I were a woman, I would be suspicious, or maybe even scared of a man like me. Yet women talk to me all the damn time. On planes they show not the slightest hesitation to sit next to me. And they tend to open up and tell me things that no one should tell any stranger.

Perhaps because I had lived in the South for so many years, or because I was close to my uncle, or because of my improbably inviting aura, I was the one person in my family, aside from my uncle, with whom Cynthia actually talked. In the greenhouse she was tending to some orchids, the blooms large and delicate, when she noticed and turned to me.

"I'm sorry to hear about your mother," Cynthia said.

"She had a good life. A little short. But really now, she didn't get cheated."

"I was there with her, you know. Just trying to help. But she didn't want my help."

"My mother was not easy to deal with, I know."

"Sasha, she kicked me out. She was screaming at me. Swearing at me, telling me to get out. I've never, I mean, I was just trying to help." Cynthia was crying, still next to the orchids, and I reached out and held her. She broke into full sobs, heaving against me. "It's been so hard, so hard," she said between the sobs.

"It'll be OK, Cynthia. We'll have the funeral tomorrow. We'll sit shiva. We'll get through this."

"And then that man today. Screaming at me in a language I don't understand. Shaking me. I thought I was going to die."

"You've had a terrible day, it's true."

"I've tried to be a good wife. I really have. I tried to be like a good little sister to your mother, too. But these people. They expect me to know Russian and Polish. They expect so much of me."

"We are difficult, I know."

She let go of me and took a tissue to wipe away the tears. Cynthia was one of those people who simply could not look bad. Her face wouldn't allow it. She always looked beautiful in some way. There in front of me, her beauty came not so much from her features but in the resolve that I could see building in her. I don't think anyone in my family knew that Cynthia possessed inner strength.

"I can't take this anymore. I sit in this house most days alone. It's a lovely house, really. It's just how I dreamed it would be. I worked on it, making it just so."

"It is beautiful."

"I know it is. But it's almost as if I've built a prison for myself here. It's cold, so cold in the winter. I've never gotten used to it. And the people. I shouldn't complain. I'm not a complainer at all. But it's not like at home. They're as cold as the weather here."

"It's not like the South, you're right."

"You understand that. You know. I try to tell Shlomo, and he says people are people, the same everywhere. But it isn't true. They aren't the same. I really can't live here anymore. I've never thought this way before. But something about that man today. I could have died. I don't want to die here. I want to be where I belong."

"Don't do anything rash, please, Cynthia. You know my uncle loves you."

"I haven't told him anything, yet. But I will. It's not something that just came to me. It's just that today I understood what I've been feeling for a long time."

"I'm sorry to hear."

"You've been the only person nice to me in this whole family. No one else. They pretend I'm a joke. I'm not a joke! I'm a real person with real feelings."

"We'll have the funeral. Then we can all talk. Maybe you and I and Shlomo all together."

"I'm not going to stay for the shiva, Sasha. I'm going home. I've already called my family. Already bought a ticket."

I looked at Cynthia, her resolve and resignation so clear and open on her face, and thought of my own marriage. I knew why I had never married again. My family is hard on people, or at least unsuspecting people who believe in following their better angels. Hopeful, cheery women may be attracted to people like me or my uncle or my father because we know how to charm and say the right thing at the right time, and we are not without a high degree of confidence and resourcefulness. But ultimately we can break people and make them doubt what they have always felt to be true. We need strong women, case-hardened. Oh, Cynthia, Catherine, and all the other blithe female spirits in the world that we have flirted with and seduced, you should know we accept the savagery of the world with open arms. How come intelligent women can't recognize this trait of ours instantly?

CHAPTER 17

A Russian Funeral

Americans expect to live forever. I've noticed how Americans deal with doctors and hospitals and how they spend money—sometimes the money of their insurance companies, and sadly, sometimes piles of their own—to try to extend their lives for a minute, hour, day, month, or year or two. They engage in a ridiculous attempt to deny their mortality.

I would expect people with such an optimistic—I should really say delusional, but I'm trying to be nice—vision of our lives on this planet to go into complete shock when the inevitable happens and a loved one dies. Their mourning should be profound, their grief total and consuming. But it isn't so. Americans are, in fact, incredibly psychologically healthy—with not a small number of exceptions no doubt—when it comes to the death of loved ones. Of course, they feel terrible, but not usually in a wail out loud, scratch the skin off your cheeks, wear sackcloth and ashes kind of way. No, Americans tend to be quite sensible about this dealing with death business, far more sensible than they are about the business of actually dying. They feel loss for a year or two, but then somehow—and maybe this is just the optimistic spirit of America at work—they just pop back up again. They begin life anew with their face and eyes forward. I salute the American attitude toward mourning. I wish I possessed it, too.

It has now been almost a dozen years since my mother died. I can say without a doubt that I still have not fully recovered. I try to be a good American—I'm a citizen and patriot, after all—and look optimistically ahead. Indeed, I have much to do and much for which to be grateful, but how can one replace a mother? How can one replace someone you love who not only loves you in return, but also possesses a brain the size of the moon? I swear it would be easier for me to reconcile my loss if my mother had been the salt of the earth, an uneducated woman who nurtured me and encouraged me to go beyond her world and achieve something with the talents I had been given. I would still possess profound grief, but it would be the ordinary grief of a son. Instead, I have to live not only with the acute knowledge that I will never see my mother again, but I will also never again know anyone with that kind of intellect. I didn't just observe that brain at work or obsess over it from a distance like Otrnlov. I was onstage with it. I interacted. I was part of that brain's consciousness, sometimes too much so for my own comfort.

Maybe I'm writing these words because I still feel something profoundly missing. It's true that I feel the spirit of my mother with me as I write this, and the fact is that it's such a comfort, this feeling like she's actually with me, that it's becoming addicting. Too bad my mother's life can't be turned into a romantic-spy serial. Instead, this is the only book I will ever write about my mother. When it is done I will undoubtedly feel sad again now and then, weighed down by the loss of the woman who gave me life.

If you come from a country where people in the prime of their lives still die from pneumonia and tuberculosis with regularity, where a national leader murdered tens of millions of his own people and was still loved (and continues to be loved sixty years later), where death falls like rain every day, an inevitable unfortunate thing, where the average life expectancy of a male is younger than I am now (a comfortable, if a bit grumpy, middle age), then you know fully that you aren't going to live forever. There is no way you can delude yourself. If a sickness comes—a little strange bump appears on your cheek, the result of too much sun as a child decades ago; or your eyes yellow and your complexion turns sallow—you know that there's a good chance it will kill you. You are not so important that God, if there is one, will lower his hand of kindness in recognition of your plight. No miracles will be bestowed.

You might think that a people with such experiences and attitudes toward their mortality, depressingly realistic, would view the death of loved ones with a sad shrug and then go on, barely impacted by Death's visits, since Death is such a frequent visitor, after all. But no, it seems to be quite the opposite. When the inevitable does happen, we break hard, or at least my family and its friends do. There is no other way possible.

We live here, we are Jewish, and we can usually pretend we are Americans, but when Death comes we might as well be in Moscow or Minsk. At Jewish American funerals the surviving family usually affixes a tastefully discreet, barely visible black ribbon on their dresses and coat lapels as a symbol of grief. In adherence to Jewish law, they take a blade and make a tiny, barely visible cut into the ribbon. I can't fathom this approach. Why should mourning be tasteful? Why should we hide our loss?

I wasn't going to wear some stupid torn ribbon. That said, I wasn't going to ruin a perfectly good piece of clothing. I was sad and depressed, but still practical. I walked up to the attic of my mother's house. Bruce shouted up the stairs as he left my mother's room, "What are you doing?"

I knew what I was looking for. "I'm getting a tie to cut."

"Grandpa Aaron's ties are still there?"

"Hundreds of them. At least a few dozen here look like they could have been made this year."

"I'm coming up."

Vintage is not my cousin's style, but still he was intrigued, if only because of nostalgia. "He did have a look," Bruce said as he fingered the ties. "How many people can say that about their grandfather?"

"This one here is good."

"Marshall Fields. Not bad. You're going to cut it, right?"

"I'll have the rabbi do it."

"Seems a shame, really. It's a good tie. Classic business look." He seemed offended by the tie's impending destruction.

"I think it closes a circle, in a way."

"Saks. Wilkes Bashford. How did he get those?"

"Every town he visited, he bought some. That's how he was."

"I'll take a few for a friend. He likes this sort of stuff. Do you mind, Sasha?"

"He was your *zaydeh* too, you know. We'll have to clean this house out eventually."

We are a people pathologically in love with mourning not only our deceased family members but our national heroes as well. Poets, mathematicians, philosophers, politicians, sports heroes, cosmonauts. I swear that the funeral is to Russia what baseball is to the United States, its national pastime. When Kolmogorov was buried in Moscow, people who couldn't add single digits together without a struggle, much less devise a trivial mathematical proof, waited in a queue to see the great man at peace, clothed in a decent (for Russia at any rate), blue suit.

And what of the death of the truly widely known? Chekhov, understanding Russia's love of mourning, said famously, "Once Tolstoy dies, everything will go to hell!" He was right. When Tolstoy did die, the tsar tried to blunt the efforts of all of Russia to turn Tolstoy's funeral into a spiritual hajj. Trains to Tolstoy's remote town of Yasnaya Polyana were canceled. This strategy backfired as people turned the streets of Moscow and St. Petersburg into public funeral homes. They wailed over the death of the great man, and used the occasion to agitate for his political causes.

Perhaps only in Russia do people formalize grief to such a degree that national leaders are pickled for decades-long public display with nary a soul saying the obvious: What kind of sick and twisted nonsense is this? If you had achieved national visibility and you didn't share this obsession, if you found it distasteful, or if you were simply a sourpuss, well then you tried your best to avoid it when it was your turn. The Nobel Prize–winning poet Joseph Brodsky was, in addition to being an outstanding talent whose poems had made him the equivalent of a rock star in Russia, a sourpuss of the first order. Though he had long left Russia for the United States, he wasn't going to let even New York Russian émigrés turn his death into a circus of grief. No, he smartly chose to have his body flown far from the potential maddening crowd in the United States to Venice, Italy. Russians living in America were shut out. Those in Brodsky's native land were left with the meager outlet of erecting a plaque at his home of thirty-three years in St. Petersburg.

In a flight of fancy before my mother died, I had actually thought of following Brodsky's model. We could bury my mother in Israel, maybe even near the Mount of Olives grave of her *landsfrau*, the nineteenth-century mystic Maid of Ludmir. But the fact is that Israeli mathematicians are as impossible and nosey as those in America.

I didn't mention this crazy thought to my mother. I knew what she wanted. "Kowalevski, where did they bury her? In Oslo, where she was a professor," my mother once said about the greatest female mathematician of the nineteenth century. Russian-born, Kowalevski had not been allowed to be educated and never taught in her homeland. "I'm no better than Sophie," she said.

That morning, the three of us—Anna, Bruce, and I—left the house together and walked slowly in our long coats. We navigated around the streaks of ice on the sidewalks with our slippery leather-bottomed shoes. It's true that Bruce, despite hearing the stories from Russia and Poland again and again, could never fathom what life was like for me as a young child. He had spent all his years in dreamy America, where stories are expected to have happy endings. But he understood enough Yiddish and Polish to know when people were talking about him, and probably understood more Russian than he realized. As for Anna, she had lived a life that was far more like that of my parents', but she had come here young enough to dip at least one toe into America and experience it freshly without always translating her experiences into the Russian equivalent. Though there were almost ten years separating us, we did share common experiences and a common mood and setting. We were here and we were there both.

"We're going to be late," Anna said.

"They aren't going to start out without us," I said.

"It's so fucking cold here. Even colder than I remember," Bruce said.

"Actually it's getting warmer. Mendota freezes over for a smaller number of days every year," I said.

"Don't piss on my shoes with lies, Sasha," Bruce said.

"That's something *zaydeh* used to say in Yiddish. Very good translation, too," I said.

"I remember. I'm not a dummy, you know," Bruce said, getting defensive.

"True, but it is getting warmer. That's a fact," I said, getting pedantic.

"I'm channeling. I'm turning into an old Jew right before my very eyes," Bruce said.

"I'm already there," I said.

"That's a fact, too," Bruce said.

"I don't like being late. It's rude," Anna said.

"We won't be late, Anna. We have thirty-five minutes," Bruce said.

"I don't like falling and breaking my leg, either," I said.

"Bruce took dance lessons. He can walk faster than this. We'll pull you along." Anna started to grab me by the elbow, but I resisted.

"I was never good at it. And besides, I don't think Sasha wants any help."

"No, I don't. You're right. Five minutes and we'll be there. Just wait."

We walked into the synagogue, the place as packed as it was

for the High Holy Days. I could feel it again instantly, just like in Van Vleck Hall, the air of overpowering sadness. No, I don't think I was projecting. These were my people. I knew their body language. Their arms swung when they were happy, and their shoulders sagged when they were defeated. If Binion's World Series of Poker would allow only Russian and Polish Jews, I would eagerly sign up and make a killing every year. Then again, as my mother had told Anna, I don't exactly possess a poker face myself.

We sat in the front row, my father, Shlomo, Cynthia, Bruce, Anna, and me. The rabbi stood on the *bima*, a man about my age who barely knew me, and I could sense his pride welling up as he surveyed the crowd before him. There are no Nobel Prizes in mathematics, which urban legend says is the result of Nobel's wife screwing a mathematician (studying the topology of curved spaces, no doubt, haha), but really now, this seems far-fetched. More than likely it's due to the fact that, while mathematics is a useful tool, the way it is studied by mathematicians is rather useless for society. Nobel was all about practical matters. I am too, sort of. My mother and my father? No. Their friends? Certainly not. Be that as it may, there is a Nobel equivalent in mathematics, the Fields Medal, which comes with five figures in cash. No woman has ever won this prize. We'll get to why this is so later, but there were eleven Fields Medal winners in that synagogue, not an everyday occurrence.

I suppose I could have been angry at seeing this rabbi—who my mother thought was a hack—full of egotism. His beard had been tastefully trimmed just that morning, and he was taking in the crowd as if he were the star of a Broadway show. Instead, I was impressed. A few minutes before we began, he walked up to me, said just the right words of condolence, pulled out a little safety razor, and in a half second was done with the ceremonial tearing of my grandfather's old tie. A real professional he was, or so I thought. In a small college town like Madison you usually got shy, tongue-tied, overintellectualizing minor leaguers. They were rabbis who couldn't possibly handle the big congregations of New York, Chicago, or even Milwaukee. My mother probably had been, as per usual, overly critical.

I half listened to the words of praise that flowed from him. My mind was racing. Unlike the rabbi, I do not enjoy performing. I simply wanted to be in my own world and think my own thoughts about my mother, about my life, about my future, and about the ones I loved. But it was expected that I make a speech, a summary of my mother's life, that I be the representative of this family for the crowd. To do less would be to shirk a major responsibility to show that this family, undeniably human, could rise above its frailties.

There is an old Jewish joke (are there ever any new ones?) that I thought about before I went to see the rabbi to discuss what he was going to say. A man dies, a complete scoundrel. His brother, also a scoundrel, goes to the rabbi the day before the funeral, and says, "I'll give one million dollars to the synagogue if you call my brother a mensch when you give your speech." The rabbi spends a sleepless night thinking about what he's going to say at the funeral. The morning comes. His heart is heavy as he gets ready. He stands in front of the congregation and says, "This man was a complete scoundrel, a swindler, a cheat, and a whoremonger. But in all honesty, compared to his brother, he was a mensch."

I didn't have to implore my mother's rabbi to say kind words.

My mother opened her heart not to most, certainly, but to many. The local community knew the stories of her generosity and commitment to charity. The rabbi was doing his job, assuring all that my mother's life on this planet was filled with acts of giving. My job would be different. There would be no tears in public, or at least not on the *bima*. I recited the words, those of my grandfather that guided me whenever I had to find the fortitude to play the part of the public face of my family. "*Shtark zich, shtark zich,*" I said over and over again in my mind. Stand tall. I swear I could feel the spirit of both my grandfather and mother in the hall strengthening me. I looked at the memorial lights on the brass plaques lining the birch-paneled walls as I walked up to the *bima*.

My voice boomed, like my mother's did. Those who knew my mother and had an ear for detail surely could hear the resemblance. A few days in Wisconsin with my family and too many Soviet bloc mathematicians had brought back roundness to my vowels. My tongue had instinctively moved back a fraction, ready at any moment to pronounce with some facility, if not fluidity, all those Russian sounds. I thanked everyone for coming, for helping my family in their time of grief, even though the presence of all these people was no solace at all.

"My mother had many mentors," I said. "Kolmogorov of course was one. There were also people from history whose works she read and who greatly influenced her. At the top of the list was Sophie Kowalevski, a nineteenth-century Russian mathematician, who like my mother practiced her profession outside her motherland.

"Kowalevski was not as much an intellectual guide for my mother as she was a beacon for how to live, how to pursue a meaningful life despite obstacles. It was Kowalevski's example that gave my mother the strength to leave the known world of Russia for something new, a potentially fruitful life in the West.

"All of you know of my mother's mathematical talent. Most of you, however, likely have little idea that she was a writer as well. Again, it was Kowalevski—who wrote a novel and a memoir in addition to her mathematical work—who inspired her. 'The mind changes as you get older,' she said to me. 'It is a different machine entirely than it is when it's young, with a different purpose.'

"My mother wrote a memoir of her childhood. She didn't know what she would do with it. It was of a lost world, she said. I don't think she ever intended this memoir to be published formally. Rather, it was a family document, a record of a vanished time and place that could be handed down from generation to generation. She wrote short stories based on that time as well, some of which have been published. Unlike her stories, she wrote her memoir in her childhood language of Polish, a language that I don't know well. She said that she received much pleasure writing in her mother tongue. She would send me chapters, and I would struggle through them, but I could sense how much she enjoyed writing each word. It was well worth the effort to read them. I learned about a side of my mother that I couldn't possibly know otherwise.

"When my mother was ten years old, she was living along the Barents Sea. It was a life of deprivation, perhaps made slightly more tolerable by the knowledge that the chances of survival were reasonable, something that could not be said for those who stayed in her hometown during the war.

"This unlikely place was where she received her first formal education in mathematics. Up until that time, she had been self-taught. Her skills were already prodigious, but in the miners' camp in the Arctic where they lived, she learned the formal language of mathematics. She learned its history. She knew then and there that she would be a part of this mathematical world for the rest of her life.

"She wrote in her memoirs, 'The war, despite all its horror for me, for my family, and for tens of millions of others, gave me an intellectual life, something I would not possibly have possessed had Hitler never lived. That was not, however, its most important gift. Before the war, I was a terribly spoiled, self-centered child. Perhaps this was a normal passing phase, but I think not. Had I not lived through the cold, the misery, the death, and the deprivation, I would have taken my life and those around me for granted for all of my days. I truly believe this. The war made me, forced me, to become human, to value life, to value love, and to strive to live every day with meaning.'

"My mother did live every day with meaning. I, like her, have had many mentors. But none have been more important to me than my mother. She was able to accomplish so much not simply because she was smart. Everything she did, she did fully and passionately, from the lofty task of making the kind of intellectual discoveries almost all would find daunting, to what some might view as the more quotidian tasks of being a good mother, wife, daughter, aunt, and friend. She will always be my guiding light. I know she will always be the guiding light of many in this room. Like her mentors Kolmogorov and Kowalevski, I am certain that she will influence lives well past our own.

"I am thankful for many things. I have led a fortunate life in many ways. First and foremost, though, I am thankful to have had a mother who taught me, patiently and with tenderness and love, how to live in this world. I have been privileged to have Rachela Karnokovitch as a mother. If anyone was an example of the miraculous gift of life and what the creative spirit can do, it was her."

I returned to my seat and took the scene in. I looked at the cut flowers so artfully arranged, not the standard bouquets of such affairs. This was Bruce's work, his eye for detail exemplary, as always. Everyone in my family was, in fact, doing what was needed to be done to keep this horde satisfied. I was deluding myself if I thought my role was somehow more important or more difficult.

I watched the faces approach the closed casket, one after another. I had no intention of staying for the entire procession, and neither did the rest of my family. Reflexively, I looked at the faces and categorized them the way my mother taught me as a child. She said it was a useful skill to know where someone was from, or at the very least, to know the birthplace of their ancestors. "Look, look," she would say to me in Russian as we approached someone on the street. "That face like an eggplant, Italian. Look carefully. That face like a ripe apple, Irish. That face like a potato, Ukrainian." Of course, in the case of Slavic faces, my mother's description wouldn't take place until the subject in question was out of earshot.

The fruits and vegetables of my childhood were transformed into a United Nations through my mother's lessons. So it was as I watched the procession, full of many potatoes and cauliflowers, with the occasional onion, plum, and mushroom. It was a good distraction. There was quite an assortment in those first fifty or so faces. But then I saw two quite unlike the others, the older one a mixture of an apple and a Bosc pear, a little long in the face, with blond, thick hair, pulled back. It was a young woman with her daughter, who was far more apple than pear, her blond hair in braids. I had never met them. But I knew who they were. They walked past the casket, and then they walked toward my family. My uncle knew too, instantly, or so he said later. My father looked at that little girl, and whatever fog he was in instantly lifted. *"Chto eto takoe?* [What do we have here?]" Me? I was at a loss for words.

CHAPTER 18

From Generation to Generation

I don't look like my mother except in my cheekbones, which are high on my face and broad, a bit like a summer squash I suppose. But from what little I know, my mother didn't look like the rest of her family. Bruce and I look like brothers, I'm told. I look like the brawn, he looks like the brains. Peasant wisdom says that family traits often skip a generation. I have my doubts whether such an assertion can be quantified and tested. But that sense of who is and isn't blood is a sixth sense that I learned I possessed the day of my mother's funeral, just like my mother could sense over the phone that she had found her brother decades before.

Of course, these things can be apparitions. Certainly I felt that, in my middle age, there was something elemental missing in my life. There is a Hebrew prayer that is recited during every daily service, *l'dor vador nagid godlecha*. From generation to generation we will tell of your greatness. It was a prayer that held little meaning to me as a child or even as a young adult. But as I recited it in my late forties, the phrase *l'dor vador* began to sting. I was the end of the line. In truth, I hadn't held up my end of the deal. I was supposed to ensure that our gene pool continued for at least one more generation in a verifiable way.

Bruce's verdict on our gene pool was a definite thumbs-down. He had said no to a friend who asked if he would donate his sperm.

"She'd have ended up with a brainy geek of a kid, or maybe worse, someone with scary ambition who'd end up in a penthouse and, in the end, a jail cell."

But me, I wasn't so negative about our traits. Certainly compared to other mathematically inclined families we were by far among the most socially adept. My mother, when necessary, could talk to the car mechanic, the dry cleaner, and the plumber. My father avoided the car mechanic, the dry cleaner, and the plumber not because he didn't possess adequate social skills, but because as a child of relative privilege who suffered little during the war, he was convinced such tasks were beneath him. While he was more than a bit aristocratic and snobby, his airs could easily be mistaken for curmudgeonliness, a behavior that, if you are above a certain hard-won age, is customarily well accepted in the Badger State.

We are smart. What's wrong with smart? We have outstanding survival skills. Our resourcefulness would peg any scale built in America. We believe that no problem, even one of Hilbert's notorious twenty-three, is too difficult to solve. We aren't bad looking. We are responsible citizens, every one of us. We pay our taxes. We are never behind on our credit cards, utility bills, and mortgages. We are hard workers, and even my father has an iron handshake, a characteristic that comes from being only two generations removed from farm work.

OK, we drink too much. You could call us alcoholics, I suppose, but if that is the case, three quarters of Russia consists of worse drunks than us. As far as I'm concerned, Americans don't drink nearly enough. A good alcoholic poisoning of the brain now and then clears it out in a way that nothing else can. Yes, it's also true that we have broken hearts. We abandon our children if we believe we are leaving them in good hands. We are not always reliable in romantic relationships, at least the men aren't. I wouldn't call that a genetic defect.

If I were to rate our gene pool like Standard & Poor's or Moody's rated bonds before the days when they began to make stuff up, I'd give it a solid honest AA. My father's rating I'm sure would be even more generous. His response to realizing in that synagogue that I had been a good son, one who had given him two generations instantly, consisted of only slightly tempered euphoria. He had, on the day that he buried his wife, won the gene propagation lottery.

On the surface there was not much of a resemblance between my daughter or my granddaughter and him, but the hair and those undeniable cheekbones of my granddaughter—my cheekbones as well as those of my mother—told him everything he needed to know. He went from being bored to ebullient in an instant.

My daughter's name was Andrea. My granddaughter was Amy. Pleasant names both. Easy to pronounce. Andrea walked up to me and I stood up instinctively and held out my hand. "I'm glad you could come," I said.

"Do you know who I am?" Her accent was a Southern hemisphere thing, either Aussie or Kiwi. Her eyes, the way she looked at me, were those of her mother. Her tone implied that I wouldn't have the slightest notion who she might be.

There are many Yiddish words that are misused in America. I don't know how, for example, the word *putz* became used to describe a man who is a clueless and tasteless idiot. It's an extremely offensive word in Yiddish, an obscene condemnation that should be used only in response to the most contemptuous behavior. I do know how another word became twisted and trivialized, *farklemt*. It became a haha-that's-so-funny signature word used by a recurring female character created and played by a male comedian on a popular TV show. But the fact is that being *farklemt* isn't a cheap emotion to laugh about. Your heart presses against your chest, your throat tightens, your eyes water, and it's nearly impossible for you to say even a single word. You could describe it as being "choked up" in English and, though that two-word description is bland, at least it isn't comical.

I looked down at the wood-tile floor and tried to compose myself. "I didn't really know about you, no. But looking at you, I know, yes." That was all I could summon up at the time. We've talked about this first meeting, my daughter and I, over the years. She has said she was so nervous herself that she didn't notice anything odd about my behavior. More than anything else, she was simply happy to have found me. Sometimes we get lucky for all the wrong reasons.

I still couldn't look up, but I took in my granddaughter again. "And her. It's amazing, really."

"She looks like your mum?"

"Uncanny."

"Well, she doesn't look like anyone from back home. Except her nose, maybe. I think that's Mother's and mine."

"I think so, yes."

"I suppose this isn't the best time to meet." She was a single mother who had traveled all the way from Christchurch to Berkeley to try and earn an advanced degree in urban planning. A very ambitious sort she was. She had chosen Berkeley because it was close to my former in-laws. "I tried to call several times actually, but your message box was always full."

"You didn't have to call. You were right to simply come. Very right. The phone messages are from a lot of mathematicians, mostly."

"That's how I heard. My landlord."

"He's a mathematician?"

"Yes. A math prof. We rent a cottage in back of his house. He was saddened. It seems your mother touched many, many people."

"Your grandmother, yes, she did." *Shtark zich, shtark zich,* I thought to myself again. Don't be a crying baby. I looked into her face, and my awareness of her happiness made me feel diminished and trivial. Uncharacteristically, I couldn't find confidence in myself. It seemed altogether likely and possible that my daughter would, at any second, pull the curtain aside and reveal me for the phony I was. "You know, I knew about you all these years," I said. "I didn't know if you were a boy or a girl, but I knew."

"She never told me about you. It was just a guess, really, on my part. I knew it would be someone here. My landlord would joke about Amy's hair, that she looked like a little Rachela Karnokovitch, and told me about your mum. Just a crazy guess. He suggested we come out here, even gave me the flyer miles to come."

"That was not a crazy guess, miss. No. It was an excellent deduction," my father said. My father had been hovering about us, staring at his little great-grandchild.

"This is your grandfather, I suppose," I said.

"There is no 'suppose.' It is a certain fact," my father said, shaking Andrea's hand. "I am so pleased to meet you, miss. You have no idea how much. My name is Viktor. Where are you staying?"

"The Howard Johnson's. We didn't know anyone, so I called the math department and asked them. It seems the place is filled with mathematicians. Very nice people, actually."

"Your mother was a fine mathematician," my father said.

"She still is. Teaches in secondary school."

"You should come to my house," my father said. "I have plenty of room for you."

"Really? Would it be OK?"

"Of course. I wouldn't want it any other way."

My father was beaming. His eyes were alight in a way I hadn't seen in a long time. Unlike me, he was pivoting with ease to a new circumstance. This is how he was, as were my mother and grandfather. Perhaps the war was what made them so. Perhaps it was just the tumult of the Soviet system. Whatever the reason or reasons, I always knew I'd never be as adroit as them when it came to change. I took pride in my resourcefulness, certainly, but only by American standards was it remarkable.

We walked out of the synagogue to the waiting limousine, which while a little tight for seven adults, could easily fit six of them and one six-year-old girl. Eight mathematicians, all former students of my mother, four men and four women—wearing the kind of clothes I seldom saw on any mathematician save for my father—easily carried the coffin with the oh-so-light load.

CHAPTER 19

From *A Lifetime in Mathematics* by Rachela Karnokovitch: The Flesh of a Bear

In this country, people buy T-shirts extolling their survival skills after snowstorms and heat waves. I used to get angry about this behavior, which I considered to be a childish display of false endurance. How can a country be so weak to think that a little snow or a little spike in a thermometer is actual hardship? But now, and maybe this is because of the mellowing of age, I'm almost pleased to see these T-shirts appear every few years. Now they indicate to me that this country is so secure and wealthy that actual hardship for many is almost impossible. These celebrations of minor calamities are in essence a signal that the people of this country feel so safe that they've turned survival into a silly game. Unfortunately, most nations are not like the United States. Danger is real for almost everyone most anywhere else, including in the nation where I grew up.

We buried my mother in April 1941. I do not know the exact day. Later, I picked the seventeenth as her *yahrtzeit*, which would have been the twentieth of Nisan, during Passover. We didn't celebrate any holidays, of course, Jewish or otherwise. We simply tried to live. To breathe another day was our goal. Survival, to my mind, implies a finite probability that without luck and cunning, you will perish. Given that definition I can definitely say that we tried to survive. My mother, however, did not possess the strength of will of my father and me. We tried to prop her spirits up, tried to keep her physically well, but we failed. It is a failure that I cannot and will not forget.

The level of sanitation in our camp was abysmal. We carried buckets of water from a hand-dug well. The pits for human waste were perhaps twenty meters away. In the wet of spring, the pits overflowed, and the mess washed along the ground. We tried to skirt the raw sewage as we walked in the camp. My father was aware of the potential danger, and made sure that my mother boiled the water before any use. But other families weren't so cautious and the extra wood necessary for precautionary boiling was almost impossible to find. Cholera erupted that spring, and it's likely that my mother, who would occasionally visit other women at the camp, had taken a drink of water from somewhere outside our apartment.

Given that manpower was so necessary for the war effort—the Soviets counted on beating the Germans' technical superiority and splendid troop training with horrible weather, long distances of travel, and superior numbers—one would think that even a work camp for minor prisoners of the Soviet state would have been designed to keep those workers alive. But the Soviet system was always chaotic and inherently lazy, a continuation of the tsarist system. The average citizen's life, even in times of peace, was made bearable only by the presence of vodka. During the war, there was not even food and basic sanitation, much less vodka.

One hundred thirty people died that spring in a camp of four hundred. Perhaps ten had died from malnutrition and exposure the previous winter. The bodies were buried in a fen five hundred meters from the camp. In this area designated for our dead there were small evergreens that clung to life in a habitat that was as unsuitable for them as it was for us.

It was my first funeral. There was talk in the camp that I wouldn't be allowed to go, but I begged my father to let me attend. It had been horrible seeing my mother in her bed, its cushioning almost gone after a year of use. Her body was motionless, her skin pale. She looked so insignificant lying there, as if her life never meant anything at all. I can never forget the bleakness of what I saw. It left me with a doubt of life's meaning that lasted for many years.

They wrapped her body in cloth—wood was too valuable for a coffin—and I held my father's hand as I watched them lower my mother into her grave. There were no words said aside from those of prayer. It was all over so quickly that I almost didn't believe my mother was actually dead. Maybe, I thought for a brief moment as we walked away, they had just pretended to bury her, that this was just a cruel little game. But the air, damp and cold against my face, told me the truth.

"Are we going to die here like Mother?" I asked my father point-blank as we walked back to our apartment.

"Absolutely not. I will not allow it."

"But how can you do that, Father?"

"I know we will survive, both of us. We will see your little brother again. But you have to listen and follow me. I need you to do what I ask. It will take both of us to live through this. I cannot do it alone. But you and I, if you promise to listen, will live through this. Will you do that, Rachela?"

"I will listen, Father. I don't want to die here. I promise I will listen."

"And I promise then we will get out of here. We two can do it.

I know we can. But first you must promise that you drink only our water. Only ours. Do you understand? That's the most important thing right now."

"I understand."

I believed in my father. I certainly did not blame him for my mother's death. I blamed myself because I felt, however illogically, that I should have watched her more carefully, that I should have ensured that she be sensible. This guilt stays with me still even though I know it makes no sense. The mind is far from a perfect machine for reasoning and logic. We have to force it to make the correct calculations.

I put all my faith in my father. He and he alone could do what he promised. When I think of it now, I wonder why I wasn't fearful of my own death. It made no sense to have such an ironclad belief that we would survive. There should have been some degree of fear of failure. But perhaps there is value in wishful thinking; not delusional thinking, but in holding a positive and optimistic view. It gives you strength to overcome long odds.

I had not thought of mathematics all winter long. Of course, I still went to school. I still studied, but there is a profound difference between charting an original intellectual path and the mechanical work of repeating what others have already done hundreds of millions, if not billions, of times. My tutor had fallen ill that winter. There were no more lessons from him. Even if he had tried to tutor me, I doubt his presence would have had much of an effect. I thought mostly about my stomach and its dull emptiness. When I went to relieve myself, I worried about where I would find the sustenance to replace the spent fuel that I had just lost. My body, I knew, was an engine. It needed energy to process and use.

We received twenty kilos of flour every month that spring. This mixture of milled wheat and I don't know what else (it was rumored to be sawdust) was nothing truly edible, but bake it and eat it we did. I learned how to bake from a neighbor. Our allotment of cooking wood for the summer was inadequate. In the night, my father would keep watch from a distance as I climbed a fence like a monkey to steal split logs from a satellite storage area I found while hunting for wild onions. We planted seeds that summer and hoped that potatoes, onions, and cabbage would actually grow. But in the meantime, we had to wait and eat what little we had and what little we could supplement from foraging the surrounding land.

The previous summer while foraging I had found a patch of what looked to be lilies. I dug around them and yanked one by its bladelike leaves. The bulb was far larger than anything I could have imagined, bigger than my fist. I hid them in my blouse, not wanting anyone to see what I had found. My father, fastidious and careful as always, washed one, cut off a sliver, and placed it against his lips and then his tongue. It was bitter, he said, but he was convinced it wasn't poisonous. We cooked them up, and when no one was watching I'd go back for more.

I went back the following summer to find some more to cook. I brought along a spoon to help me dig, and at the last second I decided to bring our one sharp knife for protection. Food was so scarce. I was worried someone would follow me and not only try to steal what I had found, but perhaps do something worse. The mood in the camp was more than somber after the outbreak of cholera. People would do anything for food.

I walked to the little rise in the fen where I had found the bulbs. My mother's grave was along the way, but I didn't have any desire to be reminded of how she had died. As at her burial ground, little trees dotted the landscape where I dug, gnarled and weather-beaten. I was digging with my spoon and wasn't aware of anything else. My focus was entirely on getting us a little sustenance. I didn't know whether the bulbs had any nutritive value, but I did know that it was exquisitely pleasing to dig for them. I can't fully describe just how uplifting it was to have the normal experience of cutting into something steaming hot at a table, putting that piece of food in your mouth, and feeling it against your tongue. It was more than just the eating of it and whatever calories and nutrients it did or didn't provide. It was about the dignity of being able to be something other than a slave to your stomach. We would be civilized again for just a little moment, reminded of what we would have once the war was over.

I dug, lost in the image of what it would be like to see that look of approval on my father's face when he saw me cooking the bulbs, and by the time I heard the noise from the short grass, it was already upon me, so close that I could sense its warmth.

It was a black bear, a cub born the previous summer, already a little bigger than I was. With me stooped over, he seemed like a giant. I flattened myself carefully and deliberately against the ground and lay still, trying not to breathe too heavily. I could smell his stench, like something rotting in a cellar. I assumed the mother bear was nearby. My heart beat loudly. I was certain that the cub could hear it.

Horrible, inconsistent thoughts raced through my mind. My father would be upset with me for going out here alone and getting attacked by a bear. He would spank me hard, I was sure. But then I thought no, he won't spank me, because I will be dead, or mauled if I were lucky enough to survive. There was something about this inconsistency that brought me to my senses. I needed to find a way to distract the cub. If the mother wasn't nearby, I could perhaps outrun him once he wasn't so close.

I slowly grabbed a bulb I had dug and then, with my wrist, flicked it so it rolled a few feet away. The cub heard the noise. Perhaps he was as hungry as I was or perhaps he thought he found a toy. I could sense him walking to where the bulb had stopped. I turned my head and watched him. He picked it up and gnawed at it. Part of me was angry and jealous at watching him eat what I wanted to have and had found all by myself, but another part was elated. He was chewing on the bulb after all, and at least for a moment I was safe. I stood up and quickly looked around. There was no mother bear to be found.

I stepped away from the cub, slowly at first, and he suddenly lost interest in the half-eaten bulb and looked at me. I stared into his eyes. He was skinnier than he should have been. He was like me, I thought. He had no mother, I was convinced. I threw another bulb at his feet. He picked this one up as well and apparently had found the first one to his liking, because he immediately brought the new one to his mouth.

I should have run away then and there. It wasn't sensible to stare at the bear like I did. Perhaps it was something as simple as loneliness on my part that made me stay. I am used to being alone. I prefer it actually. It allows me to think in an undistracted manner. But at the camp the lack of human contact was severe. My father worked long hours. My mother was gone. The other children, the ones who were left, were like ghosts. We didn't play because our spirits were low and we simply didn't have the energy. We barely talked to each other. In contrast, here I was in contact with a live being that was struggling, but still had life in his eyes. I think that I was responding to that life force inside him. He was lonely, too, with the sharpness of loss that only the young can feel. For a brief moment, a few seconds perhaps, although it seemed longer, I felt a connection to an animal unlike anything I had felt before or would feel again. He was about my size after all. He liked the food I was giving him. I was nurturing him. I could imagine him following me to camp. My thoughts went wild with possibility. Then I heard a gunshot.

I swear I heard not only the sound of the gun, but the bullet itself as it traveled, a high-pitched howl. The cub fell to the ground. I was scared that I would be next. But there would be no second shot. I turned and saw a man trudging toward me across the fen in tall boots, his gun slung across his shoulder.

"You're a brave one, little girl," he said. "What are you doing way out here?"

I looked at him carefully. His skin was dark, weathered, and full of pockmarks. With his moonlike face, he looked like he was from the East. My blond hair was in braids, so he couldn't see its curl. My face doesn't hold a hint of my religion but instead tells anyone who pays attention to such things that I come from the Russian steppes. I am a good mimic, and in the short time I had lived in Russia, had quickly shed my Polish accent. I sounded like a little Russian girl. People would tease me about how Russian I had become.

I held up the remaining bulb in my hand. "I was harvesting these."

He smiled at me. "You cook them, yes?"

"Yes."

"Smart girl. You learn fast. You won't get rickets if you eat them." He looked at the bear on the ground a meter away. "But a bear," he said. "Eating bear meat is even better. The big ones are greasy and horrible, but the young ones are tasty."

He approached the cub, a knife in hand. "You need to grow big and strong," he said to me. "When the war is over, we'll need young people like you. Who knows how many of us will be left?" He pulled out a canvas sack from a bag, thought for a moment, and then pulled out another. "I'll tell you what, little girl. You were so brave that I will share this with you. Have you ever dressed a bear?"

"No, sir, but I have a knife. I can learn."

"Let me see your knife, little girl." I knew that I didn't have a choice, that I had to give my knife to him. "This?" He laughed out loud. "This can barely cut bread. I have something better that you can use." He pulled another shiny blade from his pack. "The bloody insects will be all over us if we take too long. We need to hurry. I'll cut out the entrails. Then you watch me cut on one side. When I leave, you take what's left. OK?"

"But what about your knife?"

"Keep it, little girl. You might need it again."

I watched him carefully. He was so efficient and practiced. He placed the meat chunks in his sack and prepared to walk off. "Don't show anyone what you have, little girl," he told me. "They'll take it from you. They might take your life to get it." He pulled out a little paper box from his bag and threw it toward me. It landed at my feet. "Salt," he said. "Your mother will know what to do with it."

My first thought was to tell him that I had no mother. But then I decided that her death was irrelevant to the situation. I watched him walk away and then began to cut as quickly as I could, ignoring the blood on my hands and on my blouse and skirt. I was amazed by the sharpness of the knife he gave me. I'd never held a blade that could cut with such ease. I can't explain it, but I felt something take over me then, like I was someone different than an eleven-year-old girl. Rather, I was someone older who had been in the wild before, and I felt a rhythm take over as I cut and put the strips of meat into the sack.

The man had been right. The bugs were awful, flying around me and then biting. There weren't just mosquitoes, which were always present, but also little black flies that bit ferociously, pinching my skin in a way that seemed to find every nerve ending. I ignored them as best I could and kept filling my sack with raw meat. I sliced along the rib cage of this animal with whom, less than a half hour before, I had felt a kinship.

When the sack was so full that I knew it would be all I could carry—it must have weighed fifteen kilos at least—I stopped and began to walk back. I found a nearby tiny stream and did my best to clean myself off.

We ate meat for the first time in eight months that night. My father was worried that others would detect the smell if we cooked the bear meat on an open flame, so we boiled it instead. It tasted sweet, like cow tongue in a way, but the texture was far less firm.

I told my father what happened, although I didn't tell him about my emotional attachment to the bear. He looked astonished when I told him how I had cut into the bear myself. "The man is right. The knife will be useful. Even tonight I can use it," my father said. "You have been quite a brave young woman," he said and he looked at me in a way that I had never seen him look at me before. It was not like I was a girl, but rather like I was his equal. That night was a turning point.

My stomach was full for the first time in a long while. Afraid that we would get sick, we both made sure not to eat too much. But I had dreams that night, crazy dreams one after another. I could feel my mind waking from its hunger-imposed slumber. In one of those dreams, the cub and I stood a short distance apart, just like in the fen, and looked at each other. A bulb was in the cub's paw and he was holding it like it was a toy ball. "I like playing with you," he said to me in a squeaky voice, almost like Mickey Mouse. "I haven't played with anyone in such a long time."

PART 3

SITTING SHIVA

CHAPTER 20

The Story Hour

DAY 1

"This is wonderful," Yakov said, slurping up the cabbage borscht with a big silver spoon at the kitchen table. "Have you had any?"

"Me? Not yet," I said.

"And the *golubsti*, my lord, who brought this?"

"Jenny. She came about an hour ago."

"Which one was Jenny? Redheaded woman?"

"Yeah, that was her."

"Nice-looking woman. Cooks like this, too. Amazing." He stabbed at a *golubets*, piercing its cabbage skin, and took a taste. "This is heaven. You should try."

He took another stab with his fork and pointed it my way. I had a taste, the sour salt summoning old memories. Fuck Proust and his madeleine. If he had been born a Slav, he would have grown up eating something far superior to butter cookies, his memories would have been fuller, and by god he would have been an even better writer.

"Not bad," I said.

"Not bad? Are you kidding me? Fifteen years I've been living in this country, and I haven't had anything as good, I swear."

"Well, you have been in Nebraska."

"Exactly. You were spoiled here, Sasha. Your mother and aunt

Zloteh cooking for you, the best food in the world. Now they're both gone. You'll see what it's like."

"How many pounds have you put on since you've been in this country, Yakov?"

"Shut up. It's what they feed you in this godforsaken place. It turns you into a cow. If I were in this city, I'd be skinny again. You can't get fat on *golubsti*."

"Depends on how many you stuff in your face, Yakov. You're steaming up the windows, you're eating so much. You're on number three."

"I'm glad I came here. I was feeling miserable in Lincoln. Lonely. You walk out of the math building and there's a fifty-point IQ cliff."

"I can hear the violins. If you were in Russia, you wouldn't have a job of any sort. You'd be struggling for food, looking for used shoes that fit you halfway decently, and there would be no IQ cliff, because you'd be spending your time twenty-four/seven with people who can't handle their vodka and who can barely add six and seven together."

"Thank you for the much-needed perspective, Sasha."

"You're welcome."

"See, this is what I miss. Real people. Real food. How do you stand it in Tuscaloosa, anyway?"

"It's fifty degrees in Tuscaloosa right now. I wear a light sweater to work. I don't have to dress like I'm Nanook of the North. Madison is overrated."

"Not with me, it isn't. I would move here in an instant if I could. People like your father around. People who can understand me. Understand math. And I could chase after someone like

Jenny, eat healthy and well, lose this big tire around my waist, and be happy. I saw she didn't have a wedding ring. I notice these things."

"Between you and me, I don't think Jenny Rivkin is going to move to Lincoln, Nebraska, with her two children just so she can cook for you."

"She American?" Yakov sounded hopeful for a negative answer.

"Yes."

"Parents, too?"

"I think so, yes. Actually, I know so."

"You're right, not very likely." Yakov sighed.

Pascha, the African gray, squawked in a corner of the kitchen. "What did the bird say?"

"It's Polish."

"I know it's Polish, but what exactly?"

"She said, 'It has a singularity.'"

"She always talks mathematics?"

"No. She has a few hundred words. An assortment."

"Not a word in Russian?"

"Not a word. Mostly Polish. A little Hebrew."

"Hmmm. Your mother must have talked to her a lot over the years." Yakov stopped eating for a moment and contemplated who knows what.

There were more than twenty people in my mother's modest house on the day of the funeral. The men, more plentiful in number, had taken over the living room. The women were in the dining room. The kitchen was a neutral zone where the hungry, bored, or those who didn't want to talk about mathematics or family matters would meet. Eva Steinberg, the former student of my mother, walked in as Yakov chowed down again, lost in the revelry of his taste buds.

"So much food," Eva said.

"The Sisterhood loved my mother."

"You have no idea how good this food is," Yakov said. "Exquisite."

"I'm going to get fat. It's going to be like being on a cruise," Eva said, picking up a lemon bar from a tray.

My mother worked, like her mentor, in many different fields in mathematics. But everyone at the shiva, with the exception of Zhelezniak, who like my mother was wide-ranging in his intellect, and my father, who was a number theorist, worked principally on the theory of partial differential equations. At first I considered it fortuitous that it had worked out this way. While mathematicians can be expected to be difficult and unsuitable for human interaction even with other mathematicians, PDE people, as they are sometimes known for short, are certainly among the most normal of the lot. Topologists, for what it's worth, are the worst. Getting out of bed for them might be the most manageable obstacle of the day. OK, I'm being a little pissy on this point. Catherine, my ex, had been studying topology with my mother.

Eva knew Yakov well enough, I was certain. Everyone in the field of PDEs knew him, not so much because of his accomplishments—which were significant—but because he had a pathological need to talk and would do so with anyone. The more positive way of saying this was that Yakov, unlike most of us, genuinely loved people.

"What are the women doing, Eva?" he asked.

"Telling stories, mostly. About Rachela. Andrea is very interested. And that little one, Amy, is a very smart girl."

"The acorn doesn't fall far from the tree," Yakov said.

"No, I mean really smart. She's already studying."

"Mathematics?" I asked.

"Of course mathematics, Sasha," Eva said.

"With her landlord?"

"Yes, he's a fine man. I've met him in Berkeley."

"She's six years old," I said.

"So," my father piped in as he walked into the kitchen. "I started with you when you were five. Like you, I can tell there is something really there. A certain depth of understanding. And unlike you, she doesn't have the distraction of having to adapt to a completely different culture."

"You've seen your great-granddaughter for less than a day and already you know so much, do you?"

"I think your father is right," Eva said.

"Are you going to be pulling out the notebooks for her tonight? Give her the old lessons?"

"I wish. It was good for you. It would be good for her, too. But I think I'll leave that job to Shackleworth in Berkeley. For now, at any rate." My father flashed a smile and poured himself some tea. He was drying himself out, I could tell. Even I wasn't drinking as per usual. The mathematicians, however, were another story entirely.

I walked into the dining room. The women were seated around the table. This was like old times, people eating, drinking, and schmoozing. I did miss it. All these smart people in one place, not afraid to show their intellect, were enjoying the company of their fellow brainiacs with the warmth induced by alcohol. Anna was at the head, holding court. She was already drunk, a cheery kind of drunk. She was not melancholy or morose at all, but the way she was when she had an opportunity to perform. Many years ago, when she danced in New York, a *Times* critic praised her for her "waiflike piquancy with a delicate sparkle." The waif was gone, but the sparkle would never leave her.

"Seven years ago, I was invited by the Bolshoi for a party to honor me, of all things. I couldn't believe it. It had been over thirty years since I had left. I thought they had completely erased me from their memory. But no, they wanted me to come for the thirty-fifth anniversary of my stage debut. I think they really wanted to see how old and ugly I'd become, to tell you the truth, but I didn't care about that. I said yes immediately. When I mentioned it to Rachela, she said she wanted to come, too."

"When she told me she was going, I couldn't believe what I was hearing," I said.

"You should have come with us. She wanted that, you know. You could have seen your hometown."

"I thought it would be better for it to be a girls-only trip. Plus, it was hurricane season. I was busy." The thought of going back to Moscow had actually filled me with dread.

"Rachela was so excited to travel, as was I. I felt young again. I looked younger, too. I could feel it. And it was so good to be there with Rachela, someone who understood what I felt and who felt the same way.

"We went to the party and they tried to show off for me. I understood then that it wasn't curiosity that made them invite a retired dancer back home. They wanted a good word or two said about them abroad. This was the new Russia, they were trying to convince me. It was true, the party was indeed wonderful. The caviar, the champagne, everyone dressed in clothes they couldn't have possibly bought before the 1990s. It was fun. I had my revenge, too, the revenge of living a good life for so many years. I really did look good that night. I could see the looks of envy on the faces of people I knew back in the old days. And Rachela, when she wanted to, she could charm anyone. She impressed everyone that night. Her Russian was always so perfect and formal, free of any slang. Even the head of the Bolshoi was captivated by her. He knew without being told that he was talking to someone important."

"I can well imagine," Patricia O'Connell said. "It was like being around royalty sometimes, even when she was speaking in English."

"True. She understood about having a look. Having presence. People in America don't understand. But in Russia we know. Lots of places understand this. Not here. Anyway, we went to see the grave of Kolmogorov. She wanted to pay her respects. It was so beautiful with flowers. And visiting his grave brought back all kinds of memories for her. I said he looked like a kind man, and she said that he was like a second father to her."

"Did you go to the university, too?"

"Oh, definitely. I thought it was funny. She didn't want to tell them she was coming. Not at first. We walked into the mathematics building like we were strangers. Rachela had her hair in a scarf, I remember. It was a lovely scarf that I bought her in Rome many years ago. I was flattered that she was wearing it. But it was a sunny summer day, very warm and muggy for Moscow. There was no need to wear it, and she did have such beautiful hair, always."

"She didn't want to be recognized," I said. "That's what she told me when she came back home."

"I thought as much. We walked into the building to her old office. She knocked on the door and no one answered. Here's something funny, though. She still had a key. She took it out of her purse and it still worked. I couldn't believe it. She said Kolmogorov's office was down the hall. She remembered correctly. There was a plaque honoring him outside his door."

"No plaque for Rachela, though, I'm sure," Yakov said, walking in.

"Oh no, definitely not."

"What did she do in her office?" Yakov asked.

"We walked in. She talked about how good it had been to be a student. How she wished she could be a student again. All those smart people. All those new ideas in that one room. It was heaven, she said."

"Czerneski, Poponov, Glizsky, all in that one office. Can you imagine?" Yakov said. "It was heaven, she was right. And now they're all gone. There will never be such a group of brains in one building, much less one room, ever again."

"She said much the same thing while we stood there," Anna said. "Then she told me to stand outside her old office. She had to do something, she said. If anyone came, I should knock on the door to tell her. No one came. Maybe I was out there for three minutes. Rachela then walked out. We went to the restroom to tidy ourselves. She took off her scarf then and made sure she looked nice. Then we walked to the main office of the building and introduced ourselves. The chairman of the department walked out to greet us. You could tell he was shocked."

"What was she doing in her office?" Patricia asked.

"I don't know. It wasn't my business," Anna said.

"My mother liked her secrets," I said.

"Zhelezniak said she was known for hiding things. Poponov and Glizsky told him about this, I think. People found some papers of hers in that office years later, he said. Maybe she was looking for something she hid long ago," Yakov said.

"She didn't tell me anything," Anna said. "I didn't ask either. But when we went into the chairman's office, he recognized her immediately. People from all over the building came out of their offices when they heard the news that Rachela was there. Everyone wanted a peek, and the looks in their eyes told me everything I needed to know and everything Rachela needed to know. The admiration in that crowded room and in the hallway outside was something you could feel. I felt so proud of her. Sasha, you really should have been there. You would have been proud, too."

CHAPTER 21

From *A Lifetime in Mathematics* by Rachela Karnokovitch: Turbulence

I am a mathematician and have been one since I was nine years old. I suppose such a statement implies that I am rational and cold, but anyone who makes that inference would be incorrect. Love certainly isn't anything rational or cold and I am definitely capable of love. I also believe in miracles fervently, or at least in one miracle, the creation of life itself. There is random chance of course as well, and there is a strong tendency to interpret fortuity as being something miraculous. The war made me a mathematician. That's not a miracle. It's simply a response to a dramatic, life-changing event.

Perhaps my hunger-induced somnambulence over that winter in the Arctic Circle had been beneficial in a way. For whatever reason, the summer's daily bear meat awoke my mind almost magically. I felt so fresh and free mentally. My ability to visualize mathematics was heightened to such a degree that I felt I could understand anything. Grozslev, my tutor, sadly was gone, but he had shown me the language of mathematics over the year we studied together. He was a gifted man. Without him, I would have never been able to do anything in those early years. I wouldn't have had the necessary formal entryway into my discipline and wouldn't have known what had and hadn't been solved before me.

I would have had to use my own invented mathematical language, raw and ill-suited to making any real breakthroughs. I use the word "gifted" when describing my first mathematics tutor. I don't use that word lightly. There are individuals, rare indeed, who possess a mammoth ability for invention.

I don't see the need for modesty at this time in my life, and perhaps I've never felt that need, as others who know me have said not infrequently. At one time, I possessed the gift of creation, just as at one time my first mentor possessed it. I had a unique vision, I knew that it was unique, and I could see the world I had invented with a clarity that allowed me to identify every detail. Like an old pianist whose fingers will no longer let him create magic in a recital, I can no longer achieve what I was once able to do, at least not with any consistency. No mathematician can be expected to do so past a certain age. But because I have experienced this magic, I can certainly mentor someone who possesses the ability to create something new and vital, just like Kolmogorov and Grozslev did for me.

We, unlike all life that came before us, do have the ability to create and be Godlike, albeit in a minor way in comparison to God himself. Why not call these creations of ours miracles? They certainly feel miraculous to the creators. From out of nothing, a group of initially incoherent thoughts and images, something magically appears.

Like Kolmogorov, Grozslev was interested in the great unknown in the world of physics and mathematics, turbulence. But by the 1930s, his time had come and gone for original thinking. He could describe the problem, he could cast about for a suitable language to attack the problem, and he could, like Kolmogorov, make some definitions. But to solve any major problem in mathematics or physics requires a fresh mind, one that sees only possibilities. A mathematician, even the best of the best, will fail far more often than he succeeds. Over time, those failures crowd out the possibility for future success.

Feynman called turbulence the last great unknown in physics, and in terms of the mathematics of physical processes, it is also the last great unknown. When it is solved, one major canvas of mathematics will be complete. I'm sure minor work will continue in this area for centuries after, as it always does for mature fields.

Grozslev introduced me to the field of turbulence in 1940. Somehow, in the godforsaken land near the Barents Sea, he was managing to work on defining the essence of fluid mechanics in a mathematical sense. He was even corresponding with Kolmogorov about this work. But these two were both mature mathematicians, and who with a fresh mind was Grozslev going to find to make headway? In desperation he showed me the progress he had made, and I worked under his mentorship. It was exciting to work on something completely new and uncharted. Some of this work was published by Kolmogorov in 1941. Neither Grozslev nor I were given authorship, but this was not Kolmogorov's fault. The Soviets were not going to allow an Enemy of the People or the daughter of an Enemy of the People to receive recognition for their intellectual discoveries. Still, it made me wary, this omission, about letting anyone know about any future work of mine until it was complete.

We like to think that our lives are ordered. It satisfies us to believe that there is cause and effect, that we can make corrections to our lives as easily as we change batteries in a radio. In fact, much of our life is chaotic. There are patterns, yes, but they are unpredictable. Very little can be improved. There are no simple batteries that can fix illnesses, wayward children, poverty, hurt feelings, war, and government calamities. In response, our minds become irrational and do their best to distort our actual world. We make our present and future seem more positive and less calamitous than they are in reality. Psychologists of today, I'm told, understand our tendency to look through rose-colored glasses. The great Proust understood this well before them when he noted, "To make reality endurable, we are all obliged to encourage in ourselves a few small foibles."

Similarly, to make the physical world around us endurable, we like to emphasize that the gases and liquids that move our oceans, allow our planes to fly, and make our boats sail follow predictable, orderly paths. Often they don't, and this difference between our wish for an orderly universe and the reality of the calamity of the natural world makes us deny reality. While denial of our personal difficulties, and I know this better than Proust, can actually help us live our daily lives and give us the strength to survive under the worst conditions, our denial of the lack of order in the physical world creates havoc. Planes crash because of our false optimism. Boats turn over. As my son well knows, hurricanes destroy homes that we refuse to leave. The water and air around us can be destructive and we, more often than not, underestimate the magnitude of that destruction.

But imagine a world where we could understand these destructive forces fully, where we weren't either blindly scared of turbulence or, more commonly, blindly optimistic that we will avoid its effects. Understanding a physical phenomenon like turbulence ultimately means predicting its behavior, or at the very least understanding just what can and what cannot be predicted over time. Prediction implies quantification of the basic physical processes that drive turbulence. This is something we cannot currently do with any reasonable degree of sophistication.

From the standpoint of a mathematician, not an engineer or a physicist, the problem of turbulence is fundamentally one of being certain, to prove, that there exists in the universe a set of descriptors, in this case partial differential equations, that can encompass the behavior of fluids as they move at velocities that cause chaos. We have, in fact, such an equation that we think should work. But we don't know for sure that it does. It is a conjecture that the equation we use to describe the motion of fluids when they flow as lazily as rivers also describes the motion of fluids when they dance around an airplane wing.

It is a reasonable conjecture. But we may be fooling ourselves when we think that what works for one state of fluid motion works for all states. Like Newton's equations of motion, it may be that the equations we use, the Navier-Stokes equations, are simply approximations. If that is so, they have utility only in a practical sense. In a mathematical sense, they are dross.

Even as a girl living in squalor and deprivation above the Arctic Circle, I was fascinated by the great unknown of turbulence. Fluids behave so predictably when they move slowly. But when they speed up, they change character completely. Predicting even the average behavior of millions of fluid particles, much less the path of one elemental particle, is essentially impossible at this point in time. Who, with an intellectual focus, doesn't want to try to make what seem to be impossible problems tractable?

Early on in my work with turbulence we defined a basic lexicon. These are known today as Kolmogorov's numbers, and given that I view their creation as something rather trivial, I have no interest in trying to obtain credit. I would, however, dearly love to have Grozslev's name attached to them. The man was kind, gentle, and brilliant. The Soviets murdered him and managed to bury and ignore much of his intellectual achievement. I hope that Grozslev does, eventually, get his due with regard to this and much other work in mathematics.

Unlike many mathematicians I know, my inspiration comes not simply from the equations that define the language of mathematics. No, I need to tie these equations to visual images. Sometimes that visualization is an abstract thing. A variable in an equation will enter my mind as a colorful object on a landscape and travel along a path in the hills and valleys or across the rivers that I have created for it. I will draw these images on paper and somehow the physical act of drawing opens up even more possibilities.

But other times, and this is what happened to allow me to understand turbulence, the image is something real. One might think that these efforts at drawing—whether fanciful or realistic—are simply an entryway into understanding, but that wouldn't be right. One does not have to use the language of mathematics to make mathematical proofs. One can use simple pictures sometimes. Perhaps an example is in order for you to understand just what mathematicians mean when they say they are solving a proof.

For example, everyone has learned and many have actually used the Pythagorean Theorem, which states that for a right triangle with sides a and b, the length of the hypotenuse, c, can be described by the following relation:

$$c^2 = a^2 + b^2$$

Suppose we wanted to prove that this relationship exists for all right triangles. A triangle consists, of course, of three sides. Let's make each of those sides one side of a square:

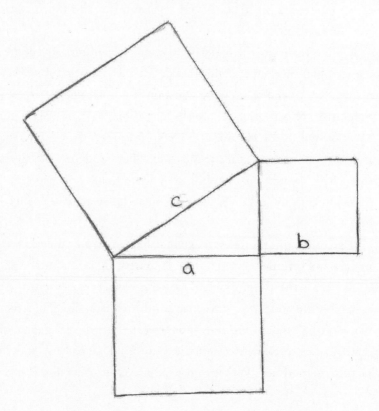

In order to compare the areas of the three squares, a^2, b^2, and c^2 and whatever relationship might exist between them, let us look at the larger square defined by the sum of lengths a and b. Its interior and exterior can be drawn in many ways. Here are two:

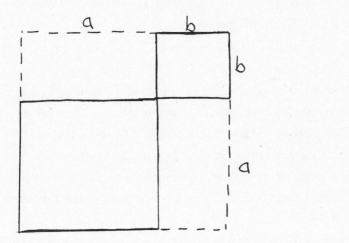

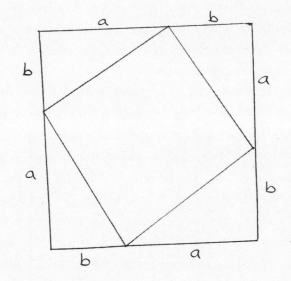

Visual inspection of the two sets of figures indicates that the interior square on the right is of length c and area c^2. The area of the square of length a plus b is $(a+b)^2$, which equals the area of the interior square, c^2, plus the sum of four interior triangles of area $0.5 \times (ab)$, or 2ab. Therefore:

$$a^2 + b^2 + 2ab = c^2 + 2ab$$

We have proven visually that indeed Pythagoras was right, if we had any doubt.

Symbolically, mathematics was easier in the time of Pythagoras, although those who created the foundations of mathematics, like God creating the first cell, were likely far more brilliant than any mathematician I have known. I cannot make simple drawings to prove anything new. But they can still be an aid. Without a visual image, I simply cannot do my work. It was so when I was nine and learning my trade on my own. It is still so today.

Two visual images that came to me back to back were the foundation of all my significant work on turbulence. At face value, they are trivial images. But that's how it always works. Just like life has its origins in ordinary elements, the foundation for human creativity is ultimately quotidian.

It all happened on one summer day. We were studying geography at the time and I suppose that our teacher wanted to make the maps of our lessons come to life. She asked all of us, "Who has seen the ocean?" No one raised a hand. Later I found out that my teacher had never seen the ocean herself. I had seen the Black Sea, of course, when we briefly lived in Odessa. But the ocean seemed to be of an unfathomable scale to my mind. It seemed improbable that I would ever be able to touch its waters anywhere, much less in the remote location to which we had been banished.

Somehow Mrs. Sharekhova, the woman whose observant eyes were responsible for the strong foundation in mathematics given to me, managed to gather three military vehicles to take us to the coast. It was a distance of approximately twenty kilometers along a crude road.

Many of us were excited, even giddy, on this trip. It was perhaps the first time any of us felt like we were real children, not adults of small size, since the war began. When the ocean came into view, I could not believe what my eyes took in. I did at first think I was seeing a mirage. You can talk about the vastness of the ocean, but until you actually see it, any discussion is inherently meaningless.

We climbed out of the vehicles onto the sand. I reached down and felt its coarseness with my fingers. I had never touched anything like it, damp and full of organic debris from the sea. The air also was new, like nothing I had smelled before, a mix of sulfur, moisture, and salt. Mrs. Sharekhova led us on a walk to the ocean while the drivers stayed near the vehicles, smoking and chatting. For us, it was magical, truly, to spend this little time on a beach, something that seemed like a vacation. It was a wonderful respite from our squalor. The wind blew against my face as I looked out at the waves crashing in the distance. The sand was mixed with seaweed. Wind-weathered branches were scattered along the shore.

We got closer and closer to the waves and I could feel the adrenaline surge in me as I looked at the water. It was so noisy and dramatic. I watched the waves swell to what seemed to be an impossible height and then crash perhaps ten meters offshore, their progress apparently impeded by an invisible sandbar.

Our teacher walked with us to the edge of the water. I could sense that she felt brave doing this. I could also sense, or perhaps I'm projecting, the pride that she felt for finding the wherewithal and tenacity to take us all there.

Mrs. Sharekhova reached down and felt the water against her fingertips. Most of us followed her lead. She took the salt water from her fingers to her lips and tasted it. I'll never forget my own taste, so remarkable it was to sense the ocean this way. I watched the waves crash and crash again. This was turbulence, the movement of water ascending and curling, the cascades coming one after another. How can one possibly solve the problem of turbulence without actually seeing it first, not in a picture, but in real life in all its dimensions and scope? I would have made no progress at all that summer and fall had Mrs. Sharekhova not made the extraordinary effort to let us witness this wonder of nature.

I don't know how long we actually stayed there. Perhaps we walked, ever so carefully, along the shore for an hour. The weather was not pleasant, but we didn't care. This visit was a true gift for us, a cherished freedom. We might have stayed longer, but the soldiers were getting so impatient that they shot their rifles into the air, and we knew it was time to go back. I cannot describe how wonderful I felt as we made that final walk.

As we approached the vehicles, insects, which apparently didn't like the salt water at all, returned to hover around our faces. They were as voracious as ever. I watched their motion intently, like I had never watched them before, because it was something fresh again and strangely unexpected. No, their paths were not, in any pure sense, turbulent. But these little creatures did not move independently. They were constrained, somehow, by the motion of their neighbors, who were in turn constrained by others more distant. Their dance was somewhat akin to the dance of fluid parti-cles. Like the particles that made up the waves in the ocean, their ascent and descent required some information to transfer from one insect to the next. I, of course, did not like the presence of these biting bugs one bit, but I was learning something from their pat-terns of flight. The equations that could describe insect flight be-havior were not the same as those that described fluid flow, but they were related. The horrible bites had a silver lining. If there had been no clouds of insects as we left the beach (and in our camp always), I likely wouldn't have been able to start to truly under-stand turbulence. Insects and an ocean. I needed both.

I drew pictures of what I saw at the ocean that day. I can still recall those images on paper from when I was young. They became the foundation of decades of work. At the age of eleven years, far from any semblance of civilization, while my father did all he could to keep us alive another day, I began an intellectual quest to under-stand turbulence. More formally, I wished to prove the following: in three space dimensions and time, given an initial velocity field, there exists a vector velocity and a scalar pressure field, which are both smooth and globally defined, that solve the Navier–Stokes equations. It would be both the most difficult and most private achievement of my life.

CHAPTER 22

The Truth, Sort Of, Comes Out

DAY 2

"How does she do it?" Yakov asked, slurping his bowl of *ukha* at the kitchen table. I sat across from him. He looked like the happiest man on earth.

"Recipes, I guess," I said.

"There are recipes and then there is talent. This woman has a feel for Russian food. Beautiful, too. I talked to her when she came this morning. She has a head on her shoulders. You sure she really is an American? Maybe she came here when she was very young." Yakov again sounded hopeful, despite the long odds.

"Definitely, she was born here. I think she was going for a Ph.D. in chemistry before she had kids. You in love?"

"Maybe. There is not one woman in all of Nebraska like her. I know. I've already looked." Yakov looked down at the soup with a baleful expression, as if the reflection from the bowl was playing a movie of his failed attempts at romance.

"I don't think you've looked that hard, Yakov. Not to diminish the allure of Jenny Rivkin."

"You have no idea. I've looked plenty. Here, taste." Yakov held out his spoon.

"You're going to do this every day? Feed me?"

"Were you disappointed last time?"

"Can't say that I was." This was undeniably true.

"Then taste again." I reached down and Yakov fed me like I was a baby.

"Really is good. You're right."

"Of course I'm right. And it's healthy. Perfect. I don't understand how you can live in bumblefuck Alabama when you could live here, be with a woman like Jenny, and be with your family. You're crazy." Yakov was trying to claim an edge over me in hard-won wisdom.

"I wouldn't have a job."

"Now that's a lie. The people in your department here. What do they call it, meteorology?" There it was: the dismissiveness of all mathematicians toward any field that wasn't mathematics.

"The department of atmospheric and oceanic sciences is what it's called."

"Whatever. People add 'sciences' to a department name only when they are worried they aren't really scientists. They would hire you in a heartbeat. Your mother told me. You broke her heart staying away, you little *moshennik*." He took his free index finger and scolded me. If I had reached over just a bit, I could have chomped on his reprimanding finger and ended our little discourse instantly.

"My mother understood my reasons."

"You and your mother. I never understood either of you. Your mother was too smart. And you, you're just perverse on purpose."

"I hope you're wrong. But it could be so."

"You have Jenny's number or am I going to have to find it in the phone book?"

"The phone book would be best. You had better be careful. She is a smart one, you're right. Used to come to our house and talk with my mother about men, right where you are sitting. One of my mother's little sisters, coming here for advice. She'll see right through you."

"My intentions are entirely honorable, Sasha." Yakov looked genuinely affronted.

"I see. What happens if she burns the food one day, Yakov?"

"Everybody makes mistakes."

"Maybe you are in love after all."

It was day two of the shiva, and people already looked tired, except for Yakov, who seemed to be thriving in the presence of all of his friends, heroes, and the good Russian food of Jenny Rivkin.

"What did you mathematicians do last night, anyway?" I asked Yakov. I was truly curious.

"We went to the conference room at the department. All of us. We drank. We worked. What the hell else can we do? It's who we are."

"And what exactly were you working on?"

"Do I have to tell you?"

"Navier-Stokes is hard, isn't it?"

"Shut up. Of course it's hard."

"But that's ridiculous. It would take years to come up with a solution. Plus, there are too many cooks working on the recipe. Over a dozen of you together in one room. It's madness." I had hit a nerve. Mathematicians are solitary creatures by nature. They sit in their offices day after day looking into space, and wait for the moment when they can actually use the paper and pencil they have on their desks. It can take days, months, and maybe years before they actually write anything meaningful. A mathematician will even dream about his or her unsolved problem, often to no avail. Then one day it happens for no apparent reason. Just like that a solution appears, or a major step to a solution is envisioned. To the unfortunate mathematicians tackling major problems like Hilbert's sixth, though, it's likely that no solution will ever come. Success will always be beyond their grasp.

"I know, I know. It sounds like something doomed to failure. But in other fields people work in teams nowadays. It's the new way of business. Look at physics. They are like armies now, with soldiers and officers clawing their way to solutions. Maybe it's time for us to work that way. That's what Zhelezniak says, at any rate."

"So by day you mourn and by night you try to solve something my mother supposedly cheated death to finish."

"Did she finish it?"

"Maybe."

"Now you're torturing me."

"That memoir I mentioned at the funeral? Last night, I translated some more. It seems she was working on it."

"I knew it!"

"Yeah, she was working on Navier-Stokes sixty years ago when she was eleven years old. That's what her memoir says."

"We already know that. Everybody knows that."

"I didn't. It was news to me."

"She never told you?"

"It didn't come up in conversation, no. My father there last night?"

"No. He was busy, he said. He is a doting great-grandpa now, did you hear?"

"I've noticed, yes. He's hogging my *nakhes*. I've barely seen my daughter and granddaughter because of him. This morning he called to say he would be late. He's making blini for Amy."

"Really? I haven't had good blini in such a long time."

"Maybe you should marry my father. He's actually a pretty good cook."

"Your father would be hell to live with."

"Tell me something I don't know."

The geographic distribution of people in the house had changed overnight. The mathematicians, both the men and women, were all in the living room. My small family, sans my blini-making father and his granddaughter and great-granddaughter, were in the dining room.

"The parrot likes Jenny, I noticed," Yakov said. "She moves to the cage door when Jenny is near, like she wants to get a better look. I can sympathize."

"Pascha likes all women."

"She doesn't like you?"

"Tolerates me, but no, she doesn't like me. And she's known me for over thirty years."

"You were competition for your mother. Why did your mother have a bird, anyway? A little thing in a cage like that. I would think it would be depressing."

"A Polish friend was moving to Israel and they couldn't take the parrot. Pascha knew a few Polish words. My mother taught her many more. She's pretty amazing, actually."

"Not like you." Yakov gave a hearty chuckle. "Your Polish is probably as bad as your Russian."

"No, it's worse."

"It's hard to believe you were born in Moscow. Impossible, actually."

"It's been a long time. I can hardly believe it myself."

He got serious and looked toward Pascha. "We're very interested in that bird, Sasha."

"Who is we?"

"The people in the living room."

"You think Pascha holds secrets?"

"We are desperate enough to think anything."

"A bird brain is not going to solve Navier-Stokes."

"No, it won't. But that bird might have memorized a few important lines from a human being who probably did solve that problem but kept it to herself."

"Now you're starting to talk like Otrnlov."

"That man is crazy. We're just crazy about mathematics. There is a difference."

"I can't tell any difference at all, to tell you the truth."

"Enough. The heavenly soup is gone. I'm going to call up Miss Jenny Rivkin, tell her how much I admire her cooking. If I'm lucky, I'll eventually convince her to move with me to my wholesome state in this gentle, warmhearted, but somewhat ignorant country. Go. You'll kill the mood. Now it's time for you to go to the living room. They want to talk to you there."

"For what it's worth, there is a list of numbers on the corkboard next to the phone. It's a good guess that Ms. Rivkin's phone number is on that list."

Someone from the synagogue Sisterhood had been thoughtful enough to bring folding chairs from the synagogue. Otherwise, there was no way this collection of geniuses and the merely super-smart could have all fit into a single living room. The only upside of their presence was that I did not have any trouble getting together a minyan for evening prayers before dinner. I stood before the mathematicians, leaned against a doorjamb—where pencil marks and notations indicated my growth as a youth—and listened.

"She should have won the Fields. It's a travesty that she didn't," Eva said. The Fields was the aforementioned Fields Medal, the international award given to two to four mathematicians under the age of forty-one every four years.

"It's true. But the time was not right," Zhelezniak said.

"What do you mean? They had until 1970 to do it. That's twenty years of her waiting in vain for an award she should have won in 1950," Eva pressed on. This was her style, and it's probably why she was successful working with my mother. She wasn't intimidated by anyone.

"It's because she was a woman. Those bastards wouldn't give it to her," Virginia Potter said.

"That's not true," one of the Karansky triplets said. "Vladimir should have received the Fields, too. It was because of the Cold War. No Russian won the Fields until 1970. All those years and just one medal." The other two triplets nodded their head in approval. It's no wonder I couldn't tell them apart.

"Enough. It's all in the past now," Zhelezniak said. "I've had a good career. I have no complaints."

"I was there in 1970 when the announcement came about Novikov," Eva said. "Rachela was furious. That was her time and the committee wouldn't do it. Novikov. It's like they knew just which name would make Rachela angriest."

"The committee blackballed her. Boyle from Oxford. An anti-Semite bastard," Ben-Zvi said. "It wasn't because Rachela was a woman or a Pole."

"Axton Boyle, oh my god," Eva said. "I forgot. Rachela hated him."

"I don't know if he was an anti-Semite, but Abraham is right, he was a bastard," Zhelezniak said. "There wasn't much to like about Boyle."

"Shackleworth was a student of Boyle's, wasn't he? So ironic. Him tutoring Rachela's great-granddaughter," Eva said.

"Shackleworth is a different man entirely," Zhelezniak said. "A true gentleman in every way."

"True, but still," Ben-Zvi said. "Can you imagine if Rachela knew about a student of Boyle's teaching her own flesh and blood? She would be on the first plane to Berkeley to strangle him."

It brought back memories, hearing the fractious gossip about this and that mathematician being discussed in the room. That anyone, much less these thirteen people, could devote such passion to opinions about others, which in effect absurdly elevated those others to celebrity status, was kind of amusing. Famous mathematicians are about as common and likely as famous auto mechanics.

"Yakov said you wanted to talk to me," I said.

"Yes, we do," Zhelezniak said. "We need your help, Sasha."

"I think I'm the one who should be getting help, quite frankly," I said. "From all of you. Or at least the small favor of not getting in the way while I try to be a good son and grieve over the loss of someone I loved."

"Everyone grieves in their own way," Ben-Zvi said.

"You're telling me that you are grieving by solving Navier-Stokes?"

"It's a way to celebrate your mother," Ito said. "It's our way."

"It's the only way we know how, Sasha," Eva said.

"Even so," I said. "If she solved the Navier-Stokes problem—which I doubt she did—and, as Yakov says, chose not to share it, then you are trespassing on her wishes."

"That would be my fault, if that was her wish," Zhelezniak said.

"My mother didn't like you, but don't think you're so important that you influenced her worldview."

"It was beyond not like. It goes back a long time. When you were young."

"A problem from Hilbert. I know about that one."

"You don't know about it. No one here does."

"Actually, I do know more than a bit. I heard my mother on the phone a long time ago. I was little, it's true, but I remember the shouting."

"With Kolmogorov?"

"You know that conversation?"

"Yes. I was listening, just like you. That's funny. Except I only heard what Andrei said, not your mother."

"It wasn't so funny, Vladimir."

"What's this about?" Virginia Potter said.

"This is old history," Ben-Zvi said. "Ancient rumors about stolen papers."

"It's not really a rumor. It's the truth, isn't it, Vladimir?" I asked.

"You and I both know what is true and what isn't," Zhelezniak said.

"What?" Peter Orlansky shouted out of nowhere, his temper flaring. "Vladimir, you really stole Rachela's papers on Hilbert's thirteenth problem?"

"It wasn't like that. I didn't steal them. Andrei had the papers. He gave them to me. I did use them, yes, but there was much more work to be done. Even Rachela, bless her soul, would admit this. Ask Viktor. He undoubtedly knows."

"Your career is a fraud, Vladimir!" Peter Orlansky jumped out of his chair. I had never seen him so angry. The others present were as surprised as I was. The ugliness of what was being revealed turned Peter into an instant champion in their eyes. All the slights and deceits these competitive people had endured over the years in their quest for recognition in mathematics were being relived.

"Calm down, Peter. Andrei had some drawings and initial work from Rachela. You know how she loved to draw. We looked at her work for months. Without her work, I would never have been able to solve that problem, I admit."

"All these years, Vladimir, taking sole credit. It's criminal," Peter said.

"Peter, Peter! We put her name on the paper. The academy forced us to take it off! They were furious. A defector as an author. It was completely unacceptable to them. Andrei couldn't say anything, or you know where both of us would have ended up."

"You should not have published, then."

"The academy already had the paper. Hilbert's thirteenth problem solved. You think they would have let such a golden achievement of Soviet mathematics go unpublished?"

"It's your shame."

"Yes, it's my shame, and I've had to live with it. Now we have this." Zhelezniak reached inside his blazer, pulled out two ancient pieces of onionskin paper, and placed them on the mahogany living room coffee table. I looked at them from afar. I knew the handwriting, of course. I recognized the style of the sketches as well.

"Where did you find them?" I asked.

"Poponov had them for thirty years. Then he died. His wife kept everything."

"It's probably what she was looking for when she visited Moscow State. And for the last twenty years, where were they?"

"I told your mother I had them five years ago. She said to keep the papers, she had no use for them."

"That's impossible," Peter said.

"Oh, it's quite possible," I said. "I'm sure she said a lot more than that."

"Nothing I care to share in mixed company," Zhelezniak said.

"I'm sure. And you need my help, do you?"

"These drawings by your mother. We know they are about Navier-Stokes. I've been staring at them for years now. There must be others. I swear, if we manage to solve this problem, there will only be one author on the paper: Rachela Karnokovitch. The Millennium Prize, too. It will all go to your family."

"Good. As of yesterday, I learned that I might have two more mouths to feed."

"It's not a joke, Sasha."

"I don't know where any papers are located, Vladimir."

"Can we look?"

"Where do you want to look?"

"Here. Rachela's office, too."

"But what if she really didn't want us to uncover her work?" a young female professor asked.

"What's your name?" I asked.

"Kelly Hickson."

"Where do you teach?"

"Minnesota."

"My mother never liked Minnesota." I laughed, remembering her insults about that school.

"I know. We'd invite her to give talks and she always said no. What was that about?"

"She gave a talk there in 1954. According to her they asked some dumb questions. That was that. Minnesota was off the list. And where did you go to school?"

"MIT."

"They must believe in ethics at MIT."

"I don't know about that. It's just that if your mother wanted to keep a secret, we should follow her wishes."

"If you all can solve this without additional help from my mother's work, that would be OK with you?" I asked.

"Yes, of course," Kelly said. "It's important work. Someone needs to solve it and make it public."

I sighed. "My guess is that my mother knew you'd all find a way to look at her papers. Maybe she knew you'd all crash this shiva."

"Your mother was not only smart. She was also a *magid atidot*," Ben-Zvi said.

"What's that mean?" Kelly asked.

"'Prescient,' which is true," I said. "You don't know any Hebrew, do you, Ms. Hickson?"

"Not a word. No Russian, obviously, either." Kelly looked a bit embarrassed.

"Eva, did you bring Dr. Hickson and the other young one—I don't know your name, sorry—for fresh blood and new ideas?"

"Of course, Sasha."

Getting through to mathematicians is never a simple thing. I decided to try a visual stunt. "OK, I want to show you something, Dr. Hickson. It's my growth chart from when I was little. It's right here on the doorjamb. Take a look at it."

Kelly quickly got up off her folding chair.

"All those numbers are from when I was five, when we moved here, until when I was fifteen. My mother always made sure painters never covered this part of the doorjamb. She said she liked to look at it and remember those times, that they were years that she thought of fondly."

"That's very sweet, actually."

"I think so, too. I probably should have covered this up for the shiva, when I think about it. At any rate, we're going to make a new mark right now. We're going to bring things up to date. Could you grab a book and a pencil?"

"What are you doing, Sasha? This is crazy," Eva said.

"Just give Kelly a book and pencil and I'll show you, Eva."

Eva pulled a book of Kandinsky artwork from the coffee table and grabbed a nearby pencil, a tool that, unlike wrenches and screwdrivers, was always in ample supply in our house.

"I think you're tall enough, Kelly. You'll just have to reach. Put the book on top of my head, make it level, and make a mark."

I stood erect while Ms. Hickson carefully and accurately took my height. I then turned around and faced the doorjamb. "That was fun, actually, brought back memories," I said. "Back then I wanted to be taller desperately. My mother would say I must have taken after my grandpa Aaron. The pencil marks went higher every year, but the incremental increases were always pitifully small."

"What happened here?" Kelly asked, pointing to a big gap

"I went away to school in Chicago. I came back nine months later. I was a foot taller. Pretty much at the height of the mark you made. I was finally taller than my mother, much taller. It made me happy. It made my mother happy, too. But I was never as smart as her. That would never happen. And all of us, smart as we are, are just down here." I pointed to my height at fifteen, before my growth spurt. "See the gap? That's the gap between our collective intelligence and my mother's. Not even close."

Kelly broke the short silence. "You're right, Sasha," Kelly said. "I've looked at some of her work. It's intimidating, but I try to make it inspire me, not depress me."

"It's good you know that, Kelly," I said. "Most people in this room cannot admit it. That was the point of this exercise. I underestimated you. I'm sorry."

"That's all right."

"You know what? You can all look wherever you want. Here. My mother's office. Even my mother viewed Navier-Stokes as potentially impossible. Look and see what you can find. It's not going to help, but it will pass the time."

"Thank you, Sasha," one of the triplets said. "But my brothers and I don't think we need your mother's help. Not directly. Rather, we should do as your mother would do to solve any problem."

"And what would she do?" I asked.

"It's obvious," he said. The brothers even smiled in unison. I noticed one of them had a chipped front tooth. Finally, I had a distinguishing feature I could use. "It's cold. There's snow," another brother with more or less perfect front teeth continued.

"A ski trip, then?" I asked.

"That's an excellent idea!" Zhelezniak said.

"What do you think, Peter?" I asked.

"I think if we don't get out of this house tomorrow we'll end up killing each other."

"That could happen," I said. "Do you ski, Professor Hickson?"

"We would go to Vail when I was a kid, but I've never done cross-country."

"It's very therapeutic. If you are a true acolyte of my mother, you must learn. Everyone in this room knows how to ski."

"Well, I run every day."

"I could have predicted that. But cross-country skiing is different. You'll see."

CHAPTER 23

The Ski Trip

DAY 3

My mother and father skied cross-country extensively every winter. It's something that all of Kolmogorov's former students living in cold climates did, and few of his students deigned to live below the forty-second parallel. Of course, cross-country skiing is also something that I grew up doing.

According to Kolmogorov, ideas needed to flow and ideas came and flowed most easily when the body was subject to a combination of punishing cold and vigorous exercise. What form of exercise was best for this combination? Kolmogorov believed cross-country skiing was tailor-made for intellectual discovery. The shiva-attending mathematicians were therefore very fortunate that the weather gods had chosen to not only dump snow on Madison, Wisconsin, before they arrived, but also to follow that dumping with the migration of a high-pressure Arctic air mass that had decided, like many Arctic air masses, to stagnate.

It was cold during the shiva. How cold was it? It was so cold that during their daily mile walk from their host's house to my mother's home, the Karanskys' considerable hair, which none of them made any effort to dry when they showered in the morning, froze into icicle-encrusted ringlets. It was so cold that, for the safety of the student body, the chancellor closed all evening classes at the university for two of the shiva days, when the night temperature fell into the minus twenties.

Bitter cold meant, as far as most of these mathematicians were concerned, absolutely ideal conditions for cross-country skiing. At these frigid temperatures, those who still preferred to use waxed skis didn't have to think about what color wax to use or worry about changing waxes in mid-ski. A thin coating of hard white polar wax and they would be on their way.

The glaciers had been kinder to Wisconsin than to the nearby states of Illinois, Iowa, and Nebraska. They had not leveled the entire landscape to the flatness of a bowling lane. Cross-country skiing in Wisconsin came with some modest challenges, huffing and puffing up inclines and gloriously careening down modest hills. The mathematicians were also blessed with a wonderful venue for skiing a mere mile from my mother's home, just beyond the zoo and ice rink of Vilas Park. The Arboretum was a twelve-hundred-acre prairie preserve maintained by the university.

Excluding my father, who certainly possessed ski equipment of his own, there were fourteen mathematicians who needed skis. Contrary to my words to Kelly Hickson, there were novices and near novices in the troupe. Those who had been students of my mother had been indoctrinated in the positive value of a good ski on the creativity of the mathematical mind. Then there was Zhelezniak, the other direct descendant of Kolmogorov. Zhelezniak was absolutely gung ho about this mission to extract a little more brain power from the group.

Zhelezniak was so adamant that he made it clear to all that refusing to confront the snow and cold would be the equivalent of treason, or at least an open admission that failure to produce a breakthrough to the solution of the Navier-Stokes problem over the course of the shiva was a possibility. News of the planned trip carried to the mathematics department and beyond. Miraculously, the necessary piles of suitable clothing, shoes, and skis appeared the night before and were deposited in my mother's storm-windowed front porch. We were good to go.

By saying we, I do of course include myself. I had no interest in solving the Navier-Stokes problem, but I was concerned about the inexperienced members of the group, Ito in particular. Plus, I felt a certain pull to get out of the house, slide on the snow, and move my bones. I thought it might prove to be emotionally beneficial. I was actually hoping for the absence of any ideas in my head whatsoever, mathematical or otherwise.

Bruce watched us bundle up with amusement. He, too, was more than competent on skis, but there was no way on earth that he was going to subject himself to such obvious misery. Instead, he pulled his own skis out of the cobweb-filled garage and instructed Ito on their use in the backyard. I did the same with my mother's skis and Jane Sempralini, a professor of mathematics from Sydney who had only recently moved to Cambridge, England. "This is an honor, quite truly," she said as I showed her how to step into my mother's bindings.

"It's cold for you now, yes?"

"Bitter cold. Already, I can't feel my nose."

"We'll get you a scarf. That will help. You've never been skiing at all, not even downhill?"

"Never."

"It's like walking in the mud. You lift up your feet to get out of the mud and then you press down and get stuck again."

"Sounds terrible."

"But there is the added benefit that you don't really get stuck. You glide. It's like ice-skating."

"Can't say I've ever done that either."

"Roller-skating?"

"That I have done."

"Good, because there are similarities there, too. You push a bit down instead of away and instead of rolling, you slide along."

I watched Bruce instruct Ito and tried not to grimace as I watched Jane try to master the push and glide of cross-country skiing in my mother's backyard. Zhelezniak, my father, Virginia Potter, who skied in the hills outside of Amherst regularly, Peter Orlansky, and the Karanskys would be one hundred yards out before either of these two managed to go ten feet. I informed Zhelezniak of the need to break into two groups.

"What do you mean? We all go out. We all ski. We all come back. It's simple."

"It's not that simple, Vladimir. It's freezing. There are people who have never been in weather this cold, much less been on skis."

"It's like walking. It's not difficult. You push. You glide. Any idiot can do this."

"With practice, yes. But you're going to want to go five miles, at least."

"At least, of course."

"Ito and Jane, they'll be lucky to make a mile. Ben-Zvi won't be able to do more than two or three. My father will show you where to go. I'll stay behind with the rest. I know the route my father will take. We'll use a shorter path and meet you at the end."

That's exactly what we did. Ito and Jane and Ben-Zvi were

thankful for a less painful, less arduous option, and I guided them as we crawled along the edge of snow-covered Lake Wingra. The cold air bit into the pores of my skin as we made hard-earned progress, and yielded a sensory memory that I thought I would rather have not elicited ever again. As we continued, though, I changed my mind. This was kind of fun. The ski track we followed was by far the gentlest and, with the near constant view of the lake, was also the prettiest. Our stops, to catch our breath or for the occasional spills into the snow, gave me the time to look north beyond the lake toward the zoo where I spent many hours as a kid. I did wish that we could move faster. It was early in the morning on a workday. The trail, which wasn't particularly well traveled even during weekends, was, lucky for us, empty. After a while, just to keep my blood circulation going, I began to ski ahead a few hundred yards at a clip, and then retreat to make sure everyone was doing as well as could be expected. I kept reminding them to brush off the snow every time they fell, lest it melt on their pants and chill their thighs or roll down into their boots.

On one of my forays ahead, I ran into an industrious skier going in the opposite direction, her rhythm steady, her breath forming little cloud puffs as she progressed across the flats. I didn't recognize her at first, but the red hair peeking out from her knit cap gave me a clue. She looked up as she approached and I moved my skis off the track.

"Sasha, what are you doing out here?" Jenny asked.

"I could say the same about you."

"I come here before work two mornings a week. It clears my head. Your mom taught me that. Are you out here clearing your head?"

"Well, not really. It's the mathematicians. They are trying to find inspiration in the woods. They're behind me a bit, getting inspired as we speak, I hope."

"All of them?"

"Yes and no. My father is leading the experts. I'm in charge of the inexperienced ones."

"I talked to one of them the other day. Yakov. Is he with them?"

"Oh, no, Yakov is actually quite a good skier. He's with my father. He's loving your cooking, by the way."

"Thanks. I'm just trying to help out. You're making us work overtime, though. We didn't know there would be so many people."

"If truth be known, neither did I."

"I know it must be hard. Your mother was important to me. It's good to do something instead of thinking about losing her."

We parted ways and I watched her shush off toward my little troop of skiing neophytes. We had another half mile to go, and if we timed things right, we wouldn't have to stand around too long before the experts met up with us. I tried to encourage the group, looking for evidence of the remotest bit of glide in their movements. It wasn't forthcoming. I stopped them to offer an impromptu lesson. I exaggeratedly lifted up and pushed down on one ski.

"This is where the rhythm for skiing comes from," I said "The planting of your foot, and then that instant feeling of effortless sliding along the compacted snow, which carries you for a second or two before you feel compelled to step down with your other foot. Back and forth, that's what it's about, the impending loss of gliding making you lift one foot and then another."

"I suppose this is a form of meditation," Ben-Zvi said without irony.

"That's about right," I said. "On a good day, if I concentrate simply on the motion of my feet, I can sometimes forget about everything else for a mile or so before I come back into the real world."

"I'm going to end up with bruises, I've fallen so much," Jane said.

"The more you practice, the better you get. One more time out here and I bet you hardly fall at all." I could barely believe the earnest tone in my voice. I must have been channeling my mother. I wasn't trying to sell snow to the Eskimos, or to the Russians for that matter, but I was certainly trying to sell it to the Aussies, Japanese, and one very skeptical Israeli.

Jane asked if we could spend some time making snowballs, and maybe even a fort. "I used to read about children doing that in books. It sounded like so much fun. Much more fun than skiing, from what I can tell."

"The snow's too dry for that, sorry," I said. "But it does make for excellent angels."

"I'll settle for an angel," Ben-Zvi said. "I'm too exhausted to do much of anything else."

To see a child make an angel in the snow can be a precious thing. There is something about watching kids, normally so erratically active, change pace and mood to splay out in the snow. But to see a burly, bearded man in Clark Kent glasses plop down, make the earth shake slightly, and imitate so ungracefully what a child of the Midwest knows how to do with ease is something else entirely.

"I may not get up," Ben-Zvi said. "This feels good."

"If Zhelezniak catches you like this," Jane said, "you'll never hear the end of it."

"Fuck Zhelezniak. I'm beat. No one brought any hot chocolate, did they? That would have been a good idea. Right here. Right now. And then some snow ambulance to take me back. They have one of those?"

"Probably not, Abraham," I said. "Unless you have a heart attack or something serious, you'll have to get back on your own."

"A heart attack isn't worth it. Does frostbite count?"

"No, I'm afraid not."

"You Midwesterners are a tough lot." He lifted himself from the snow and looked down at the depression. "I didn't know I could be so angelic."

"That's a big angel, Abraham," Jane said.

"Oh please, Jane."

"I guess this little trip isn't producing much inspiration," I said.

"Can't say it is," Jane agreed.

"It's simply cold," Ito said.

"I think you have to be born into it," I said.

"You find it inspiring do you, Sasha?" Ito asked.

"Sometimes, yes," I said.

"But it's my understanding that you live in the southern part of the United States now," Ito said.

"Heat can be inspiring, too. Although my mother wouldn't agree with that sentiment," I said.

The group of skiing enthusiasts eventually met us on the edge of the lake. I felt a tinge of envy looking at them, ruddy-faced from a good, physically draining workout. I knew how their lungs felt, raw and free from sucking in gulp after gulp of cold, dry air. My imagination was big enough to sense the collective messy rhythms of all their hearts pounding hard and fast, sometimes in unison, but usually at different tempos. For the first time in years I felt an urge to simply take off on my skis and go by myself into the woods for hours on end.

"This crew is beat," I said to Zhelezniak and my father. "It's going to take a lot of work to get them back."

Zhelezniak looked at the three mathematicians I'd moved along the shore. "They've hardly done any skiing at all and look at them! How far is it back, Viktor?"

"Two kilometers, perhaps," my father said.

"Only two kilometers they've gone, and they look as if they will die any minute. Unbelievable," Zhelezniak said. I have no problem with self-righteousness, and think it has a place when it's an honest expression of the ability to withstand hardship without complaint. If there is one hardship Russians can endure, even celebrate, it's cold, and the deprivation associated with that cold. Every hundred years or so another country forgets about this special Russian talent, declares war, and pays dearly for their naiveté and hubris.

"Why don't we cross the lake?" Ben-Zvi asked, hopeful of a shortcut to my mother's home.

"It's really not a good idea," I said. "The lake looks solid, but there are a lot of hidden springs where the ice is thin. You have to know where they are. I don't remember just where, it's been so many years. Father, what about you?"

"I haven't crossed the lake in a long time. It's usually too windy."

"We're on skis. It should distribute the weight. I don't see a problem," Zhelezniak said.

"I swear I can see Rachela's home in the distance," Ben-Zvi said.

"Is that true, Ben-Zvi?" Ito asked.

"You wish! It's too far," Jane said.

Zhelezniak looked at the defeated group next to me and didn't even try to hide his disgust. "I'm glad of one thing. That Rachela didn't have to see this display of *slabost i len*."

"My, my, aren't we full of ourselves." Jane, who didn't know Russian but could easily suss out the meaning of Zhelezniak's words, said it just loud enough for me to hear.

Zhelezniak shook his head and summoned up some pity. "We'll go across the lake, then," he said. "I'll lead. We'll get you all back and you can warm up."

"We should follow the edge of the lake, Vladimir," I said. "That way, if someone breaks through, they won't go very far down."

"It would be longer," Ben-Zvi said. "I'm not in favor of longer."

"We'll go straight across, Abraham. We'll get you back quickly," Zhelezniak said.

I said nothing as we began our journey. The wind was barely blowing. Nature wasn't being completely unkind. The sky was a wondrous dark blue shade that I never saw in Tuscaloosa, and that in the Midwest only came with frigid days in winter. I had skied on this lake many times way back when. Only once had I run into a spring-thinned patch. It was in 1966, the year when teens in my neighborhood began, for the first time ever, to take drugs for the dual purpose of mental exploration and self-medication.

I was with my girlfriend of the moment, someone with whom I was trying to maintain a long-distance relationship. It was during winter break and I was happy to be back home with her. I didn't know we wouldn't last as a couple past the spring.

I had decided that it would be fun to take a ski trip on acid. One of the advantages of growing up in a college town is that if you are inclined to take hallucinogens, supplies are ample and the quality is usually quite good. So it was with the acid we took that day, which we licked off some colorful African-themed blotter tabs labeled Safari Travels. The snow was thin on the lake as we skied. I did notice I was crossing a slushy patch, but my brain failed to understand that we were in peril. It was slushy. Hah, hah, hah. That's so cool. Hah, hah, hah. In retrospect, that year of "mental exploration" was really a year of near total mental vegetation. I guess that was the point.

I fell in with one ski. "Whoa!" I said. Speaking words longer than one syllable is quite difficult on acid. *Woe-ah.* I had truly recognized something of significance. My girlfriend was behind me.

"What's that?" she asked.

"I'm in a hole," I said.

"Oh, that's not good, I guess."

"No, it isn't," I said.

"Well, um, you want me to help?"

"Um, no, just don't get close. It's a hole, you know. You could fall in."

"OK. I won't get close."

"Good idea."

I don't remember the details of how I extracted my leg and ski from the water, but one relative advantage of being on drugs when you do something stupid is that you tend not to panic. At least that was true for me.

I thought about this as we moved across the lake with me at the end of the group, carefully watching my minions directly ahead. When I heard the shouts in Russian a few hundred yards ahead I knew exactly what had happened.

"What's that?" Jane stopped and turned to me. She was finally starting to glide along the snow, I noticed.

"Someone fell in."

"This is like *Dr. Zhivago*," Jane said. "Omar Sharif walking across Siberia, braving death."

"Hopefully it's nothing serious. I'll go ahead and check."

"Do that please," Jane said and started to hum "Lara's Theme" aloud, maybe because she was nervous or maybe because she wanted to make a joke.

I could hear Zhelezniak continue to curse. He was inspecting his waterlogged right boot and pant leg when I got to him. To his credit, the snow blanket was so thick that there was no way he could have known a thin spot was there. It had helped that he was a small man, about my weight when I was a teen. But unlike me at that tender age, there were no drugs in his bloodstream transforming danger into amusement.

"I'm happy to see you're OK," I said. "You got out yourself?"

"Of course," Zhelezniak said. "I didn't want to endanger anyone else."

"From what I remember, and that memory is fuzzy, there aren't many more thin spots near here besides this one and two others about forty meters to the right."

"Orlansky would have fallen through like a stone. You should have told me, Sasha."

"It's been a long time. I didn't remember until now."

"Let's get out of here," Zhelezniak said, and they all pushed off while I skied back to my apprentices.

They were more than a little relieved when we took off our skis and climbed the path to my mother's house. I decided to stay at the zoo for a bit while the others continued on. This was the kind of weather I liked best to observe whatever animals they allowed out at that time of year. The walruses and sea lions, their whiskers covered in a thin coating of frost and ice, seemed happy to be experiencing the near Arctic temperatures. The noisy sea lions, the alarm clocks of my youth, were active, motoring around their concrete-floored enclosure on their bellies with exuberance. If they recognized me from years before, they didn't let on.

I walked over to the bears and looked at the Kodiak, the one my mother watched while she was sick. I thought about her time in the Barents Sea, fresh in my mind from reading her memoir. She had quoted from Gorki in the chapter I had read. "The more a human creature has tasted of bitter things, the more it hungers after the sweet things in life." My mother always had that hunger, so fierce and something I couldn't possibly replicate in its intensity. My life had been—thanks to her, my grandfather, father, uncle, and aunt, who had all wished nothing but a kind world for me—not bitter in the least.

My father had taken Andrea and Amy to the zoo once already. I had heard about this trip secondhand and felt more than a bit jealous of my father enjoying our newly discovered family. Did they stop to take a look at the Kodiak? Probably they did. I thought about my mother talking to this bear when she was ill, about

Anna teasing me for doing the same. But sometimes, you need to voice something aloud just to hear yourself say it. Thinking it in your head just won't do. I stared at that huge brown bear while it paused to look in my direction. No, I'm not foolish enough to think that it was looking back with any sense of cognition when I said, "I want sweet things in life. I have a hunger, too."

CHAPTER 24

Kabbalove

DAY 4

A man knocked on the door. He wore a thick black wool coat and a knockoff Borsalino fedora, like the kind you can buy from street vendors near New York City's Little Italy. His red beard was scraggly, similar to what you find on the faces of some Hassidic rabbis, and the pale skin of his cheeks, pockmarked, also gave off a rabbinical air. He looked a little familiar. A woman, likely his wife, stood beside him. By day four of the shiva none of the mathematicians were knocking or ringing the bell. They would walk right in like they were part owners of my mother's house. A doorbell ring usually meant someone local with food, but these two weren't trying to feed us.

It took me a moment to place the man. The day of the ski trip Ben-Zvi told me that his brother was in town and wanted to pay his respects. I had met his brother long before he could grow a beard, at Ben-Zvi's wedding to Anna.

My cousin, Bruce, has an uncanny ability to detect who is sleeping with whom. I, on the other hand, have a finely tuned and less useful sense of who is a real rabbi and who is a poseur. It comes from my years of religious instruction, especially my days as a yeshiva student in Chicago. This man in front of me was trying to look like a rabbi, and may have spent a few years getting a rabbinical education after high school, but I was certain that he wasn't the real deal. At the door, he fidgeted, not out of cold, but because he was the kind of man who was easily distracted. Even the lowest of the low of Orthodox rabbis possess *sitzfleisch,* the ability to concentrate on one thing for hours at a time. Either you possess this trait naturally or they beat it into you with slaps across the face during your early education. Actually, I'm told that nowadays no slapping is allowed, but back when I was a student it was de rigueur.

Ben-Zvi's brother's wife was tall and wafer-thin, perhaps fifteen years younger than him. She wore a tan camel coat, and her long brown hair, definitely not a *sheitel,* was fully exposed to the elements. Shimon was the man's name. His wife was an American, Jocelyn.

The house was warm and inviting, I knew. A home full of people is always pleasant to find on a bitter cold day. The furnace blew in hot air constantly. Abraham Ben-Zvi put aside his thoughts of the Navier-Stokes problem and enveloped his brother Shimon with a bear hug and a kiss on both cheeks. Abraham came from a large family, and none except him possessed any mathematical ability. As Abraham hugged his brother, who he hadn't seen in more than ten years, the fat around his waist jiggled. These two were separated in age by a good many years, but anyone could clearly see that they were brothers.

My uncle peeked out of the dining room to see what the commotion was about. He caught a glimpse of Shimon and rose to meet him. Maybe it was my uncle's lack of Jewish upbringing as a child that caused him to be so enamored of those with extensive Jewish education. Even ersatz rabbis were like catnip for him. When he came to this country my uncle made it his mission to learn about his faith, to learn biblical Hebrew, and even to learn to speak a decent Yiddish with his father. In a few short years, he became a three-star Jew, at least.

My uncle was prideful of his adherence to Judaic tradition in a way that I've seen in a lot of survivors. It wasn't just about the joy of being of the faith. There was the added kicker of practicing a religion and culture that if Hitler and many others had had their way would have been annihilated. My uncle was jubilant about being a living testimony to the failure of the worst years of hate and anti-Semitism in human history.

"Reb Ben-Zvi," my uncle said. "It's a pleasure to meet you again."

"You know each other?" I asked.

"Yes, of course," my uncle said. "He's almost like *mishpuchah* to us, given that his brother was once married to Anna. We discovered our ties during his last visit here."

"I actually remember you both from my brother's wedding, and your beloved Rachela as well," Shimon said to us. When Shimon said my mother's name, he pronounced it like my grandfather did, my uncle did, and like all who came from the Jewish Pale likely would have, *Rookh-eh-leh*. Usually when I heard my mother's name pronounced this way, I'd be filled with warm nostalgia for my grandfather and his cronies. But hearing Shimon with his affected shtetl accent irritated me. "I'm so sorry to hear of your loss," he said, placing his hands on my uncle and me as if he was about to give us a blessing. My uncle seemed genuinely soothed by this gesture.

Shimon had emigrated from Israel to New York in his twenties and did god knows what for several years. One day he ventured to

Manhattan and by chance ran into an old Jewish socialist with a nostalgia for Eastern European shtetl culture who owned a book, written in a mix of Hebrew and Yiddish, detailing life in his grandfather's hometown in Poland. There are thousands of remembrance books, *yizkor beecher*, like this. They are a testimony to a life that is no more. Written after the war not by journalists but by groups of Jewish survivors, these heartfelt scrapbooks of pictures and memories describe what Jewish life once was like in most every shtetl and *dorf* in the Pale before Hitler destroyed it all. For a little money Shimon translated the book into English. The man was grateful. Out of the blue, on the day he received the translated book, the man asked Shimon what he knew about Kabbalah. Shimon, who had a genuine penchant for mysticism, began to expound on his love of those Jewish ancients who probed deeply into the meaning of life. The man, who was an assistant director of NYU's adult learning program, proposed that Shimon give a series of lectures on Kabbalistic thought. The lectures were a huge success. Shimon found his voice and his career.

Such was the story that Abraham Ben-Zvi told me about his brother. What he didn't say was that teaching the rudiments of Jewish mysticism was a competitive business, and simply informing those who were spiritually hungry about the wonders of God and his relation to the world wasn't quite enough to generate a long-term, steady, paying audience. You needed something practical, and maybe borderline salacious, to stand out from the rest. Shimon, his lecture career flagging, came upon a new idea. He called it Kabbalove, a lecture series and instruction manual for couples that mixed sex tips with relationship advice, all of which supposedly were "inspired" by the Kabbalah. Shimon traveled

around the country selling his self-published paperback bu
videos of lectures out of the trunk of his car, speaking primarily a.
"forward-thinking" synagogues. Along the way he had found his
besheret, Jocelyn. I noted that somehow over the years he had
managed to avoid my synagogue in Tuscaloosa. Apparently we
weren't forward-thinking enough.

But there he was in Madison, Wisconsin, scheduled to speak
at Temple Beth El. This was his second time in town, the first
having taken place three years before. That was when my uncle
Shlomo, attending a lecture with his new bride, Cynthia, had met
Shimon. Both of them had found the lecture and the $29.95 man-
ual captivating.

As Abraham Ben-Zvi took his brother to the flock of mathematicians, I turned to my uncle. "What do you know of this guy?"

"Shimon? Not much. You should see him talk in front of a
crowd, though. The *dveykus* just oozes from him."

"He's a trained rabbi?"

"Yes, of course."

"Are you sure?"

"Why are you always so skeptical about the Orthodox, Sasha?"

"I have my reasons. Why are you always such a sap about anything that has a Star of David on it?"

"I'm not a sap. But unlike you, I don't just say the words in *shul*.
I believe them, and I know *dveykus* when I see it." I actually admired my uncle's ironclad belief in God and his feeling of im-
measurable gratitude to *Hashem* for giving him the strength to
rise out of the earth as a young boy and live, and for returning him
to his father and sister. But I never understood how or why he entirely dropped all of his hard-earned circumspection and savvy

when he encountered ordained men of faith, be they Christian or
Jewish.

I watched from a distance as Shimon took in the crowd in the
living room. "You know, you and I share much in common," Shimon said to the group. "I, too, believe that numbers provide a con-
duit to real meaning." Abraham seemed to visibly shrink upon
hearing his brother's words. Maybe the most insulting thing you
can say to a mathematician is something to the effect that math is
all about numbers. Arithmetic is all about numbers and none of
the people in the room gave a damn about arithmetic. I got the
sense that this was not the first time Shimon had managed to
make Abraham's stomach churn in a public setting. The room's
ambience was already black because of the mathematicians' inability to make headway on the Navier-Stokes problem. No one
had patience for nonsense.

"Shimon, please tell me you aren't talking about Kabbalah,"
Peter Orlansky said. Peter had had a Jewish education similar to
mine, and not surprisingly, also shared a similar love-hate relationship with the most devout of The Tribe.

"But of course, that's exactly what I'm talking about," Shimon
said. He was smiling, completely unaware of Peter's hostility. "Do
you know Kabbalah, my friend?"

"A bit, yes."

"Well, there is always more to know. I study every day and still
I consider myself uninformed. I'm holding a seminar tonight at
the local synagogue," Shimon said. "I know this family is dealing
with a terrible loss, but perhaps some of you could attend?"

"I'm afraid we have our own work to do tonight, Shimon. We
are trying to follow through on the efforts of our lost colleague

regarding an important problem," Abraham said. The two brothers said their good-byes and, in the alcove, Shimon met my uncle and me yet again. He looked at us with kindness. "I know that this is probably of little consolation to you, but I thought I might offer it. The name of your lost loved one, Rachel. It's numerically the same in Hebrew as the words in Genesis, *viyihee or,* 'and there was light.' I am certain your mother will be a source of even greater light in the world to come."

"Thank you, Reb Ben-Zvi," my uncle said. "I may need to have a word with you while you're in town. Would you mind giving me your cell phone number?" My uncle had already whipped out his phone, ready to take the rebbe's digits. Shimon obliged.

"The man has a way with words, don't you think, Sasha?" my uncle asked after Shimon left. He was still aglow from being in the presence of someone he believed was divinely inspired.

"That man? What's with his wife, anyway? She just stands there like a Giacometti statue. Doesn't say a word, and nods her head."

"Some people are quiet. Some aren't. Who is Giacometti, anyway?"

"A Swiss-Italian sculptor who stretched all his subjects into linguini."

"Jocelyn isn't Italian. Far from it. She's related to the Baal Shem Tov on her mother's side."

"Oh please, uncle. Do you know how many Jews say they are blood relatives of the Baal Shem? Even in Tuscaloosa I can find them."

"I know. A lot. But she's the real deal. I can tell."

CHAPTER 25

On the Mend

DAY 4

When my aunt died and Uncle Shlomo fell apart, my mother was beside herself. My uncle wasn't returning phone calls, a telltale sign that he was in a bad way. Even before the invention of the cell phone, my uncle had been telecommunications obsessed. My mother had to use her own key to get into his house. She'd yank him out of bed or out of the corner of the living room where he had spent the night. Bruce, a music and classics major at Williams at the time, was still in his I-can't-see-past-my-own-nose phase, lost in a sea of cocaine and sex. While many chose that route back then, Bruce didn't view it with any nostalgia. "My music was shit and I could have fucking died," he told me once.

My mother decided that my uncle needed a change of scenery, bought him a ticket, and put him on a plane. I picked him up at the Birmingham Airport. My mother wasn't sure exactly what this move would accomplish, and I wasn't either. She had no idea what I should do to pull my uncle out of his depression, but I was given one hard rule. "Do not leave him alone."

I took this command literally. When I went shopping, he went shopping. When I went to work, he went with me. In most workplaces, even academic ones, I'm sure my uncle would not have been welcome. But the South is different, and I was a highly respected member of my community. My uncle was family, and as far as the people around me were concerned, that meant he needed care. The solicitousness over this man so obviously grieving shown by my department staff, a couple of my atmospheric sciences colleagues, a handful of members of the math department—my uncle was the brother of Rachela Karnokovitch, after all—and by the lone Slavic languages professor in my university was touching.

I had an anteroom leading to my office that was full of computer workstations. We moved two of these workstations into the offices of my students. In hindsight, I should have done this years earlier. It turned out the students loved and used those toys even more when they were in close proximity. We set up my uncle as a de facto academic. He read Polish books from the university library while he drank tea and made the transition back from a full-time alcoholic into one who, like me, drinks himself into oblivion only occasionally, after hours.

Three weeks into his visit, a hurricane began to develop in the Gulf. I got a call that I could get some time on a military aircraft at MacDill Air Force Base in Tampa to make measurements. I told them I needed to bring along an assistant, a responsible, mature graduate student. Space limitations on the small jet usually meant such requests were denied. I was relieved when they said yes. I brought my uncle along, told him to pretend that he was a student, and showed him how to deploy my instruments.

Something about the idea of flying into a hurricane excited him. It was the first time I had seen anything other than fatigue and grief on his olive-skinned face in more than a year. "It's dangerous, yes?" He kept asking me, and I kept telling him no.

"The plane is not going to shake and rattle?"

"Not really."

"Not even a little?"

"Well, a little."

"Good. How else would you know you're in a hurricane?" My uncle called my mother, called Bruce, and told everyone on campus that his nephew was going to fly him into a hurricane to make measurements. We flew down to Tampa, rented a car, and on the way to MacDill I told him that he should relieve himself before we went on the plane.

"You think I'm going to shit in my pants flying into this thing? I'm not that kind of man."

"No, I don't think so. But there is no bathroom once we're up in the air. It's a military jet. No stewardesses. No bathroom."

"And what if you have to go?"

"There's a plastic bag."

"This you didn't tell me. The most powerful country in the world and its military shits in plastic bags?"

"That's why I'm telling you now."

"Thank you. I'm not going to shit in a plastic bag. No way. You ever do that?"

"A couple of times."

"A Ph.D. big-shot professor. A mother who is a genius. And you shit in plastic bags. Unbelievable."

On the airplane, my uncle assumed the role of eager graduate student to such a degree that I began to wonder why I had come along at all. We brought four dozen sensors with us that were designed to be placed into the growing tropical disturbance and monitor temperature, wind speed, humidity, and vapor pressure every tenth of a second as they descended from the plane into the ocean below. These sensors, whose measurements were transmitted via battery-operated telemetry back to the plane, were placed in cylindrical tubes about twelve inches long and two inches in diameter. Before we took off, I told my uncle where I wanted the sensors deployed in the storm. He took to these instructions like they were military orders and he was on a vital mission to save our country.

He talked to the pilot to get information on the location of the plane and, when the time was right, would carefully place each tube into the release chamber and then press the eject button. My uncle, I understood then and there, would have made an excellent engineer.

A reporter from the *Washington Post* was on the plane as well and asked me about my uncle. "Is he a colleague?"

"Oh, yes. From the University of Warsaw," I deadpanned, and gave the reporter my uncle's name with the added title of professor. I was half hoping and half dreading that my uncle would be mentioned in the journalist's story, and that he would receive a professorship via print. Alas, it didn't happen. But I did put my uncle's name on the research paper that resulted from the data we collected. One year after his efforts at being a research assistant, I handed him a copy of the article. "Look, I'm a scientist now. It's not so hard a profession after all," he said.

That six-hour flight in and out of what would become Hurricane Frieda was the beginning of my uncle's recovery. You could see it in his step, just the way he carried himself. Sixteen days later he was back in Madison, Wisconsin, running his business again.

The death of his big sister and the certain dissolution of his marriage—Cynthia had flown to Dallas the previous morning—seemed to have put my uncle into another funk. Bruce, Anna, and

I sat in the dining room trying our best to keep him from descending any further into despair, while my father, daughter, and granddaughter sat with the mathematicians.

"I feel like the last Mohican," he said.

"You still have us," Bruce said.

"It's true. You three. The young ones. But none of you speak anything resembling a decent Polish. And I've never liked living alone."

"Well, I'm not moving back, Father. It's too fucking cold here." Bruce was aiming for forcefulness.

"Yeah, it's cold. Maybe I should move to Los Angeles. Sell my business. Get the hell out of here."

"You should sell the house, that's for sure. It's depressing. A monstrosity," Anna said.

"I should set it on fire!" My uncle's eyes opened wide, as if he had come upon a novel idea.

"You can't mean that, Father."

"You don't think I could?"

"It's not that we don't think you could," I said. "It's that we think you shouldn't."

"I don't have luck. I thought I was lucky. But no, not really. I have *Yiddishe mazel*. It clings to me. I can't shake it. I should have died in that fucking grave in Ukraine. I would have been better off."

"You should come to Tuscaloosa after this," I said. "You need some warm weather."

"You'll put me in an airplane again? Fly me in a hurricane?"

"In summer, sure. We'll fly into a hurricane." I didn't think this was a bad idea. I could always use quality help.

"And I'll have to shit into a plastic bag if I need to go. No way. That's worse than living in Poland."

"Rachela wouldn't tolerate you like this," Anna said. "Feeling sorry for yourself. I don't like it, either. It's like you're a little girl." Anna was chiding my uncle in earnest. Few had the temerity to do this.

"I'm not a little girl. I just miss my sister. I miss her voice. I wish I could talk to her again. Maybe just one more time, so I could tell her a few things I didn't say when I had the chance. A man can get sad. There's nothing wrong with it."

"It's OK to be sad, sure, but not like this. Not wishing you were dead. Look at you. A successful man with a successful son. People who love you and care about you. You're not making sense."

"You think I should be making sense now? Right now?"

"Yes. Always. There's no reason not to make sense."

"And what would make sense right now?"

"I don't have to tell you. You know what to do. You're not an idiot."

My uncle nodded, looking at his hands. "Three years with that Texas woman were like fifty."

"You were an idiot about that. But for a good reason." Anna's voice had softened. She was done reprimanding my uncle.

"She looked good, didn't she?" my uncle asked, and gave Anna a look. He wasn't lost in thought anymore.

"Not bad. No real style, though," Anna said with a touch of pity.

"She never fought. Just kept it in. If she was happy or unhappy, I never knew," my uncle said.

"You need someone who understands you. What do American women know?"

"You're right about that. Their blood runs cold. Not like us." A smile appeared out of nowhere on my uncle's face.

"It's why they can't dance."

"It's why they can't do a lot of things." My uncle's dark cloud had disappeared.

Anna smiled back at my uncle. Bruce got up and walked away from the dining room table without saying a word. It took me a few minutes before I realized why Bruce had left. I walked into the kitchen. Bruce was eyeing Pascha warily. "I was scared of that thing when I was a kid. Tried to pick her up once and she almost bit my finger off."

"You're not a pet person, it's true."

"What were you doing in there so long? Trying to kill the buzz?"

"I'm a little slower than you in social matters, you know."

"At least you're not completely clueless. You did get out of there eventually. I'm proud of you."

"Where do you think it's going to lead? You're the one with a sense for this kind of stuff."

"Well, she's not going to his house. She hates the look of that place, and then there's the Cynthia aura. Probably they'll end up at the Edgewater Hotel by week's end."

"Those two ever been together before?"

"You can't tell? Honestly?"

"No."

"You're hopeless. You can't tell which of these mathematicians have slept with each other either, can you?"

"No. Not at all."

"Fact one. The aging Soviet hipster with the goatee and the blonde with the 1980s New Wave 'do are sleeping with each other on this trip." Bruce was in college lecturer mode.

"Zhelezniak and Potter? You're like the *National Enquirer*. The triplets? Ben-Zvi?"

"The triplets are too young for this crowd. But Ben-Zvi and the one who likes business suits. That happened sometime somewhere."

"Ben-Zvi and Steinberg? I don't want to think about it. The image is not pleasant at all."

"Ben-Zvi and Anna, too, don't forget about that one." Bruce liked to stir the pot when he was back home.

"He actually looked pretty good back then. But everyone knew that wasn't going to last."

"Didn't Aunt Rachela and the shy math hunk share some time?"

"Orlansky and my mom? Just rumors."

"I never saw them together. But when he walks into this house it's not like he's just another dear old colleague." The knowing smile of his father appeared on my cousin's face.

"How can you tell about all these dalliances, anyhow?"

"Body language. The way they look at each other. It's obvious."

"So you can tell which of these women I've slept with, I suppose."

"Yeah, I can. Zero."

"You're good. Damn."

"Yeah, that was a stupid trick question. You can't tell which of these men I've slept with, no doubt."

"The triplets?" I was taking a wild guess.

"Now that would be fun. But two of them are straight. The answer is zero. At least, so far."

"I can't tell those three apart and you've figured out which holes each of them like to invade."

"That's why you're a scientist and I'm not. Jane has her eyes all over you, in case you haven't noticed. She's not bad." Bruce moved his right hand to a height that indicated his rating of Jane.

"No way am I going in that direction. She's the heir apparent to my mother, the new queen of female mathematicians. When she stepped into my mother's skis she acted like she was Cinderella being fitted for her glass slipper."

"You could be her Prince Charming." I knew Bruce was teasing me.

"She just wants me for my *yikhes*."

"I think she wants more than your *yikhes*, the way she's checking you out."

"Looking is for free. I'm flattered, but not interested."

"Ari has a certain allure, actually. I'm sure he gets bored being around his brothers all the time. Wants something new now and then."

"Which one is Ari? They look alike. They dress alike."

"Ari is the gay one. Anyone can spot the queer in the crowd, right?"

I moved toward the living room and looked at the mathematicians. The triplets weren't smiling. It was hopeless. "You should stay away from mathematicians, though."

"I don't want to live with him. I just want to fuck him. Look, it worked out for you in the end. You might have a tiny math genius to show for it."

"In a way, you're right, I guess. I'm still trying to understand my good fortune."

"Amy looks just like Aunt Rachela. Like a Mini-Me. That's amazing." My cousin was actually *kvelling*.

"It's not amazing. It's just boring genetics. But your point is well taken."

"What are you two gossiping about?" Yakov asked, walking into the kitchen.

"Love," I said.

"Lust," Bruce said.

"I don't want to talk about either," Yakov said.

"What happened to you and Jenny Rivkin?" I asked.

"*Lyubov' zla, polyubish i kozla.*" Yakov spoke as if he had grown used to failing at love.

"Got turned down, did you?"

"Without hesitation. And now look, no food from her either. I've scared her away completely."

"You and Jenny Rivkin? Really? That's funny. I went to Hebrew school with her," Bruce said.

"I don't want to talk about it. I'm going to the zoo. Take a look at the bears. I need some inspiration."

"How is the Navier-Stokes problem coming along?"

"As bad as my effort at charming Jenny Rivkin. Zhelezniak and Potter, last night both of them went out skiing, hoping the cold weather and the snow would help them understand something, anything. They plan to go out again tonight."

"They don't look like they're getting much sleep after their ski trips," Bruce said.

"That too." Yakov smiled. "Comforting each other after the daily defeat. We're getting desperate."

"I would think that crashing someone's shiva would be desperation enough," I said.

"You'd never know your mother and father and your ex-wife were mathematicians, Sasha." With that, Yakov, dressed only in a sport coat, polo shirt, jeans, and sockless loafers, went into the cold to search for the bears of the zoo.

CHAPTER 26

A Meeting of the Minds

DAY 4

For the first three nights of the shiva, Bruce, Anna, and I spent quiet time together. At dinner we would eat the food brought by the Sisterhood every day, the strange mix of Jewish, Russian, sixties-style American casseroles, and ostensibly healthy tofu-laden salads. There it was, the culinary result of one hundred years of immigration, education, peer pressure, nostalgia, and, for most, modest to impressive prosperity. After we would be like well-behaved children and read aloud scenes from a contemporary Russian play translated into English—how and why my mother had obtained the copies was unknown—each of us portraying three different characters so we could cover all the parts.

It had been a sweet time, nostalgic, and it reminded me why, or at least it gave me an initial excuse as to why, I had lived these many years without having anything close to a longtime partner. I already had enough attachments. I was filled up emotionally, or so I thought. There is only a finite amount of love I can give, was my conviction. Between Anna, Bruce, my mother, my uncle, and even my father, how much of my heart was still available? Two new people had instantly entered my family. What room in my heart was there for them, especially given that I was grieving over the loss of the most important person in my life?

This kind of thinking is, of course, stupid, and not even a good use of arithmetic. Our capacity for love isn't like a gallon jug that you fill up from rest stop to rest stop as you take a drive across the country. It can swell, and sadly, it can shrink. Less is not more. Less is less, and more is better, although I can't say that I fully understood this at the time of my mother's death. I'm a whiz at science and math. In matters of people, I am indeed a slow learner.

During the shiva, whatever efforts I would make at finding time to spend with my daughter and granddaughter alone were constantly thwarted by my father, who housed and fed my progeny. But the truth was also that I was a bit scared to meet them without the buffer of others.

I had gone to my father's house to see my daughter and granddaughter twice. These meetings seemed to me to be artificially sweet, certainly nothing like real time spent with real family. My father didn't help. Sometimes his smile was true, but I also detected a fair amount of forced conviviality. He seemed to me to be less like a grandfather and more like an upscale department store greeter giving directions. Whenever I tried to have a real conversation with my daughter, my father, either on purpose or out of the cluelessness that comes from pure selfishness, would interrupt or try to enforce a light mood.

Finally I arranged to have dinner with my daughter and granddaughter at my mother's house the night before they left. I had a sneaking suspicion that my father would try to deliver them and find an excuse to stay. When I told my father on the phone that they should come on their own, he was incredulous.

"They are new here. They might lose their way," he said.

"It's six blocks, Father. The streets go north and south, east and west. You can't get lost here even if you try."

"I don't know why you are so insistent about spending time with them alone."

"What do you mean? You've already spent lots of time with them alone."

"I'm their grandfather. Of course I should spend time with them."

"And what about me?"

"You'll live for another twenty years, at least. I could drop dead tomorrow, just like my Rachela. You, on the other hand, will have plenty of time to see them in the years to come."

"You'll be torturing me and them on this planet for many more years, Father. You've said it yourself. Tonight you can spend time with the mathematicians, or whoever you want, because you won't be allowed in this house."

As the hour of their arrival approached, I became anxious. What would I say to them when we were alone? If I managed not to be stiff or affected, how would they respond to me, someone who in all respects had been the lowest of the low on the male totem pole, a deadbeat father?

I let them in, took their coats, and for the first time ever, let my gaze linger, taking their features in fully. This effort calmed me in a way I couldn't have predicted. There were little giveaways that Andrea was indeed my ex's daughter. It was more than just her eyes. There were also the occasional gestures as she talked to me that instantly sent me back in time. The way she sat on the living room couch and brushed back her hair, the way her fingertips traced the outline of her ear when she pondered something I said. In Amy, too, there were telltale signs. She looked at me so sweetly and directly, assuming that I couldn't possibly have a drop of malice or ill intent. This might have just been the innocence of childhood, but I thought not. She was born to trust, born to be open, and I hoped no one would take advantage of her blithe spirit.

We ate the food prepared by the Sisterhood. "If you ate this stuff every day," I said as I explained each dish, "you'd turn into a blimp, but it's delicious to have every once in a while."

"Your father said the same thing."

"I understand he cooked up a storm for you two."

"He's a charming man, actually."

"I'm sure he's having a delightful time with you in his house. And I'm delighted you came to visit."

As we sat in the kitchen, Amy kept looking at Pascha, who watched us intently and occasionally said a Polish phrase.

"What did she say, Grandpa?"

"Something about mathematics."

"Can she count?"

"A bit. If you show her two groups of objects and ask her which group is bigger, she'll usually come up with the right answer."

"Sometimes no, though? She doesn't get it right?"

"Sometimes she messes up, yes."

"I bet I could teach her not to mess up."

"Maybe you could. Your great-grandma Rachela was working on it."

"How old is Pascha?"

"Older than your mom. Forty or so, I think."

"That's very old."

"Not really. I think she'll live another twenty years, if she's well cared for."

I'm not used to speaking with young children. Even when I was young, I was almost always surrounded by adults. The big exception was Bruce, the official baby of the family. He was the one who, depending on the guest list, was often stuck with the task of reading the four questions at the family seder well into his twenties.

Amy, I could tell, had a similar adult-centered life. She had also started to develop the ability (or liability) of being in one place physically but only partially there mentally. It was like dealing with a cell phone wavering between one and two bars of reception, functional but a bit worrisome. Her mind was not in the here and now but was usually preoccupied, just like my mind, just like my father's, and just like my mother's. This habit of only sort of being present can drive nonacademics crazy. But it's the only way I know that anyone can solve intellectually difficult problems. It's a constant processing of ideas and techniques in the background that happens even when you dream.

As Andrea and I talked, I knew Amy was working on some idea of hers. I could have asked her what it was, but whenever someone asked me such questions, it would momentarily break the spell. As curious as I was, I didn't want to be cruel. Andrea and I went into the living room, and Amy asked if she could stay and watch the parrot. Her mother told her not to touch it. I seconded that advice, noting that Pascha had a sharp beak and had chewed on my finger more than a few times.

"It's nice to have this living room quiet and peaceful at night," I said.

"Did you grow up in this house?" Andrea asked.

"Oh, yes. From the time I was five until I was fourteen and went off to boarding school."

"Your father lived with you?"

"Definitely. My parents didn't break up until I was in my twenties."

"Not like me then." Andrea averted her gaze. "Not like Amy, either," she said and gave a laugh.

"She see her father much?"

"Oh no. Not at all. Followed in the footsteps of Mum, I guess. Fell in love with the wrong kind of man." Then and there Andrea was looking right at me.

"I'm not a bad person, Andrea."

"I can see you're not bad now. But maybe you were back then."

"I wasn't bad. Just self-obsessed."

"Well, that sounds bad, too, though. You weren't robbing banks, I guess. You cheat on Mum?"

"No, not with another woman. Just with my work."

"Mum's like that, too. I didn't like it growing up."

"Amy probably will be like that, too." I shouldn't have hedged. I knew it was true in my bones.

"I can see that."

"It's wonderful to see her. You, too."

"I'm glad I came. I didn't know what to expect."

"I didn't know what to expect either. I'd always wondered what you were like, though."

"Me too, of course. Actually, I thought you'd have a beard. I asked Mum once when I was little what you were like, and she said you were like a cross child, someone who never listened. You were a bit wild, she said. So I thought you might be like Tarzan, in a loincloth or something like that."

"I did have a beard when I met your mother. But I shaved it just before we got married. I found some pictures of your mother and me upstairs the other day. I can show them to you if you'd like."

"I just saw the wedding pictures. I asked to see them the last time I was at Grandmother's house with Amy. She didn't want to show them to me, but I insisted."

"I have those at my home. I haven't looked at them in a long time."

"You should," Andrea said. "You look so happy in them. Mum, too."

"We were happy. Very much so."

"And then you weren't. How does that happen?"

I looked at Andrea's face carefully. She was young, it's true, but already she'd felt the world of adult hurt. I certainly had never tried to protect her, but I guessed my ex had made an effort. "People make horrible mistakes," I said. "Unforgivable ones." I walked over to a shelf where I'd placed the little box of photographs from my youth. When I had graduated from college, my parents had bought me an Olympus OM-1 camera. It was the first time I had something that gave crystal-clear pictures. I still have that camera, and even paid a little money to have it cleaned a few years ago. Back then, I would screw the camera onto a tripod, set the timer, and run into the picture to be next to Catherine. Nowadays the timer no longer works, but it still takes wonderful photos with black-and-white film, far more natural than can be achieved with a digital camera.

I placed the photos on the coffee table, and Andrea looked at them one by one. She was deeply absorbed, trying to take it all in. How well did the images correspond with the ones she had invented over the years?

"Oh my god, I'm in this one, aren't I?" she asked. She put her hand over her mouth, and I could tell that she was not just surprised. She was thrilled at this discovery.

"Yes, that bulge is you. We called you Cletus the Fetus."

"And that's your mum and dad there, yes?"

"Yes, me, your mother, your grandfather, your grandmother, and you."

"Your mum was beautiful. I never asked what your mum and dad were like. Only you."

"I should have tried to find you. Then you would have known what I was like. I shouldn't have made you try to guess."

"You seem like a kindhearted sort. Like the kind of person who would have tried."

"People change. Sometimes they get better. Sometimes they get worse."

"And you've gotten better, I guess?"

"I don't know, really. I hope so." Andrea was still holding the picture of all of us in her right hand. It had been taken at our little dacha on a lake. It was fall. In the black-and-white photo, you couldn't tell that the leaves were changing color. My father was wearing a pressed white shirt and dark wool pants. Catherine was in a flowery maternity dress that she had bought from a store that sold local handmade clothing. A few weeks before the picture had been taken, a woman came up to us beaming, saying she made that dress and that she was so happy to see it being worn. My mother was in a cotton blouse and a mid-length skirt. She was taller than all except me. I wore blue jeans and a T-shirt. At the time, I was completely certain that this picture would be followed by many more of all of us together. There was not the slightest doubt in my mind that my family would blossom and that sunshine would follow us most days. I still have moments like this. I don't understand where they come from. It's a muted form of the American view that by destiny all things in life end happily. It's a flaw of the mind really, this rosy view, but I am thankful that this flaw exists in most of us.

"Can I keep this picture?" Andrea asked.

"Of course," I said.

"You won't miss it?"

"I have negatives of them all back home," I said. "It's OK." I didn't know if that was actually true, but it didn't matter to me either way.

Amy walked into the living room. "Grandpa, how do you say, 'Which is bigger?' in Polish?"

"Która porcja jest większa?"

"Say that again, Grandpa." I did. She walked back into the kitchen.

"I wish I had come earlier. I could have met your mum."

"She would have liked that, I'm sure. But she and your mother didn't get along at all."

"So you had to choose, I guess."

"I didn't think of it that way at the time, but that's one way to look at it. Your mother know about you coming here?"

"I haven't told her yet. I will, though."

"I should talk to her. It's pathetic that I haven't."

"I don't know if that's a good idea, Sasha. I'll ask her if it's OK."

"I appreciate that. Truly do."

"Grandpa, Mum, come here, please," Amy said.

We walked back into the kitchen. Amy was standing next to

the kitchen table. Pascha stood perched on a small inverted wicker basket that was usually used to hold salt and pepper shakers. In front of Pascha were two small dishes. Amy had a box of Cheerios in the crook of her arm and reached down, putting four Cheerios in one dish and five in another.

"*Która porcja jest większa?*" Amy asked. I'd never heard Polish spoken with a New Zealand accent before. Pascha didn't seem to mind. She reached down and pecked at the five-Cheerio dish. Amy took the four cheerios off the other.

"She got it right, see? So far, she's only got it wrong once. She knows which one has more."

"That's a smart bird, Amy," Andrea said. "But what did I tell you about not touching her."

"I didn't touch her. I just opened the cage and Pascha came out. So then I had to touch her."

"It's going to be a lot of work getting Pascha back in," I said.

"Oh no, it won't," Amy said. She reached for the bird with her right hand.

"Be gentle," Andrea said.

Pascha was still in a good mood. She was bobbing her head now and then as she focused on Amy. Pascha didn't like big crowds, but having a few people in a room talking softly was something she usually enjoyed.

"I know what to do," Amy said. "Just what I did when she got out except backwards." She extended her right hand vertically and Pascha hopped on. Amy walked to the cage and stepped onto the chair that she had evidently placed there to open the cage door earlier, making sure to keep the hand upon which Pascha was perched steady. Standing in front of the black wire cage, Amy raised her arm and slowly guided Pascha through the door. I watched as Pascha hopped off and found her usual perch.

"You can close the door now, Amy." I said.

"I know, Grandpa."

"*Dobry ptaszek,*" I said. "That means 'good bird,' Amy."

"Does she speak English at all?"

"No, Amy."

"I can learn Polish. Say that again, please." I repeated the phrase. "*Dobry ptaszek*, Pascha," Amy said. "See. It isn't that hard."

CHAPTER 27

In the Wee Hours of the Morn

DAY 5

After I said good-bye to my daughter and granddaughter, I felt as good as I had felt in decades. I knew what my father thought about these instant additions to our family without even asking him. He looked at the generation beyond me and imagined being a beacon for them, an essential source of wisdom, and an occasional source of financial backing for big-ticket items, like a home.

But I had no such plans. My state of joy wasn't emanating from a vision of a happy future. I simply felt vindicated, but no, that isn't quite the right word. In Russian I might say I experienced a *nevo-obrazimaya pobeda*, a sense of relief that my past hadn't been a black mark after all, that it had, not through anything I had actively done, produced something of never-imagined value. I had a daughter with a warm heart who saw the world with clear-eyed realism and a granddaughter who possessed a rare mind capable of focusing on problems that bored or scared mere mortals.

As I write these words, that granddaughter is studying mathematics at Yale. After she won the Woodward Prize—normally awarded by the American Mathematical Society for the best paper published by a graduate student—at the ridiculously young age of sixteen, a fellow freshman clipped out a picture of my granddaughter from the *Yale Daily News*, framed it with makeshift paper Ionic columns and an arch, and pinned the whole thing on the bulletin board outside the math department office. It became an ad hoc temple where students could kneel and pray prior to their calculus and differential equation exams. My granddaughter became, for a time, Yale's unofficial matron saint of good undergraduate math grades. Of course, I couldn't have predicted such a future at the time. I was simply joyful over what she was, not what she would become.

I liken my marriage in my twenties to the ill-chosen shot by a basketball player, done without any thought from an impossible angle and motivated by a mix of pure adrenaline and ego, which his coach watches with complete despair as he involuntarily shouts "nooooo." Then, as the shot miraculously drops through the net, the coach's cry changes instantly from "nooooo" to "yessss." My marriage had been a shambles in its motivation and execution. But it had produced something wonderful and miraculous.

Anna came home that night and noticed the difference. "You had a good evening, didn't you, Sasha?"

"The best."

"You deserve some luck."

"Not really. I've been a lucky man all along."

"You think so? Really?"

"Definitely. You look like you had a good evening yourself."

"It wasn't bad." Anna looked down at the Persian carpet. I could still see her smile.

"You don't want to talk about it, do you."

"No."

"You don't want to jinx it?"

"I'm not superstitious, Sasha."

"You think you've been lucky?"

"I don't allow myself to be unlucky. I don't have any complaints. It's been a good life."

"I think so, too."

"I feel good for you, though. A man should have children. Ones he knows about, especially." Anna reached up to give me a sisterly kiss on the cheek.

Our happiness would not, however, be allowed to last through the night. The phone rang a little before 3:00 A.M., never a good sign. It was from the ranger of the Wisconsin Arboretum. "Is this the home of Alexander Karnokovitch?" Not too many people were calling me by my legal name during the shiva. Even if the call had come at a normal hour, I would have sensed that it was important.

"Yes, of course."

"I'm sorry to call you so late, but I received your number from someone. He was crazy and ranting, but he did come up with this number when I asked if there was someone that I could call for some verification."

"Big older man? Bushy mustache? Russian accent? Konstantin Otrnlov?"

"He was Russian, yeah. But no, not that name. Zhelezniak. Vladimir Zhelezniak. You know him?"

"Sure I do. Where is he?"

"Let me tell you how I met him, first. He was skiing in the Arboretum. Just in his long johns. Drunk. With a woman. Ms. Virginia Potter, according to her Massachusetts driver's license. It's twenty below outside, and he's skiing after hours in his underwear."

"That's what he does. It's hard to explain. Maybe you knew my mother, Rachela Karnokovitch?"

"Yeah, I figured that you must be related. Nice lady. Sorry to hear about your loss."

"She used to ski, too."

"Yeah, I'd see her all the time. Sometimes with your father."

"She and Zhelezniak, they both had the same mentor in Russia. He believed skiing, especially in the cold, inspired the mind."

"OK, I get that. But I don't think your mom ever came out here in her nightgown."

"Probably not, no."

"This guy, Zhelezniak, he was out here at two A.M. And he was in his underwear. Just about naked. I wouldn't have noticed except I was coming home late from a date and I saw him and that woman alongside the road. Couldn't believe it. I pulled over. He started screaming at me. I told him to get in the car. Man, he was sauced, all that alcohol just came off him. She was, too."

"Can I talk to them now?"

"They wouldn't cooperate. I've never seen anything like that in twenty years. Good skier, though."

"He's been skiing for fifty years. Can I talk to Vladimir?"

"Um, no. I mean, he isn't here. I called the cops. They picked him up. That happened about ten minutes ago. I processed a couple of forms before I'd forget the details of what happened. Then I called you."

"You had them arrested?"

"Well, yeah. Crazy guy. Screaming. Her, too. I didn't know what he was saying. Screaming in Russian. Who knows? But that woman. I knew what she was saying. She's got a mouth on her."

"She's a professor of mathematics at Amherst."

"Yeah. And I have a master's in forestry from Yale. Big deal.

You still need to treat people with respect. I don't really care who she is and where she's from, but the names she called me, I don't care to repeat them here."

"I'm sorry she was rude. We've been under a lot of stress. My mother died. Both those two came here for the funeral. Dear friends. It's been hard on us, you know."

"I'm sorry to hear."

"I hope you don't press charges. I know they were rude. They should pay a fine, I know. But I hope you'll consider the circumstances."

"Well, yeah. I suppose. A nice lady like your mother should have better friends though, sorry to say."

"Work friends, they were. Essential to her research. Personally, well, you've seen what they are like."

"No joke. Well, they'd have to apologize in person. Especially that woman, Potter. I've never been cussed out like that. There's no need for that kind of language. Plus, there's still the fine for trespassing. At least one hundred bucks, maybe more."

"I think it should be more. The Arboretum could always use some extra money, no doubt. I'll make sure she apologizes tomorrow morning. I promise."

"Your mom was a Friend of the Arboretum, you know. We appreciated all her support over the years. Good skier, too, just like that Russian dude tonight. Good form even though he was drunk as a skunk. I'll call the cops and tell them I won't press charges. But I guess you're going to have to pick them up, Mr. Karnokovitch."

"I'll happily do that. And I promise they'll come by tomorrow."

It was freezing outside, colder than I'd experienced in I didn't know how long. I drove alone in my mother's Volvo to the police station, and of course hardly anyone was on the road. The police had rounded up an orange prisoner's outfit so that Zhelezniak wouldn't be parading around the cop shop in his *kalsony*, although I think that he would have preferred his immodest attire to playing the role of prisoner. Fortunately, Potter had been appropriately attired all along.

"It's worse than Russia here. A man can't even ski when he wants. What kind of freedom is that?" Zhelezniak said in the car.

"They treated us like we were common criminals!" Potter said.

Listening to those two bitch and moan after I'd groveled to keep charges from being pressed was more than I could handle. Right then and there I hated them both. Their level of privilege and childishness was stratospheric. I knew that if Anna were with me, she would have launched into a flurry of insults. Maybe because I heard so many of these invectives from Anna, from my parents, and from all those I loved, I've always felt that there was no need for me to contribute to the family's already prodigious lexicon of barbs. That's not my role.

"How is it going with Hilbert's twenty-third, anyway?" I asked Zhelezniak in Russian. "You've been at it nonstop. Making any progress?"

"That's not the kind of question you ask a mathematician, Sasha. You should know that. And it's Hilbert's sixth, more or less."

"Six. Twenty-three. Thirteen. Fifteen. Some numbers are more difficult than others. You've been working so hard, both of you. Everyone has. And Hilbert's sixth. Navier-Stokes, whatever you call it. It's such a difficult problem."

"Are you being sarcastic, Sasha?"

"Oh no. I know it's difficult. My mother started to work on this problem when she was eleven years old. That's when she made her first insight."

"She told you this?" Zhelezniak asked.

"Sort of, yes. Those two pieces of paper you have been looking at for years now. They are from that time, I'm sure. She even talks about them in her memoirs. They've traveled a long way, from the Barents Sea to Moscow and now to the improbable location of Madison, Wisconsin. Sixty years old, those papers are. The drawings and writings of an eleven-year-old girl."

"Not just any eleven-year-old girl, Sasha."

"True. And somehow you have to go from those papers to a full-blown proof. That's a long distance to travel."

"You're taunting us, Sasha?"

"No, I'm not. I'm just telling you that I know you won't succeed."

"What are you two talking about? I don't understand a word," Potter said.

"We were talking about the fine for trespassing. Two hundred dollars each, maybe more. And the fact that you are both going to have to apologize to the Arboretum ranger tomorrow morning."

"I'm not going to apologize to that dreadful man. He treated me like I was a convicted felon."

"Yes, you will. You are going to say you were sorry for swearing at him. You are going to pay your fine. Otherwise you will be arrested. And I won't pick you up next time."

CHAPTER 28

Desperate Measures

DAY 5

Anna, my uncle, and I were in the dining room. My father, daughter, and granddaughter were planning to stop by before they went to the airport. Zhelezniak and Potter were apologizing to the Arboretum ranger and paying their fines. Bruce and Ari Karansky were, according to the rumor mill, discovering their level of compatibility. The absence of these people had temporarily lowered the noise and energy level in my mother's house. It was almost like a normal shiva. Yakov walked into the dining room, plopped down, and began to devour some *tzimmis* that the rabbi's wife had sent. "It's not as good as Jenny's cooking, but I can understand why the rabbi has been married to this woman for so long," Yakov said.

"I think it's more than the food, Yakov. A lot more," I said.

"Don't be so sure of yourself, Sasha," Anna said.

"I think Jenny thought I was crazy," Yakov said.

"Not really," I said. "And she's used to crazy, probably. Her father was in the physics department. Still is. He's emeritus."

"Academic brat, just like you. I'm probably not good enough for her, she thinks. And now I've scared the *printsessa* away."

"She's coming by to bring some dinner tonight. So you must not have been too scary."

"Really?" Yakov's mood turned hopeful.

"Yes, really."

"What is she bringing?"

"I have no idea. I didn't ask." Of course, I was lying.

"You didn't ask? Because of your lack of curiosity I'm going to be thinking about your mystery dinner all day and night. I'll be a worthless contributor to the problem at hand."

"You can't stay for dinner, anyway. Those are the rules. We pray *mincha-maariv* and then all of you have to go. I need some peace and quiet."

"You'll have lots of peace and quiet," Anna said.

"You abandoning me again?"

"Of course," Anna said.

"We have plans," my uncle said. "We're going to meet with Avi's brother, Shimon, and his wife."

"A double date?" I asked.

"Have some respect for your elders, Sasha," my uncle said and gave me the Czerneski death stare even though he knew it had no effect on me.

"Whatever involves that guy can't be any good," I said.

"You don't have any respect for religion, Sasha. For you it's all mumbo jumbo," my uncle said.

"And what about you, Anna? Do you have respect for religion?" I asked.

"I don't know if I do or don't," Anna said. "All I know is that some things can't be explained."

"I didn't think you were superstitious," I said.

"I'm not. It's just that since your mother died I've been having a crazy dream," Anna said.

"And I've been having the same one. Both of us. Your mother is talking to us in our dreams. How do you explain that, Mr. Scientist?"

"What does she say?" I asked.

"I can't make it out," my uncle said. "I wish I could. It's a strange mix. Some Russian, Polish, Hebrew, and languages I don't even know. Anna can't make it out, either. It's like she's trying to talk to us, but she can't quite do it," Shlomo said.

"Maybe it has something to do with mathematics," Yakov said.

"Yeah, right," I said. "My mother is trying to give them the solution to Navier-Stokes."

"Could be," Yakov said.

"I was joking, Yakov."

"And I'm not, Sasha," Yakov said.

"When did you start believing in ghosts?" I asked.

"I don't believe in ghosts. I believe in opportunities," Yakov said.

"Reb Ben-Zvi says maybe her soul has risen to be judged and there are complications," my uncle said.

"Her *yechida*, *chaya*, *neshamah*, *ruach*, and *nefesh* residing in the Garden of Eden, waiting for the world to come."

"See, you know the names of the souls, Sasha. Don't make light of them. You've never been close to death. You don't know anything,"

"I still say *Modeh*, thanking God for returning my soul every morning. It's a beautiful prayer. I'm not a complete heathen," I said.

"But you don't believe that your soul rises when you sleep and comes back when you wake. It's just poetry for you, but I believe it," Shlomo said. "Your mother's soul, her *neshamah*, is up on high. It can't come back down, but maybe it wants to say one last word to us."

"So you're going to try to talk to the dead tonight? That's against the rules, you know," I said.

"We aren't going to talk to your mother. Reb Ben-Zvi says there is another way. We're just going to listen."

"Listen away, Uncle. I wish you luck. At least Bruce will be here with me," I said.

"Are you sure?" Anna asked.

"Yeah, he called and said he'd be here in an hour."

"What about him and that mathematician?" Anna asked.

"Clingy. 'Very clingy,'" he said.

"Insecure. They all are like that except for your mother. The one in the living room I was married to was like that," Anna said. She shook her head in judgment.

"I wouldn't have guessed."

"Neither did I, obviously."

"You've said hardly a word to him."

"What is there to say? He was a disappointment from long ago. And now he has ballooned up. Disgusting. I barely recognize him."

"We should all stay away from mathematicians, Bruce included," I said.

"You're being mean to us, Sasha," Yakov said. "At least do me the courtesy of saving me some of Jenny's delicious leftovers for tomorrow's lunch."

"That I'll do. You really think you're going to solve Navier-Stokes during this shiva?"

"It's our best shot. She ever talk to you about it? What she was working on?"

"She hadn't published a math paper in ten years, Yakov. She was out of the business."

"One thing does not mean another. This problem would take a long time to solve. A singular effort. Total concentration would be needed, even for your mother."

"She was working on the family history, Yakov," my uncle said. "She was going to turn it into a novel. It was going to be a good one, I know."

"A multigenerational family saga," I said.

"Only Slavs know how to do this. What do the Americans have? *Gone With the Wind*? Sentimental trash with no heart. It's a shallow country," my uncle said.

"The audiences, too. They watch, but their eyes might as well be closed. They look without comprehension," Anna said.

"Yet we all came here, didn't we?" Yakov asked.

"Absolutely," Shlomo said. "It's the best place in the world for a smart man to be. All this money, all this opportunity, and only stupid, lazy Americans to compete against. It's heaven on earth."

"Your mother flourished here, Sasha," Yakov said.

"I'm very glad we came, don't get me wrong. But really, my mother did her best work in Russia," I said.

"No distractions. Nothing good to do. No fun. So you work. I danced better there, too," Anna said. She had a faraway, dreamy look, something rare for her.

"When you went with Rachela to visit Russia, and you went to Moscow State with her. Do you know what she did in that office while you were a lookout?" Yakov asked.

"Me? I told you before. It wasn't my business," Anna said.

"Probably she had some papers still there. More than just the ones Poponov found," Yakov said.

"My sister was good at hiding things," Shlomo said.

"We would like to look for the papers, Sasha," Yakov said.

"Look for them? Where?"

"In the house."

"Look away."

"We've already looked. Five days we've been here. Looking."

"I thought so far you were mostly organizing stuff upstairs. It's a mess up there."

"Organizing. Looking. What's the difference? We've looked everywhere. Here. In Rachela's office. We need to look deeper."

"Deeper?"

"Yes, deeper."

My uncle seemed keenly interested in this conversation for reasons I couldn't fathom. "It's a good idea," he said.

I looked at my uncle. "What's a good idea?"

"Look deeper. The walls. The floorboards. Open them up."

"Are you crazy? You want to tear apart this house to look for some pieces of paper that don't exist?"

"I don't give a damn about the papers," my uncle said. "But your mother. I know my sister. She's got some money somewhere in here. Cash money."

"She never told me about any money."

"She didn't have to. She knew we'd look."

"You're both crazy."

My father, who had arrived with my newly discovered family, entered the dining room. He looked a bit sad, his usual regal air absent. He'd been drinking already, I could tell, something that was as unusual for him as it was for the rest of my family. In the daytime there was always serious work to be done. But this wasn't a normal daytime. Even my father was having bouts of melancholy over the loss of my mother.

"Viktor, you knew her better than anyone," my uncle said. "Where would she hide it?"

"Hide what?"

"The money. The proof. Where would she hide anything?"

Somehow through the fog of alcohol, something clicked in my father. "Oh my god," he said. He walked upstairs. We followed. In the room of my childhood, we helped my father move a bookcase. Word spread downstairs, and the crowd of mathematicians rushed up the staircase into the hallway. A screwdriver was requested, and the two triplets present descended to the kitchen in a panic to retrieve the tool. As my father lifted the floorboard in the corner of the room next to the clothes closet, there was complete silence.

"Here," he said. He pulled up a metal ammunition box and handed it to me. The thing weighed about a dozen pounds.

"Open it!" my uncle said.

I did as I was instructed, opened the latch, and yanked on the lid, watching its sticky rubber lining stretch and finally yield. I looked inside. It was full of coins, twenty-ruble pieces from the time of the last tsar.

"In Russia, you could have bought a cow with each one," my father said.

"Great. I could have a herd of three hundred cattle," I said.

My uncle was beaming. "I knew it!" he said.

"Where did these come from?" I asked.

"She collected them. It was a long time ago. They weren't worth much back then. Gold was cheap. And nobody in America or Russia had any interest in tsarist coins. Your mother, underneath it all, was a very sentimental woman," my father said.

"But what about the proof, Viktor?" Yakov asked.

"There is no proof hidden anywhere, you idiots," my father said. Disappointment for Slavs is always more poetic and profound, as well as more frequent, than it is for Americans. The collective sigh of the eleven mathematicians in the house, for many of whom English was a second, third, or fourth language, was palpable.

The adrenaline surge caused by our mad search, so surprisingly successful for lucre but so devastatingly unsuccessful in terms of intellectual treasure, had left all of us by the time Zhelezniak, Potter, Bruce, and Ari—our shiva's lovebirds—returned. Bruce, upon hearing the news, asked to see the coins. I placed them on the kitchen table. A crowd gathered, the way it always does when something that glitters is placed in view. Bruce was sincerely impressed by the bounty.

"That's easily thirty K right there," he said. "Way to go, Aunt Rachela."

"I thought you weren't good at math," I said.

"That's not math. That's arithmetic. I could always do arithmetic," Bruce said.

"He does have a good head for numbers," Uncle Shlomo said. "He got it from me."

"What are you going to do with it?" Bruce asked.

"I don't know. Maybe I'll start a ranch."

Zhelezniak looked at the coins in the green metal box, picked one up, and rubbed it between his fingers, a rueful expression on his face. "Eighteen ninety-seven. One hundred years ago. The problems were easier to solve then."

"Only in hindsight," one of the triplets said. "Important problems are always difficult to solve."

"Perhaps."

My granddaughter, Amy, was looking up at Pascha. "Can I take her out, Grandpa?"

"There are too many people around for that, Amy," I said. "Maybe later, when things quiet down."

"She can handle Pascha?" Bruce asked.

"Apparently yes," I said.

"Amy likes Russian food, too," Yakov noted. "It's almost like a reincarnation."

"She does have a gift for math, it's true," my father said, and gave her an affectionate pat on the head.

"An *ayzene kepl*," my uncle said. "I don't feel so bad anymore. I thought this family was dead. Now look. It keeps going." He gave my daughter a patriarchal gaze that I didn't even know he possessed. "Both of you need to have children," he said. "She in twenty years. You a couple more in the next ten wouldn't be bad either."

"I need to find a good man first," Andrea said.

"It's true," said Anna. "So many men. But most aren't worth even a penny."

"I'm a good man," Shlomo said. "There are others, too. Don't be so pessimistic."

Zhelezniak looked down at Amy, who was ignoring the conversation and watching Pascha. "She's been studying?"

"Yes, with Professor Shackleworth," Andrea said.

"At Berkeley?"

"Yes."

"He's a good man. He wouldn't waste time on someone without talent. She must have a gift."

"He's why we're here now. He had a hunch we were related to Professor Karnokovitch."

"I'd like to show her some mathematics from her great-grandmother. Would you mind?"

"Zhelezniak, she's six years old," I said. "My mother was eleven when she drew those pictures."

"A gift is a gift, Sasha."

"You want to show her Rachela's papers, do you, Vladimir?" my father asked with his thin-lipped smile.

"Of course. What would be the harm?"

"What's next? You going to show the papers to Pascha, too?" I asked.

"Actually, we already sort of did this," Peter Orlansky said. He looked up at the cage at Pascha and continued, "*Chcemy zbadać skalowanie funkcji różniczkowalnej w sposób ciągły.*"

"*Następujący postulat,*" Pascha squawked.

"Pascha likes you. I've never seen her so perky with a man," I said to Peter. "I didn't know you knew Polish."

"My parents. It was their secret language—the one they used when they didn't want me to understand what they were saying—until I picked it up."

"What did they go to after that?"

"They switched to Russian. But I picked that up as well."

"What did you say to Pascha?" Amy asked Peter.

"I asked her about the existence of continuously differentiable functions," Peter said.

"And what did she say back?"

"Gibberish, really."

"Gibberish? About what?"

"Something about the existence of a postulate. Do you know what a postulate is?"

"Yes, a little."

"Do you know what a continuously differentiable function is?"

"No. But it makes sense. If you can differentiate a function, you should be able to differentiate it everywhere, I think."

"Not always, Amy. But lots of times you can," Peter said.

"When can't you?" Amy asked. Now all eyes were on my little granddaughter, whose own eyes were no longer on Pascha but directed toward the tall Princeton professor who had wished so ardently for so many years that my mother would come to Princeton and stay, whose broad shoulders and athletic build belied his lack of coordination, whose wife dressed him every morning before he went to campus, whose dress was absent of any color coordination given that he was on his own in Madison, and who was categorically incapable of looking anyone in the eye, even the great-granddaughter of his best collaborator.

"Show her the papers, Peter," Vladimir said, pulling out the thin sheets from his coat pocket.

"If he shows them to her, Vladimir, she gets to keep them," my father said.

"What?" Vladimir turned around.

"This is the work of her great-grandmother and my wife. It's only fitting that they be hers to keep."

"I need to copy them first."

"No. You've stared at them for a dozen years already. They haven't done you any good. If Amy looks at them, she keeps them. Have a seat, Amy. Professor Orlansky wants to show you something."

"Is it OK, Andrea?" I asked.

"I don't see why not."

Amy sat down, and the gentle giant, Peter Orlansky, sat next to her. He placed the two sheets on the kitchen table. "Your great-grandmother was just a little older than you when she made these drawings, Amy," my father said.

"She was good at drawing," Amy said, examining the papers.

"It's of the Barents Sea, an ocean a long ways away," my father said.

"Did she swim in the sea?"

"I don't think so. The water is very cold."

"And she drew birds that were there, too?" Amy asked.

"Mosquitoes. There were lots of mosquitoes where she was," I said.

"That's right, Amy," my father said, and shot me a look.

"That's funny that she drew mosquitoes." Amy gave a giggle. "They must have been really big."

"She was trying to understand them, Amy," Peter said. "And the waves in the sea too, I think. How they moved. She thought there was some connection between them. That the equations that described the movement of both were more closely related than any of us think they are."

"There are a lot of equations here. She wrote so small," Amy said, touching the greasy surface of each paper.

"Paper was very hard to come by back then," my father said.

"She was trying to show that the equations that described the movement of both the waves and the mosquitoes were continuously differentiable, that they were related," Peter said. "If she could show one was continuously differentiable, then by extension, the other must also be so."

"It makes sense," Amy said.

"It does," Peter said. "But we don't understand the relationship between the two. That's the problem. Your great-grandmother didn't tell us how the two equations were so close. They look too different for any of us to make any headway."

"The mosquitoes aren't as big as the waves, but she drew them like they were," Amy said.

"Exactly," Peter said. "And if you looked at the waves real close, if you really got up to them, you'd see that there were smaller and smaller waves inside the big ones."

"Waves as small as mosquitoes, even?" Amy asked.

"Yes."

"Now that's really funny," Amy said.

"We want you to look at what your grandmother wrote here," Zhelezniak said. "She was a little girl just like you. She was trying to understand this problem."

"Not all the writing is the same. The stuff on top is different," Amy said.

"That's right, Amy," I said. "She had a teacher back then, just like you have Professor Shackleworth. He wrote down the beginning of the problem. And then she started to finish it."

"It looks really hard, what she was doing."

"It was very hard," Peter said in that quiet monotone of his that made some people, those not in the know, think he was mentally retarded when he was a teen.

"Look at it very carefully," Zhelezniak said. "Start with this line first." Zhelezniak took his slender index finger to a point below the pictures of mosquitoes hovering in space.

"There are a lot of words. What language is it?"

"Some Russian. Some Polish, just like Pascha speaks," I said.

"I want to learn Polish, Grandpa. I want to speak to Pascha."

"And then you could understand what your great-grandmother wrote when she was a child, too," I said.

"Yeah, I'd like to understand."

"This is worthless," Zhelezniak said in Russian.

"You were never going to solve this problem, anyway. You're too old. We're all too old," my father said.

"What did you say, Great-grandpa?" Amy asked my father.

"I said that you can keep Great-grandma Rachela's drawings. She would have wanted you to have them, I know."

"Can I go to the ocean where she was one day? I'd like to see where she drew this. I'd like to see the big mosquitoes."

CHAPTER 29

Mama's Boy

DAY 5

Four days of relying on someone else's cooking was getting on my nerves. I understood this part of the logic of shiva. You are grieving. You are lost in thinking about your loss. Cooking is work. Someone else should do it. But cooking is also about memory, especially when it comes to the loss of mothers, at least for mothers who cook. I wouldn't say that my mother had a talent for cooking, but she did have an understanding of the basic dos and don'ts. My memories of her at breakfast or at dinner were almost always positive. Why would I not want to think about those good days while I mourned?

On winter nights, when I was a kid, the food would come to the table like a gift. Steam rose from the main dish. Dinner would take place in the early evening just after sunset. Questions would be asked about school. My mother liked to keep tabs on me. My father liked to hear about my successes. Often there would be visitors. The émigrés would speak in Russian. The mathematicians would speak in their own symbolic language. Once I turned eight years old, the expectation was that I would not shy away from participating in the interplay. I knew Russian. I knew enough mathematics to be conversant. I was a Karnokovitch. I was supposed to be smart and was not supposed to be shy about my intelligence, either.

To Americans, the outward display of intelligence is considered unseemly. The Donald Trumps of the world can boast about their penthouses and Ferraris, their women can wear baubles the size of Nebraska, and no one says boo. If you have money, you're almost always expected to flaunt it. But intellect? This is something else entirely. Women, especially, are supposed to play dumb. One of the richest men in America has said publicly that if your SAT score is too high, find a way to sell 200 points. Supposedly you don't need them.

This inability of Americans to value intellect is, to me, maddening. If someone possesses physical beauty, they will not be cloistered or hidden in dark shadows. No, they are expected to be the source of pleasing scenery to others. We are not frightened in this country by beauty. We celebrate it, as we should. But what about beautiful brains, the kind that can create amazing worlds out of nothing but thoughts, that can find a way to intricately bond elements of our lives and our ideas that conventional wisdom tells us are inert? Why should anyone hide this intellect ever? No. Fuck boring financiers like Warren Buffett. If you have a high score on your SAT, don't sell a single point. In fact, find a way to get smart enough to achieve a perfect score. There is no such thing as unnecessary beauty, whether it be physical or intellectual.

During these dinners, as in every aspect of her life, my mother was incapable of hiding just how smart she was. Her intelligence was perhaps the first thing after her long blond braids that anyone noticed. If someone was scared off, so be it. But for those who stuck around there was another side she often showed, a nurturing aspect that for some was life-changing, as it was for Anna.

She touched people, ordinary people in the community, especially women in her synagogue. When I visited Madison, women

I didn't know would sometimes, if they learned that I was Rachela's son, erupt in unsolicited praise. Jenny Rivkin was one of those women my mother influenced. I could tell from her earnestness when she walked into the house to deliver her carefully cooked meals. She'd walk in and quickly, too quickly for Yakov, be gone, her task done.

On the fifth night of shiva, I ignored the piles of casseroles, salads, cookies, and cakes and pulled out some pots and pans to make a meal, something simple but resonant of the family dinners of our past. Each utensil I touched—and they had been unchanged for decades—reminded me of what a mama's boy I was. I had watched my mother make this and that on my tiptoes next to the yellow Formica counter. I had savored the sweetness of the batters from the beaters and the bowls, removing each speck with a spatula, and then with my tongue.

"Make sure it's something halfway healthy," Bruce said as he came into the kitchen.

"You're getting kasha."

"Skip the *varnishkes*, please. A vegetable or two would be good. I haven't seen a vegetable in a week, I swear."

"There's some broccoli. I'll cook it up for you. Some chicken livers. A little onion, and we'll be done."

"What about Jenny? She told me she was coming over with a main dish."

"Oh shit, I forgot. I just wanted to cook something. The kasha is already on the stove. You get *varnishkes*, too. You can't have kasha without *varnishkes*. It's an ironclad rule."

"Those are the old rules, Sasha. We make the rules now. We're the grown-ups."

"If you're a grown-up, you don't look like you're making good rules. You've been looking like shit all day."

"Thanks for the compliment. I'm forty-one, you know. In my twenties, I could party and wake up the next day fresh as a fucking daisy. Now look at me. Takes me two days to recover."

"Your body is telling you to give up that shit."

"No, it's telling me to be more picky."

"What is your connection with Jenny, anyway?"

"Oh, I don't know. It's ancient history. We both went to Madison West, but she wasn't in my crowd. Then I was off to Williams. Probably the last time I saw her was twenty-five years ago. She had a fantastic bat mitzvah party, if I remember correctly. Brought in a DJ from Milwaukee."

"No expense spared."

"I saw her two days ago, though. That's why she's coming tonight."

"You invited her over to cook dinner?" I wanted to know who had set up this date.

"Kind of. It was her idea. But I encouraged it."

"And what exactly happened?"

"She asked about you. My idea was to figure out a way for her to find out how you were doing. She came up with dinner." This sounded both plausible and not made up.

"Well, whatever she's cooked, it better go with kasha and *vanishkes*."

"Everything goes with kasha and *varnishkes*."

"Is that a new rule?"

"No. It's a stupid excuse for ignoring that someone is cooking for us."

"I had no idea you were a *shadchan*."

My cousin smiled at the thought of being a matchmaker in a shtetl. "It's a talent that I do have, actually. I'm good at arranging and organizing all matters. Ask Barbra. Ask Reba. They'll both vouch for me. Do me a favor."

"What?"

"When Jenny comes, do not drop into that phony Russian accent of yours. You sound like a street-corner phone-card hawk in Brighton Beach."

"How do I sound now?"

"OK, that works. But I still don't understand how someone who came here at the age of four can even have a hint of Moscow in his voice. If you start saying *zees* for 'this' I'll kick you under the table, you understand?"

When Jenny came, there was no need for table kicks. Initially I had to work hard to avoid slipping into my alter ego of émigré intellectual, a warmer, kinder, and indeed softer version of my father. In my forties I had added the air of wisdom gained through experience. This addition to my bag of tricks seemed surprisingly effective for a subset of the American female public. As they say in both Yiddish and Gaelic (and doubtless another dozen languages at least), for every pot there is a lid. But that night I was just me, and that meant I was quieter than usual, more earnest, and undoubtedly a lot more boring. Take away my alter ego and what's left is the heart and soul of a typical unvarnished Midwesterner.

"I think about your mother a lot," Jenny said early in our dinner, and I understood this sentiment wasn't simply chatter to make me feel a little better about my loss. Jenny, I had inferred from conversations with my mother over the years, was a regular visitor to my mother's house. I didn't know the details of her conversations with my mother, but I could suss out their purpose and their inherent intimacy.

"I was in a bad marriage, and without her, I don't know how—I honestly don't know how—I could have made my own life."

"She was a wonderful example for a lot of people," I said.

"She was proud of you."

"We understood each other. When it's the same genes like that, lots of times you don't even have to talk. You just look at each other and you know," I said.

"I've never had that, Sasha. Not with anyone, genes or no genes," Jenny said.

"I think that's what I'm going to miss most of all."

The dinner turned out to be quiet and peaceful. Even Bruce was subdued and reflective. It was one of the few times during the entire shiva that I felt I was in the company of real adults. But it was more than that. I didn't have to explain myself to either Bruce or Jenny. I could express my emotions and be understood without being judged. I could be subtle. I didn't have to shout. They both possessed receptive and perceptive ears, and I knew it had been decades since I had a conversation like this in the company of a woman who wasn't also a relative.

Long after Jenny left, I got a call. I expected some new drama, but it was just Yakov. "How's the problem solving?" I asked.

"That's a stupid thing to ask. You know how it is. It doesn't go. It doesn't go. Then a miracle happens and it goes."

"The miracle hasn't happened yet, I take it."

"If it did, I wouldn't be berating you right now. Tell me, please,

Sasha, what wonderful thing did Jenny make that I will enjoy tomorrow?"

"You'll find out tomorrow. By the way, how was the séance or whatever Shlomo called it?"

"It's been postponed until tomorrow night."

"Really. Why? Are you waiting for a full moon or something?"

"It's not that. But I'll be there."

"You think my mother will spill the beans about Navier-Stokes?"

"No. But I do think that strange events can propel creativity. I need a change of scenery. I'm hoping my own *neshamah*, not your mother's, will speak to me tomorrow night. You want to come? Maybe your *neshamah* will speak to you, too, and you'll be able to solve a previously thought to be impossible problem in meteorology."

CHAPTER 30

The Governor

DAY 6

Ⅰn a country as profoundly anti-intellectual as ours it is predict-able that our leaders will do whatever they can in order not to appear smart in public. If they graduated summa cum laude from the finest university in the land, they will barely mention this achievement, give an "aw-shucks, I just drank a ton of beer and got lucky" response if asked about it, and even make a concerted ef-fort to drop their ending g's and add a few "ain't"s into their speeches as an antidote to their erudition and education.

This effort to appear dumb—or to put a positive spin on it, to "be a man of the people"—takes a lot of work that in a better world would be unnecessary. You have to really want to be a politician to undertake it. Plus you have to eat funnel cakes and other greasy, awful types of state fair midway food and pretend you like them all. Essentially you have to show the world that you can effectively pretend to have bad eating habits and no brains. Clearly, I don't have what it takes to be a politician, and neither do any of my rel-atives. Like my mother, none of us can play dumb, and we tend to find American food an abomination.

Obviously, I have a critical and cynical view of America's vaunted political system. It is a view identical to that of everyone in my family, including my uncle. However, my uncle, more than anyone else in our family, needs politicians to like him and grant him favors. The liquor business is highly regulated, and its taxes buttress wobbly state budgets during times of economic difficulty. The relationship between government and the purveyors of alcohol nationwide is siblinglike, and it is especially so in my home state, which leads the nation in the number of bars per capita and, it goes almost without saying, drinks more alcohol per belly than any other state in the union.

When my uncle told me that the governor was going to visit our house during shiva I cast a gimlet eye. "Is he going to *daven mincha-maariv* with us?"

"Who knows? The aide did ask if he should bring a *kipa*."

"What did you tell him?"

"That we already have many in the house. But the governor is a bit of a germaphobe, so I'm going to guess he'll bring his own."

Which is what he did. He already had his *kipa* on as he left his Lincoln Town Car and walked to our house. I was in the living room looking outside, and watched in a state of semi-disbelief. Neighbors came out of their homes—like young fleas in dormancy sensing their first chance at warm blood—to shake the hand of our governor, who possessed not only a full head of silver hair and a wondrous set of gleaming teeth, but an uncanny warm glint in his eye that quite frankly I envied.

This was the last day the mathematicians would be in the house. They would scatter to the winds on the final day of shiva and give my family one day of true peace, an act of courtesy that was not undervalued. While the governor approached, they were oblivious, still working, albeit with palpably diminished hope, on solving the Navier-Stokes problem. I had banned any food in the living room after the crumb- and plate-filled first day of problem solving. But I wasn't cruel. I let them continue to have their tea—which Yakov, being the most finicky of tea aficionados, let no one else steep—and standard gut-busting coffee. Cups had to be borrowed to keep the supply of caffeine steady, and the living room had the air and redolence of a Starbucks, a derelict one where no one bused their mugs and the sound system was on the fritz.

Hefty volumes, most of which had seen little use in the university library for decades, were on the coffee table and piled in corners of the living room. The mathematicians would pick up these volumes, seemingly at random, for information. At the end of the day the books would be carted back to the math department conference room for further evening work, when the real discussions would begin. Zhelezniak was the general leading this effort. He had systemically broken down the solution of this problem into a dozen subtasks, which eventually were going to be sewn together to make the quilt that would show the solution to the Navier-Stokes problem in all its glory. That was the plan, at any rate. If you would have asked any of the mathematicians whether they saw the governor of Wisconsin during their stay, I doubt that a single one would have said yes.

But my family saw him. We whisked the governor into the dining room. Security agents kept watch outside and tried their best to be discreet. These men couldn't possibly be confused with LDS missionaries, or even intrepid Jehovah Witnesses. Our neighbors, ever helpful and kind, brought out coffee for the security force, which it graciously accepted while the governor and our family convened to plan the state memorial ceremony for my mother.

"I'm sorry for your loss," Governor Dombrowski began, and I could feel my antagonism recede. He meant it. I could insult him for his pedestrian intelligence and whacky ideas, but even I know that there is a bit more to life than intellect. This governor, no matter how much I might malign him in conversation and in this book, dear reader, was a real human being with real feelings.

"We'd like to honor her life. I never met her personally, but I've heard many stories about just what a remarkable person she was. She's an example for all in this state. For young girls who want to be rocket scientists. For anyone who wants to pursue their dreams."

"My sister never let anything stop her," my uncle said.

"Exactly, Shlomo! That's what we want to celebrate. An indefatigable spirit. A patriot. A God-fearing woman with can-do optimism. We need more of that in this world. We need more of that in this state. I would love to see Professor Karnokovitch remembered and revered."

"We look forward to the memorial ceremony, governor. My son is very good at arranging such affairs," my uncle said.

The governor looked at my cousin, examining him carefully, and made an instant appraisal of his fit and polish. "Were you born in Wisconsin, son?"

"Absolutely," my cousin quickly replied. He was in salesman mode. "Born in St. Mary's, just down the block. Madison West graduate."

"You go to the University of Wisconsin, too?"

"No, Williams."

"Out East, huh. Speak Polish by any chance?"

"*Oczywiście!* Italian, too."

The governor gave his election-winning, teeth-baring grin. "Now my campaign funds are going to be paying for this. My understanding is that you know quite a few top-notch performers."

"That I do, dear governor."

"Now Barbra Streisand, just between you and me, is a little too much of a lefty, even though I do love her voice."

"She's very popular, it's true. Not really right for this affair, though, I agree. But what about Dolly Parton? Everybody loves her. Even my aunt loved her."

"She did?" I asked. "My mother loved Dolly Parton?"

"She did, indeed. She came to visit me when I was putting together a show at the Hollywood Bowl for Ms. Parton. Your mother came along. She was enchanted."

"It's true," Anna said. "I was there, too."

"You think she could sing 'God Bless America' if we hired her?" the governor asked.

"Of course. She loves that song, governor. She's actually a very accommodating and agreeable woman and would sing just about any song, as long as it was tasteful. I bet you she'd even sing 'Stracić Kogoś' if you asked her personally."

"I love that song. I heard it when I was visiting our sister voivodship in Poland. Very touching. I think of my own mother when I hear it. How did you know?"

"I do my research, governor."

"Does she know Polish?" He seemed excited at the possibility that the country superstar was a closet Pole.

"No, but I'll translate the words for her. I'm sure it's the kind of song Dolly could relate to. Anyone can. But you'll have to ask her personally, I think."

"I'll be glad to do that, son."

"We are, of course, talking about a big budget project, governor. I'll do this work gratis because my father has asked and I loved my aunt dearly. But still, this will not be a small production."

"I understand. Dolly Parton doesn't come cheap, I'm sure."

"No, she doesn't. But there is no one who can reach an audience quite like her."

"I think it's an excellent idea. Your father is lucky to have such a creative and dynamic son. Dennis will talk to you about the numbers later. I'm looking forward to the event."

The governor left well before *mincha-maariv*, although I'm sure he would have been game enough to recite the necessary Hebrew words in transliteration. During his little stay, he wasn't shy about mentioning that one of his grandmothers was Jewish, something I'm guessing he also noted on his occasional trips to synagogues. Being a governor requires a myriad of skills. While great hair and teeth are a good start to a political career, an ability to pretend at least half convincingly that you have an affinity to all key ethnic groups in your state is a definite plus.

"What is this all about, anyway?" I asked.

"It's to honor your mother, what do you mean what's it about?" my uncle said.

"Dolly Parton and my mother don't have a lot in common, I'm sorry."

"She did see her, Sasha," Anna said. "I don't lie. You know that. Not to you."

"She saw the Moscow Circus, too, maybe five or six times when I was a kid. But we're not having clowns and bicycle-riding bears at this ceremony."

"Tell him, Shlomo. Tell me, too," my father said. "Dolly Parton and my Rachela? You must be in trouble. Tell us what's going on."

"Close the door," my uncle said.

"Why? The mathematicians are too busy to hear anything," I said.

"They have ears. You never know what those sons-of-bitches will listen to. Six days they've been here, drinking my liquor and eating all the food, trying to solve some stupid problem."

"It's not a stupid problem, Uncle. It's probably the most important problem to be solved in mathematics in two hundred years."

"Maybe three hundred. There's not a more important problem in mathematical physics," my father said.

"OK, it's an important problem. I have problems to solve, too. Close the door. I'll tell you."

CHAPTER 31

The Listening Session

DAY 6

If you are going to attempt to communicate with the dead, I would think that the venue for this endeavor should be something quite grand in stature. There cannot possibly be an eventful meeting between someone in the netherworld and a few people seated around a Formica kitchen table. No, success requires a large room with a heavy wooden table and dim lighting produced by a chandelier or two. There must be at least a dozen people in attendance. The dead need to know that they are truly wanted, after all.

My uncle's dining room fit the bill, especially the chandeliers, which came all the way from Venice. In the new life he and Cynthia had planned together there were going to be lavish affairs, mostly charity events, held at their new house. The parties, sad to say, had turned out to be few and far between. Now the dining room had a new, if temporary, purpose. It would be the setting for my uncle, Anna, the Ben-Zvis, Yakov Epshtein, the Karanskys, Ren Ito, Vladimir Zhelezniak, and me to try to bring the ether of my mother's soul back for one last communication. The female mathematicians had declined to attend, as did Peter Orlansky. They were far more sensible than I was.

I was there strictly as an observer, I swear. It hadn't been my original intention to attend. My uncle had come to my mother's house that evening because, according to Shimon Ben-Zvi, five items that my mother held dear were needed for the ceremony. My uncle knew exactly what would be best, five of the Russian rubles from my mother's ammo box. He was partly relieved that I hadn't already put the coins in a safe-deposit box, and partly irritated. "Everyone knows that gold is here, Sasha," he said. "You need to be more responsible with your mother's hard-earned *raichkite*."

It had been my intention to stay home with Bruce, but as the evening wore on, I became more and more curious. Plus, I was getting nervous about my uncle. This event was going to be a disaster, I knew, and my uncle's response to being conned by Shimon Ben-Zvi could turn ugly. Someone needed to be there to pull him back, and I wasn't sure that Anna could do it alone.

They were all seated around the dining room table when I arrived. Shimon was at the head, his wife, Jocelyn, on his right, his brother, Abraham, on his left. Abraham looked worried. He, too, knew that this escapade would not end well. I looked at his unsettled face and regretted not contacting him beforehand so the two of us and Anna could devise a strategy for the inevitable moment when the farce became obvious to all.

Some of the mathematicians, including Yakov, had notebooks and pencils in front of them. At face value it looked like they were prepared to be stenographers for my mother, recently departed but evidently still capable of presenting an important math seminar. Perhaps one or two possessed the delusion that she would teach them somehow. I'll never know. More likely they were all like Yakov, ever ready to find inspiration and desperate enough to seek it out in even the most ridiculous of settings.

In a corner of the room stood three men with *tallitim*, ritual prayer shawls, over their heads, standing in their socks on the cherrywood floor. Rituals like this, I then understood, required a few sidekicks, in this case some old guys from our synagogue. They were undoubtedly Cohanim, members of the ancient Jewish tribe of priests.

I sat down at the far end of the table and looked directly at Shimon. I was angry but tried to appear calm. Before Shimon was a fat, well-worn Hebrew volume that looked to have been published sometime in the 1920s. Presumably this volume contained a recipe for communicating with the souls of the dead. Who did Shimon think he was going to fool? Many of us knew Jewish liturgy well, and the Karanskys had spent their formative years in Israel. Shimon was unaware that he was in way over his head, and unwilling to accept that preying upon a grieving man's sentimental desire to hear his sister one last time was well beyond behavior acceptable to a decent human being. I wondered if he was mentally touched. Or maybe he believed he could do it.

Shimon inhaled deeply before opening his book. I finally noticed the five gold coins, my gold coins, in the center of the table, thought about the possibility of never seeing them again, and decided that that was the least of my worries. Shimon solemnly began to recite in Hebrew a history, an event from who knows what century, when wayward rabbis of old managed to do successfully what we were attempting. I had a suspicion that he wasn't reading from a text at all, but was simply making up stuff as he was going along. As a stand-in for those rabbis of old, he summoned forth the Cohanim, the old men from the synagogue standing in their socks. Who had managed to convince them to come for this travesty? I didn't know. They turned their backs to us. I knew what was going to come next. Shimon was borrowing from the *Birkat Cohanim*, the priestly blessing delivered on the Jewish New Year. The old men no doubt had their fingers closed against their palms waiting for when they would be called to face us. Then they turned upon hearing the summons from Shimon, spreading out their fingers, lifting up their hands to the height of their shoulders, and reciting the Hebrew words first spoken by Shimon:

אנו בענווה עומדים לפניך מתחננים לשמוע ממך ולשמוע את חכמתך

[We humbly stand before you, beseeching to hear from you, and to hear your wisdom]

Back and forth they went in the dimly lit room. Shimon and the old men were engaged in a call and response. After a few turns they had established a well-defined cadence, and I started to gain a sense that even if what I was witnessing was 100 percent hokum, there was something inherently otherworldly, magical, and beautiful about it. My uncle's eyes were closed. He was taking it all in aurally. Shimon's high-pitched voice sang a well-known Hassidic melody. The old men followed with their droning. My uncle was perhaps fifteen feet away from me as I watched him, first reciting the words he was hearing, and then mumbling something altogether different. Perhaps other people were doing much the same as my uncle, but I wasn't watching them.

My uncle was feeling something deep inside him, I knew. I've never felt what believers hold inside their hearts, and I certainly have never felt what I witnessed happening to my uncle in that room. I heard his voice grow louder and louder, mixing with the words of Shimon and the old Cohanim. My uncle wasn't speaking in Hebrew like them, but in Polish. His eyes seemed almost forced shut by then, and he was using not his modern Polish, but the formal Polish of my mother.

In the middle of the rising din of Shimon and the Cohanim, my uncle shot up from his chair, his hands resting on the table, his eyes still closed, with tears beginning to run down from the crevices of his crow's-feet. "*Skończ z tym szaleństwem* [Stop this nonsense]!" he shouted, his booming voice taking over the room. "Stop this right now!" he then shouted out in English. The room went silent in an instant.

"Are you all right, Shlomo?" Anna asked.

"I'm more than all right." He paused to wipe the tears from his face. "Turn on the lights, Anna. All the way, please." The new brightness of the room caused me and probably everyone else to squint. "I had a memory from long ago. From Vladimir-Volynski. I'd rather have not remembered it, to tell you the truth. That place was a living hell. And not just for Jews. For Poles, too."

"What did you remember?" Anna asked.

"I don't want to say. It must have happened when I was three or so. I can't believe I can remember it now." My uncle's face was white.

"Three years old. That wasn't a good time," Zhelezniak said. "Not for my family in Russia. We're the same age, you and I. We starved, both of us. My father died that year in the army. I only know what he looks like from pictures."

"Lots of people died. Whole families. Back then I was living with my aunt, and we were on a farm. It was dangerous, I was told. A Polish farmer was taking care of us. He was a kind man. I liked him. We were in his barn, living there, I think. I knew all this before." My uncle paused to strengthen himself so that he could continue. The color in his face came back little by little. He was no longer lost in a nightmare. Instead he was a *shtarker*, a formidable man, again.

"But today, just now, I know why we left his farm. The Ukrainians. They must have come. They wanted him out, just like they wanted all Poles out of Wołyń. Maybe he resisted. Who knows? But one day we walked to his house from the barn. He was there outside. On the door." My uncle paused and looked into the hallway to his own front door.

"Nailed to the door, his arms stretched wide like he was Jesus Christ. I'd never seen a dead person before. I'd never seen blood come out of a man's mouth like that. The place was quiet. We walked inside his house. They were all dead. His whole family had been murdered."

"It was a horrible time for everyone," Anna said.

My uncle looked directly at Shimon. "I suppose I can thank you for this memory. Tonight, when I saw the faces of those children in that house, it was like I was there again. And I knew. The dead don't come back. Not to this world. This world is too cruel for anyone to want to come back. Even to speak to the ones they love. There must be a better world to go to. There must be." My uncle paused again. I could feel the anger rise in him. "What were you thinking, Shimon?"

A look of panic crossed Shimon's face. "I was trying to help you. You wanted to hear your sister. I was just trying to assist."

"No. That's not true. You were trying to make a little money. You didn't care who you hurt along the way."

"Easy, Uncle," I said. "He's not the worth the trouble."

"No, he isn't," Anna said. She put her hand on his shoulder, rubbing it slowly.

My uncle looked at me and then at Anna. "You're both right about that." He then turned to Shimon. "I want you out of here. Right now. Immediately. You, your pole dancer of a wife, and your fat, disgusting brother. Your family has caused us nothing but trouble always. Out! Right! Now!" When a Czerneski flies into a rage, a sane person understands immediately that it is time to disappear. Whatever doubts I had about Shimon's sanity left when I saw him pack up his belongings in a rush.

"I'm sorry you all had to witness me being so foolish," my uncle said to the crowd in the room as the Ben-Zvis headed for the door. "I'm not usually this way. I'm sorry to have wasted your time."

"You're still grieving, Shlomo," Yakov said. "It's hard, I know. You have nothing to be embarrassed about."

"We didn't come to hear Rachela," one of the Karanskys said. "We came because you asked us. We came for you. We're glad we did."

"OK, you think I can erase this embarrassment. I wish I could. Trying to hear the dead. I should know better," my uncle said.

"It wasn't a total waste," Yakov said. "Not for me, Shlomo."

"What do you mean, Yakov? Don't joke with me now. I'm not in the mood."

"I'm not joking. There was something about tonight. All the chanting back and forth. Like I was a child in Minsk again in our rabbi's house on Simchas Torah. It was a special day. People would sing melodies, like what I heard tonight, from the old times. The men would all be drunk. I hadn't thought about those days in a long time."

"And so, you had a good memory. I'm happy to hear someone got something good from this craziness," my uncle said.

"More than a good memory. I got an idea. A very important idea."

"What idea? My sister's problem? You understand how to solve it now?"

"No, not that one. The Navier-Stokes problem is beyond me, and beyond all of us, really. But for a long time I've been working on another problem in mathematical physics. Twelve years, actually. I had my doubts I would ever solve it. I thought I might be too old, a has-been. But here in this room, all the chanting, you saying god knows what in Polish, it came to me. An idea. A real idea. A breakthrough, really. I think I can solve this damn problem. Twelve years of nothing, and now this."

"You're not lying to me to make me feel good, right, Yakov? I don't have patience for liars anymore today."

"No, I'm not lying, Shlomo. It's true. In my head it's all there because of this crazy night."

"You think you can solve the Boussinesq equation problem?" Zhelezniak asked. "Isn't that what you've been working on all these years?"

"Correct."

"No one has been able to solve that problem in seventy years."

"I know," Yakov said. He was grinning.

"Are you sure?" Zhelezniak asked.

"The more I think about it, the more I'm sure," Yakov said.

"Well, something good came out of this, I guess," my uncle said. "Now all you mathematicians need to get the hell out of here. I need to apologize to the poor men I brought from the synagogue to help with this travesty." My uncle looked at the three Cohanim standing at the head of the table, three men who undoubtedly were staying up well past their normal bedtimes. "You can put your shoes on now. We'll have a few drinks. Then I'll be happy to drive you home."

"I'll drive them, Shlomo," Anna said. The old men seemed buoyed by the idea of a graceful woman being their chauffeur. "But first things first. I need to know where you keep the alcohol in this monstrosity of a house."

CHAPTER 32

The Truth Really Does Come Out

DAY 7

After six eventful days in which God created so very much, the story goes that he rested. The titans of mathematics who had descended upon Madison, Wisconsin, had, save for Yakov, accomplished very little over their six days in my mother's house, but they, too, in their pale imitation of Adonai, decided that enough was enough. This was all well and good as far as my family was concerned. By the end we were openly hostile to most of them. We sat in the dining room. They worked in the living room. Pascha would squawk some mathematical phrase in Polish whenever one of the mathematicians would enter the kitchen, and I had half convinced myself that these were taunts from a perceptive parrot.

There is a well-known joke—at least well known in mathematics—about how mathematicians work. A mathematician and a Starbucks barista are each placed in front of a stove with a kettle and a nearby faucet and told to make boiling water. Both do the same thing. They fill the kettle with water from the faucet, light the stove with a match, and place the water-filled kettle on the stove. Mission accomplished.

The mathematician and the Starbucks barista are next placed in front of a stove with a kettle that they are told is filled with clean water and told to make boiling water yet again. The barista lifts the kettle off the stove for a moment, lights the stove, and puts the kettle back on. The mathematician lifts the kettle off the stove, pours out the water into a sink, puts the newly emptied kettle back on the stove and says, "The problem has been reduced to the previously solved case. Q.E.D."

This joke is not so far-fetched for many mathematicians. This is indeed how they think, not just in mathematics, but in life. Solutions to problems never trespass into anything of real value. No water ever gets boiled. Living with such people can be exhausting.

The truth is, though, that not only mathematicians succumb to this trap of wanting to repeat some pleasant event from the past, the previously solved case, no matter how ridiculous it seems to an observer. We do this, perhaps, in matters of the heart most of all. We try, or at least some of us try, to revisit our past loves in hopes of bringing back that wonderful feeling of connection and passion. Some of us may spend years retracing our steps and try to win back a former lover, convinced that he or she is our one true soul mate.

In 1973, Peter Orlansky was a twenty-two-year-old Ph.D. with his first university job, an assistant professorship at the University of Wisconsin. My mother was nearly twice his age, confident, poised, elegant, and, unlike any other female mathematician in the United States, accepted as a giant in her field. In contrast, Orlansky, while obviously very, very smart, lacked anything approaching poise and confidence. Physically, he towered above all, including my mother. But his shyness was also apparent to all, and when he lectured in front of a class he seemed incapable of projecting his voice beyond the first two rows. Orlansky, despite his prodigious mathematical talent, was going to go nowhere as an academic without someone mentoring him. "He needs some work, that one," my mother said of her colleague. If anyone was capable of transforming Peter Orlansky, it was my mother. That's exactly what she did. Peter Orlansky became my mother's project for one year.

Under my mother's direction, Orlansky began to dress not like a twenty-two-year-old student but like a mature professor, complete with a dark suit, black leather shoes, and tie. He cut his shaggy Beatles 'do and sported the neat look of a Midwestern TV newscaster, combing his hair straight back to reveal his widow's peak. Making eye contact would always remain difficult for him, but my mother took him to a speech coach, and he not only began to project his voice—which it turned out could boom with authority with the best of them—but also was able, at least in front of a classroom, to sound like a real adult. The childish cadences of his former speech were barely present.

This surge in confidence, and the emergence of a man who, at least in terms of his public persona, could make a certain type of female undergraduate swoon, was noticed by all. Its cause—my mother's hard work and creative hand—was also noticed by all. It is a truism that the halls of academia, while filled with people of high intellect, are worse than high school in terms of gossip and sex rumors. It's true today. It was true in 1973, and back then in the Midwest the word for such things was still "affair." The vagueness of that word contrasted with the weight it carried. In the Midwest, sexual revolution or no, an affair between a young man and an "older woman" was not a minor thing. It was viewed as unseemly, especially in a professional environment. Within two years Peter Orlansky was gone from the University of Wisconsin, off to the less sexually prudish urban east of Princeton, where the rumor of his affair with my mother seemed to enhance his reputation. A cynic would say that since Princeton couldn't get my mother on board, they decided to settle for the next best thing, her lover. Of course, no one really knew for certain that Peter Orlansky and my mother had actually been a couple. Like the high school rumor mill, the academic rumor mill was not particularly reliable. My mother certainly wasn't going to say anything. No one was going to confront her, either.

Orlansky and my mother would work together on several highly regarded papers and many minor papers over the years. With every publication, the rumors would flourish anew. I never knew what was true and what wasn't. I was a grown man lost in my own work and personal life. Who my mother did and didn't sleep with was far less important to me than who I slept and didn't sleep with. I'd see Orlansky very infrequently, sometimes in Madison, sometimes when I went to Princeton. He was a kind, gentle spirit who never forgot to send me Jewish New Year cards and happy holiday season cards that contained pictures of his children doing cute things.

I wasn't thinking about Orlansky at all on the morning of the seventh day of shiva. I woke up and looked outside my window, saw the stars in the sky, and had the urge at the ridiculous hour of 6:00 A.M. to visit my mother's grave. I knew I'd be going home tomorrow and just wanted to say good-bye one last time, just me in that oh-so-cold cemetery, looking down at the raw frozen earth where my mother's body lay.

I quickly put on several layers of clothing and a down coat that I always kept in my mother's house, brought the Volvo back to life—noting that its battery would not likely last the winter—and drove to Forest Hill with a funeral prayer book on the seat next to me. I nursed a cup of coffee I bought along the way and, while the heater in the boxy sedan slowly kicked in, felt like a cop on duty. All I needed was a donut or two.

I made the turn into the cemetery. The oak trees were bare of leaves and stark against the sky. I slowly passed tombstone after tombstone along the skinny pavement. Then I saw him in the distance, Peter Orlansky, standing where I had imagined myself standing. He was wearing a fedora and blue wool topcoat over his sport coat and wool pants. That was it.

Orlansky was my age, give or take a year, and looking at him, I thought a bit about myself and how I looked to others. Up close, you could tell his age. There were the sags under the eyes and a loss of definition around the chin. He still looked good, don't get me wrong, but like me, I'm sure many now said "sir" as they addressed him. We were no longer young. There wasn't even a hint in our faces that we once were.

"How long have you been here, Peter?" I asked as I shook his gloved hand.

"A while," he said, looking at the ground.

"Is all night a while?" I asked.

"More or less," he said. "People were going to your uncle's house. I definitely didn't want to do that. Coming here seemed like a better idea."

"How did you get here?" I asked.

"I walked."

"It's what, three miles from where you're staying?"

"It was good. Cathartic. That hotel is really a piece of crap, by the way."

"It's always been awful. Even when it was new it wasn't much. You must be cold."

"Oh yes, definitely freezing."

"You probably could use something warm. I have some coffee in the car."

"No, I'll be OK."

"How were you going to get back?"

"The same way I came, I guess. My plane doesn't leave until the afternoon."

"How about I drive you back? Save your feet a bit."

"It's probably a good idea. Thanks, Sasha."

There is an old joke in Finland, a country proud of its collective introspective character and shyness. "How do you know when a Finnish man likes a woman? He stares at her shoes instead of his." I noticed that Orlansky was staring at my shoes.

"I came to say kaddish," I said. "How about we do it together and then drive back?"

"Sounds like a good idea."

"By the way, at the graveyard ceremony, the rabbi screwed up."

"What do you mean?"

"He said the standard kaddish, not the one for a burial."

"Why didn't you correct him?"

"I didn't want to have anyone stand there any longer than necessary. It was cold. No one would know except for me and my uncle, I thought. He's a minor league rabbi. You can't expect much."

"So you came back this morning to fix the mistake?"

"I thought I'd do that, yes. But there were other reasons."

"Well, I'm glad you came to do this fix. It's somehow, I don't know, reassuring."

I held out the little booklet that contained the burial ceremony prayers. Orlansky looked up from our pairs of shoes, now next to each other, to the open page. The sky was beginning to lighten a bit, and we both could make out the words. Orlansky's voice was loud and clear. He was, in this moment of two middle-aged men mourning the loss of someone they loved, trying to reclaim some strength. Orlansky recited the words the way my grandfather would, using a Polish-accented Hebrew that hadn't been taught anywhere in decades, and even then, only in Orthodox synagogues and Jewish schools like those I attended in my youth, "*Yiskadal, viyiskadash, shimay, rabow.*" I fell back into the old cadence and accent easily. When we were finished he said something under his breath, his eyes on my mother's grave again. I dared not ask him what he said.

We walked back to the car and I asked if he wanted to stop for some breakfast. He said no.

As we drove, Orlansky said not a word. The air was heavy. I spoke up out of desperation. "I'm glad there was someone with me this morning, Peter. But my uncle might be angry that I didn't wait for him to come along."

"You have a right to be angry, too. We just spent six days invading your life trying to solve a problem your mother solved years ago."

"Probably, yes."

"Definitely, yes. I know your mother and what she was capable of doing. She definitely solved that problem."

Peter Orlansky flew back to New Jersey that day. He still sends me Jewish New Year and happy holiday season cards every year, or at least his wife does that for him. I, of course, send him our cards in return.

CHAPTER 33

The Last Lunch

DAY 7

"**S**he had a crush on you back in middle school. I remember that distinctly," Bruce said.

"She was what, twelve? I was twenty-two already, maybe twenty-three. Gas was still twenty cents a gallon. It's ancient history."

"She asked back then if I had a picture of you. I gave one to her. She probably still has it," Bruce said.

"You can't be serious," I said.

"A girl's first love should never be taken lightly, Sasha," Bruce said.

"All of a sudden you're an expert on women?" I said.

"Do you know how much time it took to make this?" Yakov asked, his fork, which had just speared a pelmeni, extended toward me.

"You trying to feed me again?" I asked.

"No, you get your own this time. This plate is all mine. It'll be my last good meal in I don't know how long. Something like this, you have to start the night before. You need to marinate the meat. Then you have to wake up early and make the dough. Roll it out. Cut them. Fill each pelmen. Pain in the ass. Hours, it takes. I know. I saw my mother do it many times," Yakov said.

"It was Gogol's favorite," I said.

"See, she knows you like Gogol, too. I know you're not stupid,

Sasha. So I must assume that you're being purposely obtuse," Yakov said.

"He's being passive-aggressive. It's his standard pose when he knows he's on the wrong side of an argument," Bruce said.

"Somebody wonderful wants him and he has to put up a fight. What an idiot," Yakov said.

"You should see his taste in women, too. Little pieces of cotton candy that fall for his dumb 'I'm a Russian immigrant, a lost soul' act," Bruce said.

"You two are ganging up on me," I said. "And then there is Anna, telling me time and time again I have to find someone real. She put you two up to this?"

"No, we are operating independently," Bruce said. "But you should never cross Anna."

We were in my mother's kitchen. Yakov had come to say good-bye to my family, and of course have one last bite to eat. I had my doubts that he thought saying farewell was as important as eating Jenny Rivkin's food.

"You think she's been cooking for your family? You've got to be kidding. It's for you," Yakov said.

"I thought it was for you, Yakov," I said.

"Don't mock me, Sasha. If Jenny Rivkin deigned to cook for me, I'd be in heaven for the rest of my life," Yakov said.

"If you weren't interested in her, Sasha, you wouldn't be toying with us like this," Bruce said.

"It's true. He wouldn't be trying to act dumb. He knows he isn't getting any younger," Yakov said.

"Thanks, Yakov, for the reminder," I said.

"I'm just stating a fact. It's true for me, too. I feel it every morning I wake up. Then I look in the mirror. Ach. What has become of me?"

"You'll live to be one hundred, Yakov," I said.

"Not without a good woman next to me, that's for sure. I'm tired of being alone. That's why I'm going on sabbatical to the University of Manitoba next year."

"Manitoba? Why on earth are you going to Manitoba?" Bruce asked.

"There are one hundred thousand Ukrainians in Winnipeg is why. Ten thousand Jews. That means there are thousands of suitable women used to cold weather for whom Lincoln, Nebraska, would be considered a lush tropical paradise. If there is any justice in this world, I am going to make one of them fall in love with me and bring her back home."

"And what happens if you're not successful, Yakov?" I asked.

"Failure is not an option. But if God laughs at my quest, you are going to have to promise me one thing."

"What's that?" I asked.

"You're going to promise that your wife-to-be sends me CARE packages at least twice a year. I deserve at least that for talking sense to you."

"Already you have me married. That was quick. I barely know this woman."

"You know enough, more than enough," Yakov said.

"He's right, Sasha. You do know enough," Bruce said.

"She barely knows me, that's for certain," I said.

"She knows enough, too," Yakov said. "And she's smart enough to act. You sure she was born in this country?"

"Positive," I said.

"Very unusual. American women aren't like this, typically. They want to be wooed. Sweet-talked. Romanced. They want a big fantasy first. Reality comes later. I never have luck with American women. By the way, who is going to take me to the airport? If I don't leave soon, I'll be late."

"Call a cab, Yakov," I said. "We're not a chauffeur service."

"OK, OK, I'll take a cab. But I'm going to tell you, when someone makes you a meal like this, you call her. You thank her, and you don't wait seventy-two hours to do it. That's American craziness, this waiting business. Her number, as you know, is on the corkboard right there." Yakov pointed with his left hand, his right one still dearly holding onto his food-laden fork. "Jenny Rivkin. R-I-V-K-I-N. You call her. You thank her. You ask her to go to dinner with you. And you, lucky brat that you are, she'll say yes to. Do you understand?"

"Yeah, Yakov, OK, I'll call."

"Good. But call a cab for me first. I'm not getting out of this chair. I need to savor every last bite before I leave."

CHAPTER 34

The Great Realignment

DAY 7

My mother had been dead for only a week and her absence was like the disappearance of a huge planet. The moons that had revolved around her were undergoing a great realignment. An aunt, certainly my mother's least favorite moon, left her orbit altogether. Another moon, one long favored by my mother, quickly began a cozy intricate dance along my aunt's former astronomical path with a third, also favored, moon. I am, I know, going too far with metaphor here, and am also greatly distorting real physics. But as my cousin had predicted, the intricate dance was taking place not at my uncle's house, which Anna did truly detest, but at the tried-and-true location of many high-end Madison trysts, the Edgewater Hotel.

While my cousin certainly wasn't surprised by this development, we were both taken aback by just how indiscreet my uncle and Anna were about it. "After this damn memorial ceremony, I'm selling everything and moving to California," my uncle said.

We were sitting at the dining room table, having our last meal together in my mother's house. My father was at the head of the table, my uncle was at the other end. Anna was sitting next to my uncle, holding his hand. This kind of public display of affection in my family was completely foreign. My cousin and I sat together on the east side of the table just like in the old days.

"Where in California, exactly?" I asked.

"Los Angeles, of course. Anna is there. My son is there. For sixty years I've been freezing my bones. For twenty, I've been a lost soul. I'm done with that."

"You're not moving in with me," Anna said. "I don't like free-loaders." The warm tone in her voice as she scolded him was uncharacteristic, and my uncle seemed to like it.

"Not with me, either," Bruce said, with a look of genuine fear at the prospect of once again sharing a home with his father.

"I'm buying my own place, don't worry," my uncle said.

"You can come for visits then," Anna said.

"Sure, you can visit me, too, just so long as you call ahead," Bruce said.

"I won't have to call ahead for Anna."

"No. I don't have anything to hide," Anna said. "But with Bruce, I can tell you, you don't want to come unexpected."

"So important and special, he thinks his life is. I already know those secrets of his. They were a big deal once. Now even on TV they show it."

"On TV it's different. It's all in the details," Anna said.

"I suppose you're right."

"If there is a heaven," Anna said, "Rachela is smiling right now."

"If the Christians are right, Zloteh is smiling, too," my uncle said.

"You think Zloteh is happy seeing us two together?" Anna asked.

"Definitely. She wouldn't want me to be alone. She would want me happy. Plus, she even liked you."

"I'm not going back to the office tomorrow," my father announced. "I can't face the sight of another mathematician. Six days in my old house with them was enough. I need a change of scenery to finish up my project."

"Where are you going to go, Father?" I asked.

"Tuscaloosa, of course. I've been looking online. It seems like a very pretty city. It's warm this time of year, is my understanding. There is even a nice river that flows through it. Your house is next to it. I saw it on MapQuest."

"Do you mean the Warrior?" I asked.

"Yes, a strange name for a river. Black Warrior, too."

"North of Tuscaloosa it's the Warrior. South it's the Black Warrior. You're inviting yourself to my house, are you?"

"I've never been. It's time I see it, don't you think?" My father looked at me, trying to gauge my level of warmth toward his proposal.

"It's as good a time as any, I guess," I said.

"You can work in the front of his office," my uncle said. "Very nice. The department secretary is down the hall and will always make sure you get your tea and donuts."

"I don't want to go anywhere near a university. I'll work in my son's house."

"You'll be working on Navier-Stokes, I suppose," I said.

"There won't be any surprises in your house, will there?" my father asked. "I can just walk in, unpack, and work, yes? No naked women. No naked men. No dogs. No cats. No parrots."

"No. No surprises. And I'm not taking Pascha with me. Orlansky asked me if he could have her, and they seem to get along quite well. They will speak a beautiful Polish together. But you didn't answer my question."

"Why should I answer that? You already know the answer."

I shook my head and tried my best to be a scold. "For six days you let two dozen mathematicians go on a wild-goose chase in this house trying to solve a problem that you already solved. Is that right?"

"It's not solved. Well, it is. But I'm making sure it's one hundred percent correct. Technically, until I do that, the Navier-Stokes problem is still unsolved. And I didn't solve it. Your mother did."

"Why?"

"Why did I let them work so hard? It was your mother. I was honoring her wish that they have a chance to solve it. One last chance."

"But she solved this problem in what, 1945 or so?"

"I don't know when she solved it. But she told me she started it a little before then, yes. How did you know?"

"It's in her memoir, the one I talked about at the funeral."

"I wasn't listening to your speech," my father said.

"I didn't listen either," my uncle said.

"I worked hard on that thing."

"It was for other people to hear, not us. We already knew Rachela's story," my father said.

"The memoir is handwritten in Polish. She kept sending me chapters. Two weeks ago she sent me a bundle of them. In one she talks about solving this problem, among other things," I said.

"I didn't have a clue." My father smiled. "Polish, really?"

"Do you know how hard it has been for me to read? Like walking through sticky, deep mud. Without a dictionary, it would be impossible."

"Give it to me. I'll translate it," my uncle said.

"She always had her secrets," my father said.

"So, apparently, did you," I said.

"It wasn't my secret. Two week ago, she asked me to visit. She told me to go upstairs, that there was something there for me in Aaron's old room. She gave me instructions on how to find it. Just like with the gold, I needed a screwdriver. I found the package of papers. I brought them downstairs. We looked at them in her bed. That was the first time I knew."

"So it could have been 1945 when she solved it," I said.

"A proof like this? No, that's impossible. She mapped out much of it by then. I think maybe 1970 or so was when she finished it. That's my guess. Even for her it would have been a twenty-year problem at least. After she didn't win the Fields she was mad as hell. She didn't care about awards at all after that. We even had to work hard to get her to pick up that medal from Clinton. She didn't want to go."

"Why keep it a secret, though?"

"She wanted to solve it from start to finish. Completely by herself and for herself. It was the problem, I'm sure, she thought she was meant to solve. I don't think even Kolmogorov knew about it. She started working on this a little in 1940 with Grozslev. Kolmogorov published part of that work entirely as his own. She wasn't happy about that at all. Probably she started to hide this work then. I was married to her for over fifty years and I didn't know."

"So it's complete?"

"I think so, yes, but I'm still checking. Another two weeks and I'll be sure."

"Do you have it with you? I'd like to see it."

"It's in my house. We can stop by after we make the last walk for the shiva. I can give it to you then. I'll give you the original. You're her son, after all."

"You have a copy, too?"

"Yes, of course, as a precaution."

"What are the odds that there is an error, Father?"

"Zero. But still I need to check." My father poured his glass full and lifted it up high. "Every one of you played a role in this achievement. You don't think you did, but every one of you was important. You sustained my Rachela, you gave her encouragement, you made her happy, you gave her joy. I want to make a toast to all of you in her memory. This proof is a singular achievement. No one will do anything as great again. But it wouldn't have been possible without the family she loved so much."

We drank to my mother's proof, and then we drank again, too much as per usual. Everyone seemed to be happy about this turn of events. They had grown so completely inured to my mother's craziness over the years that this last trespass—keeping a secret even though it might cause troubles beyond her death for those she loved—was, to them, nothing out of the ordinary. My father was joyful, above all, about being associated with a major mathematical discovery. By the time the old guys came from the synagogue for the final prayer, including the Cohanim from the night before, we were all pretty far gone. The old guys wished us long and happy years as we shared some of our schnapps with them, sending us a little further down the slope.

We bundled ourselves up and began the final task of the shiva, the ceremonial walk around the block. There we were, all five of us in our heaviest coats, walking by house after house. I'm sure none of the people in those houses had the slightest idea why we were out and about in that cold.

For almost fifty years my mother's neighborhood, a place where few faculty members lived, had been my touchstone. There was no grandeur in this neighborhood's homes, built in the 1920s mostly to house the families of civil servants. They were all utilitarian, designed to shelter those without pretensions. For my mother and father, it was heaven in comparison to what they had in Russia, and they didn't feel a need for anything more.

As a child I could have told you the names of all of my neighbors, and they all pretty much knew mine as well. For the ones who didn't keep track of children's names, I was simply "that little Russian boy," a moniker that thankfully, during the Cold War, did not seem to cause me too much trouble. In our neighborhood, what truly mattered was not where you were from or your line of work or your religion, but simply your willingness to follow through on the community obligation to mow your lawn regularly in the summer and promptly shovel your sidewalk clear after every snowstorm in the winter. On that front, thanks to my father's fastidiousness, we always passed with flying colors.

The four people around me on the sidewalk were the ones I would always love. We would scream at each other now and then, sure. We would insult each other habitually as well. This is who we were, raw and emotional and confident that no matter how awful our behavior to each other on the surface, we belonged together, and ultimately needed each other always.

Now there was also a daughter and granddaughter, at least peripherally, in my life. I had no idea where that would lead. I would reach out to them. I would try to love them. But with those two there would be different rules that I would have to follow. They wouldn't understand this constant testing and jabbing that were so intrinsic to the world in which I grew up. I would have to be nicer on the surface. I would have to watch what I said. I thought of those two far away in California. Even if I did succeed with them and find love, they would certainly always be distant physically. I needed something more in my life, something closer and immediate.

"We need to buy something in a store owned by a gentile," my uncle said, as we were about to make the final turn back home. "It's the tradition."

"It will be another six blocks of walking. You've got to be kidding," my father said.

"Look, you don't have to go," my uncle said. "You're not even Jewish."

"I'll go, I'll go," my father said. "But promise me one thing. When I die, just put me in the ground. No shiva. No nothing. No stupid superstitions about buying things from gentiles to fool the devil, OK?"

"Yeah, that's OK, Viktor. I don't mind. It's what you want. But right now we're going to do things the right way."

After we made our purchase, we went to my father's house, where I picked up the original proof. My uncle Shlomo, Anna, and Bruce then drove off in my uncle's car as I walked inside my mother's house alone. I placed the proof on the dining room table, walked upstairs to find the chapters of my mother's memoir that I had translated during the shiva, and walked back down to the dining room. There they were, the documents that defined her life, handwritten, side-by-side on top of the weathered mahogany grain.

My mother was a careful writer, I noted. There were few corrections in either document. She thought through things fully before she wrote anything down on paper. In some ways, both of these manuscripts were opaque to me. I picked up the papers and rubbed them a bit between my fingers, trying to feel closer to them, my mother's life works.

My father knocked on the door as I held the papers in my hands. He didn't bother to wait for me to answer, entered quickly, and looked at me, still in the dining room. "I had second thoughts about giving you that proof, Sasha," he said.

"Well, here it is," I said. I held it up for him to see. "What did you think I was going to do, burn it in the fireplace?"

"Maybe. I had thoughts of doing that myself early on. It's been hell trying to check that proof. It isn't my field."

"It's been like hell translating her memoir, too. Polish isn't my field of expertise, either."

"Let me see *your* papers, Sasha." I handed him the thick stack of unlined copy paper held together with a fat rubber band. He sat down next to me at the dining room table, pulled off the rubber band, and shook his head. "This would be worse for me, that's for certain. All that emoting in a language I barely understand."

"She gave a dog's breakfast to both of us."

"Maybe, but you know if it wasn't for her we'd still be in a tiny apartment in Moscow. So we owe her this."

"Father, she abandoned us, plain and simple."

"No, that's not true. She forced us to come here because she knew it would be best for us all. She helped with the plan to get us out. She and your grandfather both."

"So now we have to struggle, Father? This is her final gift to us? To make us the worker bees of her legacy?"

"Sasha, she gave you life, and you're complaining about translating her memoirs? You should think of it as an honor. Every word is written to you. You were her audience. I have no doubt."

"She ever tell you about living off bear meat near the Barents Sea?"

"No. But I'm not surprised. Whatever it would take to survive, she would do it. I know my Rachela. She was a warrior. Like that proof you're holding. The willpower to solve such a thing, it's immense. I'm certain no American could do it."

"You think it's an honor to check her proof? You think you're her audience, too?"

"No, the audience for this proof was herself and two men, one who died of cholera in Vorkuta and one who died a happy man in Moscow. But yes, it is an honor to check her proof. She could have given the work to anyone. She chose me."

"It could have been a choice of convenience. You were close by. Plus, she knew you'd keep quiet about it until she died."

"No, don't tell me sour fairy tales. Your mother was never lazy. And we have to keep our mouths shut for a while longer, both of us. You have your work to do. I have mine. We are the worker bees. And that," he pointed to the proof in my hand, "is the work of pure genius."

CHAPTER 35

Tuscaloosa

"It's a little different than the last time we were together like this," my father said, He dropped his suitcase in the tiled hallway and looked at the interior of my home, sizing it all up.

"It was over forty-five years ago, Father," I said.

"This is nicer than our apartment in Moscow, that's for certain."

"I don't remember, but I can imagine."

"The river, is it the Warrior or the Black Warrior here?" He pointed to the water visible from the living room windows.

"The Warrior. It doesn't turn into the Black Warrior for another five miles."

"It's a nice place you have. Spacious and modern."

"No one wanted it when it was built. They said it was 'different.' In the South, different doesn't mean new and interesting. It means odd and awful."

"Different is good for us usually."

I didn't remember much about the last time my father and I lived together without my mother. I knew we had lived in an apartment in Moscow. I could remember being drilled to speak English like an American, to mimic voices on records and tapes. Most of the audio came from American radio dramas. The way the children on these shows interacted with their parents, free of shouting and so polite, seemed as foreign to me as the language of

English itself. "Are people in America really like this?" I remember asking my father.

"Yes, of course. They all are like this."

"Will we have to be like this when we move?"

"No. We can be like we are."

This answer had been reassuring. For while I was certain that I could master English, mastering American culture seemed both impossible and undesirable. To this day I don't understand this country well. The cheery optimism. The lack of concern about the past. The openness to strangers who simply show a smile and give a firm handshake. How can people be consistently unguarded and so willing to show their personalities in such an unvarnished way? How can people under a dark cloud for days, weeks, and perhaps years view hardship as temporary? Where does this blithe strength come from?

I can mimic some of the outward signs of these behaviors. I've had flashes of optimism, myself. But I cannot feel like an American. I can only admire the American spirit.

We Karnokovitches and Czerneskis are always seeing obstacles and aware that many cannot be overcome, no matter the strength of our willpower. Still, we can somehow solve mathematical problems that are accepted as intractable by nearly all and will take up decades of our time. We can crawl out of mass graves and live for untold days in a forest until we are rescued.

Sometimes our plans are created out of desperation and, despite our intelligence, are inherently rickety. We can elude the careful eyes of the KGB and, pretending to be American tourists, one supposedly hard-of-hearing adult and one loquacious four-year-old boy following instructions drilled into him, cross the border into Poland.

That was how my father and I managed to get to America. The plan required a time when tumult would reign in Moscow and beyond. We needed a day when the KGB would be too busy to bother with keeping tabs on the husband and son of a defector, small potatoes on the list of threats to Soviet dominance. My father didn't know when that day would be. He waited patiently through all of 1952, a year when the borders became tighter and tighter with every passing month. Then it came, March 6, 1953. The Russians poured out of their homes wailing in the street over the loss of their great leader, Stalin. As when Tolstoy died, chaos ruled. Grief so consumed Moscow that no one seemed to care or notice as we left our apartment, and Soviet soldiers barely looked at our false papers at the train station. They noted our American clothes made by Sears and Roebuck, asked us questions that I was schooled to answer, and let us through. At the Polish border, whatever suspicions possessed by those who examined us disappeared when I stated, in my apparently convincing American English, how sorry I was to hear of Russia's loss. According to my father, a guard broke down in tears in response. Once in Poland, my grandfather's Zionist connections found us a way into Czechoslovakia, and then to Italy, Israel, and finally the USA. I remember only one thing of this trip: sitting on a tall stone wall and looking down at the bald head of my father. My father once told me that the wall I remember was not an actual border but rather was part of a castle outside of Florence. I owe my American life to the death of Joseph Stalin. I also owe it to my father and his constant lessons.

In America, my father continued to drill me, not in English, but in mathematics. His disappointment that I did not pursue the only professional path he could imagine for me had been profound. The pain that I felt over his disappointment had been tremendous. But my father had been correct in his assessment of what our life would be like in America. We didn't change. We thrived here, certainly. It wasn't because we adapted. It was because of our strength of will.

My father took up residency in my guest room. He was supposed to be teaching in Madison in one week—it was going to be the last semester before he formally retired—but he sent an e-mail that due to the death of his wife, he would be unable to teach set theory one last time. Someone else would have to do the job. He was asked if he had any suggestions for a replacement. He said no.

He told no professional colleagues where he was. It didn't take long for those interested in his whereabouts to check out the possibilities. When I started to receive calls, I didn't deny that my father was with me. But he didn't want to talk to anyone even remotely related to mathematics. He was working, I was instructed to tell them. I was not at liberty to say exactly what he was working on. I didn't know myself, I said. How this opaqueness on my part was transmitted in the mathematics rumor mill I could well guess. So could my father. Neither of us cared one whit.

No one could ever fault my father on his professionalism or commitment to mathematics. It was his life. He was not a genius, and he held no illusions that he was. But he worked steadily on his problems, and his work was important enough that he would have received tenure at any number of high-quality institutions in the United States regardless of who his wife was.

For two weeks, he worked in my guest room every day. At night we would eat together. Sometimes he would cook, other times it would be my turn. There was no set order. One of us would simply move into the kitchen before the other and start. After dinner we would drink and play chess. Every third day or so, he would call my daughter and granddaughter and talk to them. I would talk as well, but it was actually difficult for me to get a word in when we were on the phone together, especially when he talked to my granddaughter.

All parents have their strengths and weaknesses, and listening to my father during these conversations I began to understand that, despite his formal demeanor, he was surprisingly good with young children. I could hear my granddaughter responding to his encouragement. He assumed she was intelligent, he didn't talk down to her, and you could hear the warmth in his voice. I wished then and there that I had a tape or video of my father and me from when I was that age. I'm certain that it would show two people as close and loving as a father and a son could be.

Perhaps in an American family a father and a son with a difficult past would—in late and middle age, respectively, together in a house day after day—open up and say what needed to be said to heal old wounds. There would be declarations of forgiveness on both sides. But I don't think so. It would be unusual in any culture, even one as wed to happy endings as America's. Certainly that wasn't going to happen with my father and me in any explicit way.

Two weeks into my father's stay, he announced that he needed a change of scenery. "Are you going to Berkeley?" I asked.

"No, Biloxi. I need the inspiration of sea air. I understand it's nice there this time of year."

"You want my car? It's about a four-hour drive."

"No, I understand they have buses that go there for the gamblers. I'll take one of those. I'll be back in a week or two." Just like that, he was gone.

The people in my department were solicitous of me during my first few weeks back. I also received condolence cards by the bucketful from mathematicians around the world. I would spend most of my day opening and reading them. I wasn't getting much work done.

I had called Jenny Rivkin on the day that Yakov demanded I do so. It was a short conversation. I followed that up with an e-mail thanking her for all her help during the shiva. Twenty-four hours later I received a response thanking me for my kind words. More e-mails were exchanged. Those e-mails escalated quickly into phone calls. The length of those calls, always in my office while my father was in town, stretched from tens of minutes to hours once he left, and would often last until early morning. I wasn't getting much sleep either.

One week after my father left, without a word from him during all that time, a barrage of phone messages and e-mails from reporters began—almost as extensive as the barrage of phone messages and e-mails from mathematicians with "buy me a vowel" last names—all about one thing: an abstract published online on the American Mathematical Society Web site. There was an addendum to the upcoming annual meeting, a special symposium entitled, "Sixty Years of Mathematics: The Work of Dr. Rachela Karnokovitch." The usual suspects had submitted abstracts for that symposium, including my father. The title of his abstract was "On the Solution to the Navier-Stokes Millennium Problem." The lead author on the paper was R. Karnokovitch, deceased, formerly of the Department of Mathematics, University of Wisconsin. The second author was A. Grozslev, deceased, formerly of the Department of Mathematics, University of St. Petersburg, Russia. The third author was V. Karnokovitch, of the Department of Mathematics, University of Wisconsin. The fourth author was A. Karnokovitch, Department of Atmospheric Sciences, University of Alabama. The fifth author? None other than S. Czerneski, Madison, Wisconsin, no affiliation given.

"Why is everyone calling me?" my uncle asked. "My cell phone is full. I try to delete the messages. They fill up faster than I can get rid of them. Why the attention?"

"It's because you are a coauthor of the most important paper in mathematics to be presented at a conference in a long, long time," I said.

"Oh. Interesting. Before, I was a published meteorologist. Now I'm going to be a published mathematician. How did this happen?"

"I don't know. I've been trying to contact my father to find out."

"Where is he?"

"Biloxi."

"It's in Mississippi, yes? What the hell is he doing there?"

"I don't know. He's not answering his cell."

"I got him that phone. He never uses it."

"There are also no major hotels there that have anyone registered with the name Karnokovitch."

"Maybe he's not in Biloxi."

"No, he's there. I know it. Congratulations, by the way, on your newly found fame."

"Thank you, Sasha."

"You can congratulate me as well."

"You are now a published mathematician, too?"

"Yes, just like you."

"Well deserved. Your father always wanted you to be a mathematician."

"I know."

"I'm not going to answer a single one of these messages. I'm going to get a new cell phone with a new number. I wanted a new one, anyway. They make them so good now. Those mathematicians and reporters can all fuck themselves."

"Anna still in town?" I asked.

"For the foreseeable future, yes. Until I sell this damn business and move."

A couple of reporters, nerdy science types whose articles were always buried somewhere deep inside their newspapers, actually traveled to Tuscaloosa to knock on my door. I told them I had no comment. Yakov and a few other mathematicians, in tones that were by turns indignant and joyful, left messages on my cell phone as well. My father went missing for three more days before he showed up.

"I won three thousand dollars. I had a marvelous time," my father said.

"Looks like you got a tan, Father."

"That too. Very nice sea air. You ought to think about buying a condo there. Very peaceful."

"Thanks for the real-estate advice. By the way, I don't know anything about the solution to the Navier-Stokes problem."

"Actually, you do. You don't know it, but a paper of yours, something entitled, 'On the Spatial Distribution of Velocity of Hurricane Frieda' interested your mother very much. You are very good at making graphics, by the way. There are some compelling images. I used your data as an example of the natural state of velocity under conditions of turbulence in the paper to be presented at the symposium. Your mother suggested that I do so. Blame her, if you must. I didn't ask for your permission to use the data. So out of courtesy, I included you as an author."

"And you included Shlomo, as well."

"Of course. He's a coauthor on your paper. I didn't ask for his permission, either. You've heard about the paper, I take it then?"

"I've heard about it. I didn't know you read my work."

"Not usually, no. But that paper. It was in *Science*. Your mother showed it to me. I read it. Very interesting material."

"I shouldn't have my name on this paper, Father."

"No, you shouldn't. Technically, you're right. But your mother and I are, underneath it all, very sentimental people," my father said. He was already in the kitchen pouring vodka. He poured two glasses, both full to the brim. We spilled as we drank.

CHAPTER 36

The Return

The following month, my uncle, Anna, and I sat together at two events that honored my mother. The first, the official State of Wisconsin Memorial Ceremony for Professor Rachela Karnokovitch, was originally going to be held in the capitol building. With the addition of Miss Dolly Parton and the accompanying need for a decent public address system and good acoustics, it was moved to the main hall of the city convention center, a stately facility on Lake Monona designed by Frank Lloyd Wright. My father chose not to attend, and had I not wanted to show my uncle my support, I certainly would have done the same. Before the ceremony began, we went backstage and shook the hands of the governor and Miss Parton. Then we were whisked away to our seats when my cousin said, "It's time to make the strudel."

How did this event come to be? My uncle told us he owed the governor a favor. When the governor sniffed out an opportunity to celebrate one of Wisconsin's own—with a strudel my mother would have found repulsive—my uncle Shlomo was stuck. According to him, it all went back to Aunt Zloteh's death. His liquor business originally had been registered with the state, for legal liability reasons, entirely in my aunt's name. After my aunt died, my uncle, on a bender that lasted well past one year, was in no shape to do anything. The business kept going in his absence, but certain details were ignored. One of those details was the transfer of the title of incorporation to a living person. Without that transfer, my uncle's business was technically no longer legal. That meant, among other things, that all contracts that my uncle had with the state of Wisconsin for alcohol sales at state-sponsored events were null and void.

The failure to transfer went unnoticed for three years. When it was discovered, my uncle's accountant made its repercussions known. The financial penalties and the loss of future revenue from the state of Wisconsin were enormous. Something had to be fixed somehow.

According to my uncle's accountant, there was one person who could make everything legal again, the treasurer of the state of Wisconsin, Wayne Dombrowski. My uncle went to Dombrowski's office and pleaded his case in Polish. He told his story of coming to America, losing his lovely Polish wife, and being so devastated by the loss that he forgot to do many things, including filling out the incorporation transfer form. The treasurer took pity on him. A document was drawn up that granted a back transfer of the incorporation papers to my uncle. All had been fixed.

Treasurer Dombrowski eventually became Governor Dombrowski. When the request came from the governor's office for a state-sponsored memorial service for his sister, what could my uncle do? Why would a popular governor want such a ceremony? Somehow the genius of a Polish woman whose face reminded him of his own mother's touched him to his core. This is what Dombrowski told me at my mother's ceremony. For what it's worth, he sounded sincere.

Of course, my uncle's story probably wasn't exactly true. It may have not even been mostly true. With my family, historical facts are subsidiary to narrative, and narrative must always show the narrator in the best light. Regardless, my cousin baked an excellent strudel for this show, an effort that made my uncle glow with pride.

In addition to being able to use the production services of my cousin for free, the governor had been lucky on another front. When he had proposed the ceremony, the idea was, at best, odd. Yes, my mother had won the National Medal of Science, but who outside the mathematical world knew of her? What did her obscure mathematics have to do with Wisconsin's technological innovation, anyhow?

But with her solution to the Navier-Stokes problem, my mother was, at least for a brief while, a bona fide minor national celebrity. Her achievements were noted on NPR and the *NewsHour*, and in the *New York Times* and other media sources that targeted the ever-shrinking population of citizens capable of paying attention to more than two hundred words at one time. A ceremonial event that might have baffled many suddenly seemed a stroke of brilliance. My mother's life was indeed worth celebrating.

The University of Wisconsin symphony played a movement from Beethoven's Sixth, my mother's favorite. A young Milwaukee man, Daniel Beliavsky, played a Chopin etude. Then the program moved from somber reflection to a colorful recounting of the life of my mother by the University of Wisconsin's chancellor. The brass section of the orchestra introduced the governor with a slightly muted version of "On, Wisconsin," and Dombrowski was in his element, talking about the parallels between his parents' life and my mother's, all native Poles who came to Wisconsin and enriched the state and country with their hard work and patriotism. The first time I heard the words "Badger Ingenuity" flow from his tongue, I expected to cringe, but surprisingly I was swept along by the sentiment. He mentioned Badger Ingenuity six times in his speech by my count. Three times would have been more than enough. Yet when Dombrowski walked off the stage, I was at least temporarily convinced that my mother was indeed a shining example "that the fertile ground of the Badger State was not only excellent for corn, soybeans, and cranberries, but also for technological innovation."

Then it was Miss Parton's turn to lift up the crowd. The band struck up "On, Wisconsin" again, and she picked up the tune with her instantly identifiable wavering, sweet soprano voice. She followed that with a game version of the governor's favorite Polish song, "Stracić Kogoś," the chorus translated into English by yours truly. Miss Parton introduced the number by noting that she'd loved Poland ever since she learned they named their tank armor after her. Finally, she sang "God Bless America" and "America the Beautiful" in quick succession. The orchestra's string section, playing an arrangement created by my cousin, added extra weight to the words. Maybe my mother would have approved in the end.

Despite the absence of pomp and circumstance, it was the second event, the special symposium to honor Rachela Karnokovitch at the 107th meeting of the American Mathematical Society in Boston, Massachusetts, that proved far more exciting. All of my childhood I had heard the acronym AMS. As a kid I would sometimes be carted off to these meetings and be left to run around the halls on my own while my parents attended talks. When I decided to go into meteorology, I smiled when I learned of the corresponding professional organization, the American Meteorological Society. My change in field of study would require some significant adjustments, but at least I wouldn't have to remember a new acronym.

In 2001, I had the privilege of attending both AMS meetings. I was on the roster of authors with specially invited abstracts at both, as well. But it was the mathematical AMS that was on my A-list that year.

One by one my mother's collaborators came up to the podium. Perry, O'Connell, Orlansky, Ito, Epshtein, Ben-Zvi, one of the triplets (I still couldn't tell which one), all of the people who had invaded my mother's home just six weeks before—and most of whom I had become disgusted with by the time they left—were there. Somehow on the podium they each looked completely respectable and appealing in their own way. This was their element. They said little in the way of personal stories, except for Professor Kelly Hickson. She noted that as a result of spending a week with the Karnokovitch family she had decided to take up cross-country skiing and Russian, both of which she was certain would improve her mathematics. When someone shouted out in a Polish accent, thick as sour cream, "learning Polish would be even better," the crowd roared.

Yakov presented his new proof in mathematical physics, the triumphant solution to the Boussinesq equation problem that had been preceded by twelve years of frustration. He said nothing of the origin of his breakthrough. The crowd was tense with excitement as they listened. The applause that followed was hearty. In a normal year Yakov's work might have been the highlight of the meeting. But this was no ordinary year.

I watched my father step to the podium. He stood before his colleagues, erect, confident, and without any hint of sadness or flashes of pride, presented my mother's work. The cameras of a few journalists flashed as he spoke, and he paid them no mind. He was focused on one thing and one thing only. This was my father at his best.

Following that talk, my father started to make plans for his retirement. He too, he said, was leaving for California. Everyone else was there, save for his son in Alabama. Why not him? Except he wasn't going to Los Angeles like his brother-in-law. He was going to find an apartment in Berkeley to be near his granddaughter and great-granddaughter. It wasn't meant to be, though. Three months later my father would have a fatal stroke in his office. As my mother wished, he was buried next to her.

When I think of my father, the first moment that usually comes to mind is of him delivering that talk at the AMS. He's wearing a blue suit and a white shirt. His bow tie is one that was picked out by my daughter as a present for that special day. There would be no greater moment in his life. He knew it. I knew it. Everyone did. When he was done, he walked from the podium with the cameras flashing and sat down next to me and the rest of his family. I looked at him as he sat listening to the chair of the session say a few closing words. His eyes looked straight ahead. He betrayed no emotion. But I knew exactly what he was feeling at that moment.

We, of course, don't get to choose our parents. We don't get to choose where we are born, either. We are adaptable creatures, though, and genetics often means that our families share innate attitudes, emotional responses, and intellectual traits that make us feel an intimacy much closer than what can be produced by simple day-to-day interaction alone. In a modest bungalow in a small city with a cold climate, I shared many years with two people who were more than parents, if that's possible. They were not simply guides or examples or emotional anchors. Our collective strangeness and eccentricity relative to those around us meant we were almost our own sovereign Slavic nation.

I moved back to Madison to take a position at the University of Wisconsin the year after my parents died. Jenny's two boys were still in high school, and after a lot of discussion, we both agreed that it would be cruel to yank them away from their friends and bring them to Tuscaloosa. The South was different, far different than any other place in the country. I liked it, yes, but fourteen- and sixteen-year-old boys would probably have a difficult time adapting to its unique ways.

In the South, lineage is very important, and perhaps more than in any other part of the country, Southern families are concerned with their family trees. They trace them back to the plantation days and make strange and unnecessary apologies for their great-great-grandparents' slave holdings. "I know my family was kind to their slaves, because that's the kind of people we are" is a common sentiment. Then they go back to Europe, where something strange often happens. An inordinate number of the family trees from these Scotch-Irish people who trace their lineage over one thousand years find their roots in one person, Charlemagne. I've seen these family trees in some homes in the South. Evidently there is a straight path from Hank Williams to a ninth-century Holy Roman Emperor.

I thought about these Southern family trees when I looked at my own, so carefully put together by my mother. Hers was more than just a tree. My mother was nothing if not thorough, and she had put together an epic tale, with biographies of noted people from my lineage that filled up two shelves of bookcases in my old bedroom.

Most Jewish efforts at Jewish genealogy don't try to go back more than a few hundred years. Like the Southern conceit of being related to Charlemagne, there are an inordinate number of American Askhenazi Jews who claim the Baal Shem Tov as blood kin. My mother, once she had freed her brain from the ultimate quest of solving the Navier-Stokes problem, also claimed to have found something extraordinary in our family tree.

Of pedestrian interest was that we were related to a prominent Hassidic rabbi, in our case the Grand Rabbi of Minsk from the 1850s. This was plausible. The grand rabbi had fifteen children, after all. But then her family tree marched back through the centuries, to Spain in the fourteenth century, and it hit true pay dirt. According to my mother, she and I were the descendants of none other than Rabbi Moshe ben Maimon, someone more commonly known as Maimonides.

If I were to believe my mother, the greatest Jewish philosopher and mathematician of the Middle Ages and I are blood. I don't, not for a second. My mother was the best mathematician of her time, but I am certain that as a genealogist she fell prey to the same heady embellishment of most who look at their past. She was, after all, a very sentimental woman. Still, there is always the finite probability that this blood tie does exist. If so, my mother and Maimonides are the twin towers of my lineage, my *yikhes*.

I'm of an age where I spend a good deal of time looking back. I like to take walks and retrace steps from my childhood. I look at buildings and remember what businesses used to be there and what I would buy there with my parents. Sometimes I'll walk past my old house with my stepsons or my grandchildren when we're on our way to Vilas Park and I'll just stop, look up, reminisce, and try to think how I could possibly explain all that happened inside to these people who are so utterly American. I can't do it. Maybe when they read this book they'll understand just a bit of what it was about.

On occasion, I look at my CV with my list of academic publications and note that my career is slowing down. I'm publishing far less. My grants are down to a trickle. The awards I've received as of late are not for current work but for the "body of his achievements." I'm a happy has-been. No, I haven't achieved nearly as much as my mother or my supposed patriarch Maimonides, but those are both ridiculous standards. I'm very proud of what I've done. The future is for my children. It's for my grandchildren.

Amidst the list of publications on my CV, one stands out because it isn't in *Science* or *Nature* or a geophysical or atmospheric sciences journal. It's in *Communications on Pure and Applied Mathematics*. It's true that I'm only a fourth author on this publication, but my father was right. I did play a significant role in its creation.

I'm also of an age when intellectual achievements, even those as significant as proofs to nearly impossible problems, take a backseat to friendship and family. I know that in comparison to almost all of my colleagues my "scientific impact" is considerable, but really now, it isn't much. I can search on Google Scholar and note how many times each article I've written has been referenced in the scientific literature. Aside from my mother's proof, these numbers are paltry, rarely exceeding one hundred. I am a minor footnote, indeed, in the history of science. I take much more comfort and pride in the goings-on of those I know and love. I am lucky and blessed to have a loving wife and stepchildren, and a daughter who forgave me for being absent, and ultimately cruel, during her youth.

Andrea tried to get her mother's permission to have me call. It never came. A few years ago I called Catherine anyway. She hung up the second she knew I was on the line. I then wrote Catherine a letter asking for her forgiveness but never received a reply. In Christianity, forgiveness is expected when an apology is sincere. I've never understood this concept. Apologies are, after all, simply words. They should be weighed in some way against the hurt the offense has caused.

While my transgressions have been generally of a personal nature, my mother, by holding on to a proof for decades out of pure selfishness and egotism, managed to offend the entire mathematical community. She, of course, never apologized to anyone for the trouble she caused. But in an intellectual community, genius always trumps propriety and *menschlichkite*. Bad behavior by leaders in an intellectual field is even, occasionally, celebrated and envied like a rock star's antics. The rumor mill regarding the publication of my mother's solution to the Navier-Stokes problem is still actively inventing and recycling narratives. Every once in a while I receive a call from a young professor or Ph.D. student who claims to "want to know the truth." They sound so disappointed when I tell them that I don't know what is true and what isn't.

A few years after the shiva, Yakov Epshtein came to Madison

to give a lecture in the math department. Like almost all of my parent's friends, he was not an idle talker. When he had said at the shiva that he was going to Winnipeg for the express purpose of finding a wife who understood the exquisite delights of Slavic cooking and who would not be deterred by the cold of the American Great Plains, he had meant it. I was not entirely surprised when I received a wedding invitation from him in 2002. I was also not entirely surprised to see how much he had slimmed down by the time of his Madison visit. Married life was treating Yakov well in many ways.

When he came to my office to talk, he extolled the beauty of the world and his wife. A couple of years after the publication of his major proof, he had received an offer of a chaired professorship from the school my mother always detested, the University of Minnesota. Yakov happily accepted. There was now a bit of the contented sage about him. But then he began to reminisce about the shiva, and he narrowed his eyes. "Here's what I want to know, Sashaleh. All those days. All of us working so hard. It was torture, and yet the problem had already been solved. I can't get it out of my head. Why?"

"My father said it was my mother's wish."

"I don't believe it. She wasn't that mean. Not to people she liked, and she liked most of us. Plus, she loved Peter."

"The Peter thing is a silly rumor."

"Yeah, right. A silly rumor that's the truth. You're trying to ignore my question."

"OK, I agree with you. My mother couldn't have predicted you would have crashed the shiva. Back then I wasn't so sure. But I didn't know she'd already solved Navier-Stokes. She wouldn't have wanted the craziness. Not just for the sake of the mathematicians. For everyone, her family especially."

"So why?"

"I can only guess. My father probably saw all of you wandering around the halls with your stupid plan to solve something in one week that it took my mother thirty years to do, and in a fit of pique he decided to let you carry on with your stupidity."

"Now that makes some sense," Yakov said. "Your father could be a handful. But I have a different theory."

"Which is?"

"Checking your mother's solution wasn't easy, especially for someone outside the field like your father. Plus, he was getting old, slowing down. If he faltered, if he felt he couldn't succeed, we would be there to prop him up. The bastard let us torture ourselves so he could use us as an insurance policy."

"Don't speak ill of the dead, Yakov. People do stupid things when they are angry. He didn't think his actions through clearly, if I am right. He was trying to check my mother's solution and was being bothered by all of you. Then he had the pleasant distraction of a newly found grandchild and great-grandchild. If my father could have imagined the chaos ahead of time, he would have told everyone the solution was done."

"You're probably right about that last part. No one would want to be responsible for such a mess. He wasn't a bad man. Your father was good to me. Both he and your mother." Yakov hopped out of his chair with the sprightliness of a middle-aged man who had discovered the benefits of a daily workout. "You have a nice view," he said. "What's that place with the green oval field below?"

"The football stadium. Camp Randall."

"You ever go to see such a thing? Watch young men knock each other over with reckless abandon?"

"No. Never. I don't understand the purpose of it, actually."

"See. Your parents raised you the right way. You're not distracted by nonsense. They'd be proud of you now. Married, thanks to me. Back home with a wonderful wife and a family."

"I suppose I should thank you for your efforts."

"Yes, you should. To tell you the truth, that's why I came to visit your nice little office today. I wanted to hear some belated words of gratitude from the son of Rachela Karnokovitch. You get married. OK, it was a little family ceremony, I understand. That's your and Jenny's style. I'm not insulted that I wasn't invited. But here's the important thing. Was I right with my advice?"

"You were right, Yakov."

"Of course I was. Right as rain, as they say. Now, if you don't have a bottle in your office, it's time for us to go to a bar and celebrate our good luck and fortune."

I assumed I'd never know my mother's side of the story as to why she kept the proof to herself for so long. But then last year, I got a call from the owner of my old family home. He'd found some papers written in a foreign language mixed in with the furnace manual that was attached to the back of the furnace. He thought they might be important. Did I want them?

I was both ecstatic and irritated upon hearing about this find. I was certain that before we sold the house we had combed through every square inch, expertly looking for hidden documents, jewelry, gold coins, and whatnot. What kind of Karnokovitch doesn't know how to find hidden items of value? I was turning into a lazy American in my middle age.

I went to pick up the papers immediately. Like an impatient schoolboy, I read them before I got back home. It had been ten years since my mother's funeral and shiva. In a way, my uncle Shlomo had been right. Even after her death, my mother felt the need to say a few more words.

CHAPTER 37

From *A Lifetime in Mathematics* by Rachela Karnokovitch: Untitled

O ne year when my son was a teen, my family went to the state fair. My son gravitated to the arcade, where he tried his hand, unsuccessfully, at making free throws with a basketball from a very short distance. By happenstance, the Ferris wheel was next to the basketball booth at the arcade. He wanted to take a ride, as did my nephew, who was only three at the time. I looked down from our elevated perch on the wheel and understood instantly why my son, as well as almost all others, had been unsuccessful at making free throws. The rim of the basket was distorted. It was an oval, not a circle, and while the radius of the rim's width was normal, the radius of its depth was likely barely longer than the radius of the ball. Of course, an arcade player could only discern the rim's width, and so played a game that he thought was fair, but wasn't. He had to be almost impossibly perfect in his execution to succeed.

My career in mathematics has been quite like an arcade player shooting baskets. The naïve observer might have seen me at Moscow State University and thought I was evidence that all were welcome in mathematics. But, in fact, as a woman and a Jew, the rim was distorted for me. To succeed I had to be perfect, certainly leagues better than my male and Christian mentors and colleagues.

After I left Russia I continued to work on the Navier-Stokes problem, slowly and, for the most part, steadily making progress.

Being a Jew was no longer nearly the obstacle it was in Russia, although, of course, I would still not infrequently run into anti-Semites
in my work well into the 1970s. Being a female mathematician was
also far less difficult, especially after I reunited with my husband and
son and the unwanted advances became less frequent. Still, there
were limitations. I note that the first woman to receive the Nobel
Prize in physics did so almost one hundred years ago. A woman has
yet to win the Fields Medal.

In 1970, when I learned that I would not receive the Fields
Medal in my last year of eligibility, I was furious. In the world of
mathematics gossip, there are stories about my behavior during
that year and the year beyond. Those stories are mostly true. Some
of my antics were a bit unnecessary and not productive, but I am
extremely proud of one outburst, one that drove a member of the
Fields Medal awards committee to tears. I don't have to state his
name. People who need to know already do so. I saw the fear on
his face, witnessed the baby tears on his cheeks, watched him bolt
out of his chair next to mine in a panic, and felt triumphant.

It took me two years to get over the hurt of being denied my
due. Even for me, there was a glass ceiling in mathematics. This
shouldn't have been such a shock, but through my many years of
success I had deluded myself into thinking that my talent could
overcome any obstacle. I fell hard as a result of my hubris. Still, I
had an enviable career. I had excellent students to mentor, and
perhaps one of them will receive the award that has been denied to
the women of mathematics for so long.

I decided to practice revenge in a calmer way, by living well. I
buckled down and finished my work on my career triumph, the
Navier-Stokes problem, in 1973. For over thirty years, Navier-

Stokes had been a private and exquisite journey. It was the most beautiful of work not only because it was difficult, but also because it was mine, and mine alone. Born in the most unlikely and hostile of places, my work on the Navier-Stokes problem brought out purity and innocence in me that I couldn't believe I still possessed. It was a gift to live with that problem over those decades. I believe it kept me young.

When I was done I decided that what had heretofore been private would remain private. I no longer had any need for awards and adulation. I knew that I was the best of my generation, and that personal and fair assessment was all I needed. I looked at my competition and knew none possessed the talent to do what I had done. I would assess the young ones coming up and understood that they lacked the necessary talent as well.

Of course, other mathematicians would continue to try to solve the Navier-Stokes problem. Vladimir Zhelezniak, the fiercest of them, wouldn't follow my approach and engage in a delicate dance with the mathematics. I knew his aggressive style, treating each problem as if it were a death match. What he lacked in intellect Zhelezniak tried to fortify with sheer will. I knew he had been working on the Navier-Stokes problem since the 1950s. Like when he worked on Hilbert's thirteenth problem, he was doing so with the help of my unfinished work. In this case, he had the drawings I made as a child. It pleased me, the idea that this man who had stolen my ideas once with great success would not have the talent to do so again. I thought of Zhelezniak fruitlessly trying to solve the Navier-Stokes problem year after year, haplessly trying to obtain wisdom from my drawings. I knew that I would not likely outlive him, and entertained the thought of him coming to my funeral in a vain and pathetic search for more material to purloin. It made me smile, and I must say it made me more resolute about keeping my triumph private. This, too, like living well, would be a passive yet perhaps successful final effort to extract revenge.

When the Clay Mathematics Institute formally announced the Millennium Prize for the solution of the Navier-Stokes problem in 2000, I felt wholly vindicated. I had heard rumors about this award for years and I was fortunate to live long enough to see its creation. One million dollars would not have been available to me had I announced my proof when I was young. I wouldn't be the first woman to win a Fields Medal, but I would be the first to receive a Millennium Prize, albeit posthumously. As is stated in my will, this money will be used to create the Sophie Kowalevski Chair in Mathematics at the University of Wisconsin. The chair will be held by a woman. Perhaps, whatever the number of female mathematicians at my university at any given time, there will be always one more than if I had not won the Millennium Prize.

I look back at my life as others are wont to do when the end is in sight. People commonly express regrets. But when I look back I see the beauty of what I've witnessed and done. That's what I have told people who have asked for advice through the years: focus on what is beautiful and pursue that beauty. We are not perfect vessels, certainly. I am not an exception. But I have no regrets. The love I have given and received has been pure. Driven by loss, I have both used the gift of intellect I possessed and lived my life fully. I will die wholly proud of my life and my accomplishments.

There is a real Navier-Stokes Millennium Prize problem. It has not been solved. Get to work, reader, solve it, and you will be rich. There is no Boussinesq equation problem. The University of Alabama doesn't have an atmospheric sciences department in Tuscaloosa. Kolmogorov, I was told by one of his former students, loved to jump into ice-cold lakes. So do I. The living mathematicians in this novel are all made up.

ACKNOWLEDGMENTS

My wife, Holly Welstein, encouraged me throughout the writing of this book. Editing and comments by her, Claire Rojstaczer, Jean Bahr, Rudy Bahr, Carol Booth, David Booth, Barb Gaal, Steve Ingebritsen, Hugon Karwowski, Bill Leidy, Gabriella Safran, Boris Vladimirsky, Gloria Welstein, and Michael Wex greatly improved the manuscript. Dan Menaker generously took the time to encourage and promote my early fiction writing and has always provided sage advice. My agent, Henry Dunow, and my editors, Julie Miesionczek and Lindsey Schwoeri, provided pitch-perfect suggestions and championed this book through to publication.